WYCHWOOD

This is a stunning suspense novel set in an ancient Cotswolds manor house in the 1860's. By the will of their eccentric English aunt, two American sisters inherit Wychwood House, but in order to fulfil the terms of the bequest they are required to solve an Ancestral mystery which enshrouds the house and village. Weird survivals of the Old Religion, tormented passion, legal chicanery and historical detective-work are skilfully blended in a plot full of incident and invention.

Books by Nicole St. John in the Ulverscroft Large Print Series:

THE MEDICI RING
WYCHWOOD

NICOLE ST. JOHN

Wychwood

Complete and Unabridged

ULVERSCROFT
Leicester

First published in Great Britain
1978 by William Heinemann Ltd, London

First Large Print Edition
published July 1979
by arrangement with
William Heinemann Ltd
London
and
Random House, Inc
New York

British Library CIP Data

St. John, Nicole
Wychwood. — Large print ed.
(Ulverscroft large print series: romantic suspense)
I. Title
823'.9'1F PS3560.03897W/

ISBN 0-7089-0316-9

Published by
F. A. Thorpe (Publishing) Ltd
Anstey, Leicestershire
Printed in England

for
Patricia S. Myrer
"Blessed be"

Love is
a time of enchantment:
in it all days are fair and all fields
green. Youth is blest by it,
old age made benign: the eyes of love see
roses blooming in December,
and sunshine through rain. Verily
is the time of true-love
a time of enchantment—and
Oh! how eager is woman
to be bewitched!

I

THE CIRCLE IS RAISED

1

Rossford-under-Wychwood
March, 1864

CALAMITIES come in threes, the old wives say. Once I would have shrugged off such superstition, unaware that folk wisdom often springs from the seeds of some terrible truth. The Camilla Jardine who stepped ashore in Liverpool last July prided herself on her dispassionate logic and undisciplined reserve. I saw myself as an Anglo-American gentlewoman, scholar of Tudor history and Greek and Latin. Although I knew Shakespeare as well as I knew my Scriptures, I had not yet learned that there are more things in heaven and earth than were dreamt of in my philosophy. Nor that I had a darker, shadow side beneath my cool control. But that was before I went up to Oxfordshire, that fateful summer of 1863.

Snares set to catch foxes often trap the weak and vulnerable instead, that is an old, old story in the English Midlands. And the line between victim and victimizer is so very, very fine. But none of this did I know when, in innocence and grief, I first went up to Wychwood House to make a home for Nell.

Liverpool—London
July, 1863

The locomotive shrieked and sputtered, spewing sparks and cinders. Like a giant dragon from the mythic past, the Liverpool-to-London train flung itself across the English landscape, gobbling the miles. I sat straight and tense in the first-class carriage, where the dock steward had placed me—a young American woman of the period, unattended, hurrying to the bedside of her injured sister. And *calamity, calamity* hummed the spinning wheels.

Calamity's a rock makin' spreadin' circles . . . How odd, I had not thought that way in years. Our old black nurse in Charleston used to talk like that, likening trouble to a stone thrown into water, the ripples ever widening. How fascinating I had found her maxims in the old days, when I'd first come as a child to Carolina with my English mother and the courteous, scholarly stranger who was my new stepfather. I sensed instinctively, even then, that I would be ever alien to the ways of that slow-moving Southern city; to the haunting tales spun by the mountainous slave woman in her liquid Gullah voice. Emmy was nursemaid when Nell, my enchanting sprite of a half sister, was born, and she comforted me through my mother's death soon after. And while the Colonel, my stepfather, gave me the classical education which stamped me forever as a bluestocking in Charleston's eyes, Emmy filled my lonely young girl's heart with another kind of teaching, lore which, though based on African and other local tales, sprang from some well of universal superstition. I had loved Emmy, and the world of mystery she opened to me, though there had been some dark passages between us.

I, schooled in logic and in probability, had managed for a long time to blot those memories out. I had realized, in time, that Emmy's stories had much in common with the folk myths of my native England, and that those tales of devilments and spells usually had very reasonable and rational explanations. By then a young lady, and the Colonel's assistant in his Tudor research, I had convinced myself I was much too knowledgeable for superstition. And by then Emmy was gone, and Nell off to school in England, and I had not thought of Emmy's circles for many years.

Strange how they were coming back to me, out of the dark mists, ever more insistent, as my journey across the perilous Atlantic neared its end. I had sensed it first on that day when, after seeing my beloved Martin off to war, I had returned to the house on the Battery to find the letter waiting with its English stamp and shocking news. The imagery had come back to me again that night a week later when, alone against the advice of everyone I knew, I had boarded ship to run the Union blockade to my sister's side. For Nell, I would dare anything; Martin would have understood had he been there. There had been time only for a hasty letter, which I hoped would reach him as his regiment rode north. The two-weeks' steamboat journey, dodging Federal gunboats, had been for me a blurred miasma filled with visions of my dear one going off to battle for the Glorious Cause and of my young sister broken in pain on an English sickbed.

The night we had put out to sea had been thick with mist—a good omen, the captain said. A ghost ship, slipping catlike through the dark with no lamps lit . . . I stood on the deck, wrapped in a midnight shawl. Then the mist lifted, and a breeze stirred the fringe of my shawl against my face like shrouded fingers. It was Emmy's voice I heard in the breeze, dark with somber music. And again, more strongly—like the pounding heart of some unknown self buried deep within me and filled with some prescient knowledge too profound for proof—as I saw the green hills of Ireland rise bleak and beautiful against the sky; as I disembarked in crowded Liverpool, an American woman travelling alone, to the scandal of observers; and now, in the inexorable clatter of the train wheels carrying me ever nearer London. The voice, not of Emmy now, but of that other self, telling me that there is a continuing pattern to calamity . . . and that Nell's accident was not the last.

Where had the chain begun? I wondered. Not with my parents' deaths, for those were too long past, too disparate, though each in its way had shaped the path that brought me now to London. My own father had been an Oxford tutor, gentle and consumptive, whose wealth was all in blood and brain and not in purse. I knew little of him except his name. He had been "a Lawson of Suffolk," last of a shabby-genteel branch of a family which reputedly had royal blood in its family tree. A very quiet woman ("My gracious silence," my stepfather called her, quoting *Coriolanus*), my mother never spoke of that young husband who had died soon after I was born, though I sensed that she never ceased to love him. My one memory of English childhood was of waking one night, when I was three or four, to find her laboring by candlelight at the fine sewing that earned our meager board, the tears held firmly back in her reddened eyes and her slender back upright, as a lady's should be, disdaining to lean against the chair.

Later, looking back, I understood my mother must have been near end of tether then, penniless and heartsick, but she remained always gracious, still and calm. Her godmother, Lady Kersey Lavenham, would have stepped in instantly if she had known, but this was after Lady Kersey's famous elopement into the desert with an Arab sheik, so she had no awareness of our plight, and my mother would never dream of asking aid. Then providence had arrived, in the person of Harrison Jardine, Charleston gentleman and scholar. Colonel Jardine, ending a world tour with research work at Oxford, had met my mother, loved her, and whisked us both across the wide Atlantic. I took his name, to his great satisfaction, and became to all intents and purposes American. Then, the spring when I was nine, our darling Nell was born and Mama died.

Mama died and I, like her before me, turned inward in my grief, shutting myself off from the flighty Charleston playmates who neither liked nor understood me. The Colonel, out of pity and his own loneliness, dropped his original plan to send me to Mama's own English boarding school that fall, and instead I threw myself into caring for the red-haired pixie who seemed more a daughter than a sister to me.

Then Lady Kersey reappeared in London, fantastically rich and more fabulous than ever. She learned of Mama's death and wrote most kindly, and after that there were Christmas and birthday gifts, with accompanying affectionate letters. It was Lady Kersey, I suspected, who had encouraged the Colonel in his determination to send Nell, when she was ten, to the London school.

"Nell shall go to Bedliston; she shall not be cheated out of it as you were. Your mother would wish it, and her ladyship kindly offers to take Nell under her protective eye." The Colonel had smiled at me, but he had spoken firmly. "It is best, my dear. The training and associations with girls her own age are just what our small Miss Mischief needs. You are a young woman now, and have been wrapped around Nell's fingers long enough." Poor Father (for so I always thought him), he still felt he owed me a chance to be a belle!

So my sister had sailed for England. I could almost hate the Colonel and Lady Kersey for that now, had they still been alive. For the dark finger of calamity had now stretched across the sea to touch my beloved Nell.

Nell had fallen mysteriously and inexplicably from her London window to the brick pavement below. Nell, injured God alone knew how badly, for the headmistress' letter had told so little. It had taken more than two weeks for the message to come to me from England; a frantic week of arranging affairs, bartering the last of Mama's jewels for passage on a blockade runner, writing Martin; another two weeks and more for my turbulent crossing, and now this interminable, jolting Liverpool-to-London train, though we were racketing through the countryside at an unbelievable sixty miles an hour. And all the while Nell, whom I'd not seen for three years, had been lying broken and alone in the infirmary, waiting, waiting. If only she had never gone to England. If only Lady Kersey had not passed away last winter. If only I *had* gone to her, a year ago, after the Colonel was killed in the quixotic glory of a Confederate cavalry charge that failed. But no, I had stayed in Charleston, not willing to acknowledge, even to myself, that I stayed to be near Martin, who was my love.

A memory of Nell, one of the last times I had seen her, blurred my vision now—Nell in yellow organdy and embroidered pantalettes, dancing in our garden in a patch of sun. A child of light and joy, who now might never dance again. A faintness swept over me, and I groped in my reticule for a scent bottle, intricately wrought in gold and ornamented with enamel-work and pearls. The smelling salts it contained were perfumed with English lavender, but as the sharp, spicy fragrance mingled with ammonia stung my nostrils, the picture that assailed my eyes was not of England. It was of a long, pale room, high-ceilinged, with muslin curtains stirring with breezes from the southern bay. Tall bookcases, reaching to the ceiling, filled with volumes old and rare; a baize-covered table, with presents on it, myself and the Colonel bending over them. Then the door opening and a young man ushered in.

It was on my twentieth birthday that the Colonel had given me the Tudor scent vial. It was then, too, that Martin had called to present his letter of introduction. Martin Cullen Clarke, son of an old Oxford colleague, had come to study with his father's friend; he had stayed for so much more. My twentieth birthday was the day life had turned to richness beyond all dreams—it had brought my first Tudor treasure and my first love.

I had always had an interest in English history, born of my yearning for the country of my birth and a desire to please the stepfather I revered. My studies had brought me a firm friend and mentor, a longing stronger than ever for my homeland, and an enduring delight in the scholarly pursuits that set me apart, more, even, than my alien birth, from the frivolities of my peers. The gift of the scent vial told me that I was no longer just a student, but the Colonel's colleague. And Martin . . . Martin. He called frequently when he knew the Colonel could not possibly be there. It was some time before I dared to dream he came through any personal interest in myself. Then had come a spring day when time and terror had hung suspended, like smoke from the harbor cannon, in the April air.

That had been the beginning of calamity, and I knew even then, with instinct deep as a well and just as cold, that my life was being irrevocably changed. *That* had been the beginning—oh, it had. I felt my backbone tremble and grow chill, and the plush-and-soot railroad compartment faded from my eyes. I was back in Charleston, in the smoke and panic of an April day, and my emotions were in conflict with my mind.

War. The War Between the States. We had known it was coming, ever since Secession, ever since that brave, foolhardy U.S. major had refused to turn over to the Confederacy the little brick fortress in the Charleston harbor. All through the Christmas season of 1860 an ugly tension held the city in its grip; all through an uneasy spring of 1861 the pressure built, and supplies at the fortress dwindled. Our militia marched in the Charleston streets, and I watched detachedly, caring more for the intrigues and loyalties of the sixteenth century than of the nineteenth, but holding the thought in silence; caring for Martin, but holding that in silence too. I did not even write of it to Nell, to whom I told all things.

And then came the dawn of April 12, 1861. *Calamity, calamity,* the clattering wheels sang in my ears, and I thought, Yes, that was the pivotal point, that was when it all began, like the reel of fate flung down and inexorably unrolling. I had awakened to grey murky light and the sound, afar off, of a dull roar of mortar and a crash of guns. I sprang from bed, jerking my bell-pull, and my little maid burst in, her dusky face blanched grey with panic.

A Federal fleet was at sea to bring relief to Sumter; our own General Beauregard had offered the fortress the choice of surrender or "a useless effusion of blood"; the offer had been rejected and war had come. In the streets hotheaded youths and small boys cheered with joy; on the galleried rooftops women watched and waited, and for me, for the first time, it all was real. I fell to my knees and prayed as I had never prayed before.

The Colonel was off with his regiment somewhere, and the servants huddled round me on the rooftop, gibbering with fear as rumors spread. As the day wore on, gale winds rose off the harbor; the guns of Sumter fell silent, but our own batteries kept up a barrage of shells and fires flared everywhere. Light faded, the grey clouds billowed with the stench of gunpowder, and red flames stood out distinct against the smoke. And Martin had come. Martin, with a message from my stepfather, saying he was marching off with the army, leaving me in charge and bidding me not to fear. Martin, wordlessly holding me tight in his arms, where no harm could come. Then when, some ten months later, the Colonel had been killed and Lady Kersey had kindly invited me to come to London, I had not gone.

Now it was July of 1863. The Colonel was dead, my parents long were dead. Lady Kersey had died, and I had never met her, never returned to England. Martin and I were planning to visit there on our wedding journey when the war was over, for he knew how I dreamed of putting down roots in my native soil, perhaps tracing back my mother's tale of the Lawsons, my own people, having royal blood. Never, not in my darkest dreams, had I envisioned arriving in England as I now was doing, all alone, Martin's support present only in the winking diamond on my finger. *Martin.* Why was my mind so obsessed with images of him today, when my thoughts should be all on Nell?

We were approaching London now. The fields outside the windows gave way to a welter of tenements and then to a vast engulfing station. The railed monster lurched and shuddered to a stop. I had received word at the ship's pier that a representative of Lady Kersey's law firm would meet me at the station, and here he was, a long, thin praying mantis of a man, holding the door of my compartment open. "Miss Jardine? Wilkins here, Sir Percival Parrish's clerk. I've a carriage waiting. May I have the tickets for your trunks and boxes?"

After the past weeks of coping alone with crises, I was grateful to place myself under his protection. The station was like a vast Doric temple seething with humanity of all description; I was more weary than I had realised, and being able to surrender responsibility was exquisite relief. Soon I would see Nell for the first time in three years, Nell who needed me. Wilkins assisted me into a luxurious carriage, and we rolled through the streets of a London of which I long had dreamed, yet now I scarcely even saw.

Once I roused myself to ask, "Is it much

further to my sister's school?" and my escort responded, "We are stopping by the Inns of Court first. Sir Percival expects you."

It must be the matter of Lady Kersey's legacy, which Sir Percival had made reference to in his letter. My lips tightened. How insensitive of him not to have grasped that what mattered first was reaching Nell. *Inconsideration is bred of thoughtlessness, but a gentlewoman who would point this out is herself guilty of lack of patience.* I could almost hear my mother's gentle voice saying that, and my stepfather's wry *Besides, tolerance wastes less time in the long run.* I had not thought of that in years; Nell was the one famous for quicksilver temperament, not I. But as my journey carried me further and further away from Charleston, I seemed to have less and less control of my emotions and my thoughts.

And this was journey's end now, in this narrow, quiet street in the old City, and soon, soon, in the school building on the Regency square, I would be united once again with Nell.

I allowed my guide to usher me up steep winding stairs into the musty gentility of Sir Percival Parrish's chambers. Sir Percival himself was patrician and urbane, his old face like a mask of yellowing ivory. He offered me tea, which I refused, and ushered me to a high-backed chair. Outside the leaded windows that opened on the courtyard, bees were humming among late-climbing roses. Sir Percival produced the will and read me my bequest: Lady Kersey had left me her library of books, in the hope they might prove valuable in my work.

"It is, I believe, of considerable worth, as it includes many irreplaceable first editions. Lady Kersey also made one other—er—characteristic provision for you. The books at present are stored in Wychwood House, a thatched Tudor dwelling Lady Kersey owned up in the Cotswolds. The place has long stood empty, but you are to have the privilege, if you wish, of living in it for a year. A trust fund has been set up, the income of which can provide you with a twelve-months' maintenance. If you do not choose to occupy, the house is to be let and the proceeds added to the trust, which will come to you in its entirety when you are thirty."

A thatched cottage . . . leaded windows, shoulder-high fireplaces and twisting stairs, and perhaps a garden. A wild, romantic field of flowers, like in the pictures of Anne

Hathaway's house, or one of the formal Tudor beds of knots and herbs. What a wonderful setting, one day, for our honeymoon. But at the moment my first responsibility was Nell. "Please, may we discuss this later?"

"Yes, of course. You must be anxious to reach your sister's side. We were most distressed to learn of her accident, the intelligence of which the headmistress quite properly conveyed to us. Naturally, we have made it our business to see that your sister has received the best of care. Lady Kersey would have wanted it, and frankly, anyone having once met Lady Kersey would have difficulty ever afterward in going against her wishes." The old man smiled with unexpected kindness. "But I'm afraid I can give you no further information about the accident. You must have thought me most unfeeling to have whisked you here straight away, but it occurred to me that an interval of rest between arrival and encounter might be refreshing. And ah, yes," he added casually as I rose, "we have some correspondence for you here. A letter which arrived this morning. Wilkins!"

He signaled to the clerk, who extended an

envelope to me on a silver salver. All at once the room was very still, as though even the bees beyond the window had ceased to hum. *This is why I am here.* The awareness sprang to my mind unbidden. *This is why I was brought to the Inns of Court, not for news of Nell's condition nor of the legacy, but to receive this letter.*

The envelope was black-bordered. There were many such in America these days. Doubtless one of the Charleston neighbors had suffered loss on the battlefields and was sending notice, that was all.

I longed to thrust the envelope in my reticule unopened, but one does not behave so brusquely if reared by a mother who was an English lady. One accepts the letter and the proffered paper-knife with a courteous smile, and one employs the knife.

The letter opener and the salver were heavy silver in a Queen Anne pattern. Martin would like them. Martin preferred these plainer lines to the Tudor elaborations that I favored.

Martin. Not a neighbour, but Martin, my love. Martin who had—what was the obscene euphemism polite society used to mask the rotten stench of truth?—"made the supreme sacrifice for the glorious cause" in some god-forsaken Pennsylvania field I'd never heard of and would never now forget. *Martin was gone,* and a brother officer, having found my London address in that last letter, had written with cruel kindness.

The happiness which had been so brief a dream was ended. The thin black-bordered paper fluttered from my stiff fingers like a dead moth, and I knew that for the rest of my life the scent of lemon oil on carved oak paneling and the mustiness of lawbooks would be the smell of death.

"My dear Miss Jardine! Wilkins, some water, quickly!" The room, with its late-afternoon sunlight filtering through the leaded panes, had suddenly gone black. My brooch held the lace collar at my throat too tightly. Sir Percival was fanning me with some legal papers—Lady Kersey's will. I started to laugh, irrepressibly, choked on the water Wilkins was thrusting on me, and forced myself back to a semblance of control.

"I am so sorry . . . the strain, no doubt, of the journey . . ."

"Yes, yes, of course. And it is so distressingly hot in Town this season."

Compared to Charleston in July, London

was like early spring, but I could not tell the elderly solicitor so when he was being kind, so very kind, telling me he would be at my service when I wished. When I was rested, when I had seen my sister, when I had determined what to do about the books and Wychwood House . . .

"I have already determined," I heard my own voice saying, firm and clear in the still hanging air. "I intend to live there, with my sister."

Where that knowledge came from, I do not know; it was simply there, as though some older and wiser mind were speaking through me. Sir Percival was looking at me with something akin to horror. I met his gaze. "You did say I have that privilege, did you not?"

Oh, I was right, I had rattled his reserve, and there were things which he did not intend to say. The momentary gleam of humanness was disappearing within fold after fold of legal privilege and old age. "Lady Kersey exhibited quite a determination toward the end that you should have an opportunity to occupy Wychwood House." And you did not approve, I thought acutely. "I expect she thought it would provide a suitable holiday home for a married woman. But for two young women alone . . ." Sir Percival shrugged, scattering an invisible cloud of disapprobation. "You Americans feel differently about such things."

I rose, smoothing my crinoline with a gloved hand that only will power kept from trembling. "You have been misinformed," I said carefully. "I am an Englishwoman raised abroad. And I shall certainly occupy the house." I had a sudden vivid sense of Lady Kersey's presence. How sad that I had never met her, would never be able to thank her for the gesture which I knew had been a godsend.

Sir Percival was bowing above my hand in a proper little ritual of departure. "And ah, yes, your letter. Wilkins, please."

It still lay, forgotten, where it had fallen when the giddiness swept over me. The clerk returned it to me, eyes tactfully averted, and I thrust it into the pocket of my fawn-colored traveling suit. I ought to be wearing mourning. These cream and brown and gold tones suited me, Martin told me; he said they brought out the gold tints in my caramel-colored hair and caused my olive skin to take on a flush of warmth. *Martin* . . .

"Are you sure you are feeling strong enough to leave?" Sir Percival was saying. "Not bad news, I trust."

He had seen the black border on the letter. I drew myself taller, steeling my will to hold back signs of grief. "A . . . friend of my stepfather. I am quite all right now." I bowed to the solicitor, to his clerk, and when the latter opened the door onto the street, I passed through with my head held high. A gentlewoman did not betray emotion, not if her heart was breaking, and I had been tutored well in that hard school.

I emerged from the Inns of Court into the hot light of the street. This was a man's city and a man's part of town. Messenger boys jostled one another on the pavements, and men of affairs, beautifully hatted and gloved, stood talking in threes and fours in the narrow streets. I was conspicuous, out of place, a too-slender woman, somewhat tall, in the fashionably wide golden-tan hoopskirt that swept the street dust, the leghorn bonnet with its wreath of brown pansies Martin loved because they matched my eyes. It was a street out of Shakespeare, all overhanging buildings and twisting lanes. I wished Martin were there beside me, my hand tucked through his arm. I loved to walk so; oddly, it made me feel not dependent but able to stand tall.

The narrow street opened into one wider and more bustling. To my right the road divided to embrace an old tall-steepled church, St. Clement Danes.

> "Oranges and lemons,"
> Say the bells of St. Clement's . . .

I must remember to tell Martin in my next letter. But there would be no next letter, there never would be again. I would not disgrace myself by weeping in a public street. I hurried heedlessly, this way and that, until at last I found myself at a railing by the river, my ribs in their confining stays hurting with my painful breath. It was quieter here, with a faint breeze, and below me the opaque waters moved in a kind of measured timelessness. Old Father Thames. I was really here, at last, on my native heath.

I looked to my left, downriver toward Tower Bridge, and something of its quiet endurance entered into my heart to ease its pain. This was now, this was real; Charleston and all that was a part of it now lay behind me.

How unbelievably thoughtless I was being, dawdling thus beside the river instead of rushing to Nell's side! Why had I allowed Wilkins to make me stop at Sir Percival's chambers the very moment of my arrival? I had been selfishly postponing the painful knowledge of Nell's suffering. Odd that Mrs. Bertram at the school had been so vague about the extent of the injury. Odd, too, that Sir Percival apparently knew no more than I. Doubtless he had been trying to spare me.

Martin. I must not let myself think of him, not yet. I must go to Nell. And it was as well that I had talked first with Sir Percival Parrish. Now I could face Nell with a smile and a plan already determined, could say gaily, "Guess what, darling? Dear Lady Kersey has given us a chance to live in a cottage in the country. And there's the scent of mystery about it!" Nell would like that.

Suddenly it seemed impossible to wait any longer. I hailed a cab, not caring that this was probably unsuitable, by London standards, for a young woman travelling alone. If I was to be considered a foreigner here, then I would take advantage of that fact. We rattled through narrow Tudor streets, through spacious cream-colored Regency squares.

The Bedliston School was in one of the latter, a series of austerely beautiful houses grouped together. A trim maid greeted me in the Adam entryway and showed me into a sitting room all pale green and cream. "I'll fetch the Mistress, miss," she said, retiring.

This building was so very still, like a lovely museum through which no one ever moved. When a high-bosomed woman in spreading skirts swept in, I was almost startled. "Miss Jardine. A pleasure at last to meet you. I was an instructress here, you know, in your mother's day." I hadn't known, but Mrs. Bertram was moving smoothly on. "It was most fortunate that you could come at once. Eleanor has made all the improvement she is likely to in the infirmary, and I am sure you will be anxious to move her elsewhere. We are on holiday just now, you know, and most of our young ladies have gone home."

"I noticed that the quiet was remarkable for a school."

Mrs. Bertram permitted herself a faint smile. "We pride ourselves on the quiet and decorum even when the scholars are in residence. That is one of the things, I fear, that Eleanor has found difficult to accept." She met my blank look blandly. "Often children who have been indulged after the death of a parent do not adjust easily to school routine. The sensible ones learn quickly what is required of them, and settle in. The willful ones, who are determined to maintain their own individuality rather than adopt proper form, learn their lesson later, often to their sorrow."

She flashed me an odd glance, and I stared at her. "Are you implying that Nell's accident was her own fault?"

"One feels only that she is the sort of child to whom accidents are likely to occur."

This relentlessly calm woman did not like Nell. She wanted Nell removed. Little wonder, since she herself bore responsibility for Nell's present plight. "Let me understand you," I said carefully. "You are telling me you have found my sister an unsatisfactory scholar?"

"Not at all. She is extremely clever." Mrs. Bertram made the word itself seem somehow undesirable. "I have found her mercurial, restless, prone to fancies. When she came, as of course you know, she was much given to laughter and other exhibitions of high spirits. Eleanor—"

"My sister is called Nell," I interrupted evenly.

"We do not use pet names here. I am afraid Eleanor has found it difficult to have such fancies and high spirits rooted out."

But I did not wish them rooted from her, my heart cried out. They were part of her particular enchantment. I pressed my lips together tightly. "We will speak of this later. Right now I wish to see my sister."

"Of course." Mrs. Bertram touched a bell. The maid reappeared and I followed her up the stairs, along a hall and through a green baize door to a long corridor that smelled of strong Lye soap. Twice I caught the girl glancing at me curiously. It ought not to have annoyed me, but it did.

We turned a corner, and were in the infirmary wing. The maid stopped outside a door. "She's just inside, miss, and Nurse is with her. You'll be able to see her yourself in just a minute. They've not moved her back to her own room, as she's took a misliking to it since the accident."

Small wonder, I thought with a stab of anger. I had observed the long windows with their black iron railings as I descended from the cab. They seemed most secure; only unpardonable and frightening negligence could have resulted in Nell's fall. I dismissed the maid, who looked agog for gossip, and wondered, not for the first time, what the shock of that terrible happening had done to Nell.

Nell had been so radiantly happy in her last letter. I had written joyously of my engagement, which she must have guessed was in the wind, and the next ship returning had brought a fat epistle, sounding more like my own Nell than any previous letters. She had painted an ecstatic, romantic picture of the happiness we three would share, for it was understood that Nell would always have a home with us. Then three days later had come the terse, shocking missive from Mrs. Bertram. How had it happened, why had it happened? I still could not comprehend, but at the moment it did not matter, nothing mattered but that Nell was beyond that door and needed me.

The door was of the glass-topped sort, with half drawn shade. I could make out the bulky form of an attendant bending across the bed. Then she drew back. For the first time in three years I saw my sister, and my heart stilled.

Unconsciously I had been expecting the gay bubbling child of ten in yellow organdy, dancing in the sunlight. She was here no more. In her place on the narrow pallet lay a slender girl with that evanescent beauty only the young sometimes have on the threshold of maturity. The familiar cloud of red-gold hair on the white pillow framed a little oval face too finely chiseled, and the curling lashes of her slanted eyes, that odd grey-black so striking with red hair, cast alarming shadows on her fragile skin. She was gazing somberly off across the room with an expression in her eyes too early old, and I felt a chill run down my spine. She looked like a changeling child—she looked like our mother. Then the heavy lashes lifted and she saw me. Even through the glass door I felt the magic of her presence, and she was my Nell once more.

"Camilla! Oh, I knew you'd come. But I've waited so long, so long!" Nell's thin transparent hands reached out to me, and I hurried to her, for I was alarmed by the fervour of her excitement.

"Hush, darling. I'm here now. You mustn't overdo."

"I'll do splendidly, now you're with me. It's all the medicine I need, to be with you."

Her eyes looked past me, and the ghost of her old mischievous smile flickered. "Where is your Martin? Did he not come with you? Did you leave him behind to come to me, Camilla?"

I could not speak, and in an instant her whole expression altered, becoming indescribably tender. Nell has always been sensitive to every nuance.

"Camilla, dearest, what's wrong?"

My dry lips opened, and my voice came out hard and flat. "Martin is dead."

It was real, now. Until this moment it had been just words on paper, but my own voice saying them made it real. A wave of recognition and remembrance crashed over me. *Martin was dead. Martin* . . . the gentleness of his eyes, the strength in his arms when he held me—the soft breeze that ruffled our clothing as we stood on the Battery after he'd slipped the ring upon my finger, the silver of twilight stealing in across the bay . . .

Grief poured over me in a flood, like a dam bursting. I was weeping shuddering uncontrollable sobs in my sister's arms. For she, heedless of her own pain, flung herself up to hold me tight with an intensity that almost frightened me.

"Camilla! My own dear, dear Camilla!" Her words, in a choked whisper, had a strange formality, as if she were taking a solemn ritual vow. "We must be very good to one another always, for we are all each other has now. We're all alone together. But you must not worry. I'll never, never leave you! Never!"

She clung to me passionately, her whole thin body shaking. She was crying, I knew, not just for me and Martin but for her lost mother and father, for all the life that was gone. It was then, holding her hurt childlike body in my arms, that I remembered our one haven, and the ache in my heart hardened into a stern resolve.

Wychwood House.

The old life might be ended, and with it my own dreams, but Nell's was not. Enchanting Nell, who was all the things that I could never be, who must yet have all that I now would never know. Nell's magic must not be quenched by orphan loneliness and sickbed pain.

I would take Nell up to Wychwood House and make her well and strong. She needed me so, and there was now no other claim upon me. Whatever lay before us, whatever life might hold, I would take care of Nell.

2

London—Rossford-under-Wychwood
July, 1863

"WHEREVER you run, Camilla, be very sure you know what you are running to, as well as from." Martin had said that to me when the dogs of war snapped at our heels, when I had known only that I had to flee, and had found sanctuary in his arms. That refuge was forever gone now, and I knew exactly what it was to which I ran. Serenity and peace, and a life for Nell. And work, too, the blessed grace of the quiet studies for which I had been trained. And perhaps a garden, a Tudor herb garden such as I'd read of in old books, which would restore my soul. I had loved the herb garden on the plantation when I was young, though I had turned from it after I'd lost myself in books. I found myself longing now for the healing touch of green and growing things. It would work out, I would *make* it work, and with the knowledge the tension drained from my body.

Nell must have sensed it, for after a moment she released me and fell back among her pillows, her tear-wet eyes as luminous as dark stars. "It *will* be all right, won't it? Just as soon as we are home. Oh, Camilla, how soon can you take me back to Charleston?"

Now was the time to say it. "We are not going back."

"Not . . ." Nell stared at me, her eyes a deep uncharted emptiness. "Camilla! You'll not make me stay here, even now!" I started at her phrasing, but she rushed on, childlike and frightened. "Isn't that why you came, to take me home?"

The appeal in her voice and my own grief, left me shaken. I rose and moved away a bit and searched for words. "We can't go back. There is nothing there any more for us . . . You don't know what it's like at home now, Nell." I took a deep breath, knowing I could tell this new Nell all that I had so carefully spared the child. "Everything's changed. The war . . . there is no meat in Charleston any more. Everything—quinine, not just luxuries but necessities—has to run the blockade. Confederate currency's not worth the paper it's printed on."

"Then why," Nell said in bewilderment, "why didn't you let me come home?"

"I couldn't risk your running the blockade. It had meant so much to Father, knowing you were safe here and happy."

A look I could not understand passed across Nell's eyes. "But the tuition?" she asked gently.

"Lady Kersey."

"Oh," Nell said oddly. "Well, yes, of course," as though I had given her some explanation. Then, with a little convulsive movement, she turned to me. "What then? You won't make me stay in school now I'm a cripple?"

How unflinchingly she could say it. I hurried to her. "That's what's so providential, darling. Lady Kersey owned a cottage in the country. She's given me a chance to live in it for a year, and I've determined we shall make a home there together. Did she ever speak of it to you? Wychwood House."

"Wychwood. The wood of the witches." Nell had gone off into the unknown country of her mind, her eyes remote and dreaming. Then they flickered again with her old mischief. "Yes, she spoke of it. When she last came to see me, she said she'd like to see what happened if we went there. That you would enter into the kingdom prepared for you, and *I* would likely set a cosmic battle into motion." Nell laughed at my blankness. "Lady Kersey was like that, always riddles."

"I wish I'd known her. Nell, what was she like?"

"Fabulous," Nell said. "An ugly old harridan with dyed red hair and eyes like an eagle's. And wonderful jewels. She was very kind."

"But you didn't like her?" I asked.

Nell was silent for a moment. "No, I didn't. *You* would have. She would have liked you. I was a . . . duty to her."

There was a somber, wistful look in Nell's eyes that tugged at my heart. "Doing one's duty is a beautiful thing," I said gently.

"Not," Nell said profoundly, "to the person who's the duty! How dreadful to know one's only an obligation to someone else!" She stopped. "I've been Mrs. Bertram's duty, too, haven't I? Perhaps that's why . . ."

"A shocking muddle she made of it," I added, when Nell did not go on. The relief at being able to talk unguardedly with my sister after three years' separation was intoxicating.

"She made *me* feel a sweep. Is she always like that? The grand detachment?"

Nell giggled. "Lady Kersey said it was a great annoyance to Mrs. Bertram that she was not nobly born."

Nell's voice, rich and cracked with age like old crusted port, evoked an image of Lady Kersey for me. But seeing her wince involuntarily at her slight movement, my laughter quickly stilled.

"She's hardly to the schoolroom born, judging from her appalling negligence." I sensed, rather than saw, Nell's withdrawal. She had, since babyhood, that gift for retreating deep within herself. I put my hand on her thin one quickly. "Don't. I know it pains you to speak of your accident, but we must."

"Mrs. Bertram can tell you," Nell said woodenly. "Mrs. Bertram knows all about it. Didn't she tell you?" She sounded like a wind-up toy, and her dark eyes with their golden lights were uneasy behind their lowered lashes. She was afraid. My Nell, who had feared nothing before coming here, was afraid of this formidable woman.

My anger flared, but I felt carefully for words. "She obviously prefers not to speak of it. But it is *your* story that I care about. How did it happen? You must tell me, Nell."

Her pulse leaped beneath my fingers, but her voice was low. "It was the day after I had your letter about . . . about Martin. I paid an urchin in the park a penny to post my answer. I wanted you to know how I really felt. Mrs. Bertram sent for me that evening. She had expected me to submit a proper letter of felicitation for her approval, and—"

"How did she know of my engagement?" I interrupted.

Nell looked surprised. "She reads all our mail before we see it. I knew she'd make me write you a dry, dull letter, but this time I made up my mind that I'd not do it. *She* got one of the other girls to tattle. There are ways of doing that, you know." Nell's eyelids flickered. "She called me to her sitting room. Have you seen her sitting room, Camilla?"

I nodded, not trusting myself to speak.

"She said it was her duty to write you of my insubordination and slyness. That I was an uncouth American."

"What did you say?"

Nell's eyes met mine honestly. "Nothing." No, she would have retreated, and that would only have added to Mrs. Bertram's fury.

"When she released me, I went upstairs. The students are together in the common room at that hour, but she sent me to my room, and I was glad. It was quiet there, and cool, and I . . . I'd been afraid I would faint, and I couldn't have fainted in front of *her,* Camilla. I went to stand by the open window, and leaned against the frame, and then—then everything went dark. And that's all I remember, truly!"

She had commenced trembling violently, and now with a sudden gasp she flung herself over so that her head was buried in my lap. Then pain, that shuddering pain in her hurt back that left her blanched and breathless, frightened me out of my wits until I was able to soothe her off to sleep. Then, armored with anger, I swept downstairs to beard Mrs. Bertram in her Adam chamber.

The headmistress was disengaged, the little maid informed me, but the supper bell would be ringing shortly.

"It is no matter. I wish to see her now, and I shall not be long," I snapped back crisply. And in a moment the girl, eyes big, was back saying Mrs. Bertram would receive me.

That lady rose to greet me as I entered, admirable in her British self-control. I would have liked her better had there been the faintest trace of uneasiness or concern. She must have known from my flashing eyes and heaving bosom that I was in a state of silent fury, but she merely offered me a chair and remarked that she hoped I found my sister resting well.

"Thank you, I prefer to stand," I responded coldly. I was astonished at the satisfaction I found in obliging her to remain upon her feet. "As for *Nell*"—I stressed the name—"she is not comfortable at all, but in great pain."

I had an unpleasant feeling that my passion put me at a disadvantage, but I did not care. It was my sister about whom Mrs. Bertram was murmuring, so coolly, that "the child, regrettably, still has a tendency toward exaggeration."

"Is that why you found it necessary to read her mail?"

Mrs. Bertram's eyebrows rose. "Surely you would feel us negligent in our duty if we did not supervise the children's correspondence. I assure you it is a duty expected of the better schools. Forgive me; I forget you Americans are not accustomed to the institution of finishing schools."

"You are in error. Nell is half American, but I myself am an Englishwoman. And it would seem the Bedliston School's first responsibility should be the physical safety of its scholars."

"May I ask if your sister has charged any negligence in that direction?"

"She does not wish to speak of it, and I am sure, my dear Mrs. Bertram, *you* can understand that." I could not resist the remark. "Certainly, as I am Nell's guardian, you will not be so reticent with me."

Mrs. Bertram shrugged faintly. "The child has given no explanation to us, either. She was alone in her room. The balcony rail is low, but sturdy and well-bolted. Most likely she was standing in the open window, felt faint, and fell. Girls of that age are given to swoons and weakness. They indulge in unhealthy practices, sleeping in their stays and pulling each other's laces tighter each day until they achieve thirteen- or fourteen-inch waists and wrecked constitutions."

"I should have thought," I said icily, "that supervision would prevent such excesses from occurring."

Mrs. Bertram thinned her lips but did not reply. Nell, naturally slender, would laugh at such vanities. Or would she? How much had she changed, these three years we had been parted? She spoke like one so early old; she had grown so frail and still, like Tennyson's Lady of Shalott. *"The doom has come upon me," cried the Lady of Shalott.* However fanciful, that was what Nell's fatalistic acceptance of her injury almost seemed. But I would never, never speak of that to Mrs. Bertram.

The supper bell had rung, and the wan light told me the hour was now well toward evening. "Let us continue this conversation tomorrow," I said at last. "I must engage lodgings somewhere near, and I will call again to see my sister after I have discussed matters with my solicitor."

"But you must stay here," Mrs. Bertram exclaimed, prompted, no doubt, by deference to the lawyer. "We have ample space, since our scholars are nearly all home on holiday."

So I accepted, requesting that I be placed in Nell's old room. I half hoped to find there some further insight, but if she recognised this, Mrs. Bertram did not comment. She extended an invitation to dine with her, which I refused, and said she would then have a tray sent to my room.

"And our man will go to fetch your

trunks," she said in parting, turning me again over to Sarah's guidance.

I dined in my dressing gown, grateful for solitude, and afterward made my way again to the infirmary wing. Nell was sleeping, so I retraced my steps to the prim white room that was still luminous with light. In London, so much more northerly in latitude than Charleston, the summer dark comes early. I undressed slowly, feeling the stillness settle in the near-deserted building, and pulled off the net that held at my nape the heavy twist of hair. My head felt lighter without its weight. Taking the ivory backed brushes that had been my mother's, I went to the window and pulled the narrow floor-touching panels open. A faint breeze drifted in caressingly, eddying the curtains of thin embroidered mull. Below, in the courtyard, geraniums bloomed, and another geranium, spindly from neglect since Nell's incapacity, blossomed on the sill, which was scarcely deeper than the flowerpot it held. Across the courtyard, lamps began going on in windows. I wondered if anyone had been looking out those windows when Nell fell.

There is something indescribably lonely about summer twilight when one is alone.

This building was so still. Somewhere, in a far-off wing, Mrs. Bertram was going about her own affairs. Nell was lying in the infirmary in sleep that gave a respite from her pain. The sky was darkening, and above the row of terraced houses a few stars twinkled.

In such a night as this,
When the sweet wind did gently kiss
the trees
And they did make no noise . . .
In such a night

Stood Dido with a willow in her hand
Upon the wild sea banks and waft her
love
To come again to Carthage . . .

Martin had read that to me as we stood together, looking out across the water, the last night of his leave. Now, like Dido, I was all alone. I would not think of it. What's past is past; what's done cannot be undone. Nell was right. It mattered not what lay behind, or why, or how. Martin was gone; Nell, crippled. Useless to curse my fate or seek the cause. The future was Wychwood House. The future was Nell's.

It was one thing to make such covenant in the intimate stillness of the night. Putting it into practice in hot daylight was another thing entirely. Especially insofar as its execution depended on the cooperation of strangers in an alien land. Everywhere I turned next day, it seemed, I was confronted with an impenetrable, bland façade. By teatime my head was throbbing, and I half believed that Lady Kersey had been right: to go to Wychwood House was to set a cosmic battle into motion.

No doubt it was because I was in my beloved Shakespeare's homeland that so many of his phrases echoed in my brain. The earth was more fluid, and things were not what they seemed. Everywhere was that noncommittal courtesy with which polite society conceals its walls. It commenced in the morning when I interviewed the doctor. "Mending takes time," he would only say when I pressed him for a precise prognosis of Nell's condition.

"But it has been five, six weeks now since her fall. Surely there has been progress? I don't even know the nature of her injuries."

"There were numerous bruises and contusions, which was not surprising, and a dislocated shoulder, which is healing nicely. Apparently the child took the full weight of the fall upon her heel, so that and the ankle bone were shattered. We were forced to wait until the swelling had subsided before the bones could be set right. Naturally, she was in considerable pain."

"And still is." The image of Nell in my arms last night rose up, and I pressed on firmly. "How long before she is able to walk again?"

The doctor was plump and sleek; he removed his eyeglasses and polished them on an immaculate handkerchief before replying. "A fall of some distance onto marble paving . . . it was providential that she survived at all. Fortunately, she was discovered almost immediately by another child, who stupidly, instead of running for aid, attempted to give your sister her own assistance. She, being conscious and displaying a remarkable will power, insisted on pulling herself upright with the other youngster's help. She collapsed almost at once. Useless now, of course, to speculate on the amount of damage that attempt has caused. As yet she seems unable to endure the slightest elevation without pain, but in time one hopes she will be able to sit upright in an invalid chair."

Blackness lapped at the edges of my consciousness, but I fought it fiercely. "Are you telling me she may never stand—walk—again?"

" 'Never' is a very definite word. One cannot be that sure of anything, now, can one? Remarkable cures often happen overnight. Follow the scheme you've proposed to me, Miss Jardine. Take her up to the country and make her as comfortable as you can. The journey will be difficult, but she could scarcely suffer more than she does already. Time will tell, Miss Jardine, time will tell."

"And all *you* can tell me is to wait and see?"

His "My dear Miss Jardine!" was intended to intimidate me, but it did not, for I now knew more than he cared to show: he was the best medical man in London, Lady Kersey's own physician, but he was baffled. Leave her in bed until she improved or worsened, that was his answer.

I was uneasy when I left him, and my next business, in Sir Percival Parrish's chambers, intensified that feeling. I found the lawyer prepared to be avuncular, with weighty arguments marshaled to beat down my quixotic proposition.

"I have already made my final decision," I said firmly. "I intend to occupy Wychwood House at once." I pressed on rapidly before he could recover. "The place *is* habitable, I understand?"

"Oh, yes. It has been kept up, despite standing empty all these years. Her Ladyship retained a solicitor in the village to see to matters. He also has the management of the trust fund. I wrote him of your unanticipated trip to England, but we scarcely imagined that you would intend—"

"But I do intend," I interrupted. "I appreciate your counsel, Sir Percival, but my mind is set. And frankly, I think that Lady Kersey would quite approve."

My mother would not approve the blunt manner of my announcement, nor my stepfather the rapid, illogical fashion in which I had arrived at my decision. It was as if, in running the Federal gunboats, the bonds which so long had bound me to a pattern of decorum had been snapped. I was listening now to an instinctive inner voice.

"One further question." I paused to face the lawyer. "If I had not chosen to occupy, what would have become of Wychwood House?"

"My dear Miss Jardine." There was that phrase again. Legal privilege: the mirror image of the doctor's aura of confidentiality—and intimidation. "I'm sure you can understand why it is impossible . . . All I can tell you is that Lady Kersey most definitely did not wish Wychwood House to pass directly to—ah—such as were in line."

Sir Percival looked, for a fleeting moment, quite old and troubled, and I relented slightly. "I can understand that you must be disturbed at seeing the property go out of family hands." There it was again, that odd trick of withdrawal, like Nell's own. My senses sharpened. "Sir Percival, who *were* her heirs?"

"I am afraid that, also, I am not at liberty . . . You are quite determined, then, to go to Oxfordshire? May I ask when?"

"The day after tomorrow." That again was the voice within me speaking, but I knew it counseled true. "I would appreciate it, Sir Percival, if you would inform her Ladyship's representative in the village of my coming."

I left the offices with my hands full of business papers and of timetables and maps which Wilkins, unexpectedly helpful, had produced. There was no time now for melancholy meditation beside the river. Having something definite to do would keep my mind occupied and unable to dwell on sorrow. I sensed that if once yielded to, my grief for Martin was such that I would never rise again. I knew that I was running away from the memory of his beloved voice, his touch. There would come a time when my heart could face those talismans with poignancy, not pain. But not now, not yet. Now I, like my mother before me, would dwell for a time in Oxfordshire and, embracing duty, make it a blessing to me.

"Camilla, dear." Nell's thin hand touched mine across the tea tray. She was regarding me with a grave, troubled gaze. "You're worn out, aren't you? All because of me. It would have been better if I had . . . I cannot bear to be a burden to you."

"Don't you ever, ever dare say such a foolish thing!" The words burst from me.

Nell looked at me searchingly, then reached for a volume lying near her on the bed. "Listen, dear. I found this in the book Lady Kersey gave to me at Christmas. It's a poem about a scholar who turned gypsy to learn the 'arts to rule as they desired the working of men's brains, and bind them to what thoughts they will.' It must be wonderful to have such powers. It's said the scholar gypsy's shade still walks in Oxfordshire

"In hat of antique shape and cloak of grey . . .
Leaning backward in a pensive dream,
And fostering in thy lap a heap of flowers
Plucked in shy fields and distant Wychwood bowers.

Mrs. Bertram thinks *I'm* a gypsy and you're a scholar. Now we have a scholar gypsy who's the haunt of our own Wychwood!"

How easily Nell had accepted the notion of "our Wychwood."

I kissed her good night and went wearily to bed, but it was several hours before I fell to sleep.

I awoke to a grey light and a soft relentless tapping, like a funeral tattoo. Rain. Not the quick, violent summer storms that came at home and were as quickly gone, but the slow, steady, inexorable English rain of which I long had heard. There was a raw chill in the air. I dressed and hurried down the corridors to Nell's room. Early as I was, she was awake and feverish to start our journey.

I fetched Nell's traveling clothes and helped her into them as gently as I could, for she could do little for herself and her slightest move brought pain. Nell bit her lip but made no sound, and even laughed at the expression on my face. "Poor Cam. I do hate to be such a burden to you."

"Don't talk that way," I snapped, more brusquely than I meant, for I was shaken by the thinness of the frail child's body just blooming into womanhood. Her simple dress of dark-green gauze hung loosely, and after she was dressed and her cloud of copper hair brushed and bundled in a net, she sank back on the pillows, trembling. I looked at her and was assailed by doubts.

Was it right, that voice which directed our paths toward Wychwood? Or ought I to have listened to the sensible advice of Sir Percival? Certainly I was being quixotic in the extreme. But there was, quite simply, nowhere else to go. Other than back to Charleston, which was an ordeal that I could not face. So here we were, strangers and wayfarers, going out into the wilderness in faith like Abraham. Seeking—what had Nell quoted Lady Kersey?—to enter into the Kingdom prepared for us.

"Please, miss." It was the little maid, curtseying. "The Mistress says the carriage is at the door. Mrs. Bertram begs you'll excuse her, as she's busy interviewing tradesmen in the downstairs office."

Mrs. Bertram was taking care to avoid a meeting, and I did not know whether to be angry or relieved.

Nell bore stoically a stalwart footman's carrying her downstairs. The carriage was closed, and large, chosen so Nell was able to half recline, but the dampness penetrated our very bones. Before we had gone more than a few blocks, I knew that my fears for the journey had been, if anything, underestimated. Nell gripped my hand and forced a smile, but neither of us spoke.

The carriage rattled past the tenements I had glimpsed as I approached the city. This was not the London of cloistered courts or dreaming squares; it was turbulent, choked with humanity, vehicles and debris. The streets were rank with filth, and the stench of offal reached our nostrils. Once, when we stopped at a crossing, I glimpsed a barefoot urchin, younger than my sister, plying his broom in the muck to clear a walk. Nell was silent, but her fingers dug into mine.

We careened close to a drayman, who shook his fist, muttering imprecations. The carriage lurched, halted, rolled forward a few lengths and stopped again. I rubbed the mist from the dirty window with my handkerchief and peered out at the station's bulk looming still a block away.

The driver's voice came to me hollowly. "Best I can do, mum. Been some accident, like. There's a barrow spilling all cross the gutter, an' the copper won't let us through. I got t' turn back 'ere, and y'd best 'op out an' foot it like the rest. It ain't so far."

"We can't. My sister's invalid-chair can't be taken through this muck! I must secure a porter to lift her in and out."

"Sorry, mum." Blank, closed indifference. " 'Elp you myself if I could, but I can't leave my ve-hicle and horse. 'E's in a fair take-up now, an' the copper likewise."

Indeed the policeman was already fiercely gesticulating to move along, and there was an impatient hammering against the carriage side. The door was wrenched open.

"Here, madam, you'll have to take to the curbings, like or not." A man—I would *not* call him gentleman despite his cultured tones—was addressing me with ill-concealed annoyance. "Madam, I have a train to catch, and you are blocking traffic. Will you kindly condescend to step down so your driver can turn round and allow my man to pass?"

Martin would have sent the fellow reeling in the gutter. But Martin was not here, would never be here again. I was on my own, and ironically, it was Nell who looked after me.

"I am so sorry," Nell's soft voice said. "It's my fault, you see. I . . . can't walk, and there's no way to get me to the station. We don't know how . . ."

Ignoring me, the man addressed himself directly to my sister. "Can you put your arms around my neck? Very good. If you've an invalid-chair, my man will take it in the wagon." In a minute he had swept Nell up and was striding toward the station, leaving me to pay the cabman and hurry after. I thanked my stars that I had had the foresight to ship our heavy luggage on ahead.

The stranger was fairly running; Nell's eyes were closed and I knew her back was in agony, but she gave no sign. Once under cover of the vast barnlike station, he slowed for me to fall in breathlessly beside him. "Which train?"

"What? Oh... Rossford-under-Wychwood."

Did I imagine a change in his expression? His voice gave no indication. "Get your tickets at that window yonder. I'll put the young lady and your things in a compartment."

I had no choice but to obey, though I seethed with apprehensiveness and anger. And when, after an infuriating delay at the ticket window, I at last found the compartment where Nell waited, the man was gone.

Nell's hands reached out to me swiftly. "Quick, we're starting! I was afraid you wouldn't come in time." Her pulse was pounding; her overbright eyes darted rapidly around our close compartment. "Isn't this splendid! Like a little private parlor. Can't you just see us, Camilla, fifty years from now, facing each other like this on each side of the fire—there must be fireplaces at Wychwood House—sipping tea together and pouring the cat some cream. We must get a cat, a coal-black cat with emerald eyes. And didn't that man remind you of the gypsy in that poem? The same grey cloak and hat, and appearing and disappearing like a ghost into the rain."

"We are only given Wychwood House for a year, you know. And I do not want to hear about any ghosts when we're alone in a country house together on a rainy night."

"But there are ghosts in Wychwood," Nell said.

I looked at her sharply, but she had closed her eyes. Her effervescent mood was fading and I had an uneasy feeling it had been only a disguise to hide her pain. And something more.

I shivered, feeling the rain invade my bones. For the voice within me was giving a name to that other presence, and the name that it spoke was fear.

Dampness and chill and jolting, and rain like haunted fingers on the windows—only our will power carried us through that journey. Even in the luxury of a first-class carriage, the seat was not long enough for Nell to lie down on, except bent awkwardly. I put my carpetbag flat on the seat and wadded my shawl against it to make a pillow for her. Nell endured in stoic silence, but within half an hour she was biting her lower lip and cold beads of moisture dewed her pale face. I undid her bonnet and smoothed her damp hair with my hand, and she forced a smile.

We traversed the suburbs, row on row of huddled houses to which the poorer populace had flocked, deserting the country when the mills began. Then we were in the open land, fields on rolling fields, interspersed by stands of ancient trees—an occasional farmhouse lonely in its private world; tiny villages that were no more than a market cross, a church, and a row or two of toy houses, tightly packed. Was this what Rossford would be like? Rossford-under-Wychwood. Wychwood House. Though I'd never seen it, never heard of it before, as we rattled on and I held Nell tight and tried to ease her pain, Wychwood House began to merge in my mind with the buried memories of my English childhood, with loved old legends. *Sanctuary*. That was what it was we were running to.

The rain was lightening now to a pale mist. We stopped at one small crossroad, went on to another, and came to a stop again. There was a perfunctory knock, our compartment door was opened, and the man in the grey cloak contemplated me. "You do know this is the closest rail stop for Rossford? No? I thought as much. Come along quickly, the train only stops long enough to pick up mail." He scooped Nell up without a by-your-leave, but his arms were gentle. I seized shawl and carpetbags as his servant hustled me down. We were barely on the grassy bank when the train chugged off with a farewell toot.

"Rossford is three miles further, and I take it you have not made arrangements for transportation? Caleb, fetch the wagon."

Before I knew what was happening, the youth brought a large farm vehicle from a nearby shed, and Nell was being laid carefully on a bed of hay.

"You are very kind, but it is not neces—"

"I'm not being kind at all," he snapped. "We've no livery stable, and I'll be the person called to rescue you, and I've no desire to make the same trip twice. Now, do you prefer the hay or will you sit on the front seat like a proper female?"

My fingers itched to slap him. "I shall stay by my sister, naturally," I retorted, and put my foot on the axle, glad I knew how to swing myself up without his aid. Not for nothing had I spent childhood summers on the plantation, and if our escort saw more than was proper of petticoat and ankle, well, I had other things to think about just now.

Nell reached out to pull me down beside her, and the man, whose name we still did not know, sprang to the driver's seat and took the reins. The patient grey horses began to move. Nell smiled at me. She seemed better, the strain gone out of her face, now that we had left the train. "Camilla, smell the air! The rain is gone."

Sunlight slanted through translucent depths of sky and the scent of summer came from the fields. Here and there beyond the hedgerows, people and animals moved slowly as though caught in some dreaming spell. Barns, byres, cottages and an occasional sprawling house hugged the road and seemed to have sprung from it. Now and again in the thatched roofs flowers bloomed, and the stone that formed the cottage walls was luminous—grey, rose, gold, every color of the sinking sun. We had slipped back into a painting, a pastoral world of centuries long ago.

The horses plodded slowly, their reins hanging loosely in the driver's hands. He was as much one with the animals and the dusty road as the meandering stream beside us was with its banks. I wondered whether we, too, would achieve that harmony with Wychwood Rise.

On an impulse I spoke to his slouched back. "You live near here?"

"I farm, on the other side of Wychwood Rise."

He farms, but he is not a farmer. The knowledge came to me with certainty. He had thrown off the grey cloak and removed his coat, and his rough workshirt was a farmer's smock. But his voice, despite his affectation of country phrases, was resonant and cultured.

Presently he gestured with his willow wand. "Yonder's the village."

We rounded a curve and for a moment I glimpsed a farm valley, like a toy world, beyond the hedgerows. Directly on the road, a wall of stone formed the front of cottages tightly joined—narrow windows like blank eyes, shutters and doors in faded blues and greens, geraniums in window boxes, clematis and roses. Here and there a swinging sign revealed the existence of a tiny shop, and in one or two house fronts large Tudor windows had been desecrated to make display space for butcher or for grocer. The river widened, and now a common lay beyond, with sheep and cattle grazing. At a ford crossing the road swelled to embrace a market cross, and an old tavern claimed pride of place upon the corner. On its outside bench, two ancients smoked their pipes and gazed on us curiously as we rolled by. Beside the door, a crude illustrated sign proclaimed the place's name: *The Copper Maid.*

Our driver flicked the horses with his willow wand and they turned right onto a low stone bridge. I pulled myself upright. "We are looking for a dwelling called Wychwood House. Do you know—"

"Aye."

We had crossed the river and its strip of common land and turned left onto a narrow road. Here, facing the river, was the sort of English home I had envisioned, low, sprawling to hug the ground, its thatch so thickly overhung it seemed no sun could ever touch its windows. Unaccountably I shivered. "Is this—"

"That's Quinn Cottage, the doctor's house. And back there's the Manor." The wand was raised again, pointing toward a broad parkland that ran down to meet the river. At the far end were stone walls and a high gate; to one side, a stone church, hedge-surrounded, and behind, a cemetery that ran up to meet great trees that furred the hills. Again sunlight, again that curious stillness that breathed of shadows. Perhaps it was the humming of the bees, evoking as it did an aching vision of the Inns of Court, but I felt, so strongly, that this was a village imprisoned by a spell.

The carriage stopped. Nell's fingers caught my wrists and I heard the soft susurrus of her breath.

"Wychwood House," our guide said inscrutably, and waited.

I lifted my eyes, half fearful, and felt my heart grow quiet. Here were the luminous stone, the roof of thatch, mullioned windows each of different size. Clematis flung itself thickly above an ancient door, and there were geraniums and ageratums in stone tubs. A high stone wall connected the house with the swell of Wychwood Forest; an arched gate-frame, house-high, was overgrown with climbing roses.

A figure stepped out of the entryway, and the spell was broken.

"Miss Jardine? I am Charles Roach, Lady Kersey Lavenham's solicitor." The speaker was somewhere in his forties, sturdy and upright, in well-tailored tweeds.

An odd, irrelevant thought occurred to me: *This is how the Colonel must have seemed to my mother when first they met.* There was no physical similarity between my stepfather and Mr. Roach, but they both had that enormously reassuring look of security and reason. The Colonel's face had been ascetic; the lawyer's was bluff, blunt and humorous, with a square-cut ginger beard just tinged with grey. His eyes, a pleasant blue, gave me a warming smile. Then his good-humoured gaze traveled to my driver, and those eyes grew frosty.

"Afternoon, Roach," our driver said. "I might have expected you'd be right on tap." His voice was solemn, but I could have sworn that he was laughing.

Charles Roach looked annoyed. "Afternoon, Bushel. You yourself seem not to have been exactly backward." The lawyer helped me down, then turned back to Bushel, who was opening Nell's invalid-chair. "I thank you on my client's behalf for her transportation. You may present your bill at my office."

"Now, Mr. Roach, surely a farmer can do a neighbor a good turn free of charge. You still do not know us countryfolk well, do you?" There was no mistaking the sardonic grin. He set Nell carefully in her chair and turned to me. "Miss Jardine, I salute your courage. Not many females would be brave enough to spend a night in Wychwood." Before I could find my tongue, he had flipped down the carpetbags, sprung to the wagon seat and rolled away.

I whirled to Mr. Roach. "What *did* he mean?"

Charles Roach frowned. "That is his idea of humor. Our local ghost, the Copper Maid, is supposed to flit in and out through your yew hedge, but she's never seen except by old fools in their cups."

"Who on earth was that man?" Nell demanded.

"Jeremy Bushel. He works one of the farms along the river. But he's no native; he came only last spring." He shrugged and turned back to me with a smile. "Miss Jardine, what a pleasure it is to be meeting you at last. And Miss Nell. I've heard so much of you from Lady Kersey. Amazing woman."

"She must have been remarkable," I said.

"*Formidable.*" He gave the word its French pronunciation. "Not just your run-of-the-mill aristocrat, mind you, but the 'Peerless Peeress.' That's what the penny papers called her, and I suspect she liked it. Legend has it she once danced the Dance of the Seven Veils for the Prince Regent down at Brighton. Even meeting her in her eighties, as I did, I could well believe it. She was afraid of no thing on God's green earth, and little else beyond."

For an instant an image rose before my vision, the red-haired, eagle-eyed old lady softening into a young girl with a cloud of copper hair like Nell's.

"Now you must be eager to inspect your domicile." Mr. Roach produced an enormous key. "It's cleaned and aired. I've had local women in all day working and Mrs. Giles, the doctor's daughter, ran over to approve. I'll take you through."

As he reached for the keyhole that voice within me, strong and sure, said, "No. No, thank you, you've been most kind, but from here on we can manage on our own." I was surprised, myself, to hear those words, for I found his presence reassuring. But still I stood, and waited, as with some reluctance he surrendered the key and strode off down the road.

"Camilla." Nell looked at me oddly. "Why did you do that?"

"I don't know." I let my breath out slowly. I wanted to meet the house alone, but there was something more. Something that made my hand shake slightly as I fitted the old key into the heavy lock.

Then I turned the key, pushed open the door, and stepped into a narrow passageway. A warmth, as of a living presence that was the house itself, swept round to enfold me. A sudden serenity quieted my breast and I knew, with the surrendering peace that only wanderers know, that I had at last, as from long journeying, come home.

3

Rossford-under-Wychwood
August, 1863

FOR a moment the spell held me, and then was gone, leaving me spent and trembling and filled with a quiet peace unlike any I had ever known.

I turned to Nell wordlessly, but she was lying back among her pillows. She looked pale, shrunken, as though whatever force replenished me had drained her dry. For a second the dim light performed an alchemy and her small face looked ancient, framed by the burnished waves of red-gold hair. Involuntarily I cried out, and Nell's eyes opened, staring fathomless into space. Then she turned. "I'm sorry. Something came over me . . . the air in here." She shuddered slightly, then her laugh rang out like silver bells. "Poor dear! I did not mean to frighten you. You look as though you'd seen a ghost."

"Perhaps I have," I said lightly.

Nell's eyes twinkled at me. "It would be

appropriate, wouldn't it? Wychwood Forest was a royal hunting preserve, back to earliest times, and it once stretched for miles and miles. Wych means witch, you know, in Old English."

"Wherever did you learn that?"

"I read it somewhere," Nell said vaguely. "The forest runs right down to the house, Camilla, did you see? I was looking at it while you talked with Mr. Roach. Such dense trees, and that thick yew hedge no light could pass through, ever! Camilla, don't you hope this house is haunted by the family ghosts?"

Nell's voice was becoming rapid and excited, and I said firmly, "Stop right there. I know the things your vivid imagination leads to. They'd not be *our* family ghosts, at any rate, but Lady Kersey's. *My goodness*!"

I had turned absently, my eyes traveling through the doorway to my left. The room beyond was large, low and dim, but at that moment light pierced through the mullioned windows like a slender arrow, and for the instant a woman's face glowed at me through the shadows. Her eyes, wise and knowing, looked directly into mine. It was a full minute before I realized that those eyes were painted, that the face was canvas and not flesh and blood.

"That," Nell's voice behind me said dryly, "is Lady Kersey."

I moved, as if drawn, through the low doorway, to where the great portrait hung on the side of the chimneypiece. This was, surely, the strangest portrait I had ever seen. It was not paint at all, save for the heavily ringed hands and that ugly, glowing face. The background, the period clothes, even the gold hair peeping out from under the close-cut coif—all, all were real. The Tudor gown was an elaborate appliqué of satin and brocade; winking gems had been glued onto the painted fingers and among the laces of the bodice edge I could see the upper part of an encrusted brooch.

"Lady Kersey made it herself," Nell said, watching me. "Appliqué pictures have been the fashion lately. It amused her to convert this old portrait into a great-granddam with old theatre fripperies. She told me about it the last time we were together."

"It certainly is remarkable." I didn't know if I would care for it in our private sitting room, but I could always move it later. For now, I must settle Nell for a nap and find us food for supper.

"We must see the house first," Nell protested. "I couldn't rest before we do."

"Wychwood House won't run away, you know, while your eyes are closed."

"*Our* house, Camilla. At least, for a whole year. Doesn't that excite you?" Nell looked at me and smiled. "You always stay so calm. My cool, collected sister. We're each other's mirror image, aren't we? Fire and ice, that's what Papa called us once."

Fire and ice. Strange how it could pain me to be thus contrasted to my sister's vibrant life. My heart, my body would hurt less now if I were ice. Fire and ice, air and water; the four elements of medieval metaphysics—for an odd moment I saw Wychwood House as a microcosmic "little world of man," shut off and slumbering in its high walls and the shadows of Wychwood Rise. Nell and I, the fire and ice. Water was here in the stream that cut us off from the village proper. And air . . . suddenly the air in the room was too close and too oppressive. I wheeled Nell quickly through the doorway to the right.

This room was vast, stone-paved, its hewn oak rafters black with time and smoke. The enormous chimney-breast engulfed a high-backed settle and long bench, a kettle on a cricket, great black iron pots and cranes. A high cake, delicately iced and redolent of oranges, sat on the long trestle table, ringed with flowers. "How very kind," I exclaimed, reading the accompanying note. *With welcome and best wishes. Dr. Matthew Quinn and daughter.*

"They are our neighbors, aren't they, across the green? So you may find friends here. Camilla, we will be happy here together, won't we?" There was a pinched look in Nell's face. I hurried her rapidly through the balance of our tour. Beyond the kitchen was another hall, tapestry-hung. The staircase here was more elaborately carved than the one in the other passage. Apparently this was the formal entrance, and beyond, the "best room," severely beautiful, with valuable medieval stained-glass panels in its leaded windows. Here were linenfold paneling, a high carved overmantel, brocade draperies and velvet-cushioned chairs. The remaining ground-floor rooms were a rabbit-warren of sculleries and pantries, and a long, light room which shared the chimney where Lady Kersey's portrait hung and had stone counters and a deep stone sink. A stillroom, I thought, enchanted.

Then on upstairs, where I discovered the strain and effort entailed in carrying Nell. She did not protest when I laid her to nap on the goosefeather softness of a high four-poster bed. Nell's dark eyes followed me to the door, and her voice leaped with panic. "You won't go and leave me!"

"Darling, I must. We've no food in the house. The shops are only just across the bridge." I glanced at Nell sharply, feeling my breath come quicker. "What is it? Are you ill? Don't you like it here?"

Nell's head turned restlessly on the old linen pillows. "Don't listen to me, it's just a foolish fancy."

I went downstairs slowly, deep in thought. Was it just that creative fancy of Nell's, which Mrs. Bertram deplored and I so loved? Or did houses as old as this indeed have memories, have souls? Had Wychwood House spoken in some mysterious way to Nell, as it had to me—spoken to her not of welcome but of fear?

The long summer light was cooling now, and an opalescent veil seemed to shimmer in the flower scented air. A boy in bare feet was prodding sheep into going homeward from the green. He gave me a sideways glance from under his straw hat, then looked away. Boy, sheep, and a pretty black-and-white Border collie swept across the main bridge. I followed, conscious of being watched. On both sides of the water, the buildings of that lovely luminous stone presented their blank façades.

I passed the village tavern quickly and moved toward a doorway where a shop sign proclaimed Greene's Groceries. A woman in a spotless apron, her sleeves rolled as in Flemish paintings, came forward from a back room as I entered. "Evening, miss." Eyes like the shepherd boy's inspected me with guarded animosity.

I flushed. "Good evening. I am sorry to trouble you so late, but we've just arrived and I need something for my sister's tea. She is not well."

"That be all right. Sorry to hear of the young lady's trouble. You'll want tea? Us have a tin put by of the Manor's blend." Those knowing eyes were adding up the cost of my apparel and the diamond on my finger. "A cone of sugar? Milk? Too late for dairyman, but us can spare a jug."

"Thank you. And bread, and eggs. I shall

return the jug tomorrow. My name is Jardine, I've just occupied the house across the way."

"Aye, the Americans."

It was only natural, I supposed, that news traveled quickly in a village. But there was something that troubled me about her tone. I was allowing the atmosphere of this place to lead me into leaping to conclusions, and I did know better. I hurried home . . . Home–I was using the word automatically, already. Despite my bundles, and my concern to fix Nell's supper, I found myself moving into the chamber where the portrait hung. This room *was* home, my longed-for roots, my source; I knew that during a fleeting moment in which my breathing stilled to peace and my heart grew quiet.

There was an envelope on the center table. Odd that I had not noticed it before. Inside, a single sheet of letter paper was wrapped round a thick creamy envelope, heavily sealed and addressed to me in Lady Kersey's hand. I scanned the brief letter quickly. Sir Percival, according to instructions, forwarding to me her Ladyship's last letter . . . Again, I felt that sense of presence with me in the room. Then some sound recalled me to the present, and I put Lady Kersey's envelope aside, to open at supper when Nell was there to share.

A search of the cupboards revealed an enchanting fat teapot and squat cups, all royal-blue and pale-pink roses, touched with gilt and balancing quaintly on curving legs. There were eight-sided plates, gold-rimmed and wreathed with flowers, and thin, thin silver spoons. And wood, worm-eaten with age but dry, in the kitchen bin. I lit a fire on the sitting-room's massive hearth, and lit the yellowed tallow candles on the mantel. They gave forth an odd-scented smoke, but they burned true. The room glowed in the fire-light mingled with the blue-grey filtering through the mullioned windows. I dragged a Jacobean chaise over to the hearth, heaped cushions on it, and carried Nell down big-eyed with delight.

"It's just as I imagined." Nell smiled at me across bread and milk in a pewter porringer. Her eyes traveled round the brass and pewter, the tapestried chair-seats, heavy oak dresser and fat carved tables. Her breath caught. "What is that? Up there on the rafters. Something moved."

My eyes followed hers and I laughed, my throat catching with memories of a plantation kitchen. "Herbs hung to dry, heaven knows how long ago. A draught must have disturbed them." I lifted them down, and they gave forth a faint perfume.

Nell's eyes gazed past me, black in the candlelight. "Just like in the old spells to ward off witches. We ought to burn them, oughtn't we? 'Blessed be this house, and all those in it, and keep them safe from the snares of the Evil Ones.' " She flung the nosegay to the fire, and a wonderful fragrance filled the room.

A faint, unaccountable coldness of bygone memory touched me. "Where did you learn that prayer?"

"I don't know," Nell said vaguely. "I must have read it somewhere." She sank back as though the effort had exhausted her.

I recalled Lady Kersey's letter, then, and fetched it, delighted to see some animation light Nell's face.

"If that is not just like Lady Kersey. Open it quickly, Camilla, do!"

Martin's diamond winked as I broke the heavy seal, noting its intricate device, and drew out the thick enclosure. Would it have been better, I wonder, had I read that letter when alone, when in the reality of daytime sun, when not in this house? I will never know. I could not anticipate the outcome as I began to read aloud the words which brought my mother's redoubtable godmother so vividly to life, and so changed my own.

"My very dear and I hope equally clever Camilla,

"Bravo! So you do have a daring heart, as well as a scholar's mind. I hoped you would. By now you will have crossed the threshold of the house, and set your feet into the paths the great ones and the old ones trod before. May you choose wisely which of them to follow! All my life I have gambled on human nature, and I wish in death to have one more game to roll. Hence my quixotic offer of a year at Wychwood. You must have some of the gambler's instinct, too, or you would not have come. It remains to be seen if you will win the prize. I have always been a creature of impulse, as this letter will make clear, but age has taught me that blind following of instincts is not always wise, that one must be guided by both head and heart. Dear Camilla, will you learn that, too, and how much water must pass under the bridge before you do? Have you already, I wonder, experienced the birthright that is in your blood, the pulls in paradoxical directions? And would you let me guide you to the heart of rest?"

I lowered the letter, staring at the flames, and the diamond blurred like a rainbow before my misted eyes.

"She is managing to stand here watching, isn't she?" Nell said profoundly. "That infernal picture. It's why she made it and placed it here, isn't it? So she could be here, part of this. And she's led you off into her world, the way she meant to."

"What nonsense." I shook my head to clear it.

"You did not know Lady Kersey," Nell said inscrutably.

"But enough of digression. On to Wychwood, home of my heart, and I hope of yours as well. Has it worked its magic on you yet, and do you long to have it forever yours? You shall, my dear, if you have the courage to dwell there for a year, and the wit and wisdom to discover treasure in that time. Wychwood has always been a house of secrets, and it has amused me no little to add unto that legend. It may be you will find here a token and a pledge. I have left instructions with my London solicitors that Wychwood House, as well as its treasure, shall belong to whoever finds that token. The true worth, by now, should be considerable. I have given you this year at Wychwood House to provide you with a sporting chance, and to spite the devil, since my present estimation of my lawful or unlawful heirs is, to say the least, negligible.

"So to the hunt, my dear Camilla. I am persuaded to think you have the blood and brains, and may have the heart. If not, or if you lack the stomach to run the course, you have the books to take back to your scholar's cell. You could have much, much more! Be assured that from whatever corner of heaven or hell I watch, I shall have my eyes upon you as the chain's spun out. And if, not for the first time, heads will roll, at least 'twill give the village something to think about besides their star-crossed Copper Maid.

"I charge you, speak of this to no one. This is, after all, a family affair.

Blessed be, my dear.
Your loving
Kersey"

There followed her mark, the same curious device that was on her seal, the K for Kersey blazoned clear and the L for Lavenham obscured among a superfluity of scrolls. I put the letter down and stared at Nell.

"A treasure!" Nell's eyes blazed.

"And the house." I longed, suddenly and irrationally, not just to live here for the year but to possess and be possessed by it forever. "But not a finger shall we lift to search if you're going to build palaces in the air. You know what the doctor said, rest—"

"And quiet, and time will tell, and all that nonsense, but he knows nothing. I will be good, I promise, but you must, must search."

"We have a year to do so."

"You did not know Lady Kersey," Nell said again.

Was it my imagination, or did a draft sweep through the room, sending a burst of herbal fragrance, sweet-sharp and pungent? Nell turned her face away, half covering it with her hand, and her eyes were closed. I carried her to bed, realizing that the physical burden of her care was going to be greater than I had imagined. Perhaps I could find some village girl to do the heavy work. If funds were sufficient—I must inquire of Mr. Roach. If not, surely a gentlewoman educated as uncommonly as I ought to be able to earn income in some fashion.

And then the token . . . I paused, looking across the room into Lady Kersey's painted knowing eyes. This was a Tudor house, and I well knew the Tudor meaning of that word *token*. Not small, insignificant, unimportant, as we have debased the word today, but the very opposite indeed. To the men and women who had built this house, had lived, loved, died here, token meant pledge and promise, a tangible, visible symbol of some great covenant. And such tokens, as Lady Kersey hinted, could be of great worth indeed—great enough to provide Nell with security for all her years to come.

And if the token was not found, and we left Wychwood, there was only my diamond. Martin, who would have taken care of us if he had lived, would have been glad to provide for us in that fashion after he was gone. But please, God, it would not come to that.

Unconsciously my thumb was turning the slender ring round and round my finger. Here, with no friends nor kin, stranger in a strange land, I had no link to Martin but our betrothal ring. A faint breeze from across the little river came through the open windows to cool my tears, and when I opened my eyes, my vision still was blurred. That was why, of course, when I looked at the dark crimson of the draperies so faintly stirring, I almost saw Martin's figure in the shadows, and my heart leaped with a remembered pain. I felt the touch of his fingers on my cheek, I saw the smile with which he had turned to me for one last look as he strode off to eternity along the Charleston waterfront. It was a smile of reassurance, of serenity, and some of that serenity entered my own heart. And with it a conviction—two convictions.

The first was of Martin. It was Martin's presence I felt for that brief moment, Martin's face I saw. Call it illusion, imagination, my own aching need. Martin was speaking to me, my heart knew it even as my head denied. And the word that he was speaking was farewell. Our shared world was ended; this was my home, not Martin's, he could have no part of it; he was telling me that with love and no rancor, and he wished me well. I would remember, would always remember, but I knew already, even while the salt was on my face, that soon the memory would bring no pain.

And the second conviction . . . the second presence which filled this hall with healing warmth, even as Martin's image faded—I turned toward the sitting room, toward that fantastic portrait of my benefactress, and those eyes, shrewd and knowing, promising secrets and assurance, glowed back at mine, I was very sure.

Yet, whosoever this presence was, this beneficient spirit which surrounded and upheld me, it was not that of Lady Kersey Lavenham.

4

Rossford-under-Wychwood
August, 1863

THERE is an expression I used to hear at home: being "born again." Something very like happened to me that night. I was used to a city, a circle of acquaintances, an established order, familiar black faces looking after me. All that was gone now. I had come to journey's end, here in the Wychwood hills. I lay down that first night one person and rose up another. And not I only, but my Nell as well.

"How shall we live here?" Nell asked abruptly as we ate breakfast in our dressing gowns.

I looked at her in some surprise. "Why, quite well! We shall be snug as two peas in our own little pod. I shall take care of you, have no fear!"

Her eyes darkened, and she said gently, "Camilla, don't."

"What?"

"Don't pretend. We must always be honest with one another." Her eyes traveled around the big still kitchen with its ancient, unfamiliar tools. "I'm not a child. We only have a year here, and then what? It's great fun to dream of hidden treasure round the fire, but it could all come to nothing. Tell me the truth, Camilla, can we manage?"

This was what disconcerted me most of all. I had been expecting the ebullient child who had sailed for England three years before. Through loneliness or pain, this frail girl who was my sister had grown beyond her years. I must remember that.

I answered her directly. "There will be no funds at all, I fear, from home. The war—everything is changed so, Nell. But we will manage somehow. What one must do, one can."

" 'What one must do, one can,' " Nell repeated slowly. "Yes. Like my fall; I survived that, though I thought I shouldn't. And we shall survive here, come what may!" Her smile flashed. "I shan't be a millstone round your neck, I promise. I shall look after *you*, too, you will see!"

"And I must solve the mystery of keeping house." I glanced out the window and started in dismay. "Good gracious, don't tell me morning calls are the custom here!"

A stylish equipage was drawing smartly to a stop outside our formal door. A liveried page sprang down to help forth a lady, somewhere in her late forties, whose vast spreading hoop-skirts, slightly trained, and shallow bonnet bespoke a Parisian authority. Her hair was black, smooth as satin wings, and her eyes were like black cherries. She had skin like our magnolia petals, a queenly bearing and most regal height. All this registered upon me in the winking of an eye, and with it the consciousness that I was not dressed for callers.

The knocker sounded. "She's sent the boy to do that," Nell reported. "How posh. Oh, Cam, she's seen us. She nodded most cordially."

There was no help for it. I pulled my wrapper higher at the throat, tied the sash firmly, and advanced upon the door with all the dignity I could muster.

The little lad bobbed a bow, holding forth a card. *The Lady Margaret Ross*. His eyes, slantwise, peered at me askance through a thatch of dun-colored hair. The lady advanced with her hands outstretched, and the page backed off.

"My dear Miss . . . Jardine, is it not? I fear

I come upon you importunely." I could not tell whether the expression in those fine eyes was disapproval or amusement. "Do forgive me; we are most informal in the village, and I hoped by calling early I could be of service."

Somehow I was ushering her into the orderly coolness of the drawing room, somehow I found myself upon the stairs at her courteous "Pray do not hurry yourself. I am quite content to wait." I felt like a disheveled child being sent by a governess to make repairs.

I made all speed, and it was the proper, civilized Miss Jardine who swept back downstairs in the reassuring armor of whalebone and crinoline.

"Did you find the place habitable when you arrived? These local girls are not as dependable as one would wish. So often they resist all one's efforts to improve them." Lady Margaret looked at me, her smile transforming her to warm and human. "I go too fast? My dear, you must just make do with me as the village does. My son says that my energies are such that only a ducal castle would give me proper scope. Unfortunately, though my dear father was of such rank, I did not choose to marry so. But you, my dear, how may I be of service?"

It was impossible not to respond to her vital warmth. "I don't know where to start! I've been accustomed to living in my stepfather's city house, or on the plantation—"

"And you brought no servants with you? We must procure you some at once, though I'm afraid you will think the locals poorly trained. Do you plan to stay here long?"

"We mean to live here."

"*Do* you?" Was it my imagination, or did an imperceptible change take place in her manner? "You said 'we.' Oh, yes, you have an invalid sister, I believe."

After a moment I laughed. "You have the advantage, Lady Margaret. You must know all about us from Lady Kersey."

"Oh, my dear, Lady Kersey never lived here. No one has, for over a hundred years." She smiled at my astonishment. "The heyday of these Cotswold villages was in the Wool Trade time. Since that declined, numerous fine old houses have stood empty, and the villagers eke out a miserable, catchpenny life, and resist all change. I myself have only lived here some five years. The Manor belonged to my own family, many generations back, and my dear husband was able to purchase and restore it a year before he died. We have a splendid garden; I will send some fresh produce to you, and arrange for the dairyman and baker's lad to call. That will see you started. Of course, it is too late for you to raise vegetables yourself, but there are some fruit trees, I believe, out back. And it is possible to get quite decent lamb and pork, not to mention the inevitable poultry, through Mrs. Greene. Wednesday is market day, and Laura Giles will put you on to the best tradesmen. She is quite knowledgeable about such things."

"Is there a seamstress in the village?" I willed my voice steady. "My—I need to order mourning, and have had no chance."

Lady Margaret's eyes softened, but she tactfully forebore from questions. "Mrs. Lee does excellent work, so one makes allowances for her . . . oddities. I shall send her to you. No, it would be best for you to go to her. She's in the last cottage on the right. I shall notify her to expect you at three today." She rose to leave. "You must come to dine with us on Friday."

"You are very kind, but I cannot leave my sister."

"There is no difficulty. I will send the carriage for you both. If you plan to live here, it would be well to make things clear at once." With which cryptic comment she smiled brilliantly, and departed.

When I had shut the door after her, I leaned against it, feeling weak.

In the kitchen, Nell clapped her hands softly. "Just listening made me feel like clothes being run through a wringer!"

"*I* felt like a child being called forth for inspection. I dreadfully fear we are being taken on as Lady Margaret's personal responsibility!"

Nell chuckled. "And you thought life in a village would be quiet?"

Within an hour a wagon from the Manor House arrived, laden with great green cabbages and ruffled kale, a napkin-lined basket filled with eggs, a brace of plump ducks ready for the roasting. If her Ladyship was a whirlwind, she was a kindly one. Even with my inept cooking, we made a splendid lunch. I packed Nell off to nap, but I was restless. There was yet an hour and a half before my appointed visit to the seamstress, and Lady Margaret's reference to fruit trees lingered in my mind. From the outside, Wychwood

House appeared to have no grounds at all, but we had not yet explored beyond the back door from the hall. I unlocked it now and opened it in wonder, onto a closed, still world.

Here was a farmyard in miniature, laid out with neat precision and deserted, as though in some bygone century the laborers had been summoned by a distant bell. Five or six small fruit trees were enclosed tidily in planting boxes overrun with strawberry vines. Geometrically perfect vegetable beds had long gone to weeds. The stillroom and dining-room wings, jutting at right angles, met with roof-high stone walls that connected them to a string of barns and other small structures out beyond. My eyes perceived a smokehouse, dairyhouse, carriage shed, animal housing and what were euphemistically termed the "necessaries." All together, these formed a tight enclosure, its only access through the house or the wagon-wide door set in the right-hand wall. Behind the barns, the tops of yew trees marked the boundaries of the churchyard, and off to the left, thick-growing trees rose endlessly off into the Wychwood hills.

There were no herbs, no flowers, only brambled berry canes long overgrown, fruit trees heavy with their burden, weeds parched and yellowed, the rich earth still and waiting. Off by the barn a rusty scythe rested against the wall. The stones glowed rose-gold, and from somewhere near at hand, but hidden, came the hum of bees. I had again the sensation that all things were forming together in a pattern that had waited for my coming, that something I did not yet understand was being put in motion.

It was then I saw it, on the tight barring of the carriage gate. The marks of a chisel or a crowbar. Recent marks: the raw gouges in the old wood had not yet healed. Someone had tried to force an entrance here. Someone was trying to gain entry to this house, which held a treasure.

I sat down weakly on a planting-box, wondering why the discovery should shock me so. Something in Lady Kersey's letter—something about giving me a sporting chance—should have told me I would not be the only one to seek that treasure. Someone had anticipated me, had not been willing to allow me to profit from my advantage. I looked into the toolhouse, and there was an absence of spiders where the spades were kept. Clots of earth, which looked like fresh earth, clung to the tools. When something rustled near my feet my heart lurched, but it was only a small green snake, slithering uneasily off into the weeds.

It was necessary for me to know the means and extent of this prior search. Perhaps the treasure had been already claimed—no, for if it had been, I would not be here: the house was to belong to whoever found the token. I paced off each rod of yard and garden, my eyes intent, and found several places where earth had been disturbed and then replaced. This had been no haphazard search, nor a swift one, either. When I went inside, I was deeply troubled in my mind.

The old wooden bars and latches, the great locks with their Tudor keys were picturesque, but this village must have a blacksmith, and with no time wasted I would order stout bars and chains and modern locks which could not so easily be forced. The thought of Nell and myself sleeping alone and unguarded in a house that could easily be broken into was alarming.

I must hurry, now, for my appointment at the seamstress' house. I fetched two dresses to take as patterns, then looked in on Nell, reluctant to leave her now I'd seen the force-marks on the gate. "Are you sure that you will be all right alone?"

"Of course. Just push me to the window, and bring me some books, will you, from the shelves?"

I wheeled her chair where she directed and brought a load of books, all helter-skelter. Nell pounced on one, and it gave forth a faint fragrance and a cloud of dust. "Camilla, look, a pressed leaf as a bookmark. I wonder what it is."

I glanced over her shoulder at the fine-print page. *Gerard's Herbal*, a potpourri of potions, receipts and simples. I had seen a copy of this before, in my stepfather's collection, and some memory I could not put my finger on stirred in my mind.

Nell was gazing out at the deserted street. "How still it is," she said idly. She turned back to the book and became engrossed. I let myself out, locking the door behind me.

I crossed the stream and started up the slumberous, narrow street. Rows of gabled windows, beneath steep pitched roof-lines, seemed to watch me. These joined cottages fronted flush on the road, but the interiors were invisible in darkness and the staring panes reflected the greyness of the sky.

"Be you the furrin wummin looking for my mam?" The door of the last cottage stood ajar and a girl leaned catlike against the frame, regarding me. She had the same strange eyes as Lady Margaret's page: slightly slanted, seeming to gaze askance from beneath too-heavy lids. Her lank dun-colored hair was skewered carelessly, but despite her ill-kempt appearance, she had an odd, disturbing grace.

I felt, as I had with Lady Margaret, put off-guard, and it annoyed me. "I am Miss Jardine. I am looking for Mrs. Lee."

"Her be my mam." The girl drew back slightly to let me pass, and I stepped for the first time into a Cotswold cottage.

Damp, was my first reaction, and my second that this sense of moisture came not from water alone, though I had noticed a brook running by the outer wall. The single large room, and a windowless storeroom off beyond, gave the impression of being carved out of a cave. Perhaps it was the floor of stones and earth that made it seem so, and the great stone fireplace which occupied the whole side wall. Bunches of drying herbs, some cobweb-caged, swung from the beams, and a goose-wing was impaled on a nail beside the hearth. At back, stairs ran up to a landing which held a sagging bed, then continued onward to the upper floor.

A fitful fire burned on the wide hearth, and a gaunt woman bent by it, stirring something in a kettle. She turned to face me as I entered, straightening slightly.

"Mrs. Lee?" She waited as if her silence were assent. "I am Miss Jardine from Wychwood House. Lady Margaret recommended you." Why was I rattling, and why did I have this absurd sensation that it was I who was in need of recommendation? "I need some mourning made; I have brought some gowns with me as a pattern."

Mrs. Lee took them from me, her eyes for the first time kindling. "Clever." She had turned a bodice inside out and was fingering with approval the bound edges of the seams. Apparently she did understand fine sewing.

"I shall require several dresses, and dinner clothes as well. As quickly as possible," I added, remembering the summons to the Manor. "Although I do not know how long it will take to obtain fabric."

This at least elicited an answer. "Special goods be sent from Oxford, or London, by train. Us buys from gypsies at market, and her ladyship too, if so be good enough for you, being foreign."

The languorous girl, who had been watching us, stepped forward. "If you bean't special fond of they dresses as now is, us could dye them. My mam be proper clever with the dyepots." She nodded at the sulfurous kettle in the fire.

"An excellent suggestion! And that will not take long, will it?" I was rattling again. I was very glad for interruption when a voice called, "Ah, Mrs. Lee! Is Doctor's coat ready?" and a lady appeared upon the threshold.

On second glance I realized she was scarcely more than a girl, that her face was worn with sorrow, not with age. She wore half-mourning, her pale hair inside the shallow bonnet framed a delicate oval face, and she gave me the impression of enormous quiet. Then she saw me, and her expression softened with a swift smile. "You need not tell me, you are Miss Jardine! Welcome to our village. I am Laura Giles, and I was just on my way to call on you."

"Her be Doctor's daughter," the Lee girl volunteered.

I turned quickly. "Then it is to you we are

indebted for that delicious cake! And for having Wychwood House all turned out and ready, too, I understand. I can't begin to express our gratitude."

"It was our pleasure. You can imagine how delighted we are to be having neighbors. Father and I live just across the green. It will be so nice to see lights in Wychwood House at last."

"Happen mayn't be for long," Mrs. Lee said unexpectedly.

"Nonsense. Lady Margaret tells me the Jardines will make their home here for at least a year, and we're all very glad to have them, aren't we, Mrs. Lee?" Somewhat to my astonishment, Mrs. Giles tucked her hand through my arm, and her voice was bright. "Ah, here's Father's coat. You've repaired it splendidly; he will be so pleased. Have you completed your business, Miss Jardine? Then we can walk along together, can we not?"

In some strange way a battle was being fought here, and it pertained to me. Before I could speak, Mrs. Giles fairly rushed me to the street, and not until we had gone past several houses did her feet slow, and she released my arm. "I hope you truly were finished with your business. There's no use trying to deal with Mrs. Lee when she's in a taking-on." Mrs. Giles drew a breath and shook her head. "What you must think of me, sweeping you off like that! We must seem quite mad."

"Not precisely."

"Just peculiar?" She caught my eyes and laughed. "I daresay we will seem so. Rossford was a thriving village once, but for the past century or so, especially since the Enclosures, we've been quite cut off. It does make one a bit one-sided. Your coming will liven parish society considerably."

"Mrs. Lee does not seem to think so."

"Mrs. Lee," my companion said carefully, "is a bit north-northwest, as the saying goes, since her husband died." She hesitated. "Perhaps I ought to tell you . . . Gypsy Aaron died on the hills behind your house, and she's taken a belief that the house, and anything to do with it, is evil. She still clings to the old ways; you saw her cottage. You can imagine—foreigners moving into a house that's been shut for a century or more."

"We are not foreigners, not really. My own parents were English; I was born in Oxford."

"Anyone not born in the Wychwoods is a

foreigner here. Philip, my husband, was from Oxford too. I came back when he died, and I'm still on trial, rather, as a lapsed heretic."

How quietly she could speak of him. "Mrs. Giles—"

She put her hand on my arm. "Please! Laura. We need not stand on ceremony, need we, in a small village?"

I could sense almost a starving for companionship, and it struck a responsive chord in my own nature. As sometimes happens, the barriers between strangers were swept away, and I knew, suddenly and completely, that I was no longer devoid of human friendship. We walked slowly. Laura spoke of the young scientist from my mother's Oxford, and the brief marriage which had ended in his death two years ago. I told her my parents' similar story of two decades earlier. I even told her about Martin. I did not plan to, it happened naturally, and she wordlessly squeezed my hand.

By now we had reached the threshold of Wychwood House, and I led her in to meet my sister. Laura, helping me transfer Nell to the Jacobean chaise, glanced at the portrait on the wall and laughed. "Can you imagine if both their Ladyships had resided in the village at one time? We are scarce large enough to digest one Titan, let alone two! Although Lady Margaret is more Olympian. Juno, perhaps, or Demeter measuring out the grain. Lady Kersey was definitely from an earlier world."

"Did you know her?"

"I met her once, when I was very small. She frightened my wits from me!" Laura smiled at Nell. "I see you've found her books. She was a magpie with them; she'd bring down trunksful whenever she came from town."

"I thought she never lived here!"

"She'd come down for weekends, or a full week sometimes, and squirrel herself away. No one was allowed near, the windows all were shuttered, but we'd see smoke rising from the chimneys. Mrs. Lee was sure she was burning books of spells, but the betting round the Copper Maid was that she was sequestering a fortune somewhere."

Nell's eyes met mine.

I wet my lips carefully. "Whatever made them reach that conclusion?"

Laura laughed. "Wychwood Forest's full of such stories. All legend, of course, but I daresay you'll find reference to them in those books."

Nell only nodded. Not until Laura had left did she turn to me, her eyes mysterious, and hold out the old Herbal. The pages were interlined; there were markings over the common names of herbs and writings in the margins. Kersey's writing.

"It's Latin," Nell said. "She'd have known that you could read it, wouldn't she?"

"Yes, of course." With mounting excitement I held it close, deciphering the tiny script. *Isatis tinctoria = Picts . . . Ruta graveolens . . . Rosmarinus* . . . many words were unfamiliar. What I could make out seemed to be generic classifications of the herbs in question. "But there *were* no herbs," I said aloud.

"What?"

"I explored the back garden while you were resting. There were no herbs there."

"You're thinking what I am, aren't you?' Nell said slowly. "That when Lady Kersey shut herself up here, she was burying treasure, and the herbs are markers."

Someone else, too, must have arrived at that conclusion, but I did not want Nell to worry over the digging in the garden.

"I found something else, too," Nell said.

"That leaf as a bookmark? It's costmary. It's called Bible-leaf."

We looked at one another.

Bibles were fertile fields for concealing clues, with their numbers, descriptions, place names, cryptic sayings. There was a Bible on an upper shelf above Nell's head.

"Hold on," I said rapidly. "I want to move your chaise so I can reach that corner." I pushed with what I thought was care, but the stone floor was more slippery than I knew. The couch, with Nell on it, slipped from my grasp and hit the paneling of the end wall.

Nell gasped, and I ran to her. And then I straightened, staring not at her but beyond. Nell caught her breath, and her hand grasped mine. "What is it? Camilla!"

The linenfold panel behind her chaise, the panel which had been so sharply rapped, had moved.

After the first stunned moment I began to laugh, giddily, for in the space revealed was no twisting stair or hidden passage. Through the narrow aperture filtered a shaft of daylight, to fall with welcome brightness across Nell's couch.

"It must be a side door to the yard. How stupid we were not to notice it!" My studies ought to have prepared me for the myriad of doors which the early Tudors added, wherever convenience called, when houses were enlarged. Yes, here was a latch cleverly concealed in the carving of a Tudor Rose. I pulled at it, and the door swung wide.

Here was the garden of my dreams. Here were herbs, flowers, the straw Cotswold beehive for which my eyes had searched in vain in the other yard. The panel opened onto the walled serenity of a cloistered garden that ran the whole length of the wide wing and the sheds beyond. Its further end abutted the thick dark mystery of a living wall of yew; its outer side, walled house-high with grey-gold stone, pressed directly up against Wychwood Forest. Down the two long sides ran pleached arbors heavy with vines and roses; their paths were soundless with cedar chips, and here and there seats of old wood were set into niches for peaceful contemplation.

The paths through the garden beds were of Cotswold slate, and the beds they framed— My breath caught in delight. The pattern of a Persian carpet, interpreted in the knot gardens beloved by Elizabethans, unrolled like a scroll before me. The flowers of

Shakespeare, of myth and of the Bible . . . bees and butterflies, drugged with nectar, clung to purple liatris spikes. And then, beyond the tussy-mussy and patterned beds, the beds of herbs. Herbs creeping shyly amongst the pavement, sending forth a heady burst of fragrance as I trod upon them. Herbs growing waist-high and foaming toward me, their odors released when brushed by my spreading skirts. Blossoming lavenders, yellows and pinks, a spectrum of silver-greys and greens. They stirred deep chords of memory, though my eyes could not pick out their names by sight. I recognised the scents of lavender and thyme, the tang of lemon and the pungency of mints. Someone had labored here once, long and lovingly.

Someone had labored here not long ago. I was almost as drugged by senses as the bees by nectar, but I began to realize this was no neglected garden. In the flowers, in the fresh earth, in the springing greens there was a sense of vibrant, ineradicable life. A tiny lizard sunned himself on a stone in a shaft of the warm light that had begun to filter through the greyness. A plump small bird was contentedly taking a dust bath in a path. There was peace here, the restoring peace old churches have.

I cannot say when or from what cause, but I knew suddenly that I was not alone. A tremor ran through me, my feet became as lead, and yet I was impelled slowly onward. Then I saw him, lying on the thyme-covered slope beneath the yew hedge, hands locked behind his head. He was young, perhaps sixteen or seventeen, in a white silk shirt open at the throat and a suit of some garnet-colored cloth that made him look like Lawrence's portrait of Master Lambton. But the black elf-locks that clustered at his brow, and the black eyes gazing off at the far skies, had an earlier, pagan look. I don't know what it was that gave me the impression he was not well; perhaps it was the colorless thick-cream quality of his skin that reminded me of Nell. We were so close that I could see the little pulse throbbing in his throat.

His eyes saw me but a second after mine saw him. There was that momentary shock that comes when two persons break without warning into each other's private world. After that first unguarded moment he surveyed me calmly, like a young king. When he spoke, his voice had music in it.

" 'I know a bank where the wild thyme blows, where oxlips and the nodding violet blows. There sleeps Titania sometime of the night.' Hello, Titania."

"What are you doing here?"

" 'I serve the fairy queen to dew her orbs upon the green and hang a pearl in every cowslip's ear.' " He smiled with lazy insolence. "What did you think, that I came to chop down your pretty flowers as the quarry boys would do?"

"What *are* you doing in our garden?"

"It's not your garden," he retorted coolly. "Not yet. Don't you know gardens choose whom they'll belong to, just as cats do? Just now this one belongs to me, and to the Old Ones. Whether it will become yours, too, time will tell."

I looked at him, perception quickening. "It was you, wasn't it, who brought this all back to order?" My eyes encompassed the garden's private world. "But why? And how did you get in?"

"Those skilled in the old ways need no keys, as Widow Lee would say. My dear Miss Jardine, are you really so stupid as to think this place impenetrable? Oh, yes, I know who *you* are. I hoped you'd prove to have more wit, but you're like all the others. Dull, dull, dull." His voice grew petulant, betraying his youth.

"The yew hedge," I found myself saying. "It only seems a wall. But there must be spaces between the trunks, among the branches, aren't there, if one knows where to look?"

"You *are* clever," he said approvingly. "I'm so glad. It will be refreshing to have someone sensible to talk to. The minds of persons here are as restricted as the fields by those Enclosure walls." The boy stirred, then swung back to me, his eyes intense. "You will let me continue to come here, won't you? You won't be the beast everyone expects, and banish me? I could not bear that. And the garden would wither, you know, without me. The Old Ones would be displeased."

"Of course I shan't banish you. How could I, after all you've done?"

"My *chère* Maman could, I assure you. She would point out that trespassers have no rights, as the fate of Gypsy Aaron ought to prove. But then, my *chère* Maman does not know about this garden. This is *my* kingdom." He looked suddenly frightened. "You won't tell her, will you? Say you won't!"

"I don't even know who your mother is."

He waved a hand, vaguely, towards the

hedge. "My mother's the queen of the Old Ones—by usurpation of power, not by birth. She devours people. She drinks my blood, and I grow smaller and smaller, and when I'm a tiny little man she will pop me into a bottle and put me in the window to reflect her light."

"Nonsense," I said with some asperity. "I'm sure she adores you."

"One can destroy, you know, with too much loving."

He was looking not at me but off at a great clump of ferns; he was scarcely even aware of me. Yet something had happened: we had plunged, as earlier I had with Laura Giles, into a kind of instant intimacy. But this was different, embodying something alien and disturbing. Then I glanced at him again, and wondered why I'd been afraid. He was staring still into his own world, and unaware that he was being watched, his defenses all were down. And the look on his face was the vulnerable look of those who have made peace with pain. I was seeing directly into the boy's unguarded heart.

Then Nell's voice called from the house, and the spell was broken. The youth's head snapped round. "Is that your sister? Mayn't I bring her out? She's one of the Deficients, isn't she?"

My eyes blazed, and then my anger changed to something I'd have given anything to conceal. But he had seen, and stiffened, and grew straight . . . as much as he was able. For his rising revealed what had been hidden when he lay upon the bed of thyme, explained the bitterness in his tone. Motionless, he looked a young prince; moving, he was a gargoyle, for his foot was clubbed and his back twisted, as by some dark demon of the forest, so that what ought to be a shoulder blade became a hump.

"Do you read fairy tales, Miss Jardine? The princess and the beast?" His voice was brittle, rapid. "Or is your sister also a spirit in disguise? I shall fetch her out to see the garden, shall I not?"

I opened my mouth to say, "*I'll* fetch her," to say, "Be careful with her," and knew I must not, need not, he already knew. I sat down myself on the bank, and the wonderful fragrance of the thyme rose in a cloud around me and its pungency excused what blurred my eyes.

I watched them coming along the wide slate path, he pushing the invalid-chair with infinite delicacy, Nell on her pillows looking up at him and laughing as he bent over her. The pallor of their skins, the fine-drawn marks of suffering were alike, but he was dark while Nell's bright hair and sparkling eyes gave off glints of gold. The picture they made evoked a memory of old myths—child of darkness, child of light. Something laid a finger on my heart. Then Nell laughed aloud, and I thought, he can come here as often as he likes, so long as he can make her sound like that.

Nell clapped her hands. "Who *are* you?'

He considered in lordly fashion. "You may call me Oberon, I think. Or Tristan. I rather fancy Tristan, I believe."

"Not Launcelot?" I inquired irresistibly.

He looked offended. "That blinking idiot? You think I've give up honor, fame, the quest, to be a woman's tame tabby? No bloody chance."

If he was trying to shock us, he did not succeed. "I wish I'd thought to say that," Nell said regretfully, "when I was in school."

"Where did you go?"

"Miss Bedliston's." Nell's voice was prim and careful. She did not look at him; she was pleating her wrapper between her fingers with meticulous precision.

The boy was looking at her with an expression I could not read, and when he spoke, it was to say abruptly, "My name is Stuart. Derived supposedly from the Pretender, although I doubt it. My family has a history of being careful."

Nell laughed again, and he regarded us together gravely. "One can see you're sisters, right enough. You both have the eyes of the Old Ones."

"Who are the Old Ones?" Nell inquired.

"You really are ignorant of Wychwood, aren't you? They are the People of the Forest, the Original Persons. Long, long ago they came, and raised the Stone Circles throughout the country, and set the dolmens. And then they vanished into the earth. So people *say*. But the forest's been home to strange happenings ever since."

The light in the canopy of sky was fading now; the twilight was purple above the darkling trees. In the closed garden the colors of phlox and late roses glowed like jewels. The air was still and soundless, except off in the forest where a night bird called.

"The Old Ones," Stuart's voice was as

limpid and sensuous as Orpheus's lyre. He was deliberately building his effect. "The Children of the Sun. They are the enchanters, and their eyes flash golden light. Who knows? They may come claim you as their own." He let the silence hang with transcendent skill. "And then, of course, there is the Copper Maid."

"Ah, yes. The pub," I said deliberately, to break the spell.

He shook his head. His face was solemn but his eyes were not, nor were they young. I felt suddenly as if we were playing some fantastic game of chess.

"The pub's a namesake, so-called because persons most often see the Maid after indulging there in cider and plum jerkin. No, I mean the original Copper Maid. This is *her* garden. She used to walk here, hundreds of years ago. She walks here still, people say, and on the hills, whenever doom is coming to the village. Widow Lee saw her dancing in the moonlight the night that Gypsy Aaron met his fate. If there are such things as spirits, then that would make you her tenants, wouldn't it? For the Copper Maid is the true possessor of Wychwood House."

Nell and I looked at one another. Her face

was cobweb-pale and her eyes glowed like fire. When we turned back again, it was to nothing. The boy was gone. There was no sound, only the scent of thyme.

5

Rossford-under-Wychwood
August, 1863

I DREAMED that night, for the first time, the dream that from then on would haunt my sleep. The scent of herbs, fire, a ring of figures, and myself, running, and a feeling of great conflict. And some amorphous, threatening force that suffocated, like a weight upon my breast. I awoke to a clammy fever and the pinioning constriction of the featherbed, and I crept down the hall to join my sister.

I slept at peace, then, till the early sun was coupled with insistent sounds in the street below. I flung open the leaded casements onto a bewildering and busy world.

Had I thought this town deserted? It was no more. The sounds I had heard were the sounds of sheep, thick-coated noble beasts with Roman noses. They were everywhere, cropping vegetation peacefully on the common, huddled patiently in farm carts. A docile heifer was placidly eating my geraniums. The graceful farm wagons, yellow and red, swayed like galleons along the road on each bank of the river, carrying animals, produce, whole families toward the Market Cross.

Market day . . . farmers talked and bartered, examining with critical fingertips the samples of wheat—corn, they called it here—carried in little bags. Countrywomen, sturdy or wild-flower-shy, set out baskets of eggs, jugs of cream, great wheels of cheese. Shepherds in cream-colored homespun smocks with honey-comb embroidery bargained for animals or jobs. "Carrier, farrier . . ." the old rhyming chant I had read in my mother's books rang in my ears.

Church and market were the two great crossbeam meetings which held village life together. We were not yet through breakfast when Laura's bright face smiled at me through the glass. I hurried to the door.

"Good morning! This must seem the middle of the night to you, but I thought I'd risk it. I'm off to market—would you like to come?"

"I would indeed. Come in while I fetch my hat. May I give you coffee?"

"That is right, you Americans do take it with breakfast, don't you?" Laura sat down, delighted, as though I'd offered her some exotic treat. There was a softness about her, despite her widowhood and the fact that she was, I suspected, only a few years older than I. That old-young look—Nell had it, too, and Stuart—that made one think of conservatories and plant-forcing rooms, as though a race of people, too, could be pushed involuntarily beyond the sweetness of natural maturation.

What made me think like that? I was becoming all too easy prey to fancies. I fetched a spreading leghorn hat and gloves, found a shopping basket, and turned to Laura, smiling.

"Ready? Lovely. Oh, lock the door, and keep the lower windows closed. Ordinarily we're all open in the village, but outlanders and gypsies come on market day, and as you're not natives, this house will be thought fair game."

I looked at her in alarm. "I ought not to leave Nell."

"Nonsense. She will be quite all right, won't you, dear? You must not start a house-bound pattern, Camilla. I know, believe me." Under Laura's softness there was steel. She rolled Nell's chair to a good view, pointed out a bell-pull on the wall. "Ring that if anything is wrong. It's connected to an iron bell in the yard. Have a good morning, my dear, we'll soon be back."

I found myself sailing off like a good child in Laura's wake. The warm summer morning was incredibly blue and bright, and the village stones reflected back the light. I took a deep breath and laughed aloud.

Laura looked at me and smiled. "It *is* magic, isn't it? I'm so glad; you're a countrywoman at heart, or you wouldn't feel it."

We crossed the narrow, nearer bridge in single file. My eyes were intent upon my feet, but as we reached the shore I had a prickling sensation, as though someone stared. I looked up, startled. The sullen youth I had observed before was leaning against a tree, looking directly at me with insolent eyes that pierced through the armor of whalebone and crinoline. A dizziness assailed me.

"Good morning, Raphael." Laura's voice said crisply from behind, and her hand pressed, ever so slightly, against the hollow of my back to move me on. We were swallowed up in the jostle of the market.

Laura steered me down a narrow lane.

"You wanted black dress goods. There are usually cloth peddlers at the far end here. Mind you don't consider the first price they ask. Act disdainful and offer them a quarter, or a fifth. Then you can barter."

"Perhaps you should do it."

Laura shook her head. "Oh, no. You must establish yourself as the mistress of Wychwood House."

The yard goods were of a quality better than I expected. I was able to purchase not only a dull black linen, summer-thin, but cottons for two morning dresses and a piece of fine woolen for the fall as well.

"Where shall I send it, ma'am?" the girl inquired, producing a rosy urchin. "Brother be glad to carry't for a copper."

"Very well. It's for Miss Jardine of Wychwood House."

Did everything go motionless for a moment in the summer air? Then the girl's eyes lowered, and Laura said, "Why do you not have it sent directly to Mrs. Lee's? We must look for Georgina; she's sure to be here somewhere."

The moment of tension, if it had so been, was past.

We found Georgina loitering against one of

the pillars of the Market Cross. Yes, my dress was ready, she assented. "If ye'll come up-along this afternoon, my mam'll give it you and do cutting for new gowns."

"Oh, I don't believe it will be necessary," Laura said pleasantly. "Miss Jardine has already given your mother gowns for cutting-samples. You can deliver Miss Jardine's dresses, surely, if your mother can't." There was a curious note in her voice. The girl looked frightened, the more so when Laura added, "It will not upset your mother, surely, not as much as your being with Rafe Smith beneath the cider wagon recently."

There were bits of straw adhering to Georgina's tucked-up skirts. Laura was not as sheltered as I had imagined. Georgina shot me that slant-eyed look. "Happen I will, then, and if sobeit you'm pictures of dresses you'm wanting, I'll bear them back."

She slouched off with barefoot grace as Laura gazed after her, looking troubled. "I worry about that girl," she said abruptly. "I wonder—You'll be looking for a housemaid—would you consider taking on Georgina?"

"I don't know yet if servants will be possible at all."

"Oh, you must have them," Laura said

firmly. "There are other ways to economize in villages. You'll manage *that* right enough, but not housekeeping under primitive conditions. You don't know the way of it, and you'll be lost. If you don't mind advice, take a chance and hire Georgina. You can get her cheap, and she understands how to make do."

"Why do you say take a chance?"

"Because Georgina's half gypsy," Laura said frankly. "Her mother's terrified she'll run off to her father's people, and keeps the girl on far too tight a rein. The village is hidebound in its prejudice, you know. Lady Margaret's not, and she's tried to take the Lees on and see them right, but she— How shall I put it? She has too heavy a hand. Georgina needs training but not breaking of spirit. It would be an act of charity, and she could be worth her weight in gold to you."

Nell would be fascinated by Georgina's strangeness and her gypsy blood. "I'll speak to Georgina about it this afternoon."

"Good," Laura said. "Once you have her across your threshold, that's half the battle."

The remark puzzled me, but before I could question her, an urchin rushed up and tugged on Laura's skirt.

"Oh, ma'am, please, Doctor says come

home at once. There's an outlander slipped on bridge and bruk his leg and he needs help to set it."

"I'll come directly. Camilla, forgive me." Laura hurried off.

I was alone now in the bustle of the market. The tempo was slowing now as sun and heat both rose, but there was still that sense of fresh and pulsing life. I wandered happily, ignoring covert glances, the faint drawing back from me as I approached. I looked at ducks and chickens, looked at kittens, and remembered Nell's request for one. Then I spied a display of farm instruments and went toward it firmly.

The fellow tending the stand had his back to me; he was gazing off across the throng to where Georgina Lee leaned against the Market Cross. I was struck by a similarity to a panther I had seen once in a traveling circus—there was that same mingling of sensual grace and brute power only barely caged. He paid no notice to me, and I cleared my throat. "I should like to purchase gardening tools." There was no response from him, only a kind of tension, and I wondered if I'd come upon the village natural. "Garden tools," I repeated. "A hoe and trowel."

He turned then, and it was all I could do to repress an involuntary tremor. It was the youth who had stared at me earlier. He stared now, boldly, directly into my eyes, and spoke with no pretense of civility. "These be farm gear."

"I know, but you do have some less heavy? Suitable for an herb and kitchen garden."

His eyes, with an insolence that was not even veiled, swept me up and down. "These bean't wummin's gear."

That look, slow and familiar, made me feel actually indecent; almost I began to be afraid. Then behind me, to my mingled perturbation and relief, I heard a laugh. I swung round, knowing whom I would see. Jeremy Bushel, our rescuer of the London journey, sat easily in the saddle of a spirited horse. Next to the real farmworkers of the market, he looked less than ever a man of the land. His white tucked shirt was open at the throat and his boots, though dusty, had been made by no mean cobbler. "Having difficulties again, madam? I told you the wilds of Oxfordshire were no fit harbour for lone young women."

"Can you make this person understand I wish to purchase garden tools?" I retorted icily.

"Certainly. A small slice and picker suitable for the lady, Rafe, and all accompanying. Not those; that metal's untempered and the handles are not seasoned. They won't last a fortnight. Is that all you have?" The youth grudgingly produced another set. "These are satisfactory, are they not?" He waited for my nod. "Have your father put a better edge on them at the forge, and then deliver them to Wychwood House. Take your bill to Lawyer Roach and he'll pay what's proper."

Again that pause when Wychwood House was mentioned. I paid no attention now. Mr. Bushel's eyes were dancing; he was up to something, and my own eyes shot sparks. Before I could frame a civil, frosty thanks he bowed extravagantly, clapped on his wide-brimmed hat, and galloped off up the common in a swirl of dust. The sound of his laughter carried back to me on the breeze.

I hesitated a moment, and then started home. I had gone but a few feet when a murmur of singing came to my ears.

"Heigh ho, Green grow the
rushes—oh!

One is one, and all alone, and evermore
    shall be—oh!"

The sound was so faint, so taunting, I was not sure that I even heard aright. I whirled round, but there was no one near me. Rafe was gone. Off in the pass-by of the packhorse bridge, Georgina Lee leaned on the parapet and was regarding me inscrutably with her slanting eyes.

Was it bereavement that was making my thoughts behave so strangely? My mind was like a closed cupboard of many small compartments; it was impossible to open more than one door at once. I could not even concentrate on the most important matters for more than a few moments at a time. I ought to begin seriously searching for the token, but I did not. I kept forgetting that I had to call on Mr. Roach to discuss financial matters. I wandered much too long a time in the market, but half conscious, although Nell was waiting alone at home. I scarcely even thought of Martin for hours on end—not till some small thing, sharp as broken glass, pierced through the numbness of my heart.

That had happened when I walked home

from Widow Lee's and heard Laura speak of her own loss; it happened again when Georgina brought my dresses home. One of them I had been wearing that day on the Battery when I had seen Martin off to war. The last time I would ever see him. The roses and daisies that had sprigged the thin muslin were now all gone to black. I pressed the dress tight to me in my arms and turned away from the light.

From the doorway Georgina's voice came with more delicacy than I thought she could possess. "My da's people have a saying, ma'am. 'The color of memory no dye can change.' "

This made it easier for me to bring up the matter of employment. For the first time she looked directly at me, and I saw a mixture of emotions contending there. Eagerness for work, a kind of angry pride, that curious apprehension Wychwood House evoked, an avid curiosity. It was the latter, I believe, that tipped the balance. Georgina's eyes kept skittering hither and yon all the while we talked. I named the wages Laura had advised, hinted at more if I was satisfied, and we parted on agreeable terms.

Having Georgina in the house would be a

great relief, for the secrets of the old kitchen were a mystery that baffled me, and my arms felt as though hung from broken hinges after these few days of moving Nell alone. I would feel much better having a maid, however untrained, to attend Nell in my absence.

I felt troubled about leaving Nell when I donned my new-dyed muslin that afternoon and crossed the green to report about Georgina. Quinn Cottage, inside as well as out, had that sense of shadows and foreboding. The windows, small and thickly overhung, let in little light. Laura was pleased to see me, and I was struck again by her loneliness and eagerness for friends. Dr. Matthew Quinn, who was vague, elderly and cherubic, readily agreed to look in on my sister once a week. I told Laura of my conversation with Georgina, and she produced a carefully detailed memorandum.

"It is essential that you commence on the right footing. Always know more than she does about any task, and if you do not, assign her something else in meantime and consult these notes. I've made you a weekly housekeeping timetable. Always inspect her work, and at least for the first few days try to find something that needs improvement, and point it out. She'll feel contemptuous about being able to walk all over you otherwise."

"You're an angel," I said fervently.

Laura laughed. "The fruits of experience, I assure you! Our Rosie's a great friend of Georgina's, and much like her. My first six months of keeping house for Father were miserable, and I was born here. You're a 'furrin wummin' and need all the help you can get!"

Georgina appeared promptly at seven-thirty the next morning. She was still unkempt, but I was pleased to see she had deemed it suitable to scrub her face and hands, though dark rings indicated precisely where she'd stopped. I gave her a clean apron and set her to skimming cream for the morning coffee, which struck her as a quite peculiar custom.

"My mam say nobbut tea give proper strength to blood," she observed, watching me prepare Nell's tray with the flowered china, thin toast and honey and a rosebud in a crystal vase.

"I suppose you're used to a country breakfast—porridge and eggs and ham."

Georgina looked at me in astonishment. "That's for Manor House. Us eats bread and lard. Meat's just for special, Easter and Christmas, if year's been good."

I was appalled at this extent of poverty. "I should have thought there would at least be hunting in the forest."

A shutter closed across Georgina's face. "Not no more," she said with a finality that brooked no questions.

After breakfast the garden tools arrived. To my surprise I heard Georgina speaking most venomously to Rafe for coming to the front door, not the back. "Us know why you poking here, and don't think other! This be proper lady's house, it be, and us'll thank you to treat it as you do Manor!" She shut the door upon him firmly.

"If anyone calls, I shall be in the back yard," I informed her, picking up the tools and my broad-brimmed hat. I was longing to get my fingers in the earth, and the walled garden was so perfect, so complete, it seemed courteously aloof from my ministrations. The kitchen garden, though, was an abandoned child, of good lineage but waiting to be reclaimed.

The sun was bright, the stones shone, and the sky was very blue. The faint state of melancholy which the garden evoked was only the filmiest chiffon veil, softening everything to a magical kind of peace. As soon as I dug my trowel beneath the dead-thatch surface of the soil, I uncovered a secret, living world. Ants scuttled busily, and a fat slug extended his horns to me curiously, then crawled toward the sun. I laughed aloud.

It would come back, this garden would come back, as the walled one had. I must get some of those woven bee-skeps at market for here as well. It was too late for vegetables this year, but in the spring we would plant as our neighbors did, and have our own fresh produce. For the fall, there were apples for the gathering, and late berries. Laura would teach me to make apple butter and sun-cooked jam. The outbuildings could be repaired; the market had shown me the plenitude of local labor. In time we might keep a horse—or a pony; Nell would like that. There might even be a pony trap somewhere in those sheds. We would stay here; I knew we would stay here. We would find the token and live in this house forever.

The possibilities were intoxicating. I put down my trowel and headed for the buildings in the rear. Certainly I ought to investigate before making further purchases; there were doubtless garden tools here already, squirreled away. There might be other items we could use, or clues to the treasure. I tugged all the great barn doors wide open to the sun, thinking how beautiful these simple buildings were. Those old-time artisans had been incapable of building the plainest structures without purity of line. The sun shone on chiseled stone, the silvered boards, the intricate lacework of spiderwebs that hung from rusting old farm tools whose use I did not know.

A wagon resembling Jeremy Bushel's was buried under the debris, and beyond, behind a clutter of rotting handles, I spied the curving front of what looked to be a lady's trap. I flung away rusty tools, eager to get to it, and it was then, somewhere round the corners of my mind, that I first became conscious of the smell. Insidious, sickish-sweet, as though from something that had been shut up too long.

I pulled at the side board of the wagon, and it came off in my hand, spilling to my feet a heap of moldering blankets. I reached to catch them, and then I saw, and jerked my hand away.

It was half—half only—of what once had

been a ginger cat. It had not been dead long, for it still gave off that overpowering odor of cloying sweetness, and matted fur still clung to its stiffened legs. Something had been gnawing at its tail. Something stirred now, in the blanket's revolting folds. It ran out, across my foot, and scrabbled into the debris beyond—a great grey rat. To my everlasting shame, I screamed and ran.

I fled, blindly, across the back yard toward the house, and then something solid loomed before me, and arms grabbed me, and I screamed again.

"My dear Miss Jardine! Miss Camilla!" Charles Roach, the solicitor, was gazing at me in dismay. "What is it? Georgina said you were out here—"

"I'm all right now." I threw my head back and my hat fell off, and my hair pulled loose by its passage, tumbled free. I took a deep breath, gathering the remnants of dignity. "There was . . . some vermin, alive *and* dead . . . I'm afraid I panicked foolishly."

"Not foolish at all," he responded gallantly, patting my shoulder. "That's what comes, of course, of keeping a place shut up. I warned Lady Kersey, but she never would hear of tenants. I presume she always hoped— But I digress. You must come inside and sit down. I'm sure you're longing for a cup of tea."

That was the English cure-all. "I'm longing to get that vermin out of there," I said grimly.

Georgina emerged from the house, brandishing the fire shovel. "Not to fear. Us can clear sheds tomorrow if you'm so minded, and I'll rid you'm of corpse."

I felt like a young girl again, having someone paternal and protective looking after me, and the luxury was inordinately soothing. Mr. Roach steered me into Kersey's Room and seated me in a high carved chair. "Rest a moment. I'll make you tea. Living alone, you know, one learns many things."

He made real plowman's tea, black as my coffee, and though I didn't want it I drank it, and found it bracing. "Now!" Mr. Roach smiled at me. "Do you think you can spare time from your farming enterprise to discuss some business?"

I colored. "I have been meaning to call upon you. There have been so many matters to attend to. How did you know I was farming, as you put it?"

"You bought tools yesterday from Aaron Smith's young cub. Substantial ones, not ladies' toys." His face was kindly but his eyes were earnest. "I wish you had consulted me ahead; I could have advised you what expenditures were wise."

I gazed at him in some alarm. "There is an income for our maintenance, is there not? I was told a trust fund had been set up."

"It's income will not provide for living on the level suitable for ladies of your station. To squander it on items solely for your amusement during the short time you are here would be most imprudent."

I stared at him. "I thought you understood. We intend to live here."

Now Mr. Roach's face mirrored my own dismay. "Sir Percival indicated something to that effect. I could not believe that you were serious."

"Lady Kersey's will gave me the right to occupy the premises for a year."

"Of course, but for two gently bred young women to occupy a house alone and unassisted—"

"I have already engaged a servant."

"I will come to her presently. If it were possible for you to have a proper staff, supervised by an older woman of some standing, and with the income to maintain it . . . The British pound was worth more at the time Lady Kersey set up the trust, and several of the investments on which she insisted have—ah—not lived up to her expectations. To be frank, had Lady Kersey been open to advice, had she leased this house and invested properly, there would have been a tidy nest egg now. As it is, there is only a tiny income from her speculations. I beg you, do not follow her rash examples."

"What *are* you suggesting that I do, Mr. Roach?"

"Return with your sister to your own country. You already have a life there—friends, a home. I can understand the temptation to remain here. Lady Kersey had a power of fascination and I suspect she was deliberately arranging for it to live on after her. My dear Miss Camilla, save yourself from it before it is too late. To live in Wychwood House alone not only imperils your good name but could place you in want and actual danger."

"Mr. Roach, you are under a misapprehension." I strove to speak carefully, for his warning disturbed me more than I wanted to admit. "This is not a quixotic escapade. You may have noticed I am wearing mourning. There are personal reasons why I do not wish to return to Charleston. But even if that were not the case, it would be impossible. My sister's delicate health, the dangerous passage, and our finances would not permit it. I left a war-torn city, Mr. Roach, and it took all that was left of our resources for me to do it. Wychwood House came to me as a godsend. At the moment, our life is here—or nowhere."

Mr. Roach looked deeply troubled. "Forgive me, I did not know."

I took a deep breath. "I said this was a godsend, and I . . . I believe there is some purpose to it. I was trained as a scholar of Tudor history, and I hope to be able to supplement our income by writing and other labors. Dear Mr. Roach, can you not assist us, instead of putting barriers in our way?"

Mr. Roach did not speak for a minute. He was still disturbed, but I read respect and admiration in his eyes. "What can I say, except that I trust you *will* allow me to assist, however I can. Not only as a solicitor but as a friend. To begin, will you authorize me to have the open fields belonging to Wychwood House fenced and rented? You are entitled to the profits from them, and you could never farm yourself. At present they lie fallow, open prey to poachers and an incitement to squatters and lawbreakers. To enclose and rent would be both sensible and profitable."

I assented readily, and he rose to leave. But something still seemed to prey upon him, and when I reached to open the front door, he stopped me. "Miss Camilla, I asked if I might be a friend. Now I must jeopardize that request by giving you the warning of a friend."

"What warning?"

"You come as strangers here. Do not trust too soon in associations which could bring you genuine harm. I refer to Jeremy Bushel and Georgina Lee."

I could feel a pulse beating in my neck. "I'm sure you have reasons for such an allegation."

He countered with a question of his own. "What do you know of Jeremy Bushel, Miss Jardine?"

"Nothing other than that he farms, though he seems no farmer, and that his manner, although unfortunate, is knowledgeable."

"No more do we know, and that very knowledgeability is suspicious. He appeared from nowhere and rented a derelict farm up on the hill. You are right, he is no common farmer. He works the land himself, and lets no one near it except a few men who swear by him and are close-mouthed, Widow Lee thinks he's put a spell on them. What should carry more weight with you is that he shows an extraordinary interest in Wychwood House, put in offers of rental at far more than the place is worth, and only rented Tarr Farm after discovering he could see Wychwood House from it with a telescope. He several times requested permission to inspect these premises, and was extremely insolent when I refused."

The memory of the chisel marks on the back entry shot into my mind. "And . . . Georgina?"

"Georgina is half gypsy. You have not had experience with them; we have. Why do you think she has had no employment, except of an extremely dubious nature at Tarr Farm? Aside from shiftlessness, she is the daughter of the worst poacher and thief in twenty miles. You ought not trust her even as far as you can see."

His words had made me increasingly uneasy, but at this last unfairness my sense of justice flared. "I was taught to believe in innocence until guilt was proved."

Mr. Roach shook his head. "That is a splendid theory, Miss Camilla. Unfortunately, trust in innocence offers no protection for the innocent. Your Tudor philosophers should have taught you that was true."

He bowed and went, leaving me much to think on.

The rest of the day passed in outward quiet. By afternoon Nell was in a state of such anticipation that I had Georgina carry her to her room. I tucked her between sheets cool and fragrant with lavender and said severely, "Unless you nap, I shall send word to the Manor that we shall dine at home."

Nell's eyes darkened and she pushed herself up, heedless of the pain. "Camilla, don't."

"Don't what, chickabiddy?"

"Speak to me so. As if I weren't a person." I started, and she put her hand up quickly. "Hear me, please! I know I'm a . . . a weight on you. You have to do everything for me, and it's hard. It's hard on me, too."

"I know that, dear," I interrupted swiftly. "You've been so brave. The pain will ease in time, the doctors say so."

"It's not the pain," Nell said. "That's just part of how it has to be, and I can bear that. It's what's happening to us. The way you talk to me. All the time I was lying there at school, I kept thinking, 'Camilla will come, and we'll be together once again.' But it's not been like that. You're shutting me off, not letting me share. It would have been better if I'd just not waked up after I went out the window."

I stared at her, truly shocked. "Oh, darling, darling. You must never think like that! We'll make things as pleasant for you as we can, and in time—why, in time we'll have you walking, well as ever."

"You're doing it again." Nell looked at me helplessly. "You don't believe that, Camilla, nor do I. You're just saying it, being bright and cheery, holding me off as if I weren't able any more to think or feel. Camilla, I've given up walking, don't make me give up being real!"

Her words hurt the more because they were the truth. In the blindness of my compassion, I was treating my sister like a puppet, like a doll. How ironic, when Sir Percival's kind attempts to arrange my life had made me bristle, when Jeremy Bushel's patronizing manner made by own back arch like an angry cat.

I said at last, humbly, "You can be happy here, can't you, Nell?"

Nell hesitated. "It's . . . strange here. I can't tell yet if this house is my friend. But 'happy' is not what matters really, is it?" She closed her eyes, looking white and frail. "I believe I will rest. You'll help me dress, won't you? I do want to go properly, not in a wrapper."

So, to please her, I struggled to array her in the dress that she selected, a buttercup voile that brought back memories of the old days. I choked back words that rushed to my lips to say we ought not go, as Nell bit back any sound of pain. For I was so clumsy at this nursing, and careful as I was, my efforts left her so strained and exhausted that it frightened me.

I had no heart left for my own adornment. The other dyed gown was more suitable, being low of neck and elbow-sleeved, and I pulled it on. The dull creped muslin settled round me softly, like a mourning veil. I added a jet cross hung on velvet—Martin had given it to me and it brought me comfort—and bundled my hair into a knotted net. I had to stoop slightly to see into the wavy mirror, and the room's half-light reflected back a stranger's face. My face was the color of bleached bones, and the black ribbon at my throat looked like the mark of a guillotine. I shivered, and wondered why I could not trust my conviction of that first evening, that I had at last come home.

Lady Margaret's coachman came in to carry Nell. There were cushions and a foot-rest in the carriage, but nonetheless the short ride was an ordeal. Nell's face grew paler and her hand gripped mine. The gates of the Manor House stood open, wooden gates all thick with shadows set in walls of stone. Beyond, in the winding drive, sunlight gleamed with that ephemeral quality of late English afternoon. We rolled up the curving sand-pale drive, over a low bridge furred with lichens. Quietness, that was what struck me most: a world where no thing stirred, where even the sheep on the grassy parkland seemed unreal. A white peacock, motionless, his tail a fan, posed on the greensward. It was too perfect. Then the carriage rolled to a stop before the Manor House, and my vision altered.

This was perfection attempted but gone

askew. No amount of Henry VIII grotesqueries, nor the present fashion's mock-medieval follies, could mar completely the dignity of Cotswold stone. But pseudo-French round towers, embarrassingly small and topped with conical roofs, stood at the four corners connected by miniature defensive walls. What had been intended as a moat had gone to grasses and wildflowers. Red roses foamed over crenellated walls, and a yellow rose tried to outreach the ivy at a tower window. There were geraniums and lobelias before the entrance in stiff formal beds.

It was, all in all, finely and firmly done, as though a determined will had imposed itself on what once had been an unpretentious country house. And I could not say why something choked back involuntary laughter, why something stirred me not to mirth but dread.

Nell's fingers plucked at my sleeve. "It's a gingerbread house gone all demented!"

That was it. It ought to have been amusing, but it was not.

The carriage stopped. A footman trundled out an invalid chair, and the coachman settled Nell into it under my anxious eyes. Her hair was damp and she seemed trembling, but she flashed me a stern glance.

"Her Ladyship is in the lower drawing room," the footman murmured.

We crossed the square hall with its paneling and carved stairs, high wall of windows with lovely leaded glass. The drawing room was pure and beautiful. The ceiling was blue, arch-vaulted like an abbey with the same white marble that formed the fireplace with its stepped chimney-piece. A magnificent Persian rug was on the floor. Lady Margaret was seated on a sofa, her children grouped beside her like a Nattier portrait. The dull light pouring through leaded glass behind their heads made her purple gown appear gunmetal, made them visible only as figures in silhouette.

Nell made a sound. I moved slightly, and the trick of light dissolved and I could guess why she made that cry. The girl at Lady Margaret's left was a thin child somewhere about Nell's age, dull and colorless. The slim youth at her right hand wore impeccable evening clothes, but my eyes superimposed a white silk shirt for ruffled linen, a garnet-colored cloth for the correct black broadcloth, ruffled the elf-locks carefully combed across his forehead.

Stuart. Stuart of the walled garden, who had said, "She drinks my blood," and gazed off into the darkling sky.

"May I present to you my son, Sir Philip Dudley Ross," Lady Margaret was saying.

Philip; not Stuart at all. He bowed above my hand, so properly, with that innate arrogance of social caste. But for an instant as he straightened his eyes met mine, and they were the eyes of the vulnerable, tormented child I had sensed within him when we met before. *You won't tell my mother*, he had begged me then.

I smiled with kind impersonal graciousness. "I am so glad to meet you at last," I said pleasantly. "Your mother spoke of you. I should like you to know my sister."

He murmured only, "I am honored," but for a moment relief leaped like fire within his eyes. I had an odd sense we were being bound in some secret covenant I did not understand. Involuntarily I shivered.

Then Nell, who had recovered her poise, was extending a fragile hand. His sister was being presented, Lady Amy Ross, who bobbed a curtsey and shrank back to regard us in a kind of shamefaced misery. I remembered Philip's remark about devouring, and wondered if it was of his sister he had thought.

Dinner was announced, and we all went in. It was a strange meal, and I could not pin down the cause of the uneasiness I felt. The room, so long that it seemed narrow, had a duplicate of the drawing room's fireplace and ceiling vaults, although here the interstices of the carved arches were painted red. There was red carpet on the floor, and a beautifully carved old cupboard that I coveted. The table could have accommodated twenty easily.

The food was excellent, but I ate little. I felt as though some odd and progressive enervation was taking place within me to drain resistance. No doubt it was the aftereffect of the past week's pressures, the relief of being at last where I was not obliged to lead. I experienced a sort of lassitude that was enormously alluring, despite that continuing sensation of uneasiness.

Lady Margaret was graciousness itself. She drew us out about life in Charleston and our present plans, and I found myself speaking of the scholarly work I had done with my stepfather, my hope of doing some writing here in England.

Perhaps she guessed at our financial straits. "I wonder . . . My daughter is reluctant to return to boarding school. Forgive me if the suggestion is unwelcome, but if you would consider allowing her to study with you a few hours each day, it would be a splendid opportunity for her."

And a godsend for us, was my first instinctive thought.

"*I* should be interested in exploring the classics, also," Philip said abruptly. "Are you acquainted with *Hamlet*, Miss Jardine? Or *Oedipus*?"

"You must forgive my son's teasing," Lady Margaret said with calm decisiveness. "Philip has more suitable studies, which occupy his time. He has responsibilities to prepare himself for, don't you, dear? Philip will be stepping into his father's place on the estate quite soon, and that will of course allow him little time to indulge in side amusements."

Her tone was pleasant, matter-of-fact and loving. There was even, understandably, a note of pride. But Philip had not been joking; I knew that, and I was sure his mother did, as well. The observation, such a tiny thing, lodged like a pebble in the corner of my mind.

It was Nell who picked up the dangling conversation and sent it spinning like a ball upon a polished surface. Nell's earlier exhaustion had all been transmuted into a feverish brightness and she sparkled like a precariously balanced goblet of champagne. She gave an account of our journey up from London that was considerably more amusing than it had seemed to either of us at the time.

After dinner coffee was served in the drawing room. Lady Margaret glanced at the window, where the light still glowed. "When you have finished, my son will take you out to view the grounds."

"We should be going," I demurred. "My sister is very tired."

"You must see the Italian garden, Miss Jardine," Philip said. "It is my father's masterpiece. My father was quite a designer. For my mother."

I glanced at him sharply. His eyes were expressionless.

"I am not in the least tired, Camilla." Nell's voice was very high and bright. "You must view the garden and tell me of it. Amy will keep me company, won't you, Amy?"

The girl gave a startled nod, like a frightened rabbit, and Philip said with some intensity, "I wish you to view the gardens with me *tonight*."

I could not tell whether this was arrogance speaking, or something more. In the end, of course, I went.

Philip did not, however, lead me to the garden, but across the lawn to the shadow of an enormous tree. "You can relax now. She cannot see us here."

"Who?" I asked, although I knew the answer.

"The Queen Bee. The Dragon Mantis," He gave me that penetrating stare, and his mood changed. "You do not approve of me, do you?"

"I scarcely know you well enough," I responded coolly, "to presume to judge."

"Ah, but that does not usually prevent one's doing so, does it? You are an unusual woman, aren't you?" He was deliberately baiting me, and in a peculiarly adult fashion. I chose not to answer. "I am not a riddle easily solved. Do you think that you shall ever know me, Miss Jardine?"

"Does anyone ever really know another? It is sufficiently difficult to know oneself." The shaft struck home at some point. His face altered, and I made a bold stroke. "What do you want? You did not bring me here to discuss your mother. Or did you?"

He had turned away from me toward the shadows, so I could not read him. But his voice, when he spoke again, was stripped of earlier grandiloquence. "I want to thank you for not giving me away. About trespassing on your property, I mean. It was rather more than I would have expected. But you are not the average insensitive adult, are you?"

He was back at his trick of twisting a personal comment into a question, as though erecting a wall with holes and daring me to step through. I smiled impersonally and replied in kind. "You are not the average insensitive boy, are you? Actually, I find that sort of generalization rather stupid. No one is average."

He stared at me for several seconds. "I think that I shall like you," he said at last. "It would be interesting trying to know *you*."

"Don't you think you ought to be showing me your father's garden?"

"My mother's garden," Philip corrected,

leading the way toward the far side of the house. "My mother wanted an Italian garden, so my father made it for her. My father always gave my mother everything she wanted, because she stepped down several steps, you see, in marrying him. Maman is a duke's daughter and he was only a baronet. Created, not inherited, because he did so well reviving the wool industry with his prize flock. That was my mother's doing, too, of course. My mother always knows best. My father turned out a splendid success, and died in a Florentine garden in England, instead of Italy, and I am destined to follow in his footsteps." His words were unpleasant, but there was a tautness that showed this was no detached mockery.

"I am acquainted with *Hamlet*," I said deliberately. "And *Oedipus*, too, although my own field of study is the Tudors. Curious that you should mention those particular two. What interests you, the relationships of mothers and sons?"

He stared again. "We must talk of that some time. The plays, that is. Here is the garden. Mind the stairs."

The garden was located, strangely, in a high shelf carved directly into Wychwood

Rise. Two flights of wide stone steps, separated by a landing, ran up at right angles to the house itself, and their upper reaches disappeared into greenery and vines that tangled like jungle. Beyond them, high old trees of Wychwood Forest stood like Druids.

It was now the hour before twilight when the English sky, not yet darkening, took a luminous cool light. I lifted my hoops and started up the steps and Philip followed, hovering at my elbow. Perhaps it was the height and steepness of those stairs that took my breath.

The first flight ended at a small lichen-covered landing, marble-paved. I looked back, down at the slate roof of the Manor House, at the tree-bordered common where the sheep being driven slowly home looked like toys. The town was a miniature village, tiny and perfect. To the near right a cross piercing the greenery proclaimed the church. There was the graveyard running up the slope, there the thatched roof of my own Wychwood, and faintly seen, the purple and pink of flowers in the walled garden. Pressing close, like remnants of an older world barely held at bay, were the thick-crowding black-green trees of the forest that gave my house its name.

No wonder Philip had known of the walled garden. He could see all that took place in it from here.

"To your right," Philip's voice said in my ear, and I turned, and for the first time saw the Italian garden.

I say "saw," although from this level I could only begin to grasp its form and outline. The garden rose above me in continuous terraces, and all I could glimpse from here were rails of carved white stone capped with the green of vines and hints of color. At the pinnacle, like the ornament atop a wedding cake, a small white-pillared edifice was like a Roman temple.

"Come," Philip said, and steered me down a tunnel of green vines.

The scent of moist greenery and earth rose like a cloud to swallow us. We reached a turning, went up more steps of that white stone so unlike the native ore. On a pedestal at the top of the second flight stood a stone statue of a youth with pipes. He seemed imprisoned. Further along, in a crumbling grotto, a nymph sat eternally contemplating her reflection in the clouded waters. Beyond and above, shut in by walls, lay beds of flowers. The walls were beautiful, they were low, there were openings between carved balusters which permitted glimpses in and out, but they held the garden close.

Now the nature of the garden revealed itself—a mosaic of white-pebbled walks, expanses of green turf, plots carefully "Bedded out" in sheets of color. A precisely disciplined mind had ordered it, holding it just on the edge of being too bright, too careful for the English scene.

I turned to Philip spontaneously. "Your father designed this? He must have been an artist."

"He may have been, once. I have often wondered. He was," Philip said, "one of those persons one did not really know. He did go to Italy once to study, before he met my mother. I wonder if that explains her attraction for him. Her character, I have always thought, is quite Italian—which is strange when she loathes Italy so. At any rate, he stayed in England, and what talent he had decayed. You saw the additions inflicted on our modest home. Watch that branch. It has a nasty way of clutching one's hair."

"You intend to go to Italy yourself to study?"

"I shall go one day, over *chère* Maman's dead body. It may be that, quite literally. And may the Old Ones hear my prayer that the opportunity does not come too late." He let his breath out in a burst of passion. "I will not be like my father. I want to live before I die!"

"How?"

"Every way. Taste, see, experience everything. That's what the Romans believed in, is it not?" He switched abruptly to an ordinary tone. "Actually, I want to spend a year or two abroad and study music."

"And Lady Margaret does not approve?"

He turned, and a trick of cruel light silhouetted his deformity. "Lady Margaret considers it unsuitable, considering what I was born— in all senses. Her little man must walk in his Papa's shoes, to which she has so diligently shaped his feet."

He sounded at that moment so bleak that I said impulsively, "You must come to Wychwood House. If not for lessons with your sister, then to the garden. You can visit with Nell, and we can read aloud."

Philip looked suddenly happy. He scrambled

agilely up the next stairway, and I followed at a slower pace. We walked in silence, up and up, until at last we reached the topmost level and stood before the temple-grotto backed into the very earth of Wychwood Rise.

As I crossed the grotto threshold, I had a strange sensation that I was stepping back through time, not to the Tudors or the Medicis, but to something older and more primitive. The high walls were thickly hung with vines, and their leaves pointed downward to a hollwed slab now used as a water pool, catching the flow from a gargoyle held by a crouching boy. It could have once been a sacrificial stone, and the carved figures altarpieces, embodiments of the spirits of the place. The crouching figure held the gargoyle as though to crash it down, and the water in the hollow stone was stagnant, covered with a green growth which, like the moss on the walls, was all-pervading.

Philip was watching me. "You feel it, don't you?"

"What?"

"The magic. This, like your garden and the cemetery, was all part of the Old Ones' sacred place. Those walls are believed to be part of the original dolmen. The villagers refused to move them, though they could not say why. So Father simply incorporated them into his plans. He was clever that way. Maman has her Italian garden, the village superstitions are intact, and the spirits of the place, one hopes, are satisfied."

I shivered slightly, and Philip underwent one of those mood changes which made him seem much older. "You are cold, aren't you? Come along. You'd best hold my arm, these old steps are so unsteady."

He reached to adjust my shawl, but as he did so, drawn by some force I could not name, I moved away. I stood for a moment, as though I myself were caught in stone, gazing down at the whole pattern of the garden, and surrounding country, as now revealed. Seen from above, in its entirety, the garden was too opulent. The underlying plan remained, and traces of the original order, but it was as if since its designer's death the place had been allowed to grow unchecked, the intent developing without its once-companionate discipline. It had become lush to the point of rankness.

I knew then what it was that had so disturbed me since we drove through thick shadows into the seductive golden light beyond the entrance gates. What it was that had struck me uneasily in the tarted-up romanticism of the Manor House facade. Decadence.

In a flash of most unscholarly imagery, I saw the Italian garden, sprawling on its hilltop, as a monstrous growth, feeding on the village which lay beyond in a sick enchanted sleep. And counterpoised to that vision, like an adversary, Wychwood House. Wychwood House, which was a warm and living presence, yet which, oddly, seemed somehow threatening to all but me. Wychwood House, to which, by some power I could not name, I had been drawn.

II

THE POWERS ARE DRAWN DOWN

6

Rossford-under-Wychwood
August, 1863

MORE and more strong grew the conviction that I had been brought to Wychwood to some purpose. And equally strong, and considerably more disturbing, the sense that someone—or something—was determined to keep me out.

Nell had a bad spell that night, and by morning she was twisted and stiff with pain. I sent for Dr. Quinn, despite her pleading, and his examination gave her a bad half-hour. Afterwards he spoke to me privately.

"You must keep in mind, my dear, that these chronic disabilities are not like regular illness. There is no crisis after which, if Providence so ordains, the patient is eventually as good as new. Your sister, for example, has no broken bones of which one can say, 'She will be well when that has healed.' All we can do is try to make her comfortable." He smiled vaguely and fumbled at his watch. "I will make up something in the dispensary to ease her pain."

Nell refused to take the soothing syrup when it arrived. "I've had that sort of thing before, in London. It makes me foggy, and I can't bear not knowing what's going on."

I looked at her helplessly. "Darling, you can't just lie there hurting."

"It's my bones ache. Making my head all queer will not change that." Nell gave me an odd, troubled glance. "The doctor did say so, didn't he? That there was nothing really could be done?"

How odd, and how very wrong, that it was Nell who could look the hard fact unflinchingly in the face, when I could not. She was right. I had to allow her reality because it was all that I could give her.

Or was it? I remembered half-forgotten passages in the old garden books which once had fascinated me back in Charleston. There were liniments and teas for aches like Nell's that could be made from plants in the walled garden. To think of reverting, in this modern age, to the primitive, unscientific practices of by-gone centuries seemed, on the surface of it, absurd. But memory stirred in me of concoctions old Emmy had brewed on the plantation, and how they had soothed sore throats and bruises when I was small.

I sought out the herbals Nell had found. They were filled with all sorts of instructions. There was a wash of mugwort for stiff limbs and joints, a broom and tansy tea. I could try those; they were not difficult and could not hurt her.

I took the carefully detailed line drawings with me for identification, and stepped out through the panel door. The garden welcomed me with an aloof reserve, but as I moved along the ordered rows, gathering in my basket, snipping off tips to taste and sniff, it seemed to be unfolding to me like flowers to the sun. The great stand of mugwort, shoulder-high, gave forth a camphor scent, and the yellow-button blossoms on the fern-like tansy glowed. I cut great armfuls, pausing as I did so to consult the herbals for names, histories and use.

How many of these old herbs were common to the medicines of many cultures! African witch doctors, old Hippocrates, and English Druids stirred up the same ingredients, traced the same rituals. The spells they muttered over them were doubtless different, but it was the herbs, and the will or belief that energized them, that made the magic work.

Now I must boil my harvest for an hour. "Stillroom" meant distillery; it was where good wives distilled elixirs for their household use. The name was appropriate in other ways as well. Laura had told me how everyone instinctively whispered and walked on tiptoe in a dairy house, and the stillroom had that same cloistered serenity. I lit a spirit lamp on the old stone counter and worked in comfortable silence through the cool grey afternoon.

I was at home in Wychwood now; I no longer had to stop and ask myself where each thing was. As I went upstairs later to rub Nell's aching limbs with the herb infusion, the fancy crossed my mind that I was walking in the footsteps of the bygone lady whose presence had welcomed me on that first night.

By morning Nell felt well enough to watch from her window as families passed by on their way to church. She shook her head when I wondered whether it was wise for me to go. "You'll only be gone an hour or so, and I can see the church from here, you know. No one's likely to try to break in while you're gone, for goodness sake!"

Tomorrow I must have strong new bolts put on all the doors.

"I can see up the hills into the forest," Nell said dreamily. "Did you know the Old Ones dance in the cemetery when the moon is full? And it's death to anyone who looks on them without a cross between? Georgina told me." She stretched and gave me a triangular smile. "Ah, Cam, don't look that way! I'm only teasing." But she turned back toward the window slowly. "I've dreamed about those woods."

"Is that why you could not sleep the other night?"

Nell shook her head, still gazing far away. "It was before. Before we came here. The first time I looked out at those hills, I remembered. Have you ever felt that way, as though you were moving through a pattern again in a second lifetime?"

Was it because of this conversation that the church affected me the way it did? It was so completely an English country church, with its coffin-shaped grave plots, outlined primly with stone and filled in with low flowers. The markers, usually cozily askew, bore village names: Ross, Smith, Greene. I saw no Lees; perhaps gypsies were not buried in consecrated ground. The path was edged with old-fashioned roses, and more roses clambered up the wooden arch that framed the gate. Ivy, turning red with approaching autumn, veiled the walls. I passed through the vestibule over a worn step into the church itself.

The air was close, so close. A pale light filtered through the leaded windows with their few remaining patches of admirable stained glass. The sanctuary was narrow, shoebox-small; the exquisitely carved wooden pews had name-marked doors. I hesitated, but no one moved toward me, no one smiled. A black-garbed verger studiously turned away. Then I saw Lady Kersey's arms blazoned on the empty pew before the pulpit, and I moved toward it boldly. As the door of the pew snapped shut to close me in, a similar door seemed to shut inside my lungs.

The organ swelled; the congregation rose. An acolyte in black and white bore a magnificent brass cross to lead a small procession of choir singers and a tall thin clergyman with a crimped halo of grey-white hair. The cross, as it moved forward, caught and flung back shafts of reflected light. Incense, chanting, candle smoke, unfamiliar accents blurred together into a single sensory montage. I sat back, half following the service, my eyes taking in the uneven stone flooring and the Norman walls, the special curtained pew for the family from the Manor House. Lady Margaret bowed; Philip gazed at me, his eyes black and opaque. From a pew across the aisle, like sunlight, came Laura's smile.

The pulpit before me was a carved crow's-nest reached by winding stairs. The elaborately carved altar was hung with velvet and snowy lace-edged linen. Above it soared the great window, and I stared at it with slow-growing recognition. I had thought at first that it represented the Fall of Man, but it did not; it was a Doom Window, an apocalyptic vision of the Last Days and the conflict between the angels bright and dark. The souls for which they struggled were depicted as villagers of five hundred years ago. *The principalities and powers of darkness* . . . St. Paul's words surfaced in my brain to ring there with echoes of the centuries.

The service was over. The procession wound out. The congregation rose. "Camilla, how good to see you. I trust your sister's well?" Laura's fingers closed over mine for a moment. Mrs. Lee, surrounded by her brood, did not look in my direction; Georgina broke away to slouch toward Raphael Smith. Across at the far side of the church, Jeremy Bushel was leaning against the wall, regarding me. I dropped my lashes swiftly.

"Miss Jardine, are you ill?" It was Charles Roach's voice at my elbow, tinged with concern, and I was glad to take the arm he offered. He led me out to a bench beneath a spreading tree. "You found the air oppressive? That is often the case in such old places. I was not aware of it, but then, I've had time to grow accustomed."

"You were raised here?"

"Mercy, no. I have been here three years now—just a wink in time to the locals. They scarcely acknowledge one's existence until a half-century at least."

"Yes, I've noticed." I moved to rise, and he sprang to my assistance. "I'm quite all right, really. I must not delay you."

"It is my pleasure," he responded gallantly. "And actually quite providential—if you don't feel discussing business on Sunday is improper. I have ordered the enclosing of the Wychwood fields, as we agreed, and posted poaching prohibitions. It is too late to realize a profit for farm leasing for this year, of course, but at least your rights have been protected."

"How kind of you," I said gratefully.

"Not at all. You have inherited me as your representative. And may I say that of all the commissions Lady Kersey has given me, this is the most pleasant? Now, is there no other way that I can be of service? I feel sure there are other plans fermenting in that clever brain."

"I was thinking," I said, "of chickens." I could not help laughing at his blank expression. "White chickens, like the ones Mrs. Giles has, and some of those with the plumy tails."

"Those are cockerels, actually." He was amused. "So you're thinking of indulging in egg-raising, are you?"

"Why not? We'll have our own fresh poultry and eggs for Nell. It will be a picturesque touch to the back courtyard, will it not? And Nell will like them."

"Very well, I will see about chickens. *And* white cockerels. It will afford me a reason to call on you again." We had reached my door, and he relinquished my arm, lifted his hat, and bowed. I went inside, wondering if it was weak of me to have found his masculine arm so comforting.

Georgina arrived shortly, having gone

home to change tawdry finery for the neat calico I had provided. The local pattern called for dining at midday; it was the custom, it seemed, for villagers without ovens to deliver their Sunday meal to the bakery on their way to church and collect it crisply roasted on return. Nell had been witnessing the procession from her window, and also my own approach; she teased me a bit about having acquired a beau.

It was a still day. Nell was very quiet, and I too had much to think on. We dined formally in the dining room, with candles lit, for already the sky was dark. In the afternoon Nell lost herself again in books, and I sought out histories of the Cotswold area. I had been trained in the scholar's discipline of starting one's research with general reading, allowing disparate data gradually to form into a thesis. I hoped this procedure would be effective in finding the promised treasure. I was commencing with my own Tudor field, but my mind kept straying vagrantly to earlier times. Probably that was the influence of the ancient church; the struggle between Light and Darkness was a medieval concept alien to the New Learning of Erasmus' day.

After a time Nell sighed and her book slid

to the floor. She did not demur when I called Georgina to carry her up to nap. The lower floor was very empty after she was gone. I tried to read, then picked up my bonnet and let myself out into the greyness of the empty street.

I had some half-notion of calling at Quinn Cottage, but the draperies were shut and there was no sign of life. I turned the corner and strolled up past the church. The skewed crosses and the roses waited motionless in the dull light. It was so still, so peaceful, that I felt ashamed of my earlier uneasiness. I put my hand on the lych gate, and it turned noiselessly, as though beckoning me in. My hoops whispered faintly, and as I went slowly up the deserted path I heard the sound of black muslin stirring the dry grass.

I followed the path up to the church and around behind the Norman wall. The apocalyptic window with its warring angels slumbered now, its colors gone. The formal pebbled walk marched neatly round toward the front again, but off to my left another path, scarcely noticeable save for its trodden grass, meandered off through the cemetery's gentle slopes. I wandered idly, stopping now and again to examine a curious carving or an old inscription. My feet carried me even higher, until, when I turned, I could look down on all of Wychwood's house and grounds. I could almost smell the mint of the walled garden. A lamp burned in Nell's bedroom window, a little candle in the gloom.

It was not yet time for tea, so I turned again back toward the graveyard, and then I saw the footpath went still further, under trees which overhung the slabs and crosses. It led like a winding stream to an enormous yew whose spreading arms bent almost to the ground. So high it was, so dense, that as I approached, it blotted out the sky. On the ground around its massive trunk was a ring of small white stones. To go to them was no conscious decision of my mind; my feet led me. I felt again that curious leaden weight upon my chest, choking back my breath.

The carving on these gravestones was not intelligible inscription but symbols, intricate and strange, that stirred some recognition in my mind. The blackness of the tree and its shadows seemed to swallow me and suck me down. At that moment, in the church behind me, the organ shuddered to life with a crashing chord.

The organ thundered, the bells in the tower

pealed discordantly, the lights in the sanctuary sprang to life. The window screamed at me in reds and purples, the angels flashed their wings, and I felt caught in the grip of an evil so intense and complete, it seemed to pinion me living in my tomb. The world whirled; I was rigidly upright but I seemed to fall. My lungs strained and yet I could not breathe; my heart seemed not to beat, yet its pulse thundered in my ears. All the while my eyes were fixed upon that window, until its pattern was blazoned on my brain. Everything within me was locked in mortal struggle with this power that sought possession. This was the horror, this the terror that shot like cold paralysis through my veins: I had known it all before. It was not new. I had felt it, struggled with it in some dream, some other lifetime. I had come home to Wychwood hill, to a bone-deep conflict and a terrible fear.

I became passive; I almost ceased to care. Then faintly from the church came the sound of children's voices singing. The power that had clutched at me receded and I could move once more.

Step by slow step, as though I were drugged, I came down from the hill, past the graves laid out row on orderly row, between the two neat lines of tidy roses. "Holy Saviour, calm our fears," sang the choir, and I was carried closer to reality with each surge of sound. I passed down the front path, stumbled through the turnstile and leaned against the gate-frame, shuddering, as waves of long-buried memory crashed over me.

Now I knew why the scent of herbs, the church, the dreams, the premonitions had brought such sense of panic. Another life indeed—adulthood and England fell away and I was a girl again on the Carolina plantation on an autumn night. I had waked to the sound of distant singing in the quarters and slipped, as a child would, from the sleeping house. Had beheld a ring of dusky figures round a fire, a struggling bird, a knife . . . and a known, loved face, transfixed with alien triumph, bending over it. The face had lifted, and my nurse's eyes looked across the bonfire into mine. In one bound she had reached me, was shaking me, hissing sharply. "You must never tell. You one of us now, you has felt de power. It put its mark on you!" I had nodded, blubbering with fear, stumbled back to bed and never told a soul. In the morning Emmy was the same as always, and what had occurred between us was never mentioned.

Poor Emmy, how terrified she must have been that I'd betray her. But the words she'd spoken had entered my soul. *You one of us. You have felt the power. It has put its mark . . .*

That was why I had thrust the memory deep in the corners of my mind. As a young woman, intoxicated by the world of intellect, I had seized upon scholarship's rational explaining away of all such powers; had buried, because it could not be explained, the self-recognition which had burst that night into my mind. I *had* felt the power; I had not only been possessed by it but had possessed it. What I had run from, as for my very life, had not been fear at all, but fascination.

And then, a few years after that, a book . . . I straightened, wiping the cold moisture from my brow and fumbling for my smelling salts. Not the ammonia only, but the familiar feel of the Tudor scent-vial with its memories of the Colonel, were touchstones to the real. But memory still thrust insistently—my stepfather holding a little book in long slim fingers, saying, "A Book of Shadows. This one is a really fine example. Each initiate has as an early duty the task of copying out the spells and rituals in his own hand. A procedure no doubt linked to the taking of his measure in scarlet thread, possession of which could afterwards put his fate in others' keeping." He had shown me the frontispiece adorned with cabalistic signs, had withdrawn it quickly when I reached for it. "I would not care to have you read it. To one with fine sensibilities, it could do great harm."

Childlike, I had later sought for it when I was alone, and devoured it in snatches of sick fascination. That was the year I had most sharply felt isolation from my peers. Once I had even attempted to work a spell—to make them like me? To get even? I no longer knew. Prudently, I had tried the concoction on farm animals first, and their insane behavior so alarmed me that I never experimented with such things again. When next I looked at the book's hiding place, it was no longer there. I had long since forgotten it, convinced that everything has some logical explanation, that there are no such things as dark powers.

But now, in another country, another life, I had experienced those powers once again. Say it was a kind of hypnotism; say I was overtired, too easily suggestible, had been hearing too much superstition and reading too many books. *My* mind told me all these things. But even as I clung desperately to this logic, my body reiterated the truth it had experienced. I had felt what I had felt, however much I might dispute the cause.

The twilight of this laden day was now fading. I longed to run but could not; my feet seemed caught in a slow rhythm I could not break. A few more steps . . . if I could keep going just a few more steps, I would be across my own threshold and I could let go.

The sharp scent of the geraniums came to me, and tendrils of clematis growing up the doorframe brushed my shoulder. Dimly I heard the sound of horseshoes up the road. My mind was playing tricks; my ears thought they caught the sound of a song, insidious, near at hand, but there was no one there. Now the low sloping doorstep was before me. I lifted my foot and set it down on something that slithered like jelly and caused me to grasp for the doorframe to maintain my balance. I looked down, and a wave of nausea swept me. I jerked my foot away.

Directly behind me the horse had stopped, and a familiar voice said, "Is something wrong?" I could only shake my head, for my throat was thick and I could not seem to open my tight-shut eyes. Then arms went around me, pulled me bodily off the step, and Jeremy

Bushel said matter-of-factly, "It's all right now. You're in the street. No, don't look. Take a deep breath slowly."

"What *is* it?"

"A skinned cat," he responded grimly. "Charming souvenir to find on one's way home from church. Have you had much of this sort of thing?"

"What thing?"

"Good-neighbor gifts of welcome. That's the intent of that little offering, you realize. You have come to a very pleasant village, Miss Jardine."

"Pleasant or no, I intend to stay," I muttered through gritted teeth.

He laughed without mockery. "I thought it would take more than a petty horror to drive you off. All the same, it's not nice. Had you not better go inside and sit down?" Involuntarily I shuddered, and he chuckled. "Yes, the corpus delicti. Don't worry, I'll take care of that. You have a brand new shovel, I recall. No, I'll find it. Will you be all right here while I'm gone?"

I nodded, not turning round, and I heard him lift the latch and cross the hall to the rear yard. I hugged myself tightly, staring off at the deserted street. Across the quiet water, lamplight showed faintly in cottage windows. So peaceful, so serene a scene. Yet someone in the village hated us this much. That, at least, was certain. This was more than an attempt to break in to search for treasure, it was personal. And whatever the source of that dark power that had possessed me on the hillside, the hands that had placed this grisly message here were human.

Jeremy Bushel came back and bore off the dreadful thing. I was grateful that the light was dim, for despite my cowardly resolve, I was unable to keep my eyes away. They followed, with a kind of sick fascination, as he carried the object into the woods and came back to say he had decently interred it. "Deep enough so none of the village dogs will bring it back to haunt you. We've enough tales already of cadavers that won't stay buried. Steady there! I didn't mean to scare you."

He steered me peremptorily to a chair in Kersey's Room. "Is Georgina still here?" He seized the bell on the mantel and rang it firmly.

"Hush! My sister . . . I don't want Nell to know!"

"About the cat? You're right, of course. I'll raise the girl." He strode out, and a moment later I heard his voice in the kitchen issuing commands. "Tea for your mistress immediately, and some substantial food. And you are not to alarm Miss Nell, you understand?" An incoherent murmur from Georgina followed. ". . . saw fit to revive one of the more revolting practices. . . Not clever, not clever at all, and what's more, dangerous . . . Don't try to tell me that, Gina. I know quite well . . ." The voices fell again.

Presently he returned, built up the fire, and sat down before me to rub my hands. "Georgina will be along soon. She's slow, as you must have noticed, but I've roused her." He looked at me critically. "Have you any brandy? You could use some."

"No!" I forced my voice to its normal level. "You said village customs, cadavers that won't stay buried . . ."

"I talk too much," he responded grimly. "I was trying to lift your spirits with a spot of humor, and made poor choice of subject. The forest is full of legends from the bad old days, corpses that won't lie still and mutilated animals left round as warnings. One hears them talked about as though it happened yesterday, instead of at least two centuries ago. Some of the quarry boys, when they've had too much cider, think it's great fun to make old incidents come back to life."

Georgina came in with a laden tray and a sly, defensive manner. "Miss Nell's napping. I took her up tea afore when you was so long gone."

"That will do, Georgina." My self-appointed guest took the tray from her firmly. "I will look after Miss Jardine. It's time you were leaving, is it not? You have errands on the way."

He spoke almost as if he were the master here, and I was suddenly too tired to protest. Georgina made me a grudging curtsey and withdrew, her eyes flickering from one to the other of us as she did so.

Mr. Bushel latched the door behind her. "No use putting temptation in the way of the weak," he observed. "May I pour your tea? Have some bread and cheese. This double Gloucester's very good."

His manner had changed again; it was as though he were exerting himself to be an entertaining guest. He clearly intended to make himself at home, and I was quixotically glad to have him there. It was not pleasant to think of moving about the house alone tonight.

I tried to draw him out, and I succeeded in learning exactly nothing about him. I learned rather more of local lore. He was full of stories of fortunetelling and unsuccessful poaching expeditions and love potions that went hilariously awry.

"Are you from this country, then, that you know so much about it?"

"I spent time here as a boy. Have some more tea."

"Near here? I wondered what brought you to this out-of-the way corner of the world."

"I went to school nearby."

"Oxford?"

"Oxford is not far away, that's true. You must visit there one day. It has excellent library facilities, if it is true you are planning to do scholarly research."

How had that rumor gotten round so soon? Before I could probe further he rose, as though taking leave from a party to which he'd been invited. "I must go. My employees are excellent fellows, but I make a point of always inspecting my property thoroughly before retiring. I advise you to do the same, and lock up behind me."

I would indeed. Welcome as his companionship had been, there were a few things that had not escaped my notice. He had parried my probes with a skill that bespoke much practice; no one is that clever unless he has much to hide. He denied country living, yet he had handled the cat with a country-man's lack of squeamishness. He had been talking to Georgina in the kitchen with a kind of intimacy, an implied reference to shared knowledge. He knew his way around my house and grounds remarkably well.

He tried to rent it for more than it was worth—and only took Tarr Farm when he discovered he could see Wychwood from it with a telescope. Charles Roach's words came back to confront me with a reality that I could not ignore.

An unwelcome thought followed me as I made my solitary round of doors and windows and went up to bed. Jeremy Bushel had been wanting for some time to get inside of Wychwood. How convenient that he happened to be passing by just as I made that disgusting discovery at the door. What better way to get across my threshold, to carry our relationship in one stroke from armed truce to an easy camaraderie?

Things could not have fallen out better for him if he had planned it.

7

Rossford-under-Wychwood
August-September, 1863

THE next day my panic shrank to manageable proportions. I dealt with Georgina crisply, impressing upon her that Nell, for whom she was developing a genuine fondness, was not to be alarmed by frightening tales.

I did not intend to dwell on my strange experiences, but nonetheless, and with full command of logic, I did three things. I began a journal, setting down all the events since our arrival here, differentiating carefully between fact and feeling. A journal always helped me clarify my thoughts, and if the warnings, as Jeremy Bushel called them, should be repeated, a written record might enable me to discern a pattern.

On Monday morning I went to the forge and had Black Aaron Smith come that very day to put strong bolts on all our doors. And much as I disliked being around Rafe Smith,

I watched very carefully as his father and he installed them. They were very clever bolts, which could be thrown only from within, with no keys for easy duplication. I was considerably easier in my mind after this was done.

The third thing was I did *not* go back to the graveyard on the hill to find out if my experience would repeat.

August ended in that mixture of grey and gold which was characteristic of the Cotswolds, and which I already deeply loved. Philip appeared in the garden almost daily, bringing bits of entertaining and malicious gossip. He was giving Nell an interest in life, and for that I would be forever grateful. Beneath his patronizing cynicism I could sense a hunger for affection—especially from Lady Margaret, who gave him, I gathered, great love but small approval. I could always tell when he had had a confrontation with her, for he came to us at all hours, then, in strange, wild moods. One afternoon he flung back the lid of our untuned piano, threw himself into fierce passionate chords, and played without ceasing until long past twilight. I don't think he even knew that we were in the room. He left without a word when once he'd stopped, and Nell was very silent all that evening, with an odd, exalted tenderness in her face.

Early in September came two days of lashing rain, and soon after that I embarked upon my new vocation. I must confess that I was nervous about teaching Amy; it is one thing to be a scholar and quite another to communicate learning and the love of it to others. I prepared carefully, drawing on memories of my own education. English history, of course, and literature—Shakespeare, Milton, the good grey poets. Had Amy been introduced to philosophy, to Latin, or to Greek? I queried Nell on her own studies at the Bedliston School, but she said only, "Propriety and deportment, that's all they really cared about," and it was clear that being reminded of those days troubled her.

I was continuing my systematic exploration of Lady Kersey's books for treasure clues, and I came one day upon a small volume by one Juan Luys Vives. *De Institutione foemina christianae . . . The Education of a Christian Woman.* In my mind's eye the linenfold paneling faded and I was back in the cool high-ceilinged room near Charleston's harbor. I could remember my stepfather's words so well. "Vives dedicated it to Catherine of Aragon, who led the circle of court women trained in the New Learning. Catherine brought him to England to tutor Mary Tudor and the other young girls of the court—among them, ironically, Katherine Parr, who would become Henry VIII's last queen. And Katherine, in time, passed on Vives' training to her stepdaughter Elizabeth. They were a new breed of women, witty and warm and wise, steeped in the New Learning of the Renaissance."

The New Learning—"the humanities" it was called, for it taught that only through education could man rise above the beasts to become humane. Precise research, investigation and experiment, intellectual excitement untrammeled by superstition. First the tools for acquiring knowledge—languages ancient and modern, logic and rhetoric, even music and mathematics for what they could teach of ordered form. Then the critical study of the great philosophers, historians and religious teachers. Learning as a state of inspiration and delight, the lessons illustrated with dramatic stories, delicious horror, biting satires all drawn from history, philosophy or the Bible—it was the way I had myself been trained. Those early gracious and brilliant women had first made me realize I could be more in life than a social butterfly. Now that I was here on their own heath, surely it was the way I ought to teach.

On the morning Amy first was delivered to me in her pony cart, Nell was in a state of nervous expectation, and I no less. But if we were jittery, it was as nothing compared to Amy Ross. Her face was yellow-pale, her eyes enormous, and she reminded me of nothing so much as a kicked dog. All my efforts to draw her out were to no avail; she was obedient, terrified, and silent. I soon realized that the Socratic method is not as easy as great teachers make it sound, that it is impossible to have intellectual discussion with one unwilling. My queries on philosophy elicited a whispered "No, ma'am," and my attempt at dramatically recounting the creation of the world according to Greek myth brought no response at all.

The day being warm, I suggested we withdraw to the walled garden for a botany lesson, hoping the informal atmosphere would ease Amy's tension. Even there, she was stiff, her eyes darting nervously about.

Thinking I'd arouse some spark of interest,

I even told Amy about my recent research into medicines made from herbs, and Nell launched into the tales she'd been reading of herb magic. "With a garden like this nearby, one could do all sorts of things . . . be quite an ordinary person on the outside and, inside, another one entirely, have mysterious powers. It would be quite secret, so long as no one told."

For a moment I saw fleetingly in Amy's face a resemblance to her brother. But it quickly died. By the time she was called for at one, I was exhausted. I did not realize how draining the morning had also been for Nell, until I found her shrunk into herself.

"Darling, what is it? Are you in pain?"

"Just tired. It's going to rain, I think."

Nell avoided my eyes and she held herself stiffly, as though her back was bad. By midafternoon, when rain did begin, she was crying with misery. I rubbed Nell's limbs with the herbal bath I'd made and dosed her with camomile tea, which was reputed soothing. When at last she napped, I went out in the wet garden to cut monkshood and mugwort for further distillation. This consumed the balance of the afternoon, and just as I was finishing, Laura called, bringing Jeremy Bushel with her.

"Georgina told my Rosie that Nell was poorly, so I've brought some chicken soup and that cake she liked. How is she, dear?"

"How very kind. You oughtn't to have gone to all this trouble. You have enough to do preparing dinner for your father."

"Nonsense, I was glad to," Laura responded. "Father's dining out tonight, anyway."

Naturally, after that, I asked them to remain. Mr. Bushel moved around the rooms after the manner of an old and casual friend, which I found most disconcerting. Laura's eyes went from one to the other of us with an odd expression. I had not told her of the time Mr. Bushel had rescued me; I could not bring myself to speak of it.

He inquired after the welfare of the white chickens which Charles Roach duly had installed.

"They're flourishing. The cockerels strut like kings round the back courtyard. When they carry on two-part harmony at dawn with the ones at Quinn Cottage, I feel quite the settled householder." I smiled at Laura, but she did not respond.

I gave them a humorous account of my first

attempt at teaching, and Jeremy—I could not help thinking of him that way—again exerted himself to be entertaining. Laura's earlier somberness, if it had been that, disappeared, and we had a really pleasant dinner. We were just finishing her excellent cake when an appalling racket broke out in the yard.

"Georgina!" I shouted.

"She won't come. Her mother's made her mortally afraid." Laura hurried to the kitchen as I peered out the window into black and wetness. "Where's a lantern? Hold it in the doorway, girl, so we can see."

Georgina, her back plastered firmly against the inglenook, shook her head. "It be banshees. The Old Ones send they. Bad fortune anyone try to live here, my mam say. It be cursed by Copper Maid." Her face was skeletal in the flickering light.

"Nonsense," Laura snapped sharply. "It's only ferrets in the henhouse, likely. Or else rats."

I ran to the hallway and threw open the back door, and a gust of dampness struck me. Light flickered behind me: Jeremy, a lantern in his hand. He plunged past me into blackness, but was soon back. "There's no one in the yard."

He said *no one*, not *nothing*.

"There couldn't be." I was beating my hands together as though they were very cold. "The door in the wall is strongly barred."

"Walls are made to be climbed," Jeremy said impatiently.

Then we heard it, all of us, the sound I shall remember till my dying day. The cry—I do not exaggerate—of a soul in torment.

"What is it? Dear God, what is it?" Laura swung round, her face blanched in terror.

From upstairs came Nell's voice, in panic, and at the same moment a sharp thud, as of a stake being driven into something hard.

"The front door." Jeremy dove for it. Laura and I were close on his heels, so we both saw it when he did, on the instant. Laura made a choking sound and swerved away. Automatically my arms went round her, so it was over her bent head that I gazed at the thing pinned by a knife to my paneled door.

Someone had gotten into our back yard. Someone had taken one of my beautiful cockerels, cut its throat, and impaled it like a white stain against the dark oiled wood. The feathers fluttered slightly in the night air, and blood dripped like spilled wine onto the old stone floor. It hung there like a limp puppet, and the barred knife took on, crazily, the look of a distorted cross. I could not pull my eyes away.

"*Camilla*!" Nell cried frantically.

Laura straightened. "I'll go to her. No fear, I won't alarm her." She ran up the staircase and I heard her voice calling cheerily, "It's all right, my love."

Jeremy and I stared at one another. Wet wind eddied the bloody feathers, the lamp swung, and shadows danced like witches. With a muffled oath, Jeremy jerked the knife free and flung it to the floor. As the feathered thing fell, he kicked it out, leaving a streak of blood upon the stones. He slammed the door and threw the bolt, and iron dully rang upon iron.

I started to laugh. "It's no use doing that, is it? No use at all. You said so, and Georgina—"

He grabbed me by the shoulders and shook me hard. "Stop that! Where's that cool superior logic you're so proud of? Georgina's haunts have nothing to do with this. Or with that cat, before."

"You're hurting me!"

He dropped his hands, and we stood gazing at each other. I was breathing hard.

"Don't let emotion cloud the issue. Set your brain on this as you would a problem of scholarship, and you'll see. These episodes aren't manifestations of the Old Ones. They're not even authentic, though you're meant to think they are."

But *something* was, something dredged up from that waking nightmare on the plantation by the sound of the dying cock . . . I said slowly, "It is frightening, because it's meant to be."

Jeremy nodded. "If you don't object—no, whether you do or not—I am going to engage in some investigation. The mind that dreamed these things up is not nice. Not nice at all."

We went into Kersey's Room, and there was no sound but the crackling of the flames. Laura came downstairs and lit the lamps, and I felt Wychwood House close like a shell of security around me. False security—the facile penetration of the henyard told me that.

"Georgina's making Nell hot milk. I told her she can stay with us tonight, so she need not walk home," Laura said.

"She can stay here."

"She won't." Laura hesitated. "You must know that the villagers were very superstitious about this house. It stood empty so long, and there are those three centuries of legends about the Copper Maid. Quite stupid, of course, but all the same . . . If Georgina did not need work so badly, she'd not have come here, and she'd never spend the night."

"There's more than that involved." I was thinking hard, as though struggling up from sleep. "Superstition's no reason for what happened here tonight. This is personal, it's directed against us. Someone doesn't want us here."

"Well," Laura said lightly, "in a closed-off village, there's bound to be some prejudice. You're a foreigner, you're not part of the family."

"*Is* there a family? A relative of Lady Kersey's who would want me gone?"

"Only distant relations, according to village rumour, and not well thought of." Jeremy laughed. "Can you imagine a relative of the legendary Lady Kersey having recourse to anything this crude?"

"What I cannot imagine," I said slowly, "is why this happened *now*. Why tonight, after a lapse of these past few weeks? Oh, I've felt antagonism, but it was . . . passive, not overt. Now, suddenly, these things, though nothing's changed—" I intercepted a glance between Jeremy and Laura. "What is it? *Tell* me."

"Something did change," Laura said hesitantly, and Jeremy added, "Use your deductive powers, Miss Jardine. The cat, skinned, like a legendary shepherd who once reported on poachers in the forest, was deposited on your doorstep on a Sunday. What business did you transact a day or so before?"

I fetched my journal. "Nothing. Except—Yes, I told Charles Roach to wall the fields and post a prohibition against poaching."

"On a Friday," Jeremy said. "On Saturday the work begins, on Sunday morning the news spreads round at church, and that evening the warning comes."

"But that's absurd! I don't approve of hunters killing animals and I've a right to keep them out. And the fields have to be enclosed if they're to be rented in the spring."

"So you have heard about enclosing," Jeremy said quietly.

"It was Mr. Roach's word."

"It's more than a word." Laura looked at Jeremy, then back at me. "It's different in America. Here, for centuries, the heaths and fields and forests have been common land. The people could raise crops and graze sheep even if not wealthy enough to own property. All that's changing now, the day of the large landowner's come, and this year even Wychwood Forest is being cleared."

"Of course," Jeremy added ironically, "the poor sots could be sensible and turn their lives over to Lady Bountiful at the Manor House, work at what she decides and live with hygienic regulation as she decrees. But they're quixotic enough to prefer old ways and independence, hire themselves out by the job and feel they're their own men, and subsist on hunting and squatters' crops and gleaning. Have you driven by your fine fields lately, Miss Jardine? Did you notice how empty they are compared to others? And did you notice yours are the only ones to have single stalks still standing? The rest of us landholders took our 'scarecrows' down yesterday. That's what they're called, 'scarecrows.' They're a warning no one's to glean for his own use among the leavings.

And the poor fools respect it. They leave your fields alone as you've decreed, and they go hungry, because for years that's been their only source of grain."

"But that's monstrous!"

He went on as though I had not spoken. "And hunting. I'm sorry if it offends your delicate sensibilities, but the only meat they ever see upon their tables is rabbit now and then. Of course it's poaching, and illegal, but it's such a necessity that when Gypsy Aaron started trespassing on someone else's poaching territory two years ago, he wound up hanging from that yew tree in the gypsy cemetery up on the hill. The authorities called it suicide, but his wife knew better."

I put my coffee cup down so hard that the black liquid slopped into the saucer. "The gypsy cemetery? Is that the circle of strange stones behind the church?"

"It has nothing to do with you," Laura said quickly.

"Except that every time the moon is full, Widow Lee fills herself with gin and wanders in the forest calling on the Old Ones for revenge. And this house stands, of course, on the Old Ones' meeting place," Jeremy glanced toward the door. It strikes me that someone's been aggravated by your No Trespassing notices to give the Old Ones an assist."

I drew a deep breath. "The notices will come down tomorrow. The scarecrows too. I'll drive out myself and do it."

Laura's face softened. "I am glad. I am sure, after that, the troubles will stop."

But not the antagonism, I thought. Not the suspicion. Yes—and hatred. That had come before the notices, before the scarecrows. It had been lying here in wait.

Hold on to my cool logic, Jeremy said. It was deserting me. After the others left I tested all the doors and windows, and the portrait's painted eyes watched me inscrutably. My mind told me that with the bolts shut I was in no danger, but all the while that insidious memory from my childhood told me that I was locking out some nameless evil, and that it was only waiting, not gone.

I went upstairs, and the flickering lamp illumined the red curtains and the old brocades that covered the carved beds. Nell held out her arms. "I know, Georgina told me. Camilla, are you all right?"

"She ought not have—"

"I made her. I'm not frightened, only so

very angry. I won't have you scared like that!" Nell pulled me down beside her, and her eyes were grave. "Your hands are just like ice and you're shivering."

"No, I'm not." Then I couldn't hold it back any more. My head was down on her breast and her arms went round me.

"It's all right. I promise you, Camilla, it will be all right. Nothing will hurt you." Nell held me tight, rocking me like a child, and I don't know when it was that I finally got to sleep.

All the next morning as I listened to Nell and Amy read aloud, directed them in writing, my mind was racing. At least now I had a reason for our persecution; this was logical, it could be grasped. It was not as fearsome as a mindless madness. But who? Why was the villagers' hatred directed toward me, personally, even before my enclosure of the fields? What had caused that overpowering sense of evil which I had experienced in the gypsy cemetery? Did memory of past violence linger in the atmosphere so that what I had felt was the continuing emanation of Georgina's father's murder? If so, if there *were* some scientific basis for such superstition, why did I have this persistent irrational conviction that the evil was not past but present?

I set the girls to reading *A Midsummer's Night's Dream*. In Shakespeare's comedy, at least, the air was delicate, all in fun. I stepped inside, after a time, to bid Georgina fetch some milk and cookies, and when I went back I heard Nell saying intensely, "I will not have my sister hurt. She's been hurt enough," and I saw Philip there.

Philip was there, and Nell had been telling them about last night. It showed upon their faces. I turned to Nell in dismay, but Philip said immediately, "Please don't scold. It's fearfully exciting. Now we can help you solve the mystery, can't we, Amy?"

Amy nodded. "Philip's right," she said breathlessly. "People hadn't ought to do things like that. It ought not to be allowed." What a quaint choice of words, I thought, for one so young.

"Then you don't think it's the Old Ones' doing?" Nell asked, with a wicked glance at Philip.

Philip looked superior. "Certainly not. It's a corruption of their ritual, actually. You can ask Mr. Bushel if you don't believe me."

Nell's eyes were far away. "This is an

offense against the Old Ones, isn't it? One that might provoke revenge?"

"Enough of that," I said briskly.

But Nell shook her head. "I want to ask Philip about the cat. Georgina says that means the Wychwood ghosts are stirring. What does she mean?"

And just how had Georgina known of that, I wondered.

"Gina's talking about the flayed shepherd," Philip said. "And that had nothing to do with the Old Ones at all."

"But was somebody really skinned alive?" Nell demanded. Her face was pale.

Before I could stop him, Philip nodded, his eyes gleaming. "There are two known cases, actually. In both stories they saw sheep-stealers working in the forest, and were killed in retaliation. Sheep-stealing was a hanging error in the old days. But I shouldn't worry. You have no sheep and you're not likely to have thieves. Or is there anything at Wychwood House worth stealing?"

Nell's eyes met mine, and quickly dropped.

Philip looked from one to the other of us and then rose. "I promised Maman I'd see Amy home, and we'd best be going."

Amy rose dutifully, but she looked ill and

Nell's hand reached out for hers. "It will be all right," she said gently. "We'll make it all right. We won't let harm come here any more."

Amy flashed a grateful half-smile and slipped out, but I detained Philip privately by the door. "You ought to have more sense than speak of those subjects before the girls. I won't have you alarming Nell."

"But she was not alarmed," Philip said. "You were, perhaps. You pounce like a cat whenever I speak about the Old Ones. Why is that, I wonder? Because you're so sure the Old Ones don't exist? Or because you're afraid they do? There really *were* Old Ones, you know. The people who were here before the Saxons, even before the Celts. Some say the race died out, or intermarried and was swallowed up."

"Where did you pick up this potpourri of information?"

"Mr. Bushel. He has some splendid stories. He knows how the pagan customs lived on disguised as Christian rites, and can recognize traces of the Old Religion that still are carried on."

"But do you mean anyone does"—I could not bring myself to say the word "witchcraft"—"practice the old ways?"

Philip gave me an opaque glance. "Have you never hung mistletoe? Or a Christmas wreath? Or not lit three candles from the same match? All carry-overs from the Old Religion. You've been up to the stone circle, haven't you? Then you must have felt it there. The power."

"There are perfectly logical explanations for it."

"Of course there are. But they only explain, they don't deny. Everyone who goes up there has felt it. Except my mother. She gives off so much force herself, I suppose she cancels the other out. Maman, of course, thinks it unwholesome nonsense and she's all for having the vicar preach fire and brimstone. But the vicar's a smart old bird, he manages not to tamper with the unchangeable."

He saw my expression, and his laugh was like a breath of air. "We English live in such an old country that we're more comfortable about such things. My ancestors dyed themselves blue with woad and went to Rome to negotiate with Caesar, so why should it trouble me if somebody experiments with things that my multi-great-grandpa did as a matter of course?"

The next morning I borrowed a mount from Laura and rode out, myself, to Wychwood's fields. I uprooted from each plot its scarecrow stalk; I pulled up and flung aside the signs prohibiting all trespassing. Sentiment would dictate an immediate softening, a showing of gratitude and respect from the villagers thereafter, but in truth I noticed no such thing.

A visit from Mr. Roach soon followed. "I regret, I exceedingly regret, having to report the liberties which have been taken. Were you not a newcomer and a woman, no one would have dared. I will have the damages repaired at once, and the offenders found and prosecuted. This is, of course, what comes of allowing the lower orders to presume upon unwarranted privilege. If that exasperating woman had protected the property properly long ago, this would never have occurred."

"You need not trouble yourself, Mr. Roach. I myself removed the scarecrows and the signs."

He stared at me. "You!"

"I assure you I am quite capable."

"That is not the point," Mr. Roach looked quite bewildered. "I explained to you the desirability of enclosure and rental, and you agreed."

"You did not explain the effect such action would have upon the village's economy. I am, I believe, the largest landholder here except the Manor, which already is enclosed. Were I to follow suit, the villagers' sources of food would be drastically reduced. It's not as if they were taking anything I had need of. To fence the land, just to keep it fallow, to keep them out—why, it's immoral! Even our slaves at home live better than these people! Georgina tells me—"

"Georgina!" Charles Roach snorted. "My dear young woman, pray do not indulge in sentimental notions of philanthropy. If these persons are in need, it is through their own laziness and stupidity. There is quite decent employment available for them at the Manor."

I'm not sure whether it was his avuncular attitude toward me or his callous dismissal of the villagers' need which pushed me into thoroughly reprehensible response. I drew myself up as coldly as any legendary queen. "The fencing is to stop, the notices are not to go back up. I believe that you are obliged to carry out my wishes during the year that I am living here."

His face darkened, and his manner was extremely frosty as he took his leave. Indeed, he was hard put to retain his courtesy—and I, as well. I shut the door upon him and discovered that I had a raging headache.

Behind me in Kersey's Room, Nell's voice said, "Why, Camilla! I did not know that you could be so ruthless!"

"Nor I. It must have been my headache speaking."

"Poor Camilla. You've been working too hard. Lessons with Amy and me all morning, and straining your eyes over the Latin in these old books." Nell pulled me down on the bench before the hearth. "Mr. Roach was very angry, wasn't he?" Nell was regarding me with a grave expression. "Will that make more trouble, do you think? He could have been right. Why should you turn round and give to the villagers after how they've tried to frighten us away?"

"I'm afraid Mr. Roach's anger is his problem. As for the rest—all that should change now. It's because they feared what our coming meant that those things happened."

"But it hasn't changed, has it?" Nell said soberly. "They still want us gone. They think you're only giving them what's theirs by right. Georgina says—"

"I am tired," I exclaimed waspishly, "of hearing what Georgina says! She talks far too much." I caught myself and turned to Nell with compunction. "I'm sorry. This has really bothered you, hasn't it? I ought not to have let you hear."

"It's not that." When she spoke again her face was grave, as though she were puzzling something out. "If something's wrong—if you see something bad happening, someone being hurt—you have an obligation, don't you, to set things right? To protect the . . . the victim, to stop the badness, however much it costs? Even if it hurts yourself? You can't just close your eyes?"

"Of course not. That's why I had to take down those No Trespassing signs, regardless of whether Mr. Roach approves."

"I see." Nell shut her eyes. "I'm tired," she said abruptly. I put a shawl over her and left her to her nap, and returned to my perusal of old volumes.

Each afternoon after Amy had departed, I embarked on a systematic examination of the books upon our shelves. I was determined to sort out all data relating to Wychwood House, its supposed treasure and its hold, if I could call it that, upon the village. It was apparent that Lady Kersey's tastes ran into seemingly very disparate areas. There were many books about the Tudors, a constant temptation to me to abandon myself to the joy of the sixteenth-century world. There were works of Shakespeare and his contemporaries, especially the poets. There was a quite complete collection of myths from all different cultures. Garden books; stillroom books, some handwritten and quite rare; *materia medica*. Books of English legends, such as I had dreamed over as a child. Geographies and travel books about the English country. All were fascinating, but they seemed collected without rhyme or reason by a magpie mind.

It was early in October, on a rainy afternoon when my arms ached from emptying high shelves and I longed for callers to interrupt my labors, that I made my first really promising discovery. Having no library steps, I was perched precariously on a three-legged stool, making determined stabs with a yardstick at the upper books. I sought to be careful, dislodging volumes one at a time and catching them as they toppled, but I must have prodded with too much force. A half-dozen books came tumbling, and I with them.

"Camilla! Are you all right?" Nell cried out, and Georgina, coming in with the tea tray, set it down hastily to assist me.

"Nothing's bruised but my dignity . . . and my elbow." I rubbed it ruefully. "I hope the books aren't hurt."

Georgina knelt to gather them, and it was then I saw it, a thin notebook that had fallen face-open with its cover bent. I picked it up to flatten the cracked cardboard, and my eyes fell on the frontispiece, where the ink of the Spencerian script had turned brown with age.

A Historie of the Lawson Family, Resident of Suffolk. For an instant a long-vanished memory was rekindled. I was a tiny child in that dreary furnished flat in Oxford, I could smell again the cheap varnish of the wood-work and could hear my mother's voice, a proud affirmation against the alarming tears that filled her eyes. "*We will be all right. We can never be beaten down. Your father was a Lawson of Suffolk, child, and one of your ancestors was of royal blood.*"

"What is it, 'Milla?" Nell demanded eagerly.

That beneficient spirit which seemed to watch over me at times made me say carelessly, "Just a notebook. I will show you later." Made me say calmly, "Georgina, put these other books on the table, please. And bring me the book on the history of Suffolk from the desk. Then you may leave."

Georgina had showed signs of wanting to linger, but her manner rather than being reluctant was defensive. "Which one's that, miss? They'm a-plenty."

"The title's on the spine, quite clear." Something in her tone made me look at her in surprise. "You do read, Georgina?"

"That's for gentry," Georgina said. Her head was up, and the pride in her eyes was a bright banner that defied attack.

There was a knock at the door. "I'll see to that, miss." Georgina slid out as though glad to do so, and returned in a minute to usher in Laura and her father. I thrust the notebook into a drawer and rose to greet them gladly.

"We're on our way home from a confinement case, and I thought I'd check how this young lady was faring in our wet weather."

Dr. Quinn smiled at Nell, who smiled back at him from her nest of shawls.

I sent Georgina for more teacups, for both Laura and the doctor looked chilled and tired. "How is the baby?" I asked, busying myself with the spirit lamp.

Laura shook her head and moved closer to the fire. "Not good. A difficult delivery, and it was born with a withered arm, bad misfortune in a farm-labor family."

Dr. Quinn snorted. "Malnutrition and pack-horse labor for the mother aforehand, and no medical care. What can they expect? Can't convince these people a doctor's advice is needed in anything as natural as baby-carrying, though they'd call me for an ailing animal soon enough. But they'd rather blame this young one's arm on a witch mark than on anything so rational."

Nell's eyes were large, and Laura shot her father a look I did not understand. "Have some tea and honey," I said quickly, handing round cups. The rain was beating down hard now, and I drew the curtains. Their red damask gave back an answering glow to the ruby lamp, and I gazed round the inviting room with a wave of pleasure. The silver and gold threads in Lady Kersey's portrait gleamed in the dancing light.

The sound of rain pouring off our steep-pitched roof increased and the rattle of wheels in the road was magnified. There was more rapid knocking, and Philip was standing in the hall doorway, Jeremy behind him. Both looked soaked to the skin. Philip had a muffler wrapped round his neck and huddled oddly against his shirtfront. He did not cross the threshold, but stood there, curiously defensive, and looked at me. "May Nell have this? Maman was going to have it drowned because its back is crooked, so I took it out to Tarr Farm, and Mr. Bushel said we should bring it here." He moved the muffler, and a tiny head poked out.

Nell's arms reached out at once. "A kitten! Just the kind I wanted, coal-black with emerald eyes."

"Her eyes go gold at night, just as yours do." The strain left Philip's face. He set the kitten down and it scampered in a crabwise fashion toward Nell's feet, to her great delight. "She got stepped on, that's why she's bent, but it's healed now and she's perfectly healthy. You will keep her, won't you?"

"Of course we will."

Georgina gave me her sideways look. "It be bad luck, bring a black cat into house. Be devil cat."

"Don't talk nonsense, and go heat the little thing some milk," Laura said crisply. When Georgina was gone, she looked at me and shrugged. "I am sorry. Perhaps the girl never will learn a proper servant's manner. Don't worry, Nell, she'd be just as superstitious about a white cat, too."

Jeremy grinned. "A witch cat for a witch house. I thought it would be an appropriate gesture."

Our guests did not depart until the rainstorm had diminished, and by then it was time for dinner, so it was not until evening, after Nell had been tucked in bed, that I remembered the note-book I had thrust away. Georgina was gone now and the house was chill, so I carried the little volume with me to my room. There, with curtains drawn and a fire cheerily blazing, I snuggled down beneath the featherbed and opened the bent cover with an eager heart.

A Historie of the Lawson Family, Resident of Suffolk. My hand shook slightly, as though I were opening a Pandora's box. Had this come here by chance, or had Lady Kersey placed it deliberately, a gift for me to find? Was it, indeed, my father's family, or had I leaped to unscholarly conclusion? On impulse I turned, not to the opening pages but to the end, and there, one of the last entries, I found my father's name. *Edward Lawson, b. Lavenham, Suffolk, 1783.* Page by page I followed the line back, through deaths, births, marrying, intermarrying, through varying branches that had been on different sides in the Bloodless Rebellion, in the Civil War terror of the 1630's. A Puritan killed by the King's men, a Royalist hanged by Cromwell; homely marginal notations of family happenings that brought a smile or tugged my heart. They leaped to life from the pages, these dusty ancestors, and I thought, "Well, yes, this is why I am at home here in this old house which frightens others off. I am an Englishwoman, and my roots go deep, and with these hundreds of years of history of calamity and joy, why should superstition be a threat to me?"

I came at last to a page toward the front part of the book where the writing blurred as though it had been much handled. And there I found it, sandwiched in among the other births and marriages of sixteenth-century

Lawsons, a footnote by the compiler about a Lawson's bride: "This lady was the granddaughter of Sir Edward ——" —the surname was unreadably blurred by water stain—"and his wife, Mary, who was daughter to the traitor Thomas and the royal lady of Sudeley."

What royal lady? And what traitor Thomas? My mind roamed back over English history's scandalous tales of infants born on the wrong side of the sheets, but I could come up with no rumors that would fit. I riffled through the remaining pages with some urgency, but though the volume traced the Lawson pedigree back to Plantagenet times, there were no further clues. I closed the little book with an acute frustration.

I remembered, then, my earlier thought to seek out Lawsons in the history of Suffolk. Georgina's fetching the desired volume had been interrupted by our unexpected guests. I wanted that book now, though it was past midnight and downstairs was cold and lonely.

I slid out of bed, thrusting my feet gratefully into my slippers, and pulled on my cashmere wrapper. Picking up the bedside lamp and holding it before me like a beacon, I opened my bedroom door. A rush of chill air met me in the corridor; this old house was full of drafts. Moving within that reassuring circle of light, I picked my way carefully down the uneven, creaking stairs and stepped into Kersey's Room. I went with confidence to the desk and reached for the remembered volume. And stopped and frowned, and reached again, moving with more urgency now as I sorted through the book pile again and yet again. Then, with accelerating speed, to the bookshelves, holding the old lamp high, my eyes like the beam of light sweeping along the rows. At last, stalemated, I lowered the lamp with a baffled uneasiness.

Search as I would, it was no use. The red-covered volume on the history of Suffolk was gone.

8

Rossford-under-Wychwood—Sudeley Castle
October, 1863

THE book on Suffolk, never reappeared. When I questioned Georgina about it, she repeated that she did not know the book and had no use for it, since she could not read.

"Georgina, if you would like, we can take an hour in the afternoons and I shall teach you how to read and write."

Georgina mumbled that I should suit myself, but I could discern that she was pleased. Her appearance was more personable, too, since I had taken her in hand; her hair was now combed properly into a bun, and she was clean and relatively neat, though she adhered to the custom of kilting her skirts up above her ankles when she worked.

Georgina's own explanation for the missing book came to me by way of Nell: everyone knew this was an ill-luck house, and the coming of the black kitten reinforced it.

"Georgina says she'll never touch it, no use asking her." Nell cuddled the kitten against her face. "The silly thing thinks we ought to put a curse on you and cast you out, but you're not going anywhere, are you, my darling Hecate?"

"What are you calling her?"

"Hecate. Goddess of the dark of the moon. Goddess of the crossroads." Nell's eyes were dreamy. "We are on a crossroads and this house is a sanctuary, isn't it, Camilla? Let's make it so, and draw into our circle all the waifs and strays."

I shared my discovery about our royal ancestor with Nell, and as soon as lessons were over and Amy gone, I locked the doors so Georgina could not enter, and we pored eagerly over Lady Kersey's letter.

" 'By now you will have . . . set your feet into the paths the great ones and the old ones trod before'—that must mean royalty. There is no greater rank."

"And the Old Ones. The paths of the Old Ones, Camilla!" Nell's eyes were like dark pools.

"I scarcely think Kersey was one to be addled by superstitions." My eyes ran on down the page, but I could detect no further reference to anything I did not already know. *Wychwood . . . a house of secrets . . . has amused me no little to add unto that legend.* Kersey, I thought, in your little corner of heaven or hell, you're not only watching me, you're laughing. You knew what would happen when I came here, didn't you? And deliberately let me walk into it blind? Was that why she had put in that cryptic hint that I must learn that blind following of instincts is not always wise?

I read the letter through again aloud, in the hope that could make the meaning come more clear. But when I came to the *Blessed be, my dear*, I still had discovered nothing.

I heard Nell catch her breath, and turned to her quickly. "Did you think of something?"

"No, I just moved too quickly." Nell's face was very pale and her breathing had become erratic. "I'm very tired. If I could go upstairs . . ."

She was still suffering from yesterday's rainstorm, I remembered with compunction, ringing for Georgina to carry her to her room. Though she was now much more mobile in her invalid-chair, chill or dampness affected Nell severely.

I tucked her in and offered to read to her,

but Nell shook her head. "I have books all round here I can read myself. Camilla, if Philip should come by later, may he come up? Just by himself? He always makes me laugh."

Nell was becoming very attached to Philip, and he seemed to enjoy being a surrogate big brother. So when he did appear later, I allowed him to go up, and they were closeted together for some time.

I spent my own afternoon ransacking the shelves for references to the Lawson family or Sudeley, but to no avail.

Philip, coming downstairs at this juncture, surveyed me shrewdly. "You seem all brimming with portentous secrets."

"You look remarkably bright-eyed and bushy-tailed yourself. I hope you've not been overexciting Nell. Philip, have you ever heard of a place named Sudeley?"

Philip's face changed from disconcerted to curious. "Sudeley? What is it, a town or a manor house?"

"The latter, I should judge. I am trying to trace my family," I improvised hastily, "and I understand we may have relatives who came from there."

"I'll look it up for you in the library at

home. We've lots of books about old county families. Maman puts great stock in all that sort of thing. I'll let you know if I find anything."

I checked on Sudeley in the indexes of all our own geographical volumes, but had no luck. There were, after all, so many great houses and palaces in England, each with its name; so many tiny little towns. I fared no better when I inquired of Laura Giles.

"It could be anywhere. We have so many of such places," she said vaguely, echoing my thought.

"Why don't you ask Mr. Roach?" Nell inquired with a spark of malice. "He's so eager to look after your interests."

That struck me as an excellent idea, so I paid a call on Charles Roach at his legal chambers. He was extremely cordial, as if to make amends for our last frosty parting. He escorted me with some pride to his inner office and offered me a chair. "Rather a nice piece, isn't it? I picked it up recently at a sale from one of our old estates. It takes time, of course, to acquire fine old items, as they so seldom appear upon the market, but I flatter myself on obtaining two or three."

In point of fact, his small offices struck me

as a rather pathetic attempt to imitate those of the old City legal firms. The vanity seemed a bit touching; it made Charles Roach younger and more human.

He sat down across the desk from me with some eagerness. "How may I serve you? You are not planning to make further livestock purchases, I trust!"

"I've come about a personal matter. I am tracing family history and need advice on research."

"Your best resources are at Oxford. It is unusual for a woman, of course, but I am sure that I can make arrangements for your admission to the library." He spoke with importance that was almost boyish.

"And have you knowledge of any place named Sudeley?"

He turned the name over in his mind, but shook his head. "I don't believe so. But I will inquire."

It was Philip, actually, who provided our first real clue. He appeared at teatime a few days later, to announce with triumph, "I told you I would find it, and I did! My, those scones look good."

Nell tossed one at him, but she waited till

Georgina had left the room before demanding breathlessly, "Found what?"

"Your precious Sudeley. These *are* good. Georgina really is improving, isn't she? I'll have another." He looked at our inexorable faces, and relented. "Sudeley Castle's in Winchcombe, on the far side of Gloucestershire. It's the home of persons named Dent-Brocklehurst and her papa's in Parliament."

What harm could it do to write to the Dent-Brocklehursts, introduce myself as an expatriate engaged in research of the family tree? But it took no small effort to compose a letter which established my *bona fides* while revealing nothing.

I received in reply a cordial letter in a feminine hand. "I once had the pleasure of being presented to Lady Kersey," wrote Mrs. Dent, "an exciting experience for a child! My husband and I would be delighted to have you come to Sudeley and will offer all possible assistance with your research. We are still engaged in the restoration work on Sudeley, which as you may know was 'slighted' by the Puritans. The property was purchased by our family from Lord Rivers and the Duke of Buckingham in the 1830's."

The mention of Puritan destruction recalled to mind the ancestor killed at Newbury. Was the "royal lady" perhaps an illegitimate Stuart? But certainly the *Historie* had been referring to an earlier time.

I put Mrs. Dent's letter and the Lawson *Historie* in the casket with Kersey's own epistle, locked them in firmly, and carried off the key. From then on, my mind was set on journeying to Sudeley.

How difficult this would be I did not know, and of course there was the matter of providing for Nell's care while I was gone. Armed with Philip's vague geography, I managed to locate Winchcombe on the map, and to my joy it proved not far away. Less than an hour's journey by fast train—if any trains yet wove their way crosswise in the Cotswolds. I did not mention the possibility to Nell, for I did not want to excite her with false hopes. However, inquiries through Charles Roach revealed that a mode of train travel did exist. The acceptance of Mrs. Dent's invitation might not be as impossible as I had feared.

I thought of asking Laura to look after Nell, but it turned out she and the doctor themselves were about to go away. "To an old schoolfellow of Father's in Shropshire.

It's providential, really. Father never quite recovered from a bout of pleurisy last winter, and his eyes aren't what they used to be, though he won't admit it. He *ought* to retire, but all he says when I propose it is who'll take his place? Young doctors just setting up practice won't come to villages, and I doubt the folks would trust them if they did. Not that they pay much heed to Father, either. He's been so low ever since the Greene baby was born with the withered arm. Feels he failed in not making the family see the need for proper health care earlier." Laura sighed. "A week's rest and yarning about the old days may set him up better for the winter."

At last, in desperation, I put my problem before Lady Margaret, and she said at once, "Nell shall come to us. Do not protest, my dear. I shall be glad to have her."

I was not at all sure how Nell would feel about this arrangement. She seemed to need my presence, though she was insistent I come and go at my own pleasure. In any event, I did not want to trouble her for nothing, so I could not bring myself to speak of my possible visit until I heard again from Mrs. Dent. When the date was confirmed, I told Nell of my plans. A look of pain immediately crossed her face. I said quickly, "I shall wire Mrs. Dent that I cannot come."

"Camilla, no!" Nell put her hand out quickly.

"But if you feel unwell—"

"It wasn't that. It was just, to think you hadn't felt that you could tell me . . . Of course you must go."

There was a crash on the far side of the house and a tinkle of glass. I jumped up. "Oh bother, that kitten's probably knocked over . . ."

But it wasn't the kitten. I knew that in the instant as Georgina stumbled in, blood trickling from her temple and her composure shattered. "Oh, miss, oh, miss . . ." She was shaking with fear and she held something clutched tightly in her hand. "In parlor . . . I was in parlor, on way to dining room to set table, and rock came through window . . ."

The drawing-room window with its priceless old medieval colored glass.

Georgina opened her hand. The rock lay on a crumpled piece of paper, and on the paper, crudely drawn, were figures—a woman all in black, a child with a withered arm. A cross between, in red, like a smear of blood.

Someone was accusing me of witching that poor child's arm.

Nell made a curious, almost animal cry.

"Stop it! Both of you!" I did not know I was going to shout the words out till they came. My head was pounding and my breath came in gasps. "My house—my beautiful, peaceful house. Those windows were five hundred years old, the secret of that coloring's been lost. Everything's being lost . . ." I was sobbing, I could not contain myself.

I straightened at last and dried my eyes. My lungs felt like old sandpaper when I breathed. "That settles one thing, anyway. I certainly shall not go away tomorrow."

"Yes, you shall!" Nell's words came like flame. She was very pale, but her eyes held mine and I knew what she was thinking. We had to find the secret of the token; to claim it was the only thing that could make us safe.

It felt so very strange to be alone on the journey to Sudeley. For three months I had been constantly conscious of my sister's plight, but now, as the train rails carried me away from Wychwood, that pull on me diminished.

The train meandered through the country-side: hedgerows and groves of trees; isolated manor houses with their great tithe barns; strips of houses, like toy villages, clustering round their market cross, their parish church; fields of a gold that gave back the gold of the Cotswold stone; the great shaggy sheep, the "Cotswold lions," with their amiable dignity and Roman noses. The train wheels rattled, and an odd thing began to happen. Little by little I began to feel a strong excitement, the sort of mysterious, exhilarating promise I had as a child when a birthday neared. *Expectancy, expectancy* was what the train wheels said.

The Dents sent a carriage to meet me at the station, and I was glad I was alone in the closed vehicle, for this bubbling sensation of freedom affected me like champagne. Then we whirled smartly through the entry arch in the North Lodge, and I gazed for the first time on the grounds of Sudeley.

The lawns were a vast expanse of parkland dotted with fine old trees. And there, at the end of the long drive, Sudeley Castle lifted its towers against the Midlands sky. My first castle. It *was* a castle, yet with no sense of the mystery and terror that emanated even in pictures of castles such as Berkeley. Sudeley Castle was built of the familiar Cotswold stone, but that alone could not explain—how shall I put it?—its enormous sense of light.

We drove through the old tunnel-like entry, across an inner court, and I was ushered into the castle's private family quarters. Here I was met by Mrs. Dent, a pleasant woman not many years older than myself. She greeted me charmingly, and herself showed me to my room, small in size but magnificent in paneling, bidding me when I had refreshed myself to come down to tea. I had to ring for a fresh-faced maid to guide my way through a labyrinth of corridors, their rich paneling surmounted with splendid paintings; past lovely windows in wide oriel frames. This was not only a historic landmark but a home of taste and distinction and an enviable treasury of art. Yet even as my eyes coveted, I was aware of something more, which lingered in the very air I breathed—nay, seemed to follow me like a soft whisper of breath as I walked along. A sense of presence, ever so faint as yet, which I might not have detected had it not been for those strange experiences at my own Wychwood.

Over Banbury tarts and maids of honor and China tea, Mrs. Dent told me bits of Sudeley's story from Saxon times when

Winchcombe was the capital of Mercia. "But it was during King Stephen's reign in the twelfth century that John de Sudeley began the castle here. His descendant Ralph Boteler added the second building in the fifteenth century."

There had been English nobility here when the Old Ones still held their revels in Wychwood's garden. ". . . and of course during our Civil War the castle was 'slighted'—deliberately damaged to make it unfit for military use. Until this century it lay in ruins; indeed, its stones were scavenged for local building use." It was clear Mrs. Dent felt toward this home, which was hers by marriage, much as I did toward Wychwood. "You say you are tracing an ancestor who came from here? In the days of the Civil War, or earlier?"

"About a century earlier, I should judge." My hostess' aristocratic features and kind eyes moved me to confidence. "In an old history of my mother's family I have found a reference to a Lady Mary who was 'Daughter to the Royal Lady of Sudeley and the Traitor Thomas.' I've searched my history books and can find no clue to who they are."

"But my dear!" Mrs. Dent was greatly

excited. "Surely you know— No, of course, being from America you'd not have heard the story, and with all the scandal and danger at the time, undoubtedly historians of the period swept it over."

"Swept what over?" I leaned forward eagerly.

"Why, 'Traitor Thomas' was the brother of Jane Seymour and of the Protector, whose importance was never equaled. No doubt that explains much of his conduct. He attempted to seize the power of the young King Edward and was beheaded in the Tower."

Not for the first time, heads will roll, Lady Kersey had written.

"He had been paying court, most unwisely, to Princess Elizabeth, and she almost lost her own life in consequence. But he was already in disgrace. He had eloped with Henry VIII's widow, Katherine Parr, not six weeks after the old King's death. It was for Katherine that Thomas added the Tudor renovations onto Sudeley; he brought her here as soon as the marriage became known, and it was here she died. I shall show you her tomb out in the chapel. It was vandalized a hundred years ago and we have just been having it restored."

"But was there a child?"

"Oh, yes. She died of childbirth." Mrs. Dent's lips tightened. "And young Elizabeth, who'd been like a daughter to Katherine Parr, was not even allowed to attend the funeral. That rogue Thomas needed no consolation, as the Princess herself said, but was off at once to further his future fortunes. Poor Katherine, I hope she had some tranquil moments here before her disillusionment set in."

"And the child?"

"She was raised by the charity of the Duchess of Suffolk, one of Katherine's friends. After Thomas Seymour's execution she dropped from sight, and is assumed to have died while still a child."

But the words in the handwritten booklet blazed before my eyes: . . . *the granddaughter of Sir Edward and his wife Mary, who was daughter to the royal lady of Sudeley* . . .

"Would you like to see their portraits?" Mrs. Dent inquired. She led the way down the corridor and paused before a somber painting of a pale, sharp-chiseled man with dark auburn beard. The face of an ascetic—or a fanatic. My hostess moved on, but I lingered. "Strange. There is something quite familiar . . ."

"You have undoubtedly seen pictures of his brother Somerset, the Lord Protector? There's a strong resemblance."

I followed her along the passage and up the splendid stairs, and a sense of presence, of presentiment went with me. Mrs. Dent opened a carved door and ushered me into a lovely room. The blue and gold whorls of the ceiling glowed and the crimson curtains at the low oriel windows whispered.

Even before I looked, I knew. The face of the gentlewoman in the portrait was a stranger's face, but the white satin of her pearl-edged coif, the red brocade and gold embroidery of her gown, the lace that fell about her wrists was as familiar as my own black serge. It was in the robes of Katherine Parr that Kersey, the unpredictable, had chosen to deck herself in the incredible portrait appliqué.

"This was Katherine's room," my hostess said, and quietly withdrew.

And then it came, as I had known it would, and I was not afraid. The crimson curtains whispered in the golden light, and it was as if a familiar and well-loved friend had stepped into the room. Her presence was all about me, like perfume. The presence which had welcomed me that first night in Wychwood, which since that moment had seldom been far away. Not Kersey. Katherine the Queen, last wife of Henry VIII. Without knowing what I was doing, I found myself sitting in the oriel window, and weeping. But they were tears of peace. Historians might think that Katherine's daughter had died in childhood, but I knew better. And I knew, too, that Wychwood was in some way a Seymour house, that Katherine's spirit dwelt there protecting me. For once it did not bother me that my thoughts were illogical, irrational, not subject to scholar's proof. I knew what I knew, and I needed nothing more.

9

Sudeley Castle,
Winchcombe—
Rossford-under-Wychwood
October, 1863

I WENT back to my own room presently and dressed for dinner, and talked with my hosts. But all the while my mind was some three centuries away. I was very glad when I could at last retire, and when my lamp was extinguished I lay in the great bed, my mind peopled with bright historic images. I awoke very early, still filled with that great sense of peace. The sky was yet dark, but the birds were stirring, and to the east, behind majestic trees, appeared a glow of light. I arose, dressed silently, and tiptoed through the corridor and down the stairs. A little maid, just unbarring the great door, smiled at me sleepily. I slipped outside, wrapping the shawl I had brought with me against the morning chill.

My movements led me with no conscious

design to the little church. Here, in the gracious stillness of white walls and woodlace carving, I sank into a small pew and closed my eyes. After a while the sound of bird calls drew me again outside, and I walked slowly along the east wing of the castle past the Garderobe Tower to the Queen's Garden, where the herbs of autumn still lifted their bright fragrance to the rising sun. This had been Katherine's garden, laid out for viewing from her personal apartments. To my right rose the gaunt skeleton of the old Banquet Hall, destroyed by Cromwell. I walked in history; I walked where Katherine's slippers once had trod. "Poor woman," Mrs. Dent had said, but I was conscious here at Katherine's castle of no sense of sorrow, only of joyous, ineradicable life.

I turned through a low arch in a yew hedge, across another expanse of lawn, through another hedge, and now I was within the court framed by the ruined Hall itself. To the east, the rays of early sun poured through the empty window frames, and birds flew in and out. The stones glowed gold. There was a bird's nest on the ledge of the great high window. Herbs and wildflowers grew, as in window boxes, from what had once been oriel seats and fireplaces high above my head. The grass even now was green.

I felt newborn. I felt gloriously and ecstatically free from burdens. So must Katherine, centuries ago, have come out at dawn to greet her wandering but well-loved lord. She did love him well, whatever had been his sins; I knew as if she'd told me. I crossed the grass toward the lacy shell of stone, and all the cares of Wychwood were very far away.

Then, amid the low-clipped shrubs of yew, I stopped. I was not alone. A queer prickling sensation told me that, though nothing moved. There was no sound. For a moment I stood there, somehow caught in time. Then the angle of light shifted as the sun rose further, and a golden finger illumined the farther niche where a man stood watching in the shadows. But he was no shade of some bygone courtier. He was, unbelievably but undeniably, Jeremy Bushel.

I was embarrassed and I was furious. I marched over. "What are you doing here?"

"Watching you."

"I want a straight answer."

"You have had it. When I learned of this quixotic adventure you had dashed off on, I decided you were in need of a protector. So having no pressing business of my own at home and enjoying an amble on the autumn roads, I drove on over. Pity you didn't tell me what you had in mind. You could have come with me and avoided railway cinders."

"Don't be ridiculous."

"I'm not being ridiculous. Georgina told me about that rock thrown through your window." He untied the kerchief-wrapped bundle he was carrying and spread it on the ledge. "Have some bread and cheese. It will be hours before you're served breakfast at the castle."

"I am certainly not in danger *here*."

Jeremy's eyes, if not his face, were sober. "Be realistic. For a young woman against whom highly theatrical threats are being made—"

"I don't believe in ghosts."

"No more do I, but that cockerel nailed to your door was no spectral shape. For such a young woman to set off unattended through country she does not know and in which she is all too accessible seems, at the very least, imprudent."

"Why should anything happen to me?"

"Why indeed? But it seems clear that a

person or persons unknown want to get rid of you, and get their hands on Wychwood."

"You are one of them, I'm given to understand."

"True," he retorted coolly, "but I prefer to acquire my property by legitimate means. I'll give you a rental check for Wychwood on the instant, if you'll take it." I shook my head. "Then at least be a sensible woman and allow me to escort you home. It might look improper, but it's infinitely preferable to your traveling alone." He grinned. "We can always tell any inquirers you're my sister. It's a splendid day. We can wander through back roads and you'll see all the little towns you've only read of in those books of yours."

I ought, of course, to have put him properly in his place. But the sun gilding the peaceful courtyard was intoxicating, and I was already giddy. "All right," I said. "But not until mid-morning. You can pick me up at the railway station. I've made arrangements to be driven there."

"Excellent. Meanwhile I'll to Winchcombe to purchase fruit and cheese. And a bottle of claret? It wouldn't do, would it, for us to lunch together unchaperoned at an inn?" He saluted, his eyes glinting wickedly, and departed, and I turned back to the castle, wondering what had possessed me.

It was a glorious day. I was, I think, a little bit bewitched—by my discovery of the Seymour connection and of Katherine; by being carefree in its rare true meaning, free of care. Naunton, the Slaughters, Bourton-on-the-Water—we lunched by the River Windrush's narrow stream, and Jeremy told me of the bloody days of the Puritan Rebellion when the Slaughters received their name.

"There are all sorts of tales of treachery, handed down in families, that won't bear repeating. Internal warfare seems always to be especially brutal, as though the most exquisite pain is that brought to one's own blood kin. But you in your scholar's tower wouldn't know such things, would you?"

I looked away. "Yes, I . . . know about Civil War."

"I beg your pardon. I had forgotten you had come here from such a conflict. I truly had." We were silent for several moments, and he added gently, "If I have offended you, or trod on old wounds, I am deeply sorry."

"The man I was to marry was killed in our war. I learned of it the day I arrived in London."

"I really did not know. I'm so sorry."

"You need not be. Since coming here I seem to inhabit a different world." I spread my hands. "Perhaps you can understand now why I do not intend to return again to Charleston."

"Yes, of course." He wrapped the remainder of our cheese, and in an abrupt change of mood, jumped to his feet and held out his hands to pull me up. "Those horses of mine have had enough rest and grazing, don't you think? Did you promise any especial time you would return? If we're really wicked, we could drive by way of Shipton and take tea at the Shaven Crown."

And we did, such was the spell of the enchantment that still lingered on me. The bright blue of the sky was fading now to grey, and Shipton, being one of the Wychwood villages, had about it that forest sense of immemorial sadness, but its stones still glowed. We stopped at the old inn, once a monastery, on its crossroad corner, and Jeremy ordered tea served to us in the rose-garden court.

"A bit chilly at this time of year, but perhaps more proper than having the two of us seen going together into an inn, in case any of Wychwood's gossipy ghosts are stirring." Jeremy grinned, and I tried to frown severely.

The roses were gone now, but the bronze leaves lingered and the bushes were heavy with their ruddy hips. Nell and I had been gathering rose hips to dry for tea. This garden, being enclosed, made me recall my own, and my thoughts began to run again toward Wychwood House. But by some common consent we lingered, sipping the heartening tea, as if loath to end this day.

"We really must be getting on," Jeremy said at last, rising and laying some coins upon the table.

We returned again to the wagon. The magic spell of the day was wearing off as we drew nearer home. We drove in silence; I pulled my shawl closer about me. Jeremy slouched back in the seat and seemed to have fallen into a brown study. I did not disturb him. The hills were growing steeper now and the forest thicker. Here and there on the hillside we saw sheep huddled, or a lonely shepherd walking with his dog. We passed a farmhouse clinging to the hillside among thick trees, its small windows staring blankly beneath a lowering roof. It had a bleak oppressive look to it, as Quinn Cottage did, but wilder; it made me think, irrelevantly, of gypsies.

"What is that place?" I asked impulsively.

Jeremy answered without looking up, "Tarr Farm."

Tarr Farm. His farm, then. But he had not spoken of it as if it were his home.

We were now aproaching the fields belonging to Wychwood House, and I glanced at them automatically through the gloaming. The villagers had gone back to presuming grazing rights as soon as the trespassing prohibitions had been taken down. The sheep had not yet started homeward for the night, I noted absently. And then aloud, involuntarily, I said, "But that *is* odd!"

They were not, as usual, flocked together in classical pastoral attitudes. There was some disturbance, a kind of uncharacteristic jerking activity—a pair of dogs were running among them, barking.

Jeremy's eyes narrowed. "Could be a predator of some kind. Best take a look." He turned the wagon off the road into the fields.

The barking grew more frantic now as we approached. And under it, faint but insistent, another sound. My ears comprehended it, but only vaguely, after Jeremy had already understood. With a terse "Hold these," he flung the reins to me and was running toward the sheep.

The autumn darkness was fast closing down. I leaned forward, squinting anxiously. The dogs leaped to fawn on Jeremy, anxious and bewildered. He stopped, bent over one of the massive forms that always reminded me of land-bound clouds, moved to another. I had been right, the sound had been that of animals stricken with fear and pain—stricken as though demented. Something was wrong, something was very wrong. The great beasts, like lions in their normal dignity, moved in fits and jerks, impelled by spasms. As I watched, one old Hector staggered forward, fell to his side, and lay there twitching. A dryness clutched at my throat, as it must at theirs. I dug my fingers round the wagon-rim as a wave of remembered panic crested and broke within me.

Jeremy ran back, panting, "Something's got into them. I thought at first they'd blasted themselves on clover, but that's not it. You, sir!" He snapped his fingers to the Greenes' dog. "Go home and fetch your master. Go *home*, you hear? I hope Laban will know what ails them," Jeremy added grimly as the dog ran off. "There's no vet closer than Stow."

I wet my lips. "You needn't . . . When I was a child in the States, there were some animals struck like this. There was a plant the blacks called jimson, that they used in spells." I swallowed hard. "Its name's datura."

Jeremy drew his breath in sharply. "Atropine poison. Madam, you never cease amazing me." He snatched the reins, striking the horses on their flanks. The wagon lurched.

"Where are we going?"

"To Tarr Farm. There's no time to waste, datura's part of the nightshade family. I wish to God that Doc Quinn was not away, but the poor old quack probably wouldn't know . . . I have some chemical compounds; we can just hope . . ." His voice trailed off.

We had reached the gate of the steep drive to his house, and with a muttered "Faster by foot," he jumped down. I followed, not waiting for invitation, and reached the door just as he flung it open.

The building's aura was that of a Teutonic ghost tale: dark, bare, cold. We dashed down a corridor to a locked door. He was already fumbling with his keys. "There will be a lamp, with matches by it, on a table directly to your right. Light it." Then we were inside. Jeremy plunged ahead into the blackness as I bumped against the tabletop, groped for the matches.

The lamp flared up, illuminating . . . stillroom, storeroom? "What *is* this?" I demanded.

"Laboratory. I've been doing research on some so-called spells." Jeremy was tumbling books off shelves; he seized one, flung it down beside me. "Look in that. Try datura, atropine, nightshade, anything." He was already throwing open locked cupboards filled with tall glass jars.

His tension would have communicated itself to me even had I not already been thoroughly alarmed. My fingers trembled as I ran down pages. "Here. Poisonous crystalline alkaloid . . . " I stared at the rest of the entry helplessly. "I'm sorry; I can't read chemical notation."

Immediately he was behind me, reading across my shoulder. "The gods are with us; I think I've already tried—look, can you get back to the wagon, open the gates and drive up around the back to the barn?"

"I can try."

"Good girl. I'll meet you there." He swung back to the cupboard, searching along the shelves feverishly, as I ran out.

I ought to have taken a lantern; I had not thought. It was full dark now and the drive was rutted, steep, and filled with stones. I stumbled, fell, picked myself up and went running on. My breath burned in my throat.

Dry throat; general lack of moisture; pupil dilation; stiffness, twitching; rapid pulse and respiration eventually becoming slow, weak, irregular preceding death . . . The clinical description in the toxicology book blurred with the convulsive images of the animals in the Wychwood fields, of those other animals long ago on whom the child I once had been had "tried out a spell." Why was the buried past rising to haunt me now in this other world?

I must not think like that. I must stay calm, pull the heavy gate open wide enough for the wagon. Thank fortune that the horses had stayed where they'd been left, that they knew their own way through the blackness. We reached the top of the driveway; turned. A lantern swung eerily above the barn's gaping maw. A figure ran back and forth, flinging bundles of fodder. Jeremy, hurrying to hand me up the flask of chemical solution, saying, "Pour this on the bundles as I heave them up. I don't know how one's supposed to force-feed antidotes to sheep, but the fool animals are silly over this particular fodder, wet or dry, so this may work."

The wagon loaded, we were careening down the hill again, into the road, around the curve and onto the Wychwood fields. Once I said bewilderedly, "Why should they suddenly become sick from datura *now* when they've been grazing on these fields for years?" And he was responding, "Because there hadn't *been* any datura in those fields. But I wager I know where there was, and is, some growing."

"Where?"

"In your walled garden."

"I don't understand."

"Don't you?" He looked at me oddly. "Perhaps you won't have to."

We had reached the sheep again. There were more dogs now, more noise, faint illumination from the lanterns swinging at the wagon's sides. Jeremy vaulted over the back of the seat. "Get out and spread this stuff with the rake as I pitch it down. And pray they eat it!"

We worked in taut, rhythmic silence; how much time passed, I do not know. The sheep were worse, even I could tell that. Jeremy was among them everywhere, prodding, cajoling. Even kicking, with ruthless determination, when that was needed to get them to their feet. Three or four lay still, resisting effort. I looked across at Jeremy with a sick desperation. "Do you think . . ."

"Don't waste time thinking. Concentrate on the ones that move. Stuff the damn weeds in their mouths, if necessary . . . Ahhh." He straightened with relief as one great beast gave a last shudder, stood motionless for a minute, and then went trotting off at normal rolling gait. "I think we're winning."

Why had no one come?

Faint, and far off in darkness, there were lights moving. There were voices. Only a whisper at first, but growing, swelling, surging toward us in a murmur that was not really words at all but waves of sound pulsating and vibrating in my ears. Laban Greene, holding his lantern high, his face like stone. Daniel Greene, running across the fields, stopping in stupefaction as he reached us. The towering hulk of Black Aaron Smith. Raphael, poised, legs flexed as though about to leap, a lantern dangling from his outstretched arm, eyes gleaming. Dogs, everywhere. Jeremy, stopping to rub an arm across his face: "Thank God you got here. I was wondering—"

"*They sheep's bewitched!*"

The voice came from the rear, and it was like a current passing, welding. The disparate figures had become a ring, moving closer, silent. The drumming in my ears increased and my mouth was acrid. Rafe Smith had moved behind me and his lantern threw my shadow on the ground—black, distorted, my hoop swinging crazily in the night wind. I had not realized before that I was very cold.

"What needs us more?" Another voice echoing the first. "Sheep's our'n, but land they be on's her'n, an' look upon they! There be a curse on't, as Copper Maid foretold. What her be feeding t'sheep?"

It struck me then what it looked like, our standing there surrounded by the demented sheep. What Jeremy had meant by wagering datura grew at Wychwood House. The guise of Old Religion was being used to fright me off, but in a different way; used to make it look as though *I* were the practitioner.

I stared round the rim of faces, closed, implacable, and for the first time felt actually afraid.

Jeremy looked at Laban Greene, his own expression altering. "For the love of God, man, use your head! Someone's up to something, all right, and it isn't us. You ought to be thanking your stars we happened by to help. You know me, and what I'm doing—"

"Excuse me, sir," Laban Greene interrupted with even quiet, "but us don't know, does us, other than whatsomever you tells? And as for the rest, it's not you'm fields now, is it, but the lady's?"

The words hung like a threat in the still air. Someone moved forward—Rafe Smith, his eyes narrowed. And the cold that had started at the base of my spine moved up my backbone.

For a minute, two, there was nothing but the sounds of the sheep and of the dogs, and of a scarce-voiced murmur: "*Spell . . . Old Ones . . . Copper Maid . . . Copper Maid means a doom . . . Had not walked, these many years . . .*" The men, without seeming to have moved, were closer. All it needs, the voice of reason whispered in my racing brain, is one false move; one person shoving another, or stumbling; one stone being skipped. Then one voice, over that uneasy hush, said with a firm and clear command, "Good people!"

It was Lady Margaret, whirling up in her light carriage with Philip beside her. God knew how the tale had reached her, but she was there, standing calmly, speaking in those unraised but penetrating tones. "You, Laban Greene, Aaron Smith, and the rest of you. Open your eyes! Yes, it's terrible what's happened here, but don't go looking for spells or foreigners to take the blame. You all knew something like this could happen at any time—if not bad forage, then a pox, or hard winter, or dropped wool prices. Or predators, or poachers. It's absurd to keep risking a whole year's income in this ridiculous, inefficient fashion. You know that. Don't you?"

Her eyes swept them, pinning each in turn. There was a faint wave of movement, checked at once when she put up her hand. "It's quite unnecessary to go on like this, you know. There's a decent cottage and suitable employment at fair wages waiting for everyone ready to sell his flock and move onto the Manor grounds tomorrow. I'll pay you top price for the sheep, including any who may have died in this mishap. *No*"—the hand again—"you've done enough mischief. Go home now, talk to your wives, and when you've come to your senses, see me in the Manor counting-room tomorrow."

For an immeasurable instant the scales hung in the balance. Then, in twos and threes, the men began to disappear off into darkness. She had won. Or we had. I was quite sure of nothing, except that my legs were very weak. I closed my eyes for a moment, half swaying, and Jeremy was standing behind me with his hand at the hollow of my back. Then Lady Margaret was there, her voice warm, putting a quick arm round me.

"My poor child. They were at the tavern when the call came, and drink makes them ugly. You must not let it trouble you. We shall get you home. Nell's been calling for you, you know."

Nell. I had not thought of her for hours. Shaken and stricken, I let her lead me off, and did not give a backward glance at Jeremy Bushel.

Lady Margaret bundled me into the back seat and wrapped a lap robe around me.

Philip did not look in my direction. He was very silent, as we all were.

Lights streamed from the Manor House when we arrived. The butler stepped forward, relief coloring the correctness of his tone. "Miss Jardine, how good to see you. The young lady—"But I had already heard Nell's voice, and the note of it, and was running toward the stairs.

"*Camilla.*" Nell's arms reached out to me as if the effort cost her all her strength. "Hold me, please hold me. I thought you'd never come."

While she had been lying here calling for me, I had dawdled the afternoon in Shipton's rose garden, reluctant to return. "I'm here now. I won't leave again, I promise. Try to sleep."

"No. Please take me home, tonight. I don't want to stay here." Nell's face had that pinched look that so alarmed me. "Camilla, the royal lady—did you find her?"

"Yes. Hush. I'll try to get you home, if you'll just rest." It could be unwise to move her, but she might sleep better in her own bed, and I was reluctant to impose further on Lady Margaret's kindness. So I rang for a servant to request transportation in the carriage.

We saw none of the Manor House family as we left. Philip and Amy were nowhere near, and Lady Margaret was closeted in her office with her chief steward, discussing business in anticipation of tomorrow. We rolled in silence to Wychwood's door, and I was too tired and worried about Nell to even think.

When I had her at last in bed, I gazed out the low window, but I could discern no figures in the endless night. Even the dogs no longer cried. The village was so still. That was how it was, according to old books, when spirits were abroad. Where evil brooded, no insects ventured close and no birds sang. But I knew that men were stirring, talking; not in their homes, as Lady Margaret bid them, but at the Copper Maid.

"It's happening again, isn't it?"

Nell had pulled herself up in bed and was arrested, motionless, in the grip of pain. Out of her strained face, her eyes clung to me with a kind of pitiful desperation. "It's starting up again, the . . . the hate against us. The Copper Maid's been walking again, Amy told me, and the powers of the Old Ones are being summoned. I can tell, I always get these attacks when something's happening." I ran to ease her down onto the pillows, and she burrowed against me gratefully. "You're so good to me. Why can't they understand that and let us be? God ought to punish them for being so unkind."

"Don't think like that. Nothing's wrong, just try to rest." But I was afraid she would detect the evasiveness of my tone. I made her camomile tea, and sat beside her and told her the story of Katherine Parr, and at last to my infinite relief Nell fell asleep.

I picked up the tea things and carried them wearily downstairs. The wind had risen again, and the front door swung open; I must have forgotten to latch it in my haste to settle Nell. So much for the security of my iron bolts and bars. But locks were no protection, anyway, against the power of hate.

I shut the door and walked through the still rooms, holding the hot teapot against me like a talisman. Katherine's portrait wearing Kersey's face was watching. Katherine, my beneficient spirit. Was it only some thirty hours ago that I had learned her name?

I climbed the stairs and threw myself into bed, the bright images and peace of heart of Sudeley Castle as far from my mind as if they'd never been.

10

Great Rollright
October, 1863

AFTER the excitement of the evening we did not early waken. I was still at my breakfast when the knocker sounded. Amy Ross, already. I put down my coffee cup hastily as Georgina, in slant-eyed silence, ushered Philip in.

I gazed at him in some surprise. "What brings you here so early? You can't stay, you know, to interfere with your sister's lessons."

"Amy's not coming," Philip announced abruptly. "Excitement's been too much for her. The upstairs maid's filled her up with tales of how the Copper Maid's been walking and some doom's about to fall, as witness those demented sheep. Result, Amy's scared silly and Maman's dosing her with physic. So, since you don't have to teach, I'm taking you and Nell to see the stone circle on the Rollright Ridge."

"Camilla!" came Nell's voice from above.

"Is that Amy? Send her up, do. I have to see her."

Philip bounded up the stairs before I could prevent him. "Amy's not here. I've come to kidnap you and your sister and carry you away."

"Philip, be sensible. Nell can't possibly—"

"Oh, yes I can!" Nell pushed herself up on the pillows. "We'll have one last day of sunlight before winter comes. It's what I've been longing for, too, to get away."

Fresh air and sunlight could be good for her, and I had neglected her these past few days. So I capitulated, and chased Philip downstairs while I helped Nell dress.

He stood in the lower hall muttering imprecations and requests for speed, and as soon as I gave permission he hurried up again to help bring Nell down.

"Why all the great rush?" Nell demanded breathlessly. She was filled with a hectic gaiety I had not seen often in her lately and I wondered if it was a mask for pain. "Surely the stones aren't going anywhere?"

"As a matter of fact, they do wander, according to the legend. But I'm more concerned in getting clear of the village before anyone else manages to get claws into you.

My dear mother, Mrs. Giles, Mr. Bushel, not to mention the estimable Roach. You Jardines are altogether too much in demand. Today I mean to have you to myself."

I raised my eyebrows. "You *are* being Lord of the Manor!"

"Don't say that!"

"Oh," Nell said profoundly.

"Oh, indeed." Philip negotiated a bump in the road at an all too rapid pace, but once we had passed Tarr Farm he leaned back, took a deep breath, and slowed to a more comfortable speed.

"What happened?" Nell said gently. "Is it your mother?"

"Nell," I said warningly. But Philip shook his head. "For once it's not Maman's disappointment in me that's the burden. This time *I'm* the one that's angered." He subsided, and Nell, about to speak, glanced from one to the other of us and forebore.

The sun was shining and the morning felt like spring. The forest lay beside us, and to our left the cultivated land sloped off in a patchwork of fields and tiny villages. Presently we struck due north and began to climb, and soon all vestige of Wychwood Forest lay behind. Nell's eyes were closed, her face at peace. I sat back, contemplating the brilliant sky.

It *had* been good to come. I knew it long before we rolled up the sun-dappled solitude of the high ridge and Philip pulled off into a field and said the first words he had spoken for well over an hour: "There are the stones."

In a circle they waited, in a clearing like a tiny field. Trees stood around and sheep grazed comfortably. Further up the ridge a few cows dozed in the autumn sun. Fields, animals, trees, stones—so casually at home that I could understand at last why, to the people of this countryside, the natural and supernatural were so closely intertwined. These rocks, so strangely shaped and worn by time, seemed not to have been placed but to have grown, like the surrounding forest, from the ground.

"But they're so small," Nell said quietly.

"They're as tall as a very tall man. They're unique in being so close together. As if they're holding hands. One can't count them accurately, according to the legend. Not as splendid as Stonehenge, but they're thirty-five hundred years old and they have the magic." Philip said, with an odd inflection, "They grow on one."

He carried the rugs and cushions from the carriage and spread them on the ground, making a couch for Nell against one of the taller stones. When he had her settled to his satisfaction he rose and smiled. "You must be careful here, you know. This is sacred ground. The rocks are touchstones to reveal the truths within men's hearts. Actually, this was probably one of the worship places of a Bronze Age cult of the Great Mother." He went to the carriage and returned with an enormous picnic basket.

Nell held out her hands. "Let that go now. Come and sit down and tell us."

"About the stones? This circle's the King's Men. Across the way—"

"No," I said deliberately. "About the Mother."

There was a moment's silence. I had not meant a Bronze Age goddess, and we all knew it. Philip dropped down and his jesting manner fell off like a shell. He sat plaiting the long dry grass into a braid, and he did not meet my eyes as he said, "It makes one so absolutely furious."

"What does?" Nell probed gently.

"The complacency. The self-possession. Correction, the possession of others, the assumption that one owns those of lesser quality, to 'order as seemeth right.' " He finished in a bitter parody of the liturgical prayer.

I looked at him. "Suppose you tell us exactly what is on your mind."

He was silent again for several minutes. "Those poor beasts."

"The sheep?"

"Those too, of course. I was thinking of their owners. The flocks are all they've got, poor devils, and most of them in debt from one butchering or shearing to the next. Oh, I know they'd be better off on regular wages, but who can blame the poor sods wanting to set their own hours or take a cup of cider without someone telling them whether it's right or wrong? They were frightened half out of their minds last night. And my mother drove round, pointing out the error of their ways with a gracious smile. She was out again first thing this morning, too, trying to buy them out. Can't understand why they so stubbornly hold on." Philip laughed without humor. "Laban Greene told her straight out, ' 'Twarn't no folly of our'n what killed my sheep. 'Tis someun's follicking with magicking, and you'd better poke your long nose into nudging Rector to get after that and leave we alone.' "

Nell's face was white. "Surely the sheep didn't die!"

"Some of them did," Philip said shortly.

I saw Nell's eyes, and said quickly, "But not from magic."

"From whatever it was they ate that they hadn't ought to. Which poses, by the way, an interesting question."

"But they oughtn't have died. It isn't right they died."

"It's the owners you ought to feel sorry for," Philip said bluntly. "The sheep didn't know what happened to them."

Nell's face stilled. "That's true. So it is just, isn't it? A retribution." I stared at her and she said with gentle gravity, "The villagers. They've hated you, they've been so unfair. The three calamities . . . I'm *glad* they've suffered."

Philip whistled. "Only the innocent can be so ruthless."

"Perhaps," I suggested, "you had better tell us about the circle of stones."

"After luncheon. The tale wants proper setting, and after that last remark Nell needs sweetening with treacle tarts."

So for the second time in as many days I lunched alfresco, and in the details of this, too, the two days differed. This meal was splendor, a proper English picnic for the gentry. There were silver knives and forks, and Lowestoft plates and crystal. There were delicate little meat pies and quail in aspic and hothouse strawberries. And later when we lay back on our pillows, Philip told the tale of the King of Long Compton to Nell and me.

"Long, long ago, before the law of primogeniture, when right of kingship was won by skill at arms, a tribal leader rose. He was great and strong, and he had dreams of ruling not only Long Compton but all of England. In those days, you know, we were not one kingdom. Each area had its own, or rival, kings."

"Just as there are rival queens at times now," Nell murmured.

Philip shot her a sharp look and went on. "Up from Oxfordshire he came, with his supporting army and five malcontent knights who were already plotting treason. And at the top of Rollright Ridge he met a witch. This area has always been known for witches, you know," he added casually. "She challenged him, if he wished her help in his enterprise, to take seven long strides:

> " 'If then Long Compton thou canst
> see,
> King of England shalt thou be.'

"The king laughed, for he knew he was on the highest point of land, and Long Compton lay directly below in Warwick valley. Leaving his army sitting in a circle, turning his back on the treacherous knights, he strode forward, confident that the prize he sought was about to drop by magic into his grasp."

Philip sprang to his feet with a grandiose gesture.

> " 'Stick, stock, stone!
> As King of England I shall be
> known!' "

"What happened?" Nell demanded breathlessly.

Philip froze, then he turned round, an enigmatic expression on his face. "In so doing, he must have committed an offense against the Old Ones. As he took his seventh step, a long barrow of earth—some say it was the witch herself, or that it was a rock outcropping he had not noticed—rose before him. And he heard the witch's voice sing out:

" 'As Long Compton thou canst not
see,
King of England thou shalt not be.
Rise up, stick, and stand still, stone,
For King of England thou shalt be
none.
Thou and thy men hoar stones shall be,
And I myself an eldern tree.' "

He swung his arm in an all-inscribing arc. "And so, behold! We sit within the circle of the King's Men, endlessly waiting. There to the southeast stand the Whispering Knights. And there alone, across the road, the King Stone, eternally watching over the kingdom that cannot be his."

He ceased, and a silence fell like autumn leaves inexorably drifting down.

"What offense had he committed?" I asked.

Philip shrugged. "A few against the laws of practicality, if not those of the Old Religion. One does not, if one has sense, turn one's back on potentially dangerous subordinates.

And he leaped to conclusions, taking for granted that because he stood on Rollright Ridge the view was clear. He neither checked upon the possible natural risks nor made allowances for acts of gods."

"But there was more." The words came from deep within myself. "You said, did you not, that the power of kingship had to be earned by proof and testing of the claimant's qualities? He wanted it to come to him by magic—without effort, without personal investment. He wasn't willing to pay the price of entering into his inheritance and making it his own."

Philip looked at me sharply, then turned away and was very silent.

Nell's eyes were looking off into some private vision. "That is the secret, isn't it?" She said slowly. "Whenever one longs for something, longs for it more than life itself—one has to be willing to pay the price."

I did not speak, and we remained thus in silence, locked in our private worlds yet joined, too, by our experiencing these revelations at the common moment.

Philip was regarding me with quiet eyes. "You feel it too, don't you? The peacefulness. I told you that this place was sacred.

It's a touchstone. One can know the truth here, however terrible, and not be afraid."

"As at Wychwood." It came again, that other voice from within myself.

Philip frowned slightly. "But with a difference. Wychwood House is an island, not a mountaintop. Its peace is that of the hurricane's eye, but the storm swirls round its walls."

"You are being quite fantastical."

Philip shook his head. "I wish I were. It's much more fun to make up fantasies than to have them real. You've felt it, haven't you? The quality of our village air? It seems so light and clear, but it's like a weight. It has imbibed the dark poisons of the forest. The air in a spellbound village is narcotic."

"But not in my garden," Nell said gently. "And that's in the very shadow of the forest. There the air is clear."

"Not clear. Laden with fragrances mysterious and rare, evoking bright images from illumined manuscripts." Philip was off on one of his poetic flights, but his tone was somber. "Even there, you know, there are mysteries that you know not of."

"I could learn," Nell said.

Philip laughed. "Stay with your blessed

ignorance, my child. You'll be better off. That which can cure can also kill, and vice versa."

"Perhaps sometimes the kill's the cure." Nell's eyes were far away. She shut them tight and shuddered.

"That's undoubtedly how the old hags of the forest got known both as *wicca*—the wise ones—and as witches. They knew how to use the earth's bounty either for good or ill. No doubt they occasionally, intentionally or otherwise, got it mixed." Philip stirred restively and shot Nell one of his wicked looks. "You *could* learn the secrets, I imagine. If you had the courage. And if you weren't afraid to pay the price."

"Are you?" Nell looked at him directly. Her dark eyes had that gold fire Philip had once called the mark of the Children of the Sun. For some reason it fascinated him; he seemed unable now to look away. It was Nell who dropped her eyes at last, and she was trembling.

It was not difficult to accept the concept of an older, intuitive era right here at Rollright. There was peace in this primordial ring of stones, though whether it was the peace of God or the earthly peace that comes from its having endured these thousand years, I was too close to tell. And from this place it was possible to look not only across three counties but across our lives with a detached reality of which one was incapable in our own village.

How often a teacher ends by being taught, how often the young and innocent can reveal more than they know. I opened my eyes, feeling a swell of protective affection toward them both, and was transfixed.

Philip was lying with his head pillowed in Nell's lap. She was smoothing his dark waves of hair with such naked tenderness in her face that it hurt to watch. Her defenses all were down, but he did not see. He was gazing off across the circle and his eyes were filled with a torment that was like physical pain.

III

THE CORDS ARE CAST

11

Rossford-under-Wychwood
October 31, 1863

AFTERWARD those two days were to shine sun-bright in my memory, for from then on, the autumn darkness fell. The next day, Saturday, was grey and cold, as though the false summer had never been. Nell was aching, trying to drown her discomfort in reading. I harvested great bundles of herbs for drying, and then searched the bookshelves on the trail of Katherine Parr. How little there was to find surprised me. She seemed to be regarded by historians as the least as well as the last of Henry's wives: a woman he had wed for neither lust nor heirs nor politics. She had been twice widowed before becoming queen, and her later marriage to Seymour was scarcely even mentioned. An aristocrat, a humanist, a scholar, she seemed an odd candidate for elopement and scandal. The dull word-portraits bore little resemblance, either, to the warm and gracious presence I had sensed at Sudeley and at Wychwood. Clearly, there must be more to this Katherine Parr—Katherine the Queen, KP, as she signed herself—than the world discerned.

While I was deep in my research, Amy Ross appeared. She did look sick and her eyes were feverish. I regarded her with some surprise. "I thought you were supposed to be still in bed."

"I climbed down the ivy trunk outside my window," Amy said astonishingly. "Please, please, Miss Jardine, how is Nell? I heard she wasn't well, and I had to know."

"You're a good friend, aren't you, Amy?" I said gently. "But you must not worry. Why, Amy, dear, what's wrong?"

For the child, as though all the strength was gone from her, was leaning against the newel post sobbing bitterly. "It's so awful," she mumbled through her tears. "Nell gets worse, and I feel so bad . . . It's all my fault."

"Oh, dear, of course it's not. I admit I'm stern with you when you tell Nell tales that trouble her, but that's not why she's ill. It's her poor back, and that's naught to do with you."

"But it is." Amy turned toward me a face

of abject unhappiness. "Don't you understand? Up at school . . . I was the one who told . . ."

I was dumbfounded. "The *Bedliston* School?"

Amy nodded miserably. "The letter she wrote you . . . I was made to tell. And then Nell was sent to her room, and fell." A convulsive shudder ran through her little body.

I had a stab of prescience. "Was it you who tried to help her, in the courtyard afterward?"

"I didn't mean to hurt her, Miss Jardine! Nell asked me to, she wanted no one there. But then she couldn't walk . . ." Amy dissolved into an incoherence of sobs.

"And you never told me," I said slowly. "We came here, and neither of you told me."

"I was afraid to. Mama would be so grieved, and you—you'd not want to teach me." She gulped. "Nell said it would be all right, that she'd not tell. Only it's all got worse. I've been so wicked . . ."

"Oh, darling, darling." I knelt and took her in my arms. "It's all right. You've tried to do what's right. Of course you can study here. Don't you know that I've begun to love you?

Now dry your eyes and run up and tell Nell there's no need to worry."

"Oh, yes, ma'am," Amy whispered. The kitten, Hecate, twisted round her ankles, and she gave a muffled squeak and ran upstairs, leaving me much to think on.

I turned back to my research, but could not concentrate; my mind kept darting in fragmented directions. The faint murmuring of voices came from upstairs—how fortunate for both girls that they were friends, but Amy needed love and reassurance more than I'd realized. I should have made sure Amy would not pass on to Nell the accusations made against me in the Wychwood fields. But how was it possible, even with all the care in the world, to protect Nell from reality? Was it even right? I must find a way, better than I'd devised, to protect her physically, at least. The ease with which the henyard had been broken into proved my iron bars were not a sure defense, and that moment in the Wychwood fields, surrounded by the threatening men, had brought home shockingly the need to fear. The best security of all would be to find the treasure. I could not escape the conviction that the attacks on me, the attempts to drive us out, were linked with someone's determination to claim the token and Wychwood House—Wychwood House, which we would have to leave if we did not solve its secret, and the months were passing fast; Wychwood House, which could prove too cold and damp for Nell in an English winter . . .

"You have stared at that page for ten minutes and not seen a word." The voice was Philip's; he was standing against the door in the paneling, regarding me with a superior smile.

"How did you get in?"

"It's not difficult. I've watched you work the catch from outside several times."

"I must have a bolt put upon that door at once."

Philip's face fell. "Please don't. There's no need. I'm the only one who knows the passage through the yew hedge, and I swear I'll never enter without knocking first and being sure you're here. If you put a bolt on, I'll know you do not trust me." Then, in a lightning change of mood, "Why should you? It's stupid of me to expect it."

But it mattered to him; I knew it did. One of the realizations which had come to me on Rollright Ridge was that Philip was beginning to regard me with that adoration the young so often focus on sympathetic teachers. He was so starved for approval and encouragement that I dared not risk making him feel unwanted.

"I shall think about the door." I smiled at him. "We seem to be quite popular with your family today. Your mother kindly sent down some strawberries for Nell, and your sister is upstairs."

Philip's eyebrows shot up. "Amy's here? I want to see Nell, too, may I?" He shot up the stairs without waiting for my answer.

I worried about what was happening up there, and when I realized Georgina was lingering after carrying up Nell's tea, I went to fetch her. Amy looked frightened when I entered, and both Philip's eyes and Nell's were overbright. I looked at them with some dismay, but it was to Georgina that I spoke, and firmly. "Go downstairs at once, and attend to dinner."

Georgina slid out, and I turned to Philip in the silence. He at least ought to have exercised responsibility. He knew it, too; he quailed and spoke rapidly. "Don't look so. Gina was only telling foolish tales, no more. There's no harm in them, is there, girls?"

Nell and Amy nodded quickly, and Philip raised one eyebrow in that way he had of trying to cover up discomfiture. "You had better go to church tonight. It's All Souls' Eve, you know, and the rector will be having his annual attempt at exorcising shades. You might find it beneficial."

Not for anything would I permit the children to discover the uneasiness the little church aroused in me. I attended services regularly on Sunday mornings, but the rapid heartbeat, the difficult breath and the awareness of pressing evil were always with me. Although I had learned to create a quietness within for meditation, I had no desire to experience the church at night. I said aloud, "I certainly would not leave Nell."

"Oh, but you must," Nell said, surprisingly. "Please, Camilla! It's such a special service and I'd so love to see it. *You* must go, for me. You're so interested in history, anyway. And it could be . . . good."

Her eyes were fixed on mine with a curious appeal. I wondered if she were trying not to cling to me too completely. I, too, ought to be brave enough to test myself. "Perhaps," I said slowly. But I knew I would.

Georgina served dinner in sulky silence, and then left. Philip and Amy, of course, had long since gone. Nell's eyes were still too bright, but when she saw me watching her, she smiled. "I'm all right, truly. You must go to the church, I want you to." She added, half shyly, "I shall feel better knowing you are there."

In the street beyond our half-drawn curtains, lanterns moved. Villagers crossed the footbridges on their way to church. I could hear, faintly, the sound of children's voices, the soft padding of the local dogs.

Nell snuggled down, giving me a drowsy smile. "You needn't even look in on me on your return. I shall be fast asleep."

I locked the doors behind me carefully. The night was cold and a slight wind whipped my cloak. In the darkness, figures stirred amid a murmur of voices and flickering lanterns. No one spoke to me, and if glances were turned in my direction, it was too dark to see. I followed the little procession through the lych gate, up the path and into the sanctuary, and slipped into my customary pew. The church was cold, for dampness lingered in its stone walls. But its shadows fell softly, and in the night its candles and incense seemed like notes of grace. Perhaps, I thought, I am simply becoming inured to evil. I shook my head at my own cynicism.

The pattern of ritual, the comforting words of the old service welled around me. *Lighten our darkness, we beseech thee, O Lord; and by thy great mercy defend us from all perils and dangers of this night.* And from the dangers into which the mind can wander; from fear of the unknown, of that which cannot be understood; fear of the future, fear of freedom, fear of not enduring. I thought of Nell, webbed in despite my love and warmth by the shadows of old loneliness and suffering. Of Philip, who could be as doomed to stone as his legendary King of Long Compton. Of Amy, locked in diffidence; of Georgina, trapped by ignorance and superstition. Of Nell, caught in the prison of her affliction—I must accept that reality and not cling to false, debilitating hopes. I closed my eyes and prayed for Nell, and for us all.

From all evil and mischief; from sin; from the crafts and assaults of the devil; from thy wrath, and from everlasting damnation . . . From all blindness of heart; from pride, vainglory, and hypocrisy, from envy, hatred, and malice, and all uncharitableness . . . From all inordinate and sinful affections; and from all the deceits of the world, the flesh, and the devil . . . From lightning and tempest; from earthquake, fire and flood; from plague, pestilence, and famine; from battle and murder, and from sudden death, Good Lord, deliver us.

Oh, yes, the Church knew all about human weakness, about calamity natural and unnatural. Little wonder that the walls of this small parish edifice gave off an energy that was disturbing. For a thousand years they had held within them the struggle between the forces of good and the "principalities and powers of the Evil One." The church knew all about possession. *Possession.* My mind involuntarily formed the word.

The litany was ended. The organ came to life with the same tune that had assailed my ears that evening in the churchyard, and involuntarily my eyes lifted to the stained-glass window. So it was I alone who saw, perhaps, a fleeting image as the congregation was engrossed in straggling to its feet.

During the service the great apocalyptic window above the altar had been just so much opaque dark. Now, at the instant my eyes lifted, something made two of the cataclysmic figures spring to vivid life. An angel, arms outstretched; a grasping demon. They seemed to move as lights behind them flickered. Only a moment, then the window shrank back again into dark.

I found myself sitting in the pew, my heart pounding, while all about me people were on their feet and singing. Somewhere out on the hillside behind the church, a light had been moving. That it had come at that particular moment, from that particular distance, that particular slant, had been pure chance. But I reeled from it as from some physical blow.

Faintly, above the music, I heard dogs barking. The hymn concluded; there was a benediction. We stepped out into the aisles, and I was grateful for Laura's quick hand on my arm, her soft face smiling. "Camilla, I'm so glad you came. My dear, are you all right? You seem quite pale."

"I have a headache."

"It's that incense. Camilla, stop at Quinn Cottage for a moment, can you? Goodness me, what ails those dogs?"

"Something happening up in cemetery," a voice said behind us, and Laban Greene elbowed his way past with the curtest nod.

Laura frowned. "Oh dear. We'd better see—there's been talk . . ." Her voice trailed off as she hurried out toward the side path, with me behind her.

"Miss Jardine." Charles Roach was pushing toward me but I did not stop, for an unaccountable uneasiness gripped me. The crowd of churchgoers had fallen silent, as though struck suddenly to stone like the knights on Rollright Ridge. So it was that I, still moving, with Laura and Charles Roach beside me, burst through their midst and had a clear view across the cemetery to the grave circle on the hill.

The world whirled. It was happening again; I had seen it all before. The same fire, the same ring of figures, moving torches, flash of a knife. The same view through flames, and seeing the eyes of an alien stranger in a familiar face. With the shock of recognition, I was a child again on the plantation, meeting my shadow self and needing desperately to run away.

I could not run; I was hemmed in by movement. Laban Greene's voice cried out, the figures on the hillside scattered, and the spell was broken. They were not the same figures; they were smaller, whiter; I was an adult, in an English village; and I thought that I would faint.

Laura was all concern. "Camilla, come sit down. Or let me take you home."

"No! I want to find out what is happening."

"Nothing's happening. It's all over now. Isn't it?" Laura appealed to Charles Roach, but he shook his head.

"Is it?"

The fire, the torches had been put out. The dogs had ceased to bark. The men were returning from the grave circle with an inexorable tread. The rector, moving forward to meet them, was blocked by Laban Greene.

"Us told you they was bad powers working in our midst. Happen so you're too pure of mind, or too stone-stubborn, to recognize that some among us is calling up the Old Ones under your very nose?" He thrust out his hand, and on his callused palm lay a heavy knife. Its black handle had the look of a bizarre cross, curiously carved. I stared at it, feeling ice invade my bones.

"Ei-ai-ei-ai-ei-ai . . . !" The sound, half moan, half keening, caused even Laura to whisper a shocked, involuntary "Oh, dear God."

A woman stumbled past us, clutching at the rector with a kind of guttural sobbing. "It be Aaron! Be my Aaron, can't rest, can't sleep . . . and for why? For th' righteous bezoms won't let'm be forgiven. You have to given'm peace . . ." It was Widow Lee, her words disintegrating into incoherence.

The rector was leading her, gently, toward the church. Men began gathering round Laban Greene, moving toward the bridge, toward the Copper Maid. Mothers were wrapping shawls around big-eyed children, hurrying them home. It was over, it was all over, but memory heavy with implication licked at my mind like an uneasy tide.

Laura put an arm around me. "Come for coffee. You need it. You look chilled to death."

Thank God, Nell was in bed and safe asleep. I should go home, but instead I followed Laura to Quinn Cottage, and sat in the wing chair where she placed me, wrapped in an afghan, and gradually the numbness wore from my icy bones.

Both Dr. Quinn and Laura avoided reference to the cemetery incident until I said with weary bluntness, "You needn't be so kind. I'd really rather talk about what's going on."

Laura poked the fire grimly. "I knew sooner or later something like this would happen. The rector's a dear soul and a devoted priest, but Laban's right, he does prefer not to see what's staring him in the eyes. He ought, of course, to say right out that this sort of thing's blasphemous and unchristian. But he just smiles gently and points out that being able to accommodate itself with local superstition has always been one of the geniuses of the Church."

"Accommodate itself to what?"

Laura quoted the litany. " 'Hatred and malice, and all uncharitableness.' Not to mention evil mischief."

"You mean dabbling in witchcraft." There, I had said it out. Laura swept that aside. "I'm not worried about invocations and ring-dances. Tonight was undoubtedly just Rafe Smith and some quarry roughs having fun. I'm talking about corrosion of the spirit, the sowing of distrust. To selfishly play on ignorant superstition, to take advantage of your inexperience—" She stopped abruptly.

"If you are talking about the rumor that I caused what happened to those sheep," I said carefully, "I've already heard it."

Laura lifted her hand, than let it fall. "Oh, my dear. I was hoping you would not. It will die out quickly. It's so stupid, really."

"Is it?" I said tightly. "To ignorant, superstitious, easily influenced minds? A woman comes, dressed in black, to a house reputed to be haunted. With a crooked black kitten, a sister with a twisted back."

"And an odd assortment of friends," Laura added. "Each of us twisted, too, in the eyes of the common mind."

The "differentnesses," I thought; the crippling or imprisonment of the psyche of which I'd been thinking when I'd prayed in church.

"Oh, my dear, you must not take it so." Laura knelt to put her arms around me. "It will pass, it will wear away. Such things always do."

I shook my head. "Has it ever occurred to you that some of the tales *are* true? That someone is working spells, summoning the Old Ones . . . The incident tonight, it wasn't just an innocent circle game. You see, I know . . ." My voice drained off. They were looking at me with a tolerant kindness; they could not, or would not, understand.

I don't know what we talked of for the balance of my visit. A curious numbness seemed to have afflicted me. Laura offered to walk me home, to stay with me, but I shook my head. I moved across the common like a sleepwalker, and the darkness did not affright me. I had drawn within myself.

If I had found a message on my doorstep, I should not have been surprised, but there was none. The house was locked and dark and still, and when I had let myself in I went up the stairs without even bothering to light a lamp.

It was not until I was in my own room, pulling off my clothes, that I heard a sound. It came from Nell's room, and she was weeping. I was with her in an instant, getting a match to the bedside candle with trembling fingers. At once it threw out a frail glow, like Shakespeare's "good deed in a naughty world." Nell was huddled face down on the far side of the bed, her slight body bent and tense with the effort of holding back the shuddering sobs. I took her in my arms at once, and though she cried out with the pain of being moved, she clung to me.

"I shall never be able to walk again, ever, shall I? That's the price I have to pay for living through the fall. I must just lie here, with you to care for me, forever . . ."

It had come home to her at last, the reality of her fate. And I, holding her in arms aching with pity, remembering what she had begged me about being honest, could not tell a kindly lie.

Nell's anguish drove, just temporarily, the cemetery moment from my mind. But when at last she was asleep, memory returned to confront me squarely.

Two memories, two recognitions, two knots in the cord that was binding Wychwood House and the village ever tighter in a spell of conflict. If I was right, there were not separate mysteries here, but only one.

That knife, carried by furious Laban Greene from the grave circle where he'd found it. He had held it for just one moment in the lantern light, but in that instant I had seen what I had seen. Had noticed more than one normally might in so brief a time, because I had seen just such a knife before—nailing a slaughtered cock against my door. And on this second seeing I had realized why something then had seemed disturbingly familiar. The carving, the crude symbols, bore a marked resemblance to the ones chiseled on the stones of the gypsy graves.

And then . . . the face. In that motionless moment, as in the earlier experience of childhood, my eyes by some fate had met other eyes I knew. I had felt the pull, as of a common cord, across the yards between; had recognized, for the second time in my life, a power-filled stranger in my own familiar servant.

Laura might be right that Raphael Smith was the moving spirit behind tonight's attempted ritual in the cemetery. But the face that I had seen had been Georgina's.

12

Rossford-under-Wychwood
November, 1863

I ROSE the next morning in a kind of stoic fatalism, and went to morning church. It was not easy.

The previous night stirred the rector into a stinging rebuke of those who would traffic with the principalities and powers of darkness. "And do not think I refer alone to circles and to candles and to pentagons," he thundered. "Those are but the outer trappings of an inner sickness. Idleness, jealousy, covetousness—*these* are the handmaids of the evil one. 'Put on the whole armour of God, that ye may be able to stand against the wiles of the devil. For we wrestle not against flesh and blood, but against principalities, against powers, against the rulers of the darkness of the world, against spiritual wickedness in high places. Wherefore take unto you the whole armour of God, that ye may be able to withstand in the evil day, and having done all, to stand.' "

Having done all, to stand. I had not done all my duty, not half enough. I had not yet ensured Nell's safety, or security. I had not found the treasure. I was imbued with a sense of futility, a sense of failure. I knew too little, and too much—could recognize that the Old Religion was being deliberately revived, but could not stop it or make others understand.

I could not close my eyes to the realities I'd recognized in the fields, in the cemetery. But oh, how I longed to—and realizing my own cowardice was the greatest shock of all. Yet an outsider must needs tread lightly; I stood, as it were, on a rock in quicksand, where any step I took might easily cause harm.

To do nothing could be the greatest harm.

Georgina, so ignorant and so suggestible, could not know as I did the dangers she was risking. I had seen her last night, just as I had recognized the knife. If I kept silent, I made myself in a way responsible for whatever followed. And even had I no concern for Georgina's welfare, I must think of her influence on Nell.

My thoughts were running in circles, going nowhere. I wiped my brow wearily and tried to concentrate on the rector's prayers, but I could find no peace. By the time the service was over I had, however, come to one conclusion. I needed to verify my data. My thinking was woolly because I was leaping to assumptions based on memories alone, was allowing subjective experience to interfere with objectivity. I might be sure that ancient practices were being revived and blamed on me, but I had not yet proved it.

For that, at least, I did know where to start. I had to go back to the source, to a Book of Shadows. If I was right, somewhere in this village there must be one. The logical place to look for the odd, rare literary curiosity was on Lady Kersey's shelves.

Nell was still asleep when I reached home, and the house was cold. Georgina, when she arrived, was subdued and inclined to avoid my company. So much the better; I had not yet determined how I'd deal with her. I set her to building up fires and heating soup for Nell, told her we'd not dine till evening, and then locked myself in Kersey's Room to search the shelves.

It was a discouraging business, the more so because I felt impelled to work alone. A damp chill was seeping through the walls and threatening rain, and even the fire roaring up the chimney did little to dispel it. Today I did not allow myself the luxury of browsing. Take out a book, leaf through it swiftly, replace and draw out the next; one shelf after another, climbing upward, till the ceiling was reached and it was time to move the ladder. I paused briefly over a treatise on Cotswold architecture, then put it by reluctantly. By four o'clock my arms were aching and I was forced to admit defeat. There was no Book of Shadows here. It had been only an improbable hope at best.

Rain had commenced falling in a steady monotonous rhythm, running off gargoyle downspouts to splash relentlessly into the street. Wetness was forming a strange cabalistic pattern on the wall beside the chimney. How did one go about repairing leaks in thatch? Charles Roach would simply have to make the trust fund cover that. I found myself glancing out the window in the thought that Jeremy might be coming by, but only the rain and a silent village met my gaze. I stretched, rubbing the back of my neck, and went to check on Nell. She was awake, lying among the pillows like a tired, sad Madonna. Even the featherbed seemed no defense against the clammy dampness. Something had to be done about the cold and the leaking roof. For now, the best I could do was get her downstairs by the fire.

While we were having our tea, Philip appeared within the shadows. "You did not have the bolt put on the panel, after all." He sounded pleased, but his manner was low and somber, as though he were webbed in by his private ghosts. He dropped down on the hearth fender and began cracking nuts for Nell, tossing the empty shells into the flames.

"What smells so splendid? Like all the perfumes of Arabia."

"I put some cinnamon bark and dried balm on the fire."

"No wonder persons suspect you of making magic." I made an involuntary gesture, and he looked at me. "They do, you know. Especially since that business with the sheep, and now last night. 'Never such happenings hereabouts till furrin wummin come, wi' her books an' queer learnin.' How does it feel to be thought a sorceress? *I* should find it quite exciting."

"That's because it's not you. I'd give a good deal to discover who's behind those rumors."

"Better not," Philip said soberly. "One's better off, sometimes, not knowing things, but one never discovers that until too late."

I knew that feeling; it was the one I'd had when as a child I'd read the Book of Shadows. I glanced at Philip sharply, wondering what experience he was thinking of. He had moved off restlessly, and Nell was watching him. After a while she held out her hand, and he gave her a crooked smile and went to sit beside her.

It was all a quiet Sunday in early winter ought to be, but I was filled with a sense of loneliness, of isolation, and the conflicts which had haunted me since last evening still lingered unresolved within my mind.

Sometime during the night the rain ceased, and by morning a wan November sun poked through the grey. Nell was stiff and aching, and when Amy arrived she looked as though she had not slept either. Her chocolate-brown dress with its rows of fine pin-tucking would have made Nell glow, but it only accentuated Amy's pallor, and her dark hair hung limply from its band of black satin ribbon. There were yellow-grey shadows like bruises underneath her eyes. I exclaimed involuntarily, "Why, Amy, child, are you ill?"

"Oh, no, Miss Jardine," she whispered quickly. "But Nell, is Nell all right?"

"She's suffering from the cold and damp, of course, but she'll be glad to see you. She's in the sitting room; you go right on in."

I smiled at her, but she lingered, her eyes darting nervously about. "Please, Miss Jardine." Her fingers plucked at my sleeve. "May I—I've got to ask you something. You mustn't be angry. Please!"

"Of course I shan't be angry." I took the child's hands and gave them a reassuring squeeze. "You can ask me anything you like, anytime you like. That's what a teacher's for. Do you believe me?" She nodded. "Then, what is it, dear?"

"Miss Jardine, please—is it true that you're a witch?"

Her face was so solemn, and so breathless, that I almost laughed aloud. But I dared not, for obviously the rumors had reached Amy and had troubled her. I must handle this lightly, calmly, so she would believe the matter was nothing over which to take alarm.

I was wearing the jet cross Martin had given me—a cross, the universal symbol of God's protection from all evil. I lifted it, smiling. "Of course, that's why I wear this. So you see, I'm quite safe. You need not fear. Now run along inside, Nell's waiting for you."

Our lessons did not go very well that day. They had been better lately; both girls had memorized their Greek alphabet and were well into the fifth declension in their Latin. Amy would never have Nell's quicksilver mind, but she strove diligently, with a rather touching desire to please. Today, however, work went slowly, and I was unable to spur any discussion from either of the girls. Perhaps it was because I was preoccupied myself; my personal concerns were interfering with my concentration. At last I gave up, assigned the girls a composition in their copybooks, and sat thinking my own thoughts as they wrote. The small monograph on Cotswold architecture was lying near and I picked it up idly.

Tithe barns . . . Jane Seymour's reception, at her wedding to Henry VIII, had been held in the family's tithe barn down in Wiltshire. What splendid edifices those old tithe barns were. There had been the ruined shell of one at Sudeley, dating back to long before Katherine's day. *Talluts* . . . that was the name given to the right-angled out-shots such as housed our still-room. Often, apparently, increasing prosperity had led to their being made two stories high, although that had not happened here; there was no additional room behind Nell's bedroom. Some of these old houses had hidden chambers, early lofts or storerooms which had completely vanished from sight as new wings were added on. I wished we had something of that nature here; I would feel safer than sleeping in an unguarded house. My fear was growing more and more strong each night.

I left the room to fetch the girls a treat of milk and cookies; I was using every excuse these days to get Nell to eat, for her appetite was poor. As I returned, I heard the murmur of their voices, quite intent, but they broke off quickly as I entered. Perhaps I ought to have pursued it, I do not know. I let the moment pass. And after lessons ended and Amy left I decided I needed fresh air and activity. There were yet some herbs unharvested for winter, if the rain had not ruined them. I put on a heavy cloak, took up basket and clippers, and went out into the walled garden.

The rain had left deep pools of standing water, and many of the smaller plants were ruined. The pointed leaves of mint and balm had turned to rust, but mugwort and wormwood still lifted their tall feathers. I cut quickly, intent upon my task, trying not to think or to look beyond the yew hedge to the grave circle on the hill. How bleak and oppressive it was here, with the summer gone. The forest rose dark and somber, and even the faceless walls of my own house seemed threatening. There were no windows on this side, save for the small quatrefoil high under the eaves.

The quatrefoil beneath the eaves. Strange it had never struck me to investigate that small window from within. Where was it, anyway? Not in Nell's room; there were no casements facing on the forest. The attic, then? But Nell's room itself had an attic's sloping roof.

My eyes wandered idly to the chimney with its rows of pots. How endearingly English was this construction method of miniature chimneys within the great one. Smoke rose from four pots: Kersey's Room, the still-room, the upper hall, Nell's chamber. Other rooms used the chimneys at center or far side of the house.

There was another, fifth chimney pot here from which no smoke rose.

I stood staring at it, and an unreasoning, excited giddiness rose within me. I had just been reading of "lost rooms" in these old houses. A chimney, a window unaccounted for—what could be more likely than that a house of secrets, of a hidden garden and a door-concealing panel, should have a chamber concealed within its walls as well?

I ran inside, banging the panel shut, and up to Nell.

"For goodness sake, what is it?" Nell pushed herself up quickly, and her voice sparked. "Have you found something? Camilla!"

"I think so. I don't know." My eyes darted rapidly around the chamber. It should be there in the chimney wall, so the two fireplaces, as downstairs, could share a single trunk. The bedroom walls were for the most part stucco, with timbered beams, but on either side of the fireplace were carved panels. I rapped them with my knuckles, and they sounded hollow.

"No. Wait." I flew to the door, shut it, turned the key. The last thing I wanted was Georgina coming in. Then back to the panels, to explore the familiar motifs with trembling fingers.

"Here's a letter opener," Nell urged. "Try prying at the cracks."

"I don't want to damage anything. This

Lancaster rose looks carved more deeply than the rest." I tugged at it, and it came off in my hand, revealing a finger-hole. Thrust in; pull; the panel opened. There was an empty cupboard behind it, that was all. The most careful examination, by fingertips with lamp held close, showed nothing more.

"Not even a scrap of paper," Nell murmured in dismay.

"There may be a matching cupboard on the other side." I found the hidden catch more easily this time. And now our careful searching was rewarded. This back wall was more skilfully furnished than the other, but there was a knothole that did not look quite right. It took strength and deftness, and the paper-knife, to dislodge the plug. A small door, shoulder-high, swung inward into darkness.

"Hold the lamp up," Nell whispered, and we gazed into a small square room. "Camilla, please, I have to see it," and I nodded. I undid my hoop petticoat, stepped out of it, scooped her up, and squeezed us through into a little chamber filled with a poignant quietness. There was a small carved bed with quilted coverlet, a narrow chair, a chest. It had an air of touching tidiness, though all was veiled with a faint grey film of dust. In the side wall, facing toward the garden, was the quatrefoil window.

"There's writing on the glass," Nell whispered.

I laid her on the bed and moved toward the window eagerly. The writing was Latin, and my mind translated swiftly the Catullus poem:

> I hate and love, Why . . . I do not
>   know, but
> I feel it, and I am in torment.

Someone knew her classics. *Katherine*, my heart told me. And perhaps as well, a clue to our hidden treasure.

Never had I felt so close, so hopeful of finding it. Never had I looked so diligently. But after two hours of exploring every inch of the room's surface with lamp and fingers, I turned to Nell, and all my bright confidence had vanished. "I'm sorry," I said gently.

"I'm glad we found this chamber, all the same." Nell's eyes traveled around the serene small room. "I should like to sleep here."

It was the first thought that had flashed across my mind: here at last was a secret place in which Nell could be hidden, safe, any time I had to leave her in the house alone. Or safe at night, if anyone should try to break in while we slept. That night-fear was never far from the corners of my mind. I at least could run from intruders, but Nell could not.

"That might be a very good idea," I said carefully. "But you must not tell anyone. No one, not even Georgina. There is still the chance the treasure may be hidden here somewhere." I did not believe that, but I did not want Nell frightened by the real reason for my secrecy.

"You mean not tell Philip or Amy either."

"It would be best."

Nell nodded slowly. "It would not be wise, would it, to trust them with real secrets? Philip . . . likes to tell things. And Amy believes anything she hears."

There was such a note of troubled disillusion in her voice that I looked at her sharply. "What has she heard?" Nell would not meet my eyes, and I regarded her with a sinking heart. "Are you telling me Amy actually believes the stories going round about us?"

Nell was pleating the frill of her wrapper with meticulous precision. "She says you told her straight out you are a witch. That that's why you wear your black cross. We had quite a row about it."

I cursed myself for the stupidity of my clever answer.

"And then there's other things she's sure are proof," Nell went on reluctantly. "The medicines you make for me in the stillroom. The fact you burn four candles on the table when we read aloud at night."

"Where on earth does she hear these things?"

"The upstairs maid at the Manor has it from the kitchen maid." Nell and I looked at one another. Jo, the kitchen maid, was one of Georgina's cronies and kept company with Daniel Greene. "It's wicked," Nell said doggedly. "They oughtn't be allowed to speak of you that way."

"I do not think you need be troubled about further rumors starting," I said grimly. I left Nell and went downstairs, and my blood was boiling.

I found Georgina in the stillroom, poking among the jars. When she heard me she stopped as though the herbs had burned her, and backed off. I blocked her path. "Just a moment, Georgina."

Any other servant would by now have

been gabbling protestations of innocence. Georgina merely waited.

"I understand there are a good many rumors going round about the things we do here. I hope you realize that so long as you are in my employ, you are bound by a . . . a certain loyalty."

Georgina's eyes flickered uneasily. "No call to blame I for what folk think. How I to know what you'm do hereabouts?"

"You know, at any rate, certain things that I have *not* done. It was not *I* up at the grave circle on Saturday night." That stopped her dead. I seized my advantage boldly. "I saw you there, dancing around the bonfire. I recognized you, Georgina, and you know it."

Oh, that shook her. Georgina's eyes darted up, then down. She made no response, but two can play that game, and so I waited. Waited. Until at last she murmured sullenly, "Ye'll have told them, then."

"No, I have not. I wanted to hear your story first. Georgina, how could you? I know it must have seemed exciting. But it's unwise, if not downright dangerous. You gave your mother quite a fright, you know. She thought it was your father calling her."

Georgina shuddered, and then to my surprise two grimy tears trembled down her face. She dashed them off, her face stiff with pride. "What is it, Georgina?" I queried gently.

"Happen I have a right to be there, then. My da—my da lie there. That's gypsy graveyard. Dig a hole in the ground, they did, and put him in it, and never a prayer said over him, nor a blessing. Because him not baptized, and Rector say him kill himself. He never! And my mam walks the hills moaning and grieving, growing more and more foolish, acause why? Acause my da can't rest, she say, less'n somebody do for him, as is right and proper." She made a vicious gesture toward the church. "He won't do it. Happen the gypsies have own ways, and they just as good."

"Was that what you were trying to do last night, Georgina? Give rest to your father's spirit?" She did not answer, but she bowed her head. I patted her shoulder awkwardly, a lump in my throat. "Very well,. Georgina," I said at last. "We'll say no more. But you are not to carry off accounts of what takes place in Wychwood House, and there must be no further occurrences in the cemetery, do you understand? It is fine to want to do honor to your father, but the way you chose was not good at all. It causes fear and suspicion and could do real harm."

She was silent, and I thought to appeal to her better nature. "My sister is very troubled by the stories that have been going round. And I am grieved and disappointed, Georgina, that you yourself have seen fit to add to them. I've tried to be your friend, to help you. I've given you work and clothes; I'm teaching you to write and read."

"Happen some think that's a bad magic." Georgina looked at me at last, directly, and I sensed a pleading. "Bean't fitting a woman should know more than her man."

"Whom do you mean, Georgina? Raphael Smith?" A frightened truculence appeared in her face, and she did not reply. "Raphael was with you in the cemetery, wasn't he? He doesn't like my helping you, giving you new ideas. He's been spreading stories."

Fear flared in Georgina's eyes. "You'll not tell my mam? Oh, please, miss. She not trust Rafe, he too like my da. She say he come to same bad end. Bean't no chance for him here, less'n he break away and work in quarry. That's why he not want me to learn more than he."

"Raphael cannot read or write, is that it?" I looked at Georgina, and all at once my duty leaped out clear. I did not like Rafe, did not trust him, but what right had I to judge? The gradually emerging picture of these people's lives more than explained their superstition, their imprisonment in the past. Ignorance could indeed create a spellbound village.

This was the answer Katherine would have taught me. There was no way, after all, to disprove suspicions. One could only rise above, and bear witness to the real truth by acts of goodness. If my mission here drew me from the cloistered luxury of my beloved books into teaching the ignorant and unwashed, how dared I let personal distaste stand in the way? It was, certainly, a way of combining giving love and doing duty, for a teacher, as I well knew, had many chances for beneficient influence.

And so Rafe Smith, as well as Georgina, began to con the alphabet at the kitchen table. He came at night, when his day's work was done, wary and surly; but when I had showed him how to write simple numbers and to reckon sums, when he was able to put *Raphael Smith* boldly on the quarry work-sheet instead of marking an X, his guard dropped somewhat. On the evening he brought Daniel Greene along, I knew that I had won.

Next it was Georgina's little sister, Dorothea, and then Laura's Rosie, and Jo, the Manor kitchen maid. All this took a great deal of my time and an effort which was both a physical and spiritual drain. But there was something almost exhilarating about knowing that my labors were going to good purpose.

So November moved along in grey days and raw wet rain, and the winds of winter swept down with lashing force from Wychwood Rise. And in Kersey's Room, around the fire, my circle grew. Laura came often to sit and talk and sew, her feet warming on the hearth. Her father liked to drowse contentedly in the wing chair, occasionally startling us by droning out stanzas of poetry remembered from his student days. Jeremy appeared in the evenings when his work was done; he would sit and talk with Nell until the lessons of my "free scholars" were completed.

I remarked to him with some amusement, "One would almost think you were hovering here as a protector."

"Now that you mention it, that is not at all a bad idea."

"It's quite unnecessary. I'm overcoming my antipathy to Raphael Smith. There's no reason, really, for one to be afraid."

Jeremy started to say something, looked at me, and stopped. He took out his knife and commenced to whittle, whistling. The tune plagued me, and it was not till after he was gone that I recognized the nursery rhyme: *Who killed Cock Robin . . . ?*

I wished he hadn't done that. Charles Roach called, with a diffident correct formality, to ask if the glazier had satisfactorily repaired the broken window. He did not, to my secret relief, come when my "free school" was in session. I knew that he would not approve. My scholars themselves, perhaps through some embarrassment, kept the matter silent. Lady Margaret did not know, but Philip did, and he was not pleased.

"How can you let those persons impose on your valuable time!"

"I am glad to help them. Surely they have as much right to try to improve themselves as you."

It was an unfortunate remark. He wheeled on me. "I thought our studying together was special. But it wasn't, was it? You're just tearing round doing good so you can see yourself as Lady Bountiful. The people don't really matter to you at all."

The savagery and unfairness of the attack left me breathless. Then my brow cleared. "You must not worry. The others don't replace you; I will still have time—" But he was gone, through the hidden door. It was, in a way, rather reassuring to find that at heart Philip was just a young boy who resented sharing the attention of his teacher.

Winter settled like a still blanket over Wychwood, and the village and the disturbing forces within it slept. Nell grew steadily more frail. She had a touching sad serenity that tore my heart, but the spiritual struggle of attaining it had left upon her its indelible mark. She seemed—I do not know how to put it less fancifully—to dwindle, as though some sucking mouth was draining out her life.

I was counting on Christmas to kindle Nell's vitality again. As I stitched and knitted and compounded pomander and potpourri, I felt my spirits rise. Nell and Georgina, and Philip too, had assisted in cutting fruitcake fruits and nuts, which gave forth a wondrous fragrance when I turned them in their crocks of rum.

Philip, who was clever with his fingers,

introduced us to ornaments made of gilded walnuts, to quill-work snowflakes and lacy stars carved from the thinnest wood. Almost daily, as early twilight fell, I would look up and find him, his dark eyes shining, ready to show us some new contrivance for the Wychwood tree. He appeared one day with grand plans for a yule-log-cutting expedition in the forest.

"As soon as this snow stops. It must be special wood for a Christmas fire, you know. Preferably from a tree hung with mistletoe. That's the Old Ones' blessing."

I pointed to a big log in the corner. "We already have our yule log. Mr. Bushel brought it."

"Mr. Bushel, Mr. Bushel!" Philip burst out darkly. "Why do you let that fellow hang around so, monopolizing your time?"

"I thought you liked him."

"He's a good enough chap, but it's time he took himself back again to the city. Why does he want to stay around here, anyway? I wouldn't, not if I were free, as he is. I do think it's odd."

"He seems countryman enough. Look how he cured those sheep."

"And that's another odd thing," Philip

said. "He's a rare bird, is our Mr. Bushel." He wandered to the window and peered out. "It's snowing hard. The drifts in Manor drive will soon be waist-high."

"Then you'd best be off before it gets much worse."

"Do you think so?" Philip said innocently. "On the contrary, the storm may stop, and the wind abate, in a few more hours."

"Oh, let him stay to dinner," Nell said from her corner, laughing.

"Your mother will be worried."

"Maman has gone to Town to order Christmas gifts. She won't be back for three more days. And the servants," Philip finished with irony, "are used to my vanishing when she's away. So it does seem a shame to make me venture forth in all that storm."

I capitulated, glad to see Nell stirred to life. "Very well. We shall roast apples by the fire, and later we can string popcorn for the tree."

"And I shall tell you tales of Cotswolds Christmas." Philip was effervescent. "Christmas here is medieval, at the very least, and the Rossford Morris, our little local mummers' show, undoubtedly goes back to the Old Ones' time. It has all the traditional accoutrements, the Hobby-Horse, the Betty and the Fool. It's as pagan as the very devil, but nobody admits that."

Nell was watching him, her face intent. As if feeling her gaze, Philip shrugged self-consciously and moved away. "There's sleighbells outside. You've got more callers."

It was Jeremy, stamping snow off his heavy boots. "I've brought a ham from the Tarr Farm smokehouse to tide you over if you're housebound. You're not used to this sort of winter, I imagine. If you're having a party in there, I can be enticed to join you. It's bitter out."

"Stay for dinner," I invited recklessly. It was a night that called for friends round the fire and blazing logs. Georgina had made meat pie and oxtail soup. On impulse I sent her to the cellar to fetch some claret. Wychwood had a wine cellar that would have done credit to a medieval abbey, and I had found a recipe for a flaming bishop that I longed to try. It was just the night for it, and would be good medicine for the chill in my sister's bones.

It was a lovely, an absolutely perfect evening, everything I'd dreamed of when as a young girl I'd longed for England. I had Georgina set a table before the fire in

Kersey's Room, and we dined by candlelight. The honey-clove-and-cinnamon-flavored wine steamed on the hearth, and its scent alone had the power to intoxicate.

Jeremy was in one of his flamboyant moods. He held my chair and poured my cups of wine with a swashbuckling air, and Philip, after a few moments' observation, began to devote himself to Nell in a similar fashion. As for my sister—it was like having the old Nell back again, I thought with an overflowing heart. She sparkled, she coquetted, her eyes flashed their golden fire.

It pleased me to see Philip paying her those brotherly attentions, his dark head bent over her red-gold hair that glowed in the flickering light. What extraordinarily beautiful children they really were. Almost too beautiful to seem quite real, I thought hazily. That was the wine talking; I put my cup down firmly. They were extraordinary, Nell and Philip: exceptionally gifted in intellect and sensitivity, and so tragically afflicted. But here, in the warmth and magic of firelit circle, the handicaps were somehow mitigated and transcended. How blessed it would be if I could make that circle strong enough to sustain them and keep them safe. I felt Nell's questioning eyes upon me, and lifted my cup in a private salute, and smiled.

It was so intense that night, the sense of love and warmth, family and safety. Perhaps that is why, without realizing it, I dropped my guard. Philip was telling of village Christmas customs, wassailing and bell-ringing and candle-lighting, and Jeremy contributed memories of childhood Christmases in London when the goose hung high.

"Tell them all about Charleston," Nell prodded me, and I wove a spell of holidays in the Low Country, oyster stew and rice and benne seeds and New Year's calls.

"The Colonel, my stepfather, made a famous punch. It took him days to prepare it by himself, and he flamed it with brandy in a silver spoon." All at once it did not hurt any more to think of Charleston. Almost I could have been a girl again, in the happier childhood I had longed for. I threw back my head and laughed. "I always wondered why that punch was reputed the most popular in Charleston. One day I tiptoed down the stairs and took a taste, and then another, and another . . . and oh, did I regret it the next day!"

Jeremy was looking at me with approval. "Do that again."

"What—sneak the punch?"

"Laugh like that. It's refreshing," Jeremy said wickedly, "to find you're human, after all. Do you know, except for that day driving home from Sudeley, I've never seen you laugh?"

I protested, but he overrode me. "It's true. You are always so sedate, so very much Miss Jardine of Wychwood House. You could be forty-seven, at the very least. I wondered if a human heart beat somewhere beneath that inky armour. I've never known so young a body with so old a head!"

"Oh, she is human," Philip said with a superior air. "Though she's usually not quite so silly as she is tonight."

"It's the wine. It's muddled my wits, I think."

"Then I salute the wine. And I approve the silliness." Jeremy looked at Philip. "You know, young man, the ancients regarded the ability to be childlike on occasion as a gift of grace. That's what enthusiasm means, of course. *En theos*: in God."

Oh, he was not just a farmer, not with that education. As if sensing my thoughts, Jeremy turned to me, lifting his cup on high. "You remind me tonight of one of the Old Ones' deities. The Mother Goddess, the all-giving, all-perceiving. And the all-entrancing. Madam, when you allow yourself, you can be very witching."

"Don't say that." The words slipped from me involuntarily.

Jeremy looked at me. "Have I trod on a raw nerve? Do not fret, my sweet. There is good magic as well as bad, you know. You do have the glamour. The Stranger always does, you know, and you more than most. I've always thought one had a . . . duty, as you would put it, to use one's power for good ends and let the chips fall where they may. Provided, of course, that one does not become so bewitched by one's own power that the means become the ends." He lifted his wine cup, and I felt his knowing eyes watching me through the fragrant steam.

At length the storm abated somewhat, and Jeremy announced he would drive Philip to his door. Philip's face fell; he had, obviously, been hoping he could linger. Nell was very silent after they had gone. When I had tucked her in, I went back downstairs where the fire still burned, and moved quietly about, putting the gracious room in order. Such a lovely evening it had been, with all shadows held at bay. How good to see Nell happy, to watch Philip trying to copy, even outdo, Jeremy in savoir-faire. More than once, when Philip's youth betrayed him into some grandiloquence, my eyes had met Jeremy's in shared private laughter. As if we were a father and mother taking pleasure in our lovely children.

As if we were father and mother—I stopped, struck dumb.

Oh, Camilla, Camilla, how could you have been so blind? I gripped the back of a chair and leaned against it, trembling, but as the room whirled, two things stood sharply clear.

The part of me that felt and responded as a woman had not died with Martin, after all. It had only been slumbering, but I could no longer delude myself it was not perilously close to being wakened. And I didn't want it wakened. Everything in me that had ever loved and lost cried out against it. I wanted the safe, secure existence I had so carefully been carving out—studying, teaching, being a surrogate mother to the young I loved. If that made me an early-old forty-seven, then so be it. I wanted the quiet warmth, the measured heartbeat, not the fire and ice in which one froze or burned.

In willful or unconscious ignorance, secure in the protection of my mourning weeds, I had allowed Jeremy to come too close. I did not intend to make that mistake again.

13

Rossford-under-Wychwood
November, 1863

IT should not be difficult to dampen that intimacy which had too easily sprung up. I would be less free with hospitality, would spend my leisure in my upstairs chamber, telling Georgina to inform callers I was not at home. Jeremy Bushel would soon understand; he was not a fool.

That led inexorably to another question. Why had he devoted himself, like a craftsman patiently chipping away layers of stone, to piercing through my armor, winning my trust? I knew why; I had always known. Jeremy Bushel wanted to get into Wychwood House. He had done so through cultivating me when his earlier efforts to acquire the place had failed. There could be but one reason—Lady Kersey's treasure.

I had realized the night of the circle dancing that there were not separate mysteries in the village here, but one, like a rope made of three cords intricately intertwined. To unravel a rope, one could untangle any thread, and from either end. Had I pursued this, as reason and responsibility both dictated? No, I had shied away like a bedazzled girl.

Three threads, three clues: Katherine the Queen and her story, somehow involving both the token and Wychwood House; the attempts to drive me off; the outbreaks of the Old Religion, which were being blamed on me. Connecting all of these was the knife, the familiar knife, which had been carried off so casually—by Jeremy, who knew too much, who lived in a strange house where he compounded antidotes to witchcraft poisons.

And always, omnipresent, that sense of impending, overpowering evil. The irrational was no less real, less potent, than the rational. Deep within myself, I must have known it. Oh, Jeremy saw too far, he had put his finger directly on it—that was why I took refuge in being early-old, would not allow myself a woman's feelings. If I did, the walls of my ordered intellectual universe would come tumbling down.

Katherine Parr had learned that. Katherine's heart, for all her wisdom, had betrayed her into loving a man who was not worthy. I delved feverishly into the history of Katherine Parr; it felt a good deal safer than researching the Old Religion, as I ought to do. One can hardly be armed, after all, against something one does not understand. Sooner or later I would have to wrestle with the force that gripped me in the grave circle, in the church. But I was faced, flat, with the unpleasant realization that I was afraid.

Three days after our disturbing dinner, fate intervened to knock down the barriers of my disbelief. I had spent the afternoon reading a history of the Queens of England in my room, having told Georgina I was not at home to guests. I had uncovered a cryptic account of the young Princess Elizabeth being sent away from the Dowager Queen's household for some un-named transgression. It seemed to be another instance of Katherine's giving love to someone and having that trust betrayed.

After dinner, while we were reading by the fire, I finished my book and went to place it, not where I'd found it on an upper tier, but in a more convenient location on a lower shelf, near to the fireplace, where I had been installing the books of Tudor history. Nell, engrossed in her own reading, was not looking. I thrust the book in carelessly, my mind still preoccupied, and the volume jammed. Something, somehow, had become wedged behind the orderly row. I reached behind, probed with my fingers, and pulled it out. A slim, soft-covered, hand-sewn volume—I knew at once that it was very old. I must have made a sound, for Nell said immediately, "What is it, Camilla?"

"Nothing." Some deep impulse made me lie; made me, before I knew a reason, conceal the little booklet in a larger one. I sat down by the lamp on the carved table, and within the leather-bound larger volume, opened the brittle pages. It was a Book of Shadows.

Thank God, I found it, and not Nell, was my first thought. And the second, hard upon it: How did it come here? I was absolutely certain it had not been there when I searched the shelves but a few weeks before. Not there, nor anywhere else in Wychwood House. Someone had, deliberately, brought it here. As threat? As warning?

I shut the cover quickly and sat for a long time staring down at it. It was all there beneath my fingers, the proof of whether my suspicions were sick fancies only, or all too real. A voice rang in my ears like Old Testament conscience: ". . . be like gods, having the knowledge of good and evil." But another voice, too: "Ye shall know the truth, and the truth shall make you free." I turned the page.

I was back, at once, in that side of the Tudor world which I had so carefully been avoiding all these years. Tudor, and even older, stretching in unbroken chain back to the Old Ones and the Rollright stones. Words have power, I have always known that, and the words of the Book of Shadows wove a spell. Here were the rituals of Equinox and Solstice, here the Five-Fold Blessing, here the ceremony of Initiation and the mysterious Great Rite. I went from revulsion to a shocked fascination and beyond, to a shattering realization that even I, for all my armor of scholarship and Christian faith, could still respond. This was the Old Religion in pure form, stripped of outsiders' horror-filled surmise of Satanism, orgies and black rites. Despite aspects which offended and repelled me, it *was* religion, and had features in common with all genuine spiritual experiences—communion, exaltation, great beauty.

There were healing ceremonies involving the laying-on of hands, there were spells for bringing one in tune with nature. There was the Fire Festival of Samhain—that was what we must have witnessed up at the grave circle on Hallowe'en.

Dread Lord of Shadows, God of Life, and the Giver of Life . . .
Open wide the Gates through which all must pass.
Let our dear ones who have gone before return this night . . .

I shuddered, thinking of Georgina, and involuntarily my fingers groped for the black cross on my breast.

And the Five-Fold Blessing:

Blessed be thy feet, that have brought thee in these ways.
Blessed be thy knees, that shall kneel at the sacred altar.
Blessed be thy womb, without which we should not be.
Blessed be thy breasts, formed in beauty.
Blessed be thy lips, that shall utter the sacred names.

It was beautiful, and it was very pagan. Not because of its accent on the physical, but because it worshipped the human as divine. "You shall be like gods . . ."—the sin of Adam. It sought to make men and women not channels only, but wielders, of the power that should be God's alone. No wonder it was sin, seduction and temptation.

Blessed be . . . Those haunting, beautiful words, employed by Lady Kersey (*Lady Kersey*?) in her letter, by Nell in her own prayers. I must not allow Nell to use them any more.

On the next page I found what I had been seeking. A drawing of a dagger, or athame, the ritual knife, with mystic symbols. *Let the handle be black, and let there be carven upon it by its owner the symbols of his Craft.* There the symbols were, drawn large and meticulously labeled: the Pentagram star, the Waxing-Waning Moon, the Mother Goddess, the Horned God, belonging not alone to the Old Religion but to all primitive mysteries which sought to explain and control the force of life. How potent they were, even so crude and simple, that here in warmth and firelight they could make my neck feel cold and my pulse beat faster.

And let not the ritual or sacred knife stray from its owner's keeping, but let him cherish it as an implement of the Power. One knife at least had strayed. I was quite sure Laban Greene had not tossed the one he'd found carelessly aside. But the knife that had been in my door—where had it gone? Had it made its way from Jeremy's keeping to the grave circle on the hill? Or were the suspicions racing through my brain a sign of *my* corruption, of my succumbing to belief in evil and distrust?

It seemed important, all at once, to examine the evidence with correct detachment. Then, quite likely, one could say, "Of course. There are similarities common to all primitive art, and that is all. There is no devious and suspect thread connecting Wychwood House to Tarr Farm, to the faceless persecutors, to the graveyard circle."

"Camilla." My eyes focused, to find Nell gazing at me urgently, her whole face troubled. She had picked up my perturbation, as surely as I was able to experience her anguish and her pain. But I didn't want Nell exposed to the shadows that plagued me now.

"I've just been daydreaming," I said aloud—oh, with what calm, deceiving guile. It pained me to lie, but I could not bear the thought of Nell's mind haunted as mine was.

Ye shall know the truth, and the truth shall set you free. Even from the seducing knowledge of the Old Religion? Ye shall know the truth . . .

"I'm going to step outside," I said, "for a breath of air. It's close in here. I may run over to Laura's for a moment. You'll be all right, won't you?" Before Nell could answer I ran out, snatching up my shawl. And I carried the Book of Shadows concealed within its folds—why, I do not know, other than a determination it should not fall into my sister's hands.

The moonlit evening was as bright as day and very still. The wind had fallen and no sound broke the silence. The perpendicular tower of the church gleamed from the reflecting radiance of the snow. The cemetery was blanketed in its soft whiteness, on the edge of the encroaching forest. It was all so peaceful, so placid. The yew tree stood on Wychwood Rise like a magnet on the hills, and I let it draw me, shutting the door to the disturbing other side of self that murmured caution, murmured fear. So I went, calmly but without forethought, through the yard door, up through the lych gate veiled in snow.

Perhaps because I was prepared, I felt now no sense of struggle, no wave of evil. I reached the circle of stones and knelt beside them, my skirts making a dark circle round me on the white-covered earth. The carvings were smothered with snow, which I had to brush away.

I did not have to bring the Book of Shadows out to see. Pentagrams were common enough to be coincidence, but here were the Dark Goddess, the Horned God, the Waxing-Waning Moon.

Even now, having faced the truth, I still did not want to believe that Jeremy was in any way involved. Not with the Old Religion—no, he couldn't be, not with his skepticism, his common sense. But with all the rest . . . Oh, that was another matter, wasn't it? Dissembling, contriving, using the aura of superstition already present for his own cool purpose. Jeremy wanted Wychwood House, that much was known. The cat on the step, the cock on the door—stripped of their superstitious trappings, they had caused me no harm but fright, and had effectively, each time, turned me to Jeremy for support, gaining him admission to the house. The rock in the window, anyone could have done; the rumors had to have been started about me by someone familiar with signs of the Old Religion. The poisoning of the sheep, ascribed by the village to my vengeful spirit—yes, Jeremy could have done that; Jeremy knew too much.

I wanted him, terribly, standing there beside me, telling me that none of this was so. I wanted to believe him in the face of evidence, and discovering this was the greatest shock of all.

I rose, numb, as though my energy had all been drained. A wind had risen, and on its whispered breath a sound came, carried to me from the forest. So faint it was at first, and so inhuman, that I felt my hackles rising as at some dreadful dream.

A figure, wrapped in dark, stumbled toward me from the forest, hugging itself like some archetypal grief-figure out of the mists of time. Stumbled toward me, mumbling and keening, as I drew back, first in fear, then in pity; passed me, with no flicker of recognition, to circle round the tree. It was Mrs. Lee, gin-propelled, calling for Gypsy Aaron.

I felt the cold more now as numbness faded, and I rushed home. I had been gone, at the most, ten minutes, but how thoughtless of me to have left Nell in that equivocal fashion. And how irresponsible that without a thought I had left the yard-door standing open. I shut and locked it tightly and hurried to the house, grateful at occupying tasks, for my whole self was trembling.

There were voices in Kersey's Room as I entered the house through the back-hall door. Nell's, and another's. Even before I crossed the threshold of the room, I knew. Jeremy was lounged back in his accustomed chair, his boots on the fire's brass fender.

"Good evening! Rather a cold night for walking, is it not? The yard-door's being open struck me as unusual enough to demand investigation. But your sister assures me there's nothing wrong. She and I have been amusing each other till your return."

Now was when I should confront him directly with my suspicions, but I did not, and hated myself for my own inability to speak. Nell knew that something was amiss; her eyes went from one to the other of us searchingly, but she said only, "Mr. Bushel says the wall dampness and the ceiling leak should be repaired before more rain or snow."

"I know. I intend to speak to Mr. Roach tomorrow." I spoke abruptly, and Jeremy's eyebrows lifted.

"Since all is well, I'd best be getting on."

He rose, but lingered—in expectation, no doubt, of being asked to stay, as I so often, so unguardedly, had done before. I turned away, and after a moment he went to the hall and donned his coat. "I'll go along, then. If you need assistance with the roof, you can consult me, too, you know. I'm a bit more experienced with thatch than the estimable Mr. Roach. Miss Nell, take care, and blessed be."

That phrase, that freighted phrase. I swung round sharply. He was standing framed like a portrait in the doorway. An odd sensation of déjà vu assailed me. Then the fire leaped up, and by some trick of light his profile was thrown into sharp relief. The room whirled, the scales fell from my eyes, and I knew, I knew. As I had almost known before, in a corridor in Sudeley. *This* was why that strange half-recognition had tugged me then from Thomas Seymour's portrait, had done so again at dawn when I beheld Jeremy's face framed in the ruined arch. Not in full face, but profile, our enigmatic Mr. Bushel and "Traitor Thomas" Seymour were as one.

The heir, the missing, mysterious heir. Pursuing the treasure, cultivating me, using me. That sense of companionship, of friendship, upon which I had been more and more relying, and to which I had given way that one enchanted day—it had all been a fraud, a sham. A calculating, manipulative game, like the maneuvers between men and women that had so revolted me in Charleston. Some of the gentlemen had tried them on me then, but with no genuine interest, no real respect, only for the sport of catching the cool Miss Jardine off her guard. It was no different now, except that the prize was bigger game. I was nothing but a pawn to Jeremy Bushel, was I? What a fool I had been to imagine otherwise.

The whirling world righted, the mist cleared, but I was seeing now through very different eyes. The words of Princess Elizabeth's epitaph on Traitor Thomas rang in my brain: *A man of much wit—and very little judgment.* That was true here, too; that had been my first evaluation, before my senses had been all beguiled.

As I stared at him in strange fascination, Jeremy turned slightly and his eyes caught mine. What he read there, God only knows, but I could not move away. Then I felt the intensity of Nell's gaze upon me, and that freed me. I jerked round toward the fire, my hands like ice. I ought to have demanded the truth of him, right then. But one thing stopped me: Nell was looking at me with the look of a mother seeing her child step into danger she could not prevent. It frightened me so that I could not speak.

By morning I was so angry at my own impotence that I resolved to try using the old stillroom book receipts to bring out that unreadable name in the Lawson family book. After Amy's lessons were completed I told Georgina, "I do not care for lunch. See that I am not disturbed," and swept into the still-room and locked the door. I felt rather absurd, which did not improve my disposition.

This was a delicate task. I could do irreparable damage if I were rushed or careless, so I spent some time in willing myself calm. Then I set to work, compounding the solution "To Bring Forth Ink, It Having been Faded or Dissolved." One step at a time, meticulously measuring not allowing my attention to be distracted or my thoughts to wander—the discipline quieted my body as it did my mind. At last, with a fine sable brush, I painted the solution on the brittle page and held it, so carefully, above the flame. The letters formed, leaped out as though they burned.

This lady was granddaughter of Sir Edward Bushel and of Mary Seymour . . . Mary Seymour. Sir Edward Bushel. Jeremy Bushel.

I felt as though I had been putting together an intricate puzzle and had stumbled on one piece which not only tied all the disparate ones together but suggested possibilities I could not comprehend.

I returned the *Lawson Historie* and the Book of Shadows to my little chest and locked it firmly, pocketing the key. *This is, after all, a family affair*, Lady Kersey had written in her letter. Family: Jeremy, Kersey and I, all of one blood and bone? What had seemed so improbable seemed now the only possible explanation. If Queen Katherine was my father's ancestor, as I now knew to be true, then so was Thomas Seymour. And the resemblance between Thomas and Jeremy, which had nagged for recognition and now seemed so striking—family traits of bone structure can endure through so many more generations than mere facial resemblance, as old portraits proved. I did not for one moment believe Jeremy's name was really Bushel . . . but it could very easily be Lavenham. Lady Kersey Lavenham . . . Jeremy Lavenham. Lady Kersey's god-daughter, all unaware, marrying a distant relative of Lady Kersey's husband. Lady Kersey, much later, making the same discovery I had made in her old books, but saying nothing, gloating over the coincidence in secret. I, my mother's daughter, also unaware, becoming fascinated by Kersey's errant grandson. And through no coincidence, through his deliberate effort to exploit me.

The cords of connection were so entangled that had I run across a similar circumstance in a novel, I would have considered them too far-fetched to be believed. Jeremy and I, not only competitors for Kersey's buried treasure, but also joint heirs, much further back, to Katherine.

There was only one person in the village in a position to have information on Lady Kersey's family history or mine, and a possible link between. That was Charles Roach. Why had I never pursued the matter, never probed beneath his turning aside my initial questioning? The lawyer's professional reticence, I had assumed: it could have been protection of client confidentiality or ignorance; it could as easily have been deliberate evasion. But Charles was supposed to be representing my interests, was he not, as well as Lady Kersey's?

I jerked on my cloak and bonnet and ran upstairs to Nell. "I'm going across the river to talk to Mr. Roach."

Nell took one look and pushed herself up on her pillows. "Camilla, what is wrong?"

"Nothing. I want to find out if we can get money from the trust to fix the roof."

"You had better find out if he can do something to stop the kind of talk that's been going round." She met my startled gaze steadily. "Camilla, don't pretend. You can't close your eyes; it's making you more worn and worried all the time. Someone's trying to make you look responsible for all the village's bad fortunes, and it can't go on."

"One can't disprove rumors."

"No, but one can find out who's in a position to profit from them, or who'd have known how to make suspicious happenings occur." She hesitated, giving me an uneasy glance from beneath lowered lashes. "We do know who could have witched those sheep, and done the other things to drive us off. But you won't want to hear it. Mr. Bushel."

I did not answer, and after a moment she shrugged wearily. "I knew you wouldn't like it, but it's true. Perhaps it's just as well people *do* start to think it's dangerous to cross you. Then they may think twice before they do you harm."

So Nell had suspected all along what I'd been too blind to see. I went downstairs into the raw wet afternoon, filled with frustration and self-disgust and discouragement, and by tortuous paths I came at last to anger.

I meant to approach Charles Roach with calculated guile, knowing it would take as much to pry revelations from his professional reserve. But it took only one kind word from him and my determined reasoning detachment fled.

"Miss Camilla, what a nice surprise. What brings you out on such an unpleasant day? My dear, what is wrong? You look tired to death and deeply troubled."

"Just . . . disheartened." I moved to the small fire and held out my hands to it, grateful to have my back to him, for my mouth was trembling.

Behind me I heard furniture being moved. He touched my elbow. "Do sit down. And please have some sherry. It will warm you." I was guided into a heavy chair. Then Charles stood before me, holding out a slender glass on a silver tray. The expression on his face was of such concern, it was all I could do not to break down completely.

I took the glass carefully, striving to keep the tremor from my voice. "This is very lovely, and quite old."

Charles sounded embarrassed. "I came into a bit of money last year—bought a small house, have been collecting a few nice pieces. As one grows older, one values such things more, even in a village. But it is your concerns we should be speaking of. You've not had bad news from home, I trust."

"*This* is my home now." But could it be much longer? My voice shook, despite my sternest efforts. "I have had, can have, no news from the other side at all. Our assets all are gone. The fortunes of war." I meant that to sound gay and gallant, but it did not work. "And now I watch my sister growing steadily more frail. The cold is not good for her; there are drafts everywhere, leaks in the roof, moisture in the walls. Surely there must have been funds provided for repairs."

He walked away from me, looking very grave. "This is what I was afraid of. I tried to warn you. The house was allowed to deteriorate, stood empty for so long. It demands funds and stewardship, which for all your bravery and effort, you cannot provide. There is no allowance for maintenance, other than the income you are already being paid."

"That is barely enough to keep a cat alive." I was shocked at the viciousness of my own tone. So need could strike a common denominator of ruthlessness in us all; I was not immune. I turned my head away, and Charles' tone became very kind indeed.

"When you came, you had had hopes about your writing . . ."

That was the opening I had prayed for, and I leaped at it. "I *have* been working on the family history I told you of. There may be a market; so many persons are fascinated by Lady Kersey's colorful life." I held my breath, but he did nothing to contradict this assumption of a common relationship, so I went on. "I've been able to trace my father's family tree to the common ancestor with the Lavenham branch, but I've had difficulty locating Lady Kersey's immediate kin. A . . . a nephew, or a grandson, is it not? Do you feel it would be necessary to obtain his permission before I publish?"

"I don't see why," Charles said reassuringly. "It is, as you point out, your family story, too." So it *was* true, then, and he knew it, the relationship that I suspected. Not only Kersey as Mama's godmother, but Lord Lavenham as my father's distant kin. I veiled my eyes quickly, but he was going on, unconscious of the information he had let slip. "You're not planning anything of a libelous nature, I daresay? There's only the grandson, and he's not been heard of, I understand, these several years. He broke with her completely when she refused to finance what she regarded as more useless studies. I believe he threatened to ride into the East and outdo the exploits of his famous grandmama." Charles smiled. "In my opinion, the old lady secretly hoped he would. At any rate, you need not worry over him."

Were those useless studies by any chance a delving into the lore of the Old Religion? It would explain the strange laboratory at Tarr Farm. Could explain, too, the village sheep being stricken on my neighboring fields—he could have done that, could have put on the act of later deep concern. It had served two purposes: made me suspect, and established him even more, in my eyes, as my protector.

If he were Lady Kersey's grandson, the villagers could know him, trust in him, protect him in a conspiracy of silence . . . A chill ran through me.

Charles leaned forward quickly. "You are cold. More sherry—or shall I send for tea?"

"No. I must go home." I clasped my hands together tightly. "About the trust—will you get the papers together for me, and a list of the securities being held? It will all come to me eventually anyway; there *must* be some way to break the provisions now and sell some holdings. If you aren't sure how, then perhaps Sir Percival . . . but I must have money soon." I had to get out of there before I broke completely. I rose, bowed, thanked him for his kindness, not daring to meet his eyes. Then I was outside in the raw rain that stung my face, mingling with the hot salt of my tears.

I stumbled across the bridge unseeingly, and hesitated on the corner by Quinn Cottage. Laura's presence would be comforting, but I could not give way to the luxury of weakness; I needed to do hard thinking on my own. Each door that opened in my mind led to labyrinths as intricate as the spell-binding cords of the Old Ones' rituals.

No lights showed from Wychwood's windows, and the afternoon was already growing dark. I pushed the door open quickly, calling, "Nell? Georgina?" Only silence answered. Then my ears caught a barely audible sound, like a faint, tired crying. Like a lost animal—the kitten, no doubt, had gotten herself shut up somewhere again. I stepped into Kersey's Room, pulling off my wraps. And stopped, the cloak and bonnet falling from my fingers.

Nell was lying on the floor before the fireplace, her legs twisted under her and her back bent. I ran to her, shouting for Georgina. I could not imagine what had happened, but as soon as I caught her in my arms Nell's eyelids fluttered. "I fell from my chair. I was reaching for a book, and fell." When I tried to lift her she screamed with pain and clung to me. I was forced to lay her down again, and her fingers scrabbled for mine. "Please! Don't ever leave me!"

"I ought not have left you alone, I knew it. Why wasn't Georgina with you?" I flew to the bell-pull and tugged it violently, shouting out her name. But it was not Georgina who appeared but Philip, bursting through his private door.

"I heard you shouting as I came through the hedge." His eyes fell on Nell, and he whistled. "How did this happen?"

"That's what I'm trying to find out. She was lying on her bed when I went out. Where *is* Georgina?" I caught sight of her then, sauntering through the hall, and flew at her. "You are never to leave Miss Nell alone when I am out, do you understand? Why is she down here? Why did you not answer?"

Georgina shrugged. "I scrubbing kitchen good afore holidays come. I not know—"

"Georgina brought me down." Nell's face was white with effort. "I asked her to. I was all right when she left me. It's not her fault." She tried to move, was caught again in a spasm of pain, and cried for me.

I knelt beside her helplessly as she clung at me. "Someone must fetch the doctor."

"I'll go," Philip said instantly, but Nell grabbed at him, too, her voice a whisper.

"No. Don't leave me."

"I go," said Georgina, now considerably subdued, and vanished.

Philip and I looked at each other across Nell's still figure. "We can lift her, I think, between us, without jostling her."

Had I not been so worried, I would

have been touched at Philip's solicitude. Both grandiloquence and vulnerability were absent, and he gave promise of the man he would become, lifting Nell gently, superintending our laying her carefully on the couch. Once Nell's eyes opened and she looked at him directly, and she seemed to draw strength from his answering gaze.

Dr. Quinn came at last, and looked Nell over; he was comforting to her, and to me noncommittal. "She'll have mighty sore limbs and back for quite some time. You might continue that herbal rub you two concocted. It will do for her as well as any." His eyes were kind, confirming what I already knew: Nell's condition was such that nothing could change it much for ill or better.

We got Nell at length upstairs and into bed, Philip lingering until I finally sent him home. Nell's eyes followed him as he went. "He can be so kind, when he cares to," she said slowly. She looked back at me with an odd expression. "You would have liked it to be Mr. Bushel, wouldn't you, who came to help?"

My head came up sharply. "Whatever made you think of that?"

Nell did not answer. Her eyes held still gold fire, and she was watching me with that look she had had before, of being twice my age.

14

Rossford-under-Wychwood
December, 1863

I WONDERED that night if we were entering another cycle of calamity. I had been living the past month in a false peace, living in the one illusion to which the intellectual is prey—the myth of the ivory tower, the utopia separate from the world. But my eyes were opened. One can never take security for granted, nor blindly trust.

Nell had a very bad time after her fall. She was panicky and frightened, and she clung to me and to Philip, from whom she seemed to draw a kind of strength. Sitting up with Nell in the dark reaches of the night when the house creaked and whispered, holding the thin fingers that gripped mine tightly as the pains racked her, I think I would have sold my soul to help my sister.

Christmas was approaching. There must be gifts and a real Christmas feast. But more important, and infinitely more expensive, there must be warmth and comfort, a freedom from drafts and cold. If Wychwood was not repaired, Nell could not live here—and we had no funds and nowhere else to go.

It was all very well to say, in anger born of desperation, that there had to be a way to draw on the principal in the trust. I had learned too well that what was possible had no relationship to need. So I sat down alone, that cold December, and grappled starkly with reality.

Wychwood was our only refuge; Wychwood was not, in its present condition, safe for Nell. There were no funds available from Lady Kersey's trust, no funds from Charleston. As for employment—I racked my brains for hitherto unperceived opportunities and ended precisely where I had been before. There were no other likely "paying pupils" in the neighborhood, no salaried position for which I was equipped. Nell, in her failing physical health, needed me more and more. I had had such bright hopes for an income gained from writing, but months had gone by and I was still engaged in the most preliminary of research.

I felt as if I stood at Avernus, the mouth of hell, watching rivers run off to vanish unprofitably into darkness. What other means were there of obtaining money quickly? Borrow? I came from a class of people whose code dictated struggle and starvation before such dishonor. Sell something? What? The house and its valuable furnishings were not mine.

What *did* I own of marketable worth? Lady Kersey's books. But I dared part with none until absolutely sure I had extracted from them all hidden clues. The Tudor scent vial the Colonel had given me. My betrothal ring. They were so tied up with sentiment that the thought of parting with them was a kind of death. But Nell's needs came first. If only there was a way to sell them and later buy them back. I did not know where to begin. Perhaps Sir Percival Parrish would; I must write to him today.

My thoughts were interrupted by the entry of Georgina. "Her Ladyship's come to see how Miss Nell be."

"Oh . . . show her into the drawing room, please, and light the fire."

I smoothed my hair, hoping I could as easily blot out the worry lines on my brow. But I was not successful; as soon as I entered the room Lady Margaret rose and held out her hands. "My dear, you look so troubled and so tired. Why did you not call me? Is your sister worse?"

"We cannot tell; there is so little that can be done. The cold is so bad for her, and this old house is leaking like a sieve." I had not meant to say as much, and I stopped quickly.

"Would it not be wise, then, to take her back to Charleston?" Lady Margaret asked gently.

I could not help myself, I laughed, and there was a note of hysteria in my tone. "Everyone keeps saying that, everyone's so anxious to get rid of us, and it's quite impossible. I'm sorry. I did not wish to come apart before you in this fashion."

"Please do not be embarrassed. It is quite understandable, in your position." Lady Margaret paused. "It is finances which are worrying you most, child, is it not?"

I dropped my eyes, and in my breast necessity struggled hard with pride. At last the vision of Nell lying helpless upstairs drove me on. "I don't know how to say this. I have thought of . . . of selling my diamond ring, and a valuable antique scent bottle that I own. If you could find it in your heart—"

"To purchase them? Oh, my dear, I am

afraid . . ." When I forced myself to lift my eyes, Lady Margaret was smiling sadly. "My own funds, you know, are tied up in investments, and it would not be wise . . . But there is one other possibility, you know." As I looked at her, she went on quickly. "Give up this romantic notion of living here and come and take up residence at the Manor. It would be quite suitable, as you are teaching Amy, and we would be glad to have Nell as well. She would be safe and warm.

But if we once left Wychwood House, by the terms of the will we never could return. We would forfeit all chance of claiming it, and the treasure.

I could not speak, and after a moment Lady Margaret added, "You are like the rest. You want security *and* independence. Oh, my dear, you have a fine brain and an education; use them! For you to be able to live here on your own is as unlikely as that your sister will ever recover the full use of her limbs. One must eventually accept such realities, as I have had to accept the handicaps of my son; create a more limited existence for oneself and dwell within it." She hesitated, went on firmly. "Forgive me, but is it right to let your pride stand in the way of meeting your sister's very real need?"

She was right, damnably right. I understood suddenly why Philip found it so very difficult to fight her. Common sense, rationality, logic, all said I ought to yield, just as the other voice within me kept insisting that I keep on trying.

But I could not, for Nell's sake, hold out much longer. I knew that even as I steeled myself to go on with the proper social formalities, saw her out, promising to think carefully on what she'd said. I did not need to think; I knew the reality she spoke of all too well. Soon, very soon, unless it was possible after all to tap the trust, I would have to sell my independence for Nell's security, and with it would go all hope of inheriting Wychwood House. Our only other hope was for a miracle—the discovery of Lady Kersey's promised treasure.

If that was to come to pass, it must be soon—before anyone else found it, before the village antipathy led to serious harm, before the cold wrecked what was left of Nell's frail health. I did not know how to approach a further search. I was discouraged, tired, could not, as the saying went, see the forest for the trees. Then very faintly, the ingrained voice of scholarship spoke through my weariness in my stepfather's words: "When one is confused in research, it is always wise to go back again to the primary source and re-examine it in the light of knowledge gained."

The next afternoon, when I had succumbed to Nell's plea to be carried down for tea, I went back once again to Lady Kersey's letter. I read it through to myself, beside the fire, and wondered why I'd not had the sense to return to it before. How much now leaped out at me which I had not on first reading been able to understand. *The great ones and the old ones*—Katherine Parr and Thomas Seymour were the former. The old ones—Old Ones—had Lady Kersey known all about the Old Religion? *Which of them to follow*: Katherine's path of wisdom, or the superstition and fears that possessed the villagers? But even Katherine had been beguiled by a fortune hunter of glib tongue and great charm. *One must be guided by both head and heart . . . will you learn that too*? Oh, I had, I had, and she might have been more explicit in her warning!

The birthright that is in your blood, the pulls in paradoxical directions. Head and heart;

Lady Kersey was a witch. She had foreseen, all right, that I would be tempted, even as Katherine. *To spite the devil*: that superstitious blight supposedly on Wychwood House, or Jeremy? She had made it plain that she held a dubious opinion of her heirs.

Kersey had said this was a house of secrets. The hidden doors, revealing secret places; the writing etched on the windowpane in what I was sure must be my Katherine's hand.

Home of my heart . . . It struck me suddenly how often Lady Kersey's letter referred to heart. Was she only, as I had belatedly realized, warning me about my own fallible emotions, or had the words another, simpler reason? *The heart of rest . . . may have the heart . . . a token and a pledge* . . . jeweled hearts were often given as love tokens in the Tudor days. How lovely if Kersey's treasure should prove just such a thing, all diamond-encrusted. How lovely, too, to have a heart of rest, I thought heavily, putting the letter down and gazing out the window at the rain-soaked twilight. My heart, this bleak December, was far from easy. It was disillusion in Jeremy and myself, but it was more than that. I knew it, with instinct passing logic, in my blood and bones.

Something was going to happen again. I did not know what it was any more than I had known when I'd had that strange sense of calamity while travelling to London. I could feel danger coming, but was gripped by that same fatalistic passivity which, in the intervals between her flares of rebellion, enveloped Nell.

"How dead it is." She was silent for some moments, then said quietly, "I thought that Mr. Bushel would be here. He has not been here for several days now, has he?"

"No." He had called the previous afternoon, but I had sent down word I was not receiving guests.

Nell was looking at me closely. "You miss him, don't you?"

"I'm sure Mr. Bushel has other things to do." I turned away so she could not see my face.

Behind me, I heard Nell sigh. "I hope Philip will come by."

"He won't if he has any sense, not in this weather."

But he did appear, wrapped in a dark cloak and knocking properly on the front door. "I hate to make such an ordinary entrance, but the yew hedge in such seasons lacks all charm. Lord, Lord, what a day is this." He threw off his cloak and went to stand somberly before the fire. Nell held out her hands to him and he took them, his face softening. "How are you faring? You ought not be here in our English winters. You should be in Italy, all warmth and flowers."

Nell smiled. "We *will* go one day, and you shall be our guide."

Philip brightened. "I should like that. You shall travel in a gondola, or a sedan chair like the Florentine ladies of quality. I shall dedicate a concert to you in the great opera house." He broke away, his face darkening. "Whom am I fooling? There will be no Italy, no concerts. Not ever."

"You must not say that!"

"Yes, indeed I must. I think with the New Year, I must turn over a leaf of reality. I shall be seventeen soon, you know, and I must face the truth. *She* will never allow me to be free."

"There is no way she can keep you, once you are of age," I said.

Philip turned to me, smiling queerly. "You still do not understand it, do you? Some persons have power, even though they have no right. And the longer I stay here, the more I feel all my own power slipping out of me and into her. It's now, *now*, I should be in Italy. But I never shall."

"No." Nell spoke low and rapidly. "No, she must not be allowed to win. You must never give up the dream, however much it costs." She was silent a minute, then went on more gently. "Anyway, I'm glad you cannot go to Italy just now. For I could not. And I need you; you make it possible for me to go on growing stronger." Philip looked at her gratefully, and she added, "I really don't think, you know, that I could bear to lose or even share you."

The words seemed to have some meaning to Philip; he straightened and looked more resolute, I was glad to see. He drank his tea, and painted fantastical pictures in his conversation, much as always. But the somber note remained an undertone, and when he left, Nell's eyes looked after him for a long time.

"That woman is a witch, a black one."

She said it with such force that I gazed at her in surprise. "Darling, you must not say such things!"

"Why not?" Nell asked squarely. "She's no proper mother. She doesn't care about him, nor anyone, not really. All she really thinks of is herself." She took a deep breath, and sank back on her pillows as if exhausted.

Nell had another bad night, whether from the damp or worry over Philip, I could not tell. Her body was like a barometer of the emotions of those around her, and so was mine. I began that week to have the strangest headaches and faintnesses of my life. It was as if they were not happening to me at all, as if I were the key on a lightning rod and all the physical and spiritual anguish Nell was prey to was somehow able to drain out of her through me.

I had had this experience before, with Nell, with Martin, but this was different. This was a giving which exhausted rather than energized. When I dragged myself up to bed I felt like the carcass of an animal whose blood had been drained in some strange sacrifice. I cannot continue this and stay well myself, I thought, then felt ashamed. If for me, a mere bystander, the strain could be so bad, how very much worse it must be for Nell!

Nell continued asking me about Jeremy, and when I avoided answering I would find her watching me with that odd, grieved expression. Fortunately, her attention was much occupied with Philip, who was often at

Wychwood. I left them together, feeling they could minister to each other's needs, and immersed myself in my search of Lady Kersey's books.

Since the disappearance of the Suffolk book, I had taken the precaution of doing my studying in the stillroom. If I was called away, I could lock the door behind me and leave the volumes currently in use still spread out, without fearing they would be disturbed. I should have kept the door barred, also, while I was in there working, for one grey cold day Georgina walked in on me without knocking.

I concealed the book I was reading quickly behind my back. "What is it? I told you I was not to be disturbed."

"Miss Nell said I should. It's Mr. Bushel, miss. I told him what you said, and he pushed right in."

"Very well, Georgina, I will see him." I sailed out after her, locking the door behind me.

Jeremy was standing by the fireplace in Kersey's Room, and he watched me, grinning. "Not a good idea, is that, locking a stillroom door? It might give rise to talk you're brewing something diabolical in there.

You need not glare at me in that fashion. I'm not going to interrupt your scholarly pursuits, though I'd dearly love to. I've come to fix your roof."

"To . . . what?"

"Repair the thatch and rid the walls of leaks. I told you I would be more use to your purpose than would Lawyer Roach." His eyes told me he knew full well he was heaping coals of fire.

How I longed to throw a refusal flat in his face, but I dared not do so. Was this not, after all, the small miracle I had prayed for—not money for repairs, but the means of having them without need for cash? It took care of the immediate emergency and deferred a while longer the surrender to Lady Margaret's inevitable reality. But why did miracles always have to happen in such ironic fashion!

Jeremy was smiling, so charming and so kind. I know you, I thought grimly; it's not good will at all that prompts you but a desire to explore some more inside this house. Make your repairs. I will exploit you as you exploited me, but do not for an instant think you will wander around alone. I picked up the nearest book and followed him upstairs.

He knew what he was doing, I must grant him that. He found the source of the leak quickly and began to make repairs with a dispatch that showed real skill. A Jack-of-many-crafts—the Old Religion was known to its practitioners as the Craft. What *was* his background? Strange, indeed, for the aristocrat that he must be.

He felt me watching him and looked up, smiling. "Is it my great charm or my dexterity that makes you unable to tear yourself away?"

"The house is my responsibility while I'm tenant; I simply want to be sure the job's well done." He could see too much. I dropped my own eyes swiftly.

The book I carried had been plucked at random; I opened it to discover a quaint tome on the significance of jewels. I began to read assiduously, feigning interest. Then I turned a page, and my heart began to pound.

Irony, indeed. I had spent so much time in my systematic search, and here by chance, by accident, was what I'd been seeking. A whole stanza of verse in Kersey's hand, and the briefest glance made me swing round so Jeremy could not see. My eyes raced over the words, on a blank page at the end of a chapter on memento mori, those ornamental memorials to the dead.

> Almost memento mori 't did become.
> Thy head, not mine. Not dice alone do roll,
> And thus I learn't King Death hath ass's ears.

Memento of the dead, a head that rolled. Thomas's, not Katherine's, as it easily could have been for her elopement. My pulses quickened. I scanned the balance swiftly.

> My premier Lord to many ladies gave
> Such letters, and they often, poor frail fools
> (E'en my own lady), to their fools did give
> Their most immediate jewels. And now Thou,
> *My* premier Lord, with many oaths to me,
> Do give the letter she didst give to thee,
> Which she, of such an one, did have before.
> So lightly didst thou value what for her

Meant risk of life. So lightly thou
took'st me.
From this day forth, so I account thy
love.
What's of great price, must first be
greatly prov'd.

It *was* a letter, then. Some letter from Henry VIII, her greatest lord, to Katherine Parr. No, not to Katherine, but to Jane Seymour, Thomas's sister, whose lady Katherine once had been. Henry to Jane, to her brother Thomas, to his bride Katherine, who was Henry's widow. Any letter from Henry VIII would be of great value, even in his own day. Especially if it contained state or private secrets. *For her meant risk of life.*

"Madam." I came back to the present with a start. Jeremy was regarding me, a twinkle in his eyes. "I am about to climb the roof and lay on thatch, if you intend to watch."

I thrust the book in my pocket and followed him without a word. The wind beat at me, whipping my cloak and pulling down my hair, but up on the gables he worked steadily, intent, oblivious of the cold. Lay on a bundle of thatch, line it up neatly, lace it down and trim the edge; down the ladder for another bundle and repeat. By the time he had finished the sky had grown quite dark. His face and bare hands were raw with cold, and quite as a matter of course, he followed me inside. "I see Georgina's just bringing in tea. How opportune. You are planning to offer me some, are you not?"

I could scarcely do otherwise, and he knew it. He sipped with maddening slowness as Nell watched him.

"Is the roof repaired?" Thank fortune, she at least was able to speak normally.

Jeremy nodded. "It will take some time to season. I'd be careful of sparks from that chimney, until spring." He turned to me. "I observe your scholarly pursuits are not, after all, so all-engrossing as you led me to believe. I plan a jaunt this week to Oxford. If you care to come along, I can arrange for you to have research privileges at the Bodleian."

He was the devil itself when it came to offering temptation. I said through gritted teeth, "You really could not expect me to leave my sister."

"You did before."

"Things are different now." I wished, fervently, that Nell was not there to hear, but there was no help for it. "She has grown worse since then. I could not possibly—"

"You are suffering from Philip's delusion." Jeremy's tone was blunt. "No one should flatter himself that he has total responsibility for another's life."

"You can scarcely deny my sister needs me."

"Yes, she needs you," Jeremy retorted roughly. "But what earthly use will you be to anyone, if you continually allow yourself to be drained dry?"

" 'Allow' is scarcely the word—"

"It is precisely the word. It could not happen to you unless you permit it—or I should say, want it. Even the most bountiful pitcher needs to go back to the well at times to be replenished. Unless, of course, one is determined to make oneself into a god. You aren't allowing yourself any time for your own nourishment, Camilla. Why is that, I wonder? Or do you need Nell's dependency upon you as a shield to hide behind?"

He was gone before I recovered my ability to speak. Nell was watching me, deeply troubled. "You wanted to go, Camilla, didn't you?"

I ought to have denied it then and there, but my head was throbbing. What I did was say waspishly, "Pray let's not discuss it. You know it's quite impossible."

Nell was silent, but I could sense her thoughts. I felt quite ill, myself. Irrationally, I had a longing to just run away; I was tired of being everyone else's reservoir. *But that was just what Jeremy had tried to tell me, wasn't it?*

I fell that night into a restless, dream-spattered sleep. Katherine Parr walked endlessly down corridors that were now in Wychwood, now in Sudeley, murmuring "Memento mori," searching for a letter. Traitor Thomas, his head beneath his arm, stalked the slopes of Wychwood Rise. The scene shifted, and they sat on the stones of the grave circle—Katherine, her Henry, Thomas, a copper-haired maiden with her back to me. The scene dissolved again, and the figures in the circle now were five. A pentagram, the figures linked by their tight-held cords, as in the Book of Shadows—Jeremy, Charles Roach, Philip, Lady Margaret, myself, while on the outside in a larger circle hovered Laura and her father, Georgina, Raphael Smith. In the center, like the pawn and focus of all energy, was Nell, her head bent so her hair flowed to her shoulders and hid her face. I felt again that surge of malignant energy, was trapped once more in that paralysis I had experienced that first time on Wychwood Rise. And all the while, through the chill mist, Mrs. Lee keened endlessly for Gypsy Aaron.

The keening turned to screams. I struggled upward through the thrall of sleep. It was the weight of heavy quilts that held me captive, and for a moment I lay dazed, unsure whether I waked or slept. Then I was out of bed, and running through the icy hall, for the screams were real and coming from the secret room.

My fingers were stiff with cold and I broke a fingernail clawing at the latch device in the cupboard's hidden door. Then it swung open, and I stumbled in. Nell was half in, half out of bed, her frail body shuddering with spasmodic sobs. The sounds kept coming, almost animal-like now in their dumb hopelessness. I tried to catch her to me, but she struggled and screamed out in real panic. I piled covers round her and managed, with shaking hands, to light a lamp. She recognized me then, and clung to me.

"Help me . . . don't let him get me!" Her fingers dug into my arms and she shook with fear.

I eased her back into the bed and cuddled her. "Darling, you're in your own bed, safe.

You were having a nightmare. There's no one here."

"He is, he is! He warned me . . . he's come back to get me." She had pulled herself bolt upright and was trying to use me as a shield. Her eyes stared frantically beyond my shoulder, darting toward the shadows. She shivered. "It's so cold . . . so cold . . ."

I wondered whether by some thought transference my dream of the icy hillside had communicated itself to her. "You were asleep. It was a dream, no more." I pulled a hand free and turned the lamp wick higher, dissolving shadows. Nell's shudders diminished then, and she looked at me dazedly. "You see? There's no one here. It was a dream."

"He was here."

"Who?" I asked. Perhaps it was best, after all, to let her talk it out.

For an instant Nell stared off into that private world. Then her eyes fell and her voice was flat. "You won't like to hear it. It was Mr. Bushel."

A chill ran down my spine, and I felt around us that inexorable evil like a sucking tide. Then my head cleared. Of course, I already knew, did I not, that we were receptors of one another's emotional states. I must be still, calm, so Nell could draw upon my serenity.

I laid her back on the pillows and smiled at her. "Darling, it had to be a dream, for it couldn't have been real. The only entrance here is through a hidden door. *My* room is at the head of the nearest stairs and my door was open. If anyone had passed it, I would have heard. In any event, the house is tightly locked."

Except Philip's door, a voice inside me whispered. Perhaps I should be more careful of that in future. How could I make him understand, without betraying to him all my fears? "Those stairs creak. No one could have come up them without my knowing it," I repeated.

"You don't want it to be possible." Nell was quiet now, and her eyes, very dark with their rims of gold, were watching me. "Camilla, why don't you want to believe it could be true?"

"Because it's nonsense, like frightening oneself with ghost stories for the sake of being scared." I sat by Nell and sang to her until she fell asleep. But when I went back to my own room for the rest of the wakeful night, the dark images from Nell's mind haunted me.

The next day Nell felt ill and stayed in bed. My morning was taken up with Amy's lessons, and immediately after lunch Doth Lee arrived for hers. We had scarcely started when Georgina interrupted. "It's Mr. Bushel, miss, come back to finish the work on the inner walls."

So I dismissed Dorothea and once again followed Jeremy on his rounds, sitting primly on a nearby chair, my gaze severely focused on a book. My forbidding aspect must have had an effect upon him, for he said little, nor did he ask for tea; he only grinned sardonically when he departed.

Now, when I at last was free to commence my search, I found my energy was drained away. I dropped down on Nell's chaise by the fitful fire and pulled an afghan over me. My intention was just to rest a bit, but as I lay there gazing out at the gathering darkness, I felt my eyelids drooping. How long I slept I could not say, but I dreamed again, a pale shadow of my sister's dream. I was in a place that was very dark and cold, but oddly, I was not afraid. There was only that sense of inevitable fate against which one no longer had the will to fight. Through the dark came a shaft of black light and a sibilance of feet, and through an aperture that was not there a figure loomed. I could not see its face, but I looked where it should be, and I felt a sense of recognition.

There was a sound, not of feet but of a voice. I opened my eyes, heavily, into the darkened room. No lamp was lit, but the fire on the hearth gave forth a feeble glow. There was a figure before me, and its face was Philip's.

"I did not want to wake you." Philip's tone was grave, as though he, too, were webbed with shadows. He picked up a log and with a murmured "May I?" threw it on the fire. A shower of sparks shot up and the flames caught, illuminating the familiar features of the room. Philip's eyes roved around it, almost hungrily. "Where is Nell?" he said at last.

"Upstairs. She had another bad night. She oughtn't to be awakened, if she's napping."

Philip ran his fingers through the elf-locks on his forehead. "Actually, it was you I came to see."

"How nice." I sat up, forcing myself awake. "It's a long time, isn't it, since we've had a chance to talk? What would you like to do—read aloud or just sit quietly and have tea before the fire? We never did finish discussing *Hamlet*, did we?"

"I've rather given up on *Hamlet*."

"Then let's have some tea while we decide what we should start on next." I reached for the bell-pull, but Philip put out a swift hand to stop me.

"No! I won't be staying. I shan't be going on with Shakespeare." He walked over to the windows and stood hunched, his hands thrust in his pockets, gazing out. "That's what I've come today to tell you, really. I can't—I mean I won't be studying with you any more."

For a moment I just looked at him, then my anger surged. "Your mother has said you are not to do it, is that it?"

"Maman has not said a word against it, you must understand that." For some reason, that seemed to matter to him very much. "And you mustn't think I don't appreciate what you've done for me. You've changed my life. I'll never forget that, never. I'm very grateful."

"Don't speak of gratitude!" I threw the afghan off me and rose. "I've tried to help you, I've *wanted* to help you. It's mattered to me too, you know." I frowned. "Is that it? Because you're still resentful of the others?

That doesn't interfere with us, you know."

"It's not that. You've done—you do—so much, it's not fair to ask for anything more."

"But you're not asking. Can't you accept a gift that's freely given?" I stopped. "That's it, isn't it? You're being made to feel"—I was careful to avoid any mention of his mother—"as if your coming here is an imposition. But it's not. So there's no reason at all for you to stop—unless you want to."

"I don't *want* to stop coming!" Philip flung himself round to face me, his eyes tormented. "You're my good angel. You think I don't know that? But it's not right. *I'm* not right."

"Whoever told you that?" He did not answer. "Was it your mother?"

"She doesn't have to tell me. I know myself."

"No, you don't, not if you can think such foolish, wicked things." He started, as though I'd drawn blood, and I pressed advantage. "Philip, don't you see? You've been letting people influence you, with their own values. False ones for you, but you've been judging yourself against them." He shook his head as if to clear it, and I raced on. "Philip, the King of Long Compton, do you remember? Can't you see, you're letting the . . . the witch rise up in front of you to block your own clear view? Can't you understand, just as with the would-be king, it's only the weaknesses within your own self that can hold you back?"

"That's exactly what I'm trying to tell you!"

"But you're seeing weaknesses that do not exist! You've been listening, haven't you, to the idea that you're taking up too much of my time? And that you're wrong, undutiful, to have desires other than the ones Lady Margaret has mapped out for you? Oh, my dear, I know you, and you're *not* unfair, undutiful, unkind. You're brilliant and sensitive and thoughtful—"

"Please don't make this harder than it already is! You don't know me, not really. There's another side of me, too, that harms everything it touches."

He drew a ragged breath as if it hurt him, but when I moved to reach for him, he drew away. He stared at me in anguish from across the room. "Those things you said—I'm all of that with you, because you *make* me that. You're my . . . my touchstone. But don't you know what happens to a touchstone? If one tries to hold on to it, the magic dies.

Somehow, some way, I have to find those qualities in myself, not just drain them out of you. I have to start giving, not taking. If I can. If it's not too late."

"But of course you can. It's never too late." I was speaking very quickly, for I was afraid that any moment he would bolt and run. "Philip, my dear, that's what I want for you, too, what I've always wanted. To help you grow into the man, fine and strong, that you can be—"

"*You can't*! Not *you*! Can't you understand?" Philip's face was filled with torment, but after a moment it drained away and his eyes dulled. "No, of course you don't understand. You're too good."

He picked up his hat while I watched him in a kind of curious numbness. At the garden door he stopped and turned. "Maybe I can do something to even the score. You've been delving into our old Wychwood superstitions. Did it ever occur to you many of them could have arisen because there are more ways than you know of to get about in these old medieval houses?"

My mind flew at once to Nell's nocturnal visitor. "What do you mean?" I demanded sharply.

But it was too late. He had vanished through the paneling door as swiftly and silently as he was wont to through the old yew hedge.

He would not be coming through either entryway again. I knew that with a presentiment that lodged within me as heavy as a stone. I had failed him. In some mysterious way I could not understand, I had failed him. There was some force pulling at him, pulling toward destruction; I knew that as clearly as I knew my own ability to be a force toward good. I had to find a way to reach him, to draw him back within the circle of my influence, or he would be forever on my conscience, and my heart. But no more through the secret door, never again so freely that he could just appear in a child's sublime confidence of welcome.

I threw the iron bolt on the paneled door and it settled with a sick finality. There was no reason any more to leave it unbolted.

15

Rossford-under-Wychwood
December, 1863

FROM that night on, cold thickened like the storm clouds over Wychwood Rise. The village was drawing in upon itself, wrapped in the coil of impenetrable winter, and with Philip's departure the circle round my hearth was broken.

Rafe and Dan did not appear one night for their usual lesson. I thought little of it, but when for a second time they did not come, I questioned Georgina about it the next day.

She avoided my eyes. "Reckon they ought to've told you, then. Rafe's learnt good and sufficient for his needs, he say, and he needs naught more."

"And Daniel?"

"That be his feeling, too."

"I'm disappointed," I said at last. "I had hoped they came for more than just minimum skills. I wanted to give much more."

"Reckon you tried, miss." Georgina looked

at me with something akin to pity. "Us have our own ways, howsomever strange they seem."

"At any rate," I said with lifting spirit, "you and your sister have a chance to go much further. It is fortunate we were able to start teaching Dorothea while she is still young. She is a clever girl, Georgina."

"My mam says there be all sorts of clever, and some not fitting." A note in Georgina's voice made me prick my ears. "My mam fear learning put ideas into our Doth's head and give her notions unsuited to her station." I looked at her, and she added, with embarrassed truculence, "Her not want our Doth to come here any more. Not a right house, she say, and never was."

The old superstition, again. Tears of frustration rose in my eyes. "That is ridiculous. It is not right to deprive Dorothea of a chance to learn. Surely you can make your mother see that!"

But Georgina had retreated behind a blank mask, and there was nothing to be achieved by arguing. I left her at her kitchen work and returned to my own employment. But as I went about my meticulous searching, inch by inch, of the spare bedrooms, a surge of liberating anger built within me. At length I went to my own room, changed my gown and recoiled my hair. I stopped to see Nell as I tied my bonnet strings. "I'll be out for a time, how long I cannot say. Ring for Georgina if you need anything."

Nell surveyed me shrewdly. "You're wrought up. Your cheeks are like red apples, and not from cold, and your eyes have that gold fire Philip talks of."

"Little wonder." I jerked on my gloves.

"Where are you going?"

"To Mrs. Lee's. I'll explain why later," I retorted grimly, and hurried off.

The afternoon was lowering, in echo of my mood. The shops were putting forth bits and tats of Christmas temptation now, and Mrs. Greene had hung a gaudily colored Advent calendar in the bakery window. The peaceful unreality of the snowbound stable was like an ironic commentary. No doubt first-century Bethlehem, even without the snow, had also seemed quaintly beautiful, betraying no sign of the tension and drama beneath its surface.

There was a drama being played out here, more somber and more urgent than what I first had thought. And there was more at stake than the Wychwood token. The network of village relationships, with their strange mixture of evasiveness, servility and threat, was tightening. Possession, that was it: the old, old struggle between beneficient and malevolent influences. And it was the children, especially, who were the innocent and helpless pawns.

The notion was absurd, and I could not shake it off. Perhaps that was why when I stepped into Mrs. Lee's cottage I felt a chill. She could have been a figure from an earlier time, bending over her dye cauldron on the hearth. A wan light filtered through the weaver's window, making her face seem cadaverous. She straightened and turned, but did not speak.

What an annoying trick of hers that was. I forced myself to speak pleasantly. "Good afternoon, Mrs. Lee."

"Be you wanting party gowns for holidays?"

"What? Oh no, I'm still in mourning. I want to speak to you about Dorothea."

"Thought you'd be in scarlet soon," she said bewilderingly. "Our Doth's up at Manor dairy, learning proper work."

"That's splendid. But it needn't prevent her having an education, too. Mrs. Lee, you don't understand. There's no need for the village children now to stay illiterate just because their parents were. It's immoral to stand in the way of children learning."

Mrs. Lee seemed to grow taller in the shadowed room. "Happen us knows what's fitting for our own. And no call to speak to us of moral, neither. Us knows a thing or three, us does. Sitting like a spider in a bad house what's not proper your'n, and black things happening a' night. Whole village know what I seen, a-coming home from seeking my Aaron in the forest. The stranger creeping out of your walls by dark of moon!"

I stared at her as the image of Nell's nightmare flashed back to me. My lips were dry. "Who was it?"

She looked at me with contempt. "You be not knowing it was Mr. Bushel?"

The room grew very dark. Mrs. Lee turned back to her dipping and stirring, like an archetypal Fate. "Not for us to speak of," she said with finality. "Us keeps with our own."

There it was again, that impenetrable façade. There was nothing I could do but leave. A mist was falling, penetrating through my woolen garments to the very marrow of my bones. Along the village street lamps began going on in windows, and the far edge of the common vanished into fog. Mrs. Lee was imagining visions in gin-soaked fumes. Unless Nell had told her dream to Doth or Amy? She would not have; Nell was so fiercely protective of me. But of course, she would not have understood how the incident could be interpreted.

Had Philip heard this tale and, hurt, cut himself off? Or had his mama, with Machiavellian skill, used it as proof that I had other interests, that his monopolizing my time was an inconvenience to me?

I had sensed a dissonance, a seething restlessness, as if there were some active force beneath the surface of village life. Was it possible that Lady Margaret was its source? The world of the Manor was too small a scope for her, Philip had said. Perhaps her energy, with no outlet, had grown malignant—not through deliberate evil, but through perverted love, through the need to control, to be the fount of power. I had failed in my efforts with Philip, Georgina, Mrs. Lee, because they were only rooks or pawns. It was the Queen Bee whom I had to see.

The entrance to the Manor drive was shrouded in the fog that rolled down from

Wychwood Rise. I picked my way slowly, feeling the damp chill against my face. At last a yellowish glow emanated through the grey. The walls of the house loomed, the door was opened at my knock, I was relieved of my wraps and ushered into a sitting room that had never seemed so welcoming. A hearty fire crackled cheerfully in the fireplace, and the brass and silver gleamed. Lady Margaret, sewing in an easy chair, looked up with such motherly hospitality that I almost laughed at my earlier sick fancies.

"My dear child, have you walked all the way in this raw weather? How nice of you to have come! You must have hot tea at once, and dry your feet." She bustled me into a chair opposite her at the hearth.

The tea came, a delicate bergamot-scented blend in a heavy Georgian pot. Lady Margaret insisted that I drink it slowly. "Then you shall tell me what is troubling you. Something is, I know, to bring you out on such a day."

The warmth of her concern enveloped me. It felt so good, to sit back and let the burdens drop. I found myself telling all my concern about the village children, my longing to be of help, my frustration at mistrust and indifference. When I had finished, tears starred my eyes, and for some moments there was no sound save for the crackling of the flames.

Then Lady Margaret's voice said, so kindly, "My dear child, what could you expect?"

She was smiling. That was what I most remembered afterward; she kept on smiling through it all, and her head was tilted to one side. She was regarding me as an adult does a misguided child, and her voice remained so very kind.

"My dear Camilla . . . May I call you that? You are young, and have no one to guide you, so may I speak to you in a mother's place? You have had a shock, I know. I'm sure you were acting with the best intentions in the world. But you see, my dear, it has been your own impulsive deeds which have brought about all the calamity that has come upon you."

She means the rumors, the accusations, my mind thought numbly. So she knows all about them, too. She would. I said aloud, "I don't see how."

"No, of course not. And that is the very proof of your different viewpoint. You have not been here long enough to understand us yet. It is your American idealism that tries to change twelve centuries of tradition overnight. Mrs. Lee is quite right. It is most unsuitable for you to be teaching Dorothea Lee."

I stared at her. "*You* try to uproot people from their cottages and work and settle them on your model estates. Why is it right for you to try to improve their bodies, and wrong for me to try to stretch their minds?"

"But that is just it," Lady Margaret said gently. "I am trying, as is my duty, to improve the lot of our lower orders. What you would do is make them dissatisfied with that lot itself. Where is Dorothea to go if you cultivate in her a frame of mind that makes her unfit to enter into service? To the factories? Do you really believe she would be better off in a city slum? We are a structured society in England, and there is a great security in being at home in one's proper sphere." She saw my face, and added quietly, "This is hard for you to understand, I know. But life in a village teaches one to be realistic. I fit my workers for what is possible. Tell me, my dear, are your newly emancipated slaves going to be any more welcome as they try to improve their station than Dorothea Lee would be here?"

There was no answer to that. I felt suddenly very tired. My head was throbbing, and I longed for some of Nell's camomile tea. I took a deep breath. "You are right, of course. It is so very disheartening to want so much to help others and to feel one's efforts rejected at every turn . . ."

"How well I know." Lady Margaret looked very human. She hesitated a moment. "Perhaps the difficulty is that you care too much. You are an excellent scholar, but you lack detachment. It is a grave mistake, my dear, to become personally involved with one's pupils."

I frowned. "Are you dissatisfied with Amy's studies?"

"Not with her *studies*. All of us must learn the discipline of accepting our proper lot. It is a cardinal error to sow the seeds of dissatisfaction, or to create, in the delicate sensibilities of children, an uneasiness of mind."

"I do not," I said carefully, "know what you mean."

Lady Margaret sighed. "I did not mean to bring this matter up, but may I speak frankly?"

I looked at her, willing my expression to be bland.

"I have a concern that the stimulation of your little circle is perhaps too intense for my children's minds." She said "children," in the plural, my brain noted automatically. "The study of philosophy and abstract questions, and then all the talk of local superstitions . . . Your sister is a charming child, but her personality has a peculiar intensity that cannot help having an effect on the impressionable young. And then of course there are the personal relationships . . ."

She *had* heard the story about Jeremy. My breath hurt me. "You are saying that Nell and I—that Wychwood House—are an unhealthy influence on your children?"

"My dear, I am not saying anything so strong! Only that as adults we must recognize the possibility and—ah—take precautions that schoolroom fantasies are nipped in the bud."

She was still smiling. I thought numbly: *This* is evil. This is the true evil in the village, not the dabbling in spells and conjuring of horned gods, but this overpowering kindness that is so self-righteous. It never dreams there are truths other than its own, never allows for any diversity. It destroys souls, not with hate or daggers, but with impersonal warmth. It mummifies its victims, wrapping them in cotton candy, cotton wool. It destroys the hearts. "She eats me," Philip had said when first we met.

"My son Philip," Lady Margaret's voice said as though she had read my mind. "I am sure his schoolboy attachment is an embarrassment which cannot but have been a burden to you. Forgive me, my dear, but your own vulnerability—if I may put it so—has left you open to a failure of detachment which would not have happened in an older woman. Philip has such romantic fantasies. Naturally, coming from outside, you were caught off guard and the child has read undue significance into commonplace remarks. I know your intentions have been of the best, but really it is heartless to encourage him against his own best interests."

"If you are speaking of his music," I said through stiff lips, "Philip cares deeply for it. It is his whole world, and was long before we came here."

Lady Margaret lifted her brows. "My dear Camilla, surely you will concede a parent's knowledge of what is best for her own child! Philip's dream of studying music in Italy is as impossible as it is unsuitable, considering his station."

"And his wish to go away to school, as other young men of his station do?"

"Philip has had excellent tutors here, who understand his limitations. There is no need for his handicap to be brought home to him, as it would in the Spartan atmosphere of a boys' school."

But Philip was already too conscious of his handicap, and he longed for the masculine camaraderie of school.

"In another few years," Lady Margaret was saying, "when he has settled down, he will step into his dear father's place and forget this nonsense."

My head pounded, and the room was going round, I rose with some difficulty. "I take it, then, that you do not wish your children to study with me any longer."

"My dear child, nothing of the kind! I only suggest more carefulness in subject matter. And perhaps it would be well for the relationship to be limited to the classroom. You are young, Camilla, dear, and, I should judge, quite sheltered. No doubt that is the result of a scholar's life. But my son is—how shall I put it?—not of the cloistered temperament. Has it never occurred to you that his attachment for you is not all that of a student for his tutor?"

He is infatuated with you, Miss Jardine, and in no wholesome way. A wave of heat rushed over me and the scales fell from my eyes. That was it, wasn't it? Had Philip seen? Of course he had; he was far more mature than his actual years, and my folly lay in my forgetting that. This was why he had needed to cut himself off, and in my blindness I had totally misunderstood—making his task more difficult, seeing myself as a mother-figure to him. Was this why he felt that affinity to *Hamlet*, and now would not delve into it any more?

And the irony of it all, I thought, was that Lady Margaret's mother-hen rush to her son's defense was quite unneeded. He had seen it himself, before either one of us. Oh God, I was going to be sick.

"If you will excuse me . . . I have left Nell alone too long . . ." I rose blindly to my feet.

Lady Margaret was all motherly concern. "My dear, you are ill. I ought not to have upset you. I will ring for the carriage to drive you home."

"No. Please." I needed solitude and fresh air. Somehow I was able to get out of there with the proper civilities of leave-taking. The butler wrapped me in my cloak and I plunged out into wet and mist.

Raw and wet was the world through which I stumbled blindly; raw and weary were my thoughts. This life I had been building, like a precariously constructed house of cards, now seemed so foolish, an ironic joke. I had erected it, I thought, on a firm foundation of logic, rationality, scholarship—the gifts I had to give. They had turned out to be but shifting sand. How had the melancholy Dane expressed it? *How weary, stale, flat and unprofitable seem to me all the uses of this world.* Now I was thinking after Philip's fashion. *Philip* . . .

I had come here with such high hopes, such devout resolves. To care for Nell, to make a home, to win a place for us. But this climate of dampness and suspicion was not good for my sister, and as for the rest . . .

Jeremy had said I was using Nell's need as a shield to hide behind, and doing her no benefit in the process. *Jeremy* . . . My thoughts were chasing themselves in an unholy circle.

I was sick unto death of all of it. To really care for Nell, I should find a way to take her south, where the sun could warm her bones and the shadows of Wychwood Rise could never touch her. I could have done so, had I not needed to sink my own roots in the Tudor past, had the house-presence not twined its tendrils round my heart.

Now, groping my way through swirling mist, I simply no longer cared. I never wanted to look into the face of any village inhabitants again. I wanted to run away. It was the suffocating feeling I had had on a roof in burning Charleston. The same swirling fog, the same sense of inhaling poison vapors. But then there had been Martin to run to; there was no one now. I would not allow myself to succumb again to the illusion that love did not mean loss.

The distance to the Manor gate seemed endless, but I dared not trust my sense of direction to cut across the parkland in this mist. It was impossible to see more than a few feet; trees loomed up suddenly like sepia shadows. The slush dripped down the curve of my bonnet onto my neck. I ought to have a muff. I turned my collar up as high as I could and hunched myself within it. I should not have been too proud to accept Lady Margaret's offer of the carriage.

I almost stumbled into a tree, but it was not a tree. Hands reached out to steady me. "My dear Miss Jardine, you are indeed courageous to walk out in this weather," Charles Roach's voice said. And then, "Miss Camilla, are you ill? Lean on my arm, so, and I will see you home."

I did lean, with enormous gratitude. "I am taking you out of your way. You were going to the Manor."

"That can wait. We are almost to the gate now, and you will soon be home."

I laughed at that, I could not help myself. "Will it ever be my home? I wonder. The end of the year's a time for taking stock, they say. I've embarked upon it early, and feel as though I've failed. Do you have that list for me of properties in the trust? I'm writing to Sir Percival tonight. There has to be a way I can convert some of them to cash, and quickly! This climate is so bad for Nell. We have to get away."

We had reached my door, and Charles Roach stopped, taking my hands to hold for a moment in his warmer ones. "You are wet and tired. I'll not stay, but I'll call soon, if I may, to see how you are. Dear Miss Jardine, do not act in haste, and do not be discouraged."

He smiled, bowed, and was gone into the fog. I let myself in wearily. The lamps were not lit, and I reached for the bell-pull, then stopped. I had no wish at present to see Georgina, or to see anyone, although when I had spread my wet garments out to dry I dragged myself up to Nell. A small fire burned on her hearth and Nell was lying on her bed, rimmed in with shadows. She looked at me questioningly, and I sat down beside her.

"I'm sorry I was so long."

"It was all right. Philip came to see me." When he had known I was not there? I wondered. "We talked of Christmas."

"Dear, would you mind terribly if we do not go to the Manor House for Christmas?" At Nell's look of dismay, I hurried on. "I would so like to spend Christmas here, in our own house. We could invite Dr. Quinn and Mrs. Giles, and trim a tree." Nell had been fascinated over accounts she'd read of the royal family's following this German custom.

Nell's eyes were searching, but her fingers tightened on mine. "Of course, if it would make you happy. I want you to be happy here with me, Camilla." To my relief, she did not ask about my interview with Mrs. Lee.

Nell did not feel equal to coming back downstairs, so we dined on trays before the fire in the secret room. The small chamber had, like Katherine's rooms at Sudeley, so much the feeling of a little cloistered world. Had Katherine felt the same when she was fitting up the nursery for Lady Mary, and had she realized her folly before she died?

I always thought of Katherine when I felt weak or troubled, and always that sense of her presence came to comfort me. That, as much as anything, perhaps, spurred me to go back downstairs to Kersey's Room when Nell had gone to sleep. It was my intention to write Sir Percival, but lassitude overcame me. I threw myself down in my high-backed chair. The fire on the hearth had burned down low, and as I watched, the last log burst in two, sending forth a shower of sparks and one long tongue of flame. It was reflected in the mirror above the lowboy across the room and refracted back at Lady Kersey's picture. The inscrutable mouth seemed to be smiling.

"I wish you had not been so clever," I said aloud. "I wish we had met. Then I might understand better how your mind worked.

Was it, I wonder, as labyrinthine as my own? Oh, Kersey, Kersey, why couldn't you have been more explicit in your letter?"

Letter. Katherine, too, had written convoluted letters. Mrs. Dent had shown me some at Sudeley Castle, signed even during her fourth marriage with her maiden name. *Katherine the Queen, K.P.* P for Parr—Katherine had been a most progressive woman for her time, or mine. But all her wisdom had not protected her from being hurt.

> My premier Lord to many ladies gave
> Such letters, and they often, poor frail fools
> (E'en my own lady), to their fools did give
> Their most immediate jewels . . .

A letter could signify an initial as well as an epistle. *Katherine the Queen, K.P.* This was the home of Katherine's heart, as well as mine . . . Hearts, broken by too much idealism and too much trust; hearts, jeweled ones, given as token of some pledge . . .

I gazed at the appliqué portrait and my breath rasped like fire inside my lungs. This fantastic montage incorporated an initial, a golden K forming a brooch upon the bosom. *K for Kersey, K for Katherine.* I dragged the fire bench over to the picture, and feeling as though I might faint, stepped up upon it.

I had not realized how heavy the picture in its weighty frame would be. It was all I could do to even slightly lift it to disengage the wire. Absurd to have driven a nail through this priceless paneling, rather than have suspended the picture properly from the molding. Only Kersey the iconoclast would not have been troubled by such a thing. The air became even warmer and more close, it almost seemed to sing in my dazzled brain. *Yes, Katherine, yes, I hear you, and I'm hurrying.* The room grew both bright and dark.

I had placed the bench in my haste too close against the wall. I was pressed so near the picture that with its weight upon my arms I was bent backward, and my foot stumbled and I slipped. Went down, bench, burden and myself, in an instant of fear and pain, onto the flagstone floor.

The bench had not been high. If I was hurt, it was not badly, though my ankle throbbed and the bones of my back and elbow shrieked a pale copy of what my sister had endured.

But the glass was shattered. I heard the silvery tinkle even as the particles stung my face and glittered in the lamplight.

By some miracle, I had not cried out. By some miracle, I was able dazedly to surmount the pain and sit up slowly, to tilt back the gilded frame with its broken pane and lean it carefully against the wall. Kersey's eyes still gazed out at me inscrutably. And in among Katherine's ruffles at Kersey's throat . . .

Slowly, delicately, I stretched out fingers that were both numb and trembling. Pressed back the frill of antique lace and drew it out. It came easily, for it had been caught down with loose stitches. Then it lay there, so quietly, in my hand, and my heart was pounding. A heavy gold locket, like a skewed heart, with an enormous, a priceless baroque pearl hanging from it. Surmounting all, the elaborate raised initial. *K for Kersey, K for Katherine.*

Like a sleepwalker I rose and pushed the damaged picture into the cupboard in the fireplace wall, locked it tightly and took away the key. I swept up the glass and disposed of it tidily. And all the while, the token was in my hand. It fitted into my palm as if it belonged there, a legacy from Katherine the

Queen. I had read somewhere that men and women often thus carried jewels, that holding them gave a kind of reassurance in perilous times, and I could now believe it.

It occurred to me at last to look inside, and I carried the token over to the lamp. From somewhere beneath the monogram, a secret spring sprang open. Within were two familiar locks of hair, the one a pale-gold replica of that Mrs. Dent had shown me as rescued in the last century from Katherine's coffin; the other a dark auburn I had seen in Thomas's portrait. There was another, too, a pink-gold copper that reminded me heart-breakingly of Nell. Snipped perhaps from the head of the young child who had vanished, had survived to be my many-times great-grandmother. A lump formed in my throat and tears starred my eyes.

The Wychwood token—Kersey's gift, and Katherine's. I closed the locket slowly and clasped it close. If the pearl were real, as I had every reason to believe, our financial worries now were over. It was not that which mattered most to me at that moment but the locks of hair, the sense of family and roots. I turned out the lamp and sank down on the chaise by the dying fire, and the shadowy room was warm, so warm. Even the air seemed to sing, like the vibrating hum of bees.

I drifted off into a sleep that was peopled with bright images. Katherine was there, and Thomas, and an enchanting child the age of Nell with copper curls. The pictures shifted, changed. Katherine was no longer there, just the child and Thomas. Then the child only, sorrowful and deeply troubled. Something was wrong, something was gravely wrong. I felt that same turbulent tightness in my body as when I was picking up negative vibrations in the village. But withal, constantly, that strong sense of Katherine's warmth and love.

Was it the muscle spasms of my own body, or some sound, that woke me? I opened my eyes with a sudden start. It was long past midnight and the fire was dead. The room was icy cold. The golden heart was still clasped tightly in my stiffened fingers. I pulled myself up, set my feet on the chill stones, and groped for the slippers which I had kicked off.

A draft swirled through, sending a wave of pungent fragrance from the bowl of dried herbs on the table. Strange that there should be such a strong air current, for the curtains were tight-shut. I took a few steps forward, heedless of my slipperless feet, till I could see through seried doorways to the far side of the house. My throat tightened in a grip of ice.

The drawing-room front window was swinging open. I had locked it myself, some hours before, had felt the familiar pang over the clear new glass that now replaced the earlier glowing colors. Yet now it stood ajar, and through that aperture the wind was eddying, lifting the curtains so that they puffed and swayed like ghostly robes. A prickle rasped my scalp. More vandalism . . . I willed myself one step forward and then stopped, frozen.

I was not alone. It was no beneficient spirit like Katherine's that was just beyond the hall, but a human presence. I knew this not by sixth sense only, for a faint sound reached my ears. So slight a sound that I would not have heard it had my hearing not been sharply tuned by fear. A tiny creaking. There was a floor-board before the kitchen fire which creaked if trod upon.

If I could make it to the hall, could fly upstairs to Nell in the secret room and slam the hidden door, we would both be safe . . . My feet were like lead. I forced one up, like pulling it from quicksand, took one step forward. Stopped again. There was the sound of a foot on flagstones in the hall. I was trapped, now, into this far side of the house.

There was a way out, through Philip's door into the garden, through the yews. I could flee across the common and hammer on Laura's door. All this flashed through my mind within the instant, and with it the picture of Nell upstairs, crippled, defenseless and alone. The door of her secret room was not shut and latched; I had insisted it remain swinging open ever since her nightmare when I almost could not reach her. I could not leave Nell unguarded now while I fled for help.

There remained two courses. Hide here mute and motionless, trusting in the concealing darkness to shield me from the intruder's eyes. And if need be, if I heard him going near Nell's room upstairs, create some disturbance to frighten him or lead him off. *Cat and mouse* . . .

The bell. The farmyard bell . . . If I could once reach the pull, it would, Georgina had once told me, wake the dead. Surely the villagers, despite their antagonism, would come to see . . .

It was too late. The presence came closer; I could feel a breathing in the dark. I crept backward, step by step, toward the stillroom, but there was no place to hide there. Toward the fireplace, toward the inglenook beside the fire.

The token, still in my hand, dug sharply into my trembling fingers and I tightened my grip upon it. I was on the hearth now; my stockinged toes recognized the difference in the stone. I hit my head sharply against the mantel stone. A flash of pain shot through it, and also fear. Had the crash, had I, caused any sound? Had it been heard? There was a faint whisper of fabric as of garments moving, coming near.

I ducked and shrank into the inglenook. My hoopskirt billowed. Frantically, with my free fingers, I clawed at my waistband and the hoops dropped off like a collapsing cloud. I stepped out of them backward, onto the ingle-seat. Praise God for the blackness of my garments; I was hidden now, as well as one could be, for my head was concealed now behind the mantel. I flattened myself, tightly, against the chimneyside's iron panel.

Something moved behind me. Then a draft came against my neck that was not the chimney draft. The iron panel had shifted slightly; creaked.

It had been heard. There was a silence like a thunderclap, and then the faint fast whisper of a moving figure. A rasp, a high-pitched shatter like a violin string pitched crazily off key. A thud, a muttered curse.

But he would recover himself in another moment. The fingers of my free hand searched desperately behind me, encountered nothingness. Cupboard-high, body-wide nothingness. Another secret door. I did not know where it led, I did not care, I ducked backward, half falling through the aperture, and slammed the iron panel shut behind me. There was a latch-bar on the inner side and I threw it firmly.

I had fallen, heavily, onto tiny twisting stairs. It was black as Hell; I could not see; my hands explored rapidly and my brain raced. A hidden passage upward, winding round the chimney . . . I thrust the locket in my bosom and crept upward, cautiously, on my hands and knees. A flat, blank wall . . . I discovered I could stand, and did so, and my fingers searched. An uneven place, a muffled click, a half-high door swung open. I stumbled through it—and was in the secret room.

In the faint light from the high window I

could make out my sister's sleeping figure in the bed. Thank God, she had not wakened. I darted soundlessly across the little room and slammed the swinging door, and leaned against it, my whole body trembling.

We were safe, and I was able now to listen to the question which had been pounding in my brain. Or, rather, no longer could avoid it as I had half been able to while the necessity for action was upon me. The question—if it was a question—throbbed insistently in my aching head. *Who*? Who was the intruder?

My mind demanded, and my heart gave back the answer. Or perhaps it was the other way around. There was but one answer, could only be one answer. A vision formed behind my burning eyes. The figure had a face, and the face had a name, and its name was Jeremy.

Jeremy—who wanted Wychwood House. Jeremy—who was, like me, a descendant of the Lady Mary. Jeremy—who, if he was Kersey's grandson, must know this house. Jeremy—who Nell had insisted had been in her secret room.

If he had found this room before, he could find it now. This was a house of secrets, and he knew them. We were not safe here. I must not stay here, must slip into the hall, ready to lead him off if necessary. I must wait there, hiding in the shadows, and when I was sure he was gone, creep down and bar the window.

My mind told me all these things. But I knew better, knew my true reason even as I hid the golden token beneath Nell's pillow and moved as if hypnotized back to the door. I was impelled by a need beyond the need for safety, which had driven mankind to risk disillusion, death, damnation since the dawn of time. The need to *know*.

Like an automaton I unlatched the hidden door, crept through, shut it tight behind me. Like an automaton I moved, so silently, across the larger bedroom to the hall. It was cooler here, with the drafts blowing upward from the floor below, and I was gripped as well with the iciness of fear.

The stair creaked, the sense of presence mounted, and a wave of irrational terror washed over me. I flattened myself against the wall as a figure passed me, brushed me, stopped. Hands grabbed my shoulders in a bruising grip. I screamed aloud, but the sound was faint and faraway.

Then a voice said, "Miss Camilla, is that

you?" and I laughed aloud. I laughed, and laughed, and could not stop.

For the voice was not Jeremy's, not the voice of danger. It was the ordinary, kind, unfrightening voice of Charles Roach, come to my defense.

16

Rossford-under-Wychwood
December, 1863

HE had to seat me on a high-backed bench and light a lamp before I was able to stop laughing, and I still was trembling. I stared at him dazedly, and he knelt before me. "It's all right now. You're safe. Whoever broke in must have been frightened off by my appearing. I saw the window swinging open and thought it would be wise to investigate."

"You were . . . just out walking at this hour?"

"I was on my way home from dining at the Manor." I shivered, and Charles took my hands in both of his and rubbed them. "When I asked if I might call, I did not expect it would be so soon or so informally. But I was right in thinking you need someone making sure you are all right."

"It was providential that you were passing by."

"Indeed," he added grimly. "You have no notion, do you, who the intruder was?" I did not answer, but a chill ran through me, and after a moment he said, "Come downstairs. We do not want to wake your sister, and we must talk."

I was still shaking, and he had to help me down the stairs. He threw a log upon the hearth and added kindling, and in a moment the flames blazed high. Involuntarily I glanced toward the inglenook, but it looked as always, with no sign of the hidden passage.

I sank down on the chaise, and Charles drew the afghan across my lap. I was grateful for his reassuring presence. He paced back and forth for several moments, and at last planted himself before me bluntly.

"Miss Camilla, I must say it plain. I tried that once before and you took offense, but you must listen. It's not safe for you here. I know you don't like to face that, but certainly tonight should show you that you're in no position to know whom to trust!"

"You are referring," I said through stiff lips, "to Mr. Bushel?"

"Dammit, woman, I'm referring to the whole benighted village!" Charles ran his fingers through hair that bristled in exasperation. "You still think it's all quaint and charming, don't you? High revels in the graveyard and undressed cats upon your doorstep. I daresay you tell yourself it's all outsiders doing that, or some of Widow Lee's forest apparitions, not folks you know. Does it interest you that your precious Raphael Smith and Daniel Greene, whom you've been coddling, bought a dead cat from Squeaky Thomas the afternoon before that one appeared here? Or that Rafe was 'assisting,' so his father claims, when the bars were installed on your back entrance? No doubt he could get into your hen-yard with great ease."

So the village grapevine knew all about the incidents I so carefully had concealed. My head was throbbing as the bang on my nape began to reassert itself.

"And the party in the graveyard," Charles went on. "A Lee graveyard, as you might have noticed. One could make out a justification for Georgina on that base, no doubt; she's sucked superstition from both the gypsy and Saxon side of her unpleasant family. But I doubt if that's her whole reason for indulging. It's certainly not Rafe's. There's always been talk about how Gypsy Aaron's hanging came so suddenly on the heels of his horsewhipping Rafe for making free with Georgina. No doubt Rafe found a Hallowe'en bonfire admirably suited for that purpose. The Old Religion was a fertility cult, you know. Its rituals have much in common with the barnyard, and the cider wagon beneath which Aaron caught Rafe and Georgina. That's the sort of persons you've tried befriending, Miss Camilla, and a man can't stand by and let a woman he respects be pinned with the blame for what such persons do!"

The old clock ticked in the stillness.

"Rafe and Georgina . . ." I spoke with difficulty. "They couldn't even read. They wouldn't know how to revive an Old Religion ritual."

"No, but either Bushel or that young Ross would," Charles said bluntly. "I've tried to tell her Ladyship she'll drive him peculiar by keeping him penned up, but she won't listen. He's fascinated by queer things, and he's a great admirer of Machiavelli. He loves to throw out rocks and watch the ripples. And so does Bushel. All right, I'll say no more in that department. I doubt *he* was involved in this anyway; I fancy our bucolic belles are too unwashed to suit his taste, despite the rumors about him and Georgina. But I suspect he's shared with the locals more knowledge than they can cope with, and had it boomerang on him, just as you have."

My world lay in shards around me, like the glass of Lady Kersey's picture. It all added up. Myself and Jeremy, each in our own way, opening the village's eyes. Perhaps giving them, as the Bible said, strong meat before they were able to digest their milk. A little knowledge is a dangerous thing. I had criticized Lady Margaret for good intentions gone astray, but had I been any wiser? I, too, had wanted to be the source of my circle's wisdom, forgetting that when one teaches, one must also learn.

Somehow, in the tangled fashion such things always happen, a Pandora's box had been opened in the village. And the evil lay in the way ignorance was being manipulated, exploited for private ends. *Evil and mischief . . . blindness of heart . . . pride . . . envy, hatred, and malice, and all uncharitableness* . . . Just as, in the Old Religion, the danger lay not in what was done, but in its purpose—to make human beings not instruments of the Divine Power, but power-users.

Somewhere beneath all of this, a malignant

force was moving. Not causing our weaknesses—oh, no, we contributed them quite on our own—but using them, working through them. For possession. For corruption. What that force was, I still did not know. Once, reason would have supplied instant explanation, but no more.

"I'm so tired," I said suddenly. To my dismay, tears began spilling from my eyes. I pressed my knuckles against my lips, but could not hold them still.

He saw, of course, for I could not help myself. His ire vanished; he hovered over me paternally. He poked a handkerchief into my hand; he fetched brandy, which he insisted that I drink.

"I didn't want to upset you. But damn all, it's time someone did something besides just talk!" Charles ruffled his hair again into a ginger crest, and his language was a measure of his concern. "It's not right for a gentlewoman to have to face such things unprotected. I tried to tell Lady Kersey she was putting a hornet's nest into your hands, but she'd not listen. Having to stand by and watch what's going on fair made my blood boil. I ought not to speak of it. I have no right, but in the absence of any male relatives, I wish you would allow me the privilege of protecting you."

I did have just such a relative in Jeremy Bushel, and it was he whom I had most cause to fear. But I didn't say so. "As a lawyer protecting his client's interests?" I asked aloud.

"My feelings are more those of a man toward a lady he admires than what is suitable for solicitor to client." He actually flushed. "Forgive me, I am taking advantage of this irregular situation, and I have no right. If I might call, at a more convenient time, and express myself better . . ."

He stopped, and the burning log cracked in the stillness. A flame shot up, and the diamond on my finger sent out a quiet fire. I gazed at it, too weary now for thought. He was asking permission to call upon me with intent to eventually become a suitor. The year of my mourning was now near half spent, and Martin was part of an existence forever gone. I had come here looking for a corner in which to hide and heal.

Being in Charles's company was like sitting in a comfortable old chair beside the fire, able to kick off one's slippers and toast one's toes upon the fender; a restful haven from effort and emotion. Not exciting, certainly;

not stirring to my blood as Martin once had been. I still felt a startled gratitude for having known that feeling, but I no longer mourned. And I no longer cared to know such a thing again. I had not the motive nor the cue for passion; I sought a quiet peace. And if, as I could not deny, Jeremy Whatever-his-name-was had power to kindle that burning in my veins, why, I preferred sitting beside the fire to being in the fire itself.

"Yes," I said aloud, quietly, "yes, you may call."

He left, then, with a tact that I appreciated, after we had first made the rounds of doors and windows together with dispatch and little speech. I went, at last, to bed.

I showed Nell the token in the morning and she gazed at it in awe and wonder, cradling it in her hands. When she lifted her face, her eyes held the reflected glow of gold. "We must not sell it. We can manage without that, can't we, for as long as possible a time? And you must wear it, Camilla, at your throat."

"I'm still in mourning."

"But you'll not be, shall you, forever?" She was looking at me with grave and too perceptive eyes. Despite myself, I blushed, but she made no question, only continued watching me with a troubled look. "The token is yours, and you must wear it," she repeated.

"Not for some time. It shall be put away, as a . . . a talisman, to provide care for you when it is needed. For the present, we shall not speak of it." I had a curious reluctance to share the knowledge that it had been found. It seemed, in some way, as though the token yet had more to tell me.

It was nearly Christmas now. On choir night, we could hear the old anthems being practiced at the church. Special pastries appeared in the bakeshop windows, and men and boys made excursions into the forest for greens and holly. It was bad luck to bring the latter into the house until Christmas Eve, according to Georgina, and she put the allotment she had procured for us out in the yard. Nell and I wove evergreen garlands, though, and made ornaments for the tree that I had promised. Nell's slender fingers were deft at such pretty pastimes, and it was pleasant to see her, these dark afternoons, hovering over her little store of jeweled baubles. I had more time to assist her, since I was no longer employed with my "free scholars," and though the holiday evoked in me only a bittersweet nostalgia, I tried to summon enthusiasm for it, for her sake.

I extended an invitation to Charles Roach for a Christmas meal at our home. He made no effort to conceal his pleasure. The next afternoon, at teatime, I donned cloak and bonnet and crossed the common to Quinn Cottage.

Laura was surrounded by a sea of tissue and colored ribbons. She looked up with gladness as I entered. "Camilla, how nice! It's been so long since you've come by for a real visit."

"I've been busy."

"Yes, of course. All your students," Laura responded without rancor. "I do think it's splendid, what you've been doing. And what satisfaction in seeing Rafe Smith working at something constructive for a change." She had not heard, then, how my school had dissolved around me. "Come sit down. I do love Christmas bustle, but I've been pining for a break in labors. One misses access to city shops at holiday time. How are you coping with our village Christmas?"

"That is why I've come. We hope, Nell and I, that you and your father will come to us for dinner on Christmas Day."

"We would be happy to, if you really wish

it." Laura's face was troubled. "Forgive me, dear. Of late it seemed . . . there has been a difference, a quality of reserve. One could not help but wonder . . ." she colored. "There seemed at first to be an affinity between us, but loneliness can lead one sometimes to leap too rapidly to conclusions."

"Oh, Laura, no."

"I have offended you. I am sorry. But we have been able to be honest with one another—"

"Have you, always?" I could not help myself, the words slipped out. Laura's eyes widened, and I knew I must finish what I'd started. "You've known Mr. Bushel a very long time, you told me. Then you must know there *is* no Jeremy Bushel. Only old Sir Edward. I've traced the Lawson and Lavenham branches of our family tree."

Laura walked in silence toward the window. When she turned, there was moisture in her eyes, and something like relief as well. "I knew you would. It was a fool's pretense. I told Jeremy it would not work, but he would not listen. Jeremy has always let his impetuosity rule his head."

"He's the missing grandson, isn't he?" I asked.

Laura nodded. "He said you'd guess, but that all he needed was a little time. Lady Kersey always promised him Wychwood House, you see, and it wasn't till the will was read that he learned she'd changed her mind."

" 'A little time'?"

Laura looked frightened. "I did not mean that. Camilla, please don't think badly of him, or of me. It seemed different when you were across the ocean, and a stranger. Lately, since I've known you, I've been so torn. But Jeremy and I were children together, he's always turned to me as a younger sister."

But I had known for some time that whatever his feeling for her, hers toward Jeremy was not that of a sister. I put my hand on her shoulder. "Do one thing for me, please. Don't tell him that I know. And I hope you will come to us for Christmas."

When I went home I found Nell stringing berries. "Philip picked them for me from the yew tree. He's sending the closed carriage for us, on Sunday, to take us to the mummers' play."

Christmas was now only three days away. On Christmas Eve, Lady Margaret kept Amy home to greet arriving relatives, and I was not sorry. I was engrossed in holiday food preparation; I had determined to introduce our guests to some Charleston Low Country delicacies at our Christmas feast. The goose had been delivered, and Georgina was plucking it amid a welter of white down. More white began sifting down outside our wreath-hung windows, but the snow diminished by mid-afternoon, though the sky was grey.

I was caught in a burst of frenetic energy and a compulsion to summon Christmas spirit. When Nell was settled for a nap, I flew about tending to odds and ends. Eventually, feeling the need for air, I put on my wraps and went across the bridge. The shops were busy, and delirious odors emanated from all the houses. I spent my slender resources recklessly, purchasing ribbons and sweetmeats and odd, intriguing novelties I hoped would bring a light to my sister's eyes. On a last impulse I added a book for Charles, for instinct warned me he would come bearing gifts, and another as an additional peace offering for Laura. Snow was falling again now, in thick white flakes that tangled in my lashes. I had just emerged, haphazardly, with a load of bundles and was slipping on the path when I bumped into something tall and solid, and a too-familiar voice said, "And so we meet . . ."

It was Jeremy, and he could not have caught me at a less propitious moment. I groped for my falling bundles, striving for control. "I beg your pardon. I could not tell where I was going."

"That is moderately obvious," Jeremy said dryly, "and has been for some time. What is more obvious is that you have been avoiding me. Don't bother reaching for those packages, I have no intention of returning them until we've talked."

"We have nothing to discuss."

"Oh, yes, we do. 'Miss Jardine is not at home this afternoon.' I thought humanist gentlewoman scholars scorned such lies."

My temper snapped. "A social lie is at least intended as a kindness. What is your excuse, Mr. Jeremy Edward Bushel Lavenham?"

Whatever response I had expected, it was not what I got. After a startled second, he threw back his head and roared. "A hit, a very palpable hit!" He tucked his hand firmly through my arm and steered me toward the bridge. "The church is open; that is more neutral territory than Wychwood House, and we are most definitely going to have a talk. So come calmly, cousin. Oh, yes, you are, you know, however distant. Kissing cousins, as you Americans so quaintly put it."

Persons were watching, so I could not struggle. He did not release me until we were through the lych gate, up the path and in the sanctuary fragrant now with greens. "Sit down like a good girl now, and catch your breath. And keep you voice low. The place looks empty, but the women have been in and out all day with their decorating."

"How dare you—"

"Oh, I dare all right," Jeremy said calmly. "You might say I've been dared to. Tell me something. Did you by chance receive a cryptic posthumous epistle from my grand-mama?"

My jaw dropped. I recovered quickly, but it was too late. He sat down, and his teasing manner dropped off like a shell. "That was not fair. If I'm right, as I believe I am, you could hardly answer. But I think it's time the air was cleared before more harm's done, so I'll break the silence. *I* had such a letter."

My gaze flew upward involuntarily, and he added. "One of her cleverest and most mad-dening, full of cryptic comments, and barbs enough to have finished off St. Stephen. But one fact stood out sharply clear. She'd changed her will. Ever since I was a boy, you see, she'd been telling me how she was leaving me Wychwood House and a noble income with it. The place had a hold on me, but it was more than that. She used to say I was the only one who understood her, who had the old family flair. Everyone told me she was a Machiavelli, not to be trusted, but she was never that way with me." He hesitated, and added flatly, "It seems that they were right."

I could not speak.

"Oh, we had our fallings-out from time to time," Jeremy said. "She couldn't understand my wanting to be a farmer. Or, considering that, burying myself at Oxford in research into the roots of British witchcraft. I had a notion, you see, that one could prove a scientific basis for the Old Ones' magicking, not only in herbs but in the power of suggestion."

"So that's the reason for the laboratory."

"That's the reason. It would have made more sense to Grandmother if I'd planned to exploit such discoveries, rather than seek them just for the love of knowing. Despite her exoticism, she was a very practical old girl. Hence her unexpected testamentary disciplining."

"Just what *did* your letter say?"

Jeremy looked at me. "Honesty for honesty? All right. Bluntly, that if I'd inherited a shred of the brains, as well as the impetuosity, of my ancestors, I'd hustle myself down here and 'earn the right to call myself Lavenham.' That Wychwood House contained a treasure of great price, which proved neither head nor heart was worth anything without the other, and if I could be first to find it, then token and house and the lord's income she'd promised me would all be mine. If not, then I deserved no better than our ancestor, Traitor Thomas. Also, that she was sick and tired of seeing me live my life in anticipation of my future prospects—an anticipation which, I might have pointed out, she had encouraged," he finished bitterly.

"And all this time"—I groped my way through a flooding tide of realization—"you've been down here, working your way into the house, hiding who you are—and everyone's known, everyone's gone along with the pretense."

"Not Roach or the people of the Manor House," Jeremy said quickly. "They came since my time. But the villagers—yes. They've not known the reason, but they automatically protect their own, and I was one of them, you see, when I'd come here as a boy." He was silent for a moment. "Can you understand how it seemed only justice? I was Lord Jeremy Lavenham, after all, and she'd brought me up to consider myself as the young heir. Then she suddenly turns round, without word of warning, and drops my birthright into the lap of an old maid bluestocking American." Jeremy grinned slightly. "That description was before we met, of course. Afterwards—to be honest, I have felt a bit of a heel. But by then I was into it, up to my neck and over; I poured every cent I could lay my hands on into Tarr Farm, in the blithe confidence I'd be able to find the treasure long ere now."

Oh, Kersey, Kersey!

My anger burst into a chain of rocketing emotions that in the end left me only spent and tired. "So it was you Nell saw that night," I said dully.

Jeremy's face changed; he looked at me closely. "She told you about that? What did she say?"

"Only that she'd waked and found you

there. I told her it was a nightmare. But it wasn't, was it? And the other night, how did you find a way to break in through the window?"

"I never did that." He was in dead earnest now. "Nor do I go in for skinned cats and slaughtered cocks and stones, if that's what you're thinking. Yes, I want the treasure, and I've as much right as you to claim it. But I like clean races. I'd never do anything that would harm you, *or* that house, and you should know that. I'd never have been prowling round the secret stair that night if the rent weren't due on Tarr Farm the first of the year, and I'm getting desperate. It gave me the start of my life when I found Nell staring at me that night, you can believe!" He stopped abruptly. "You mean someone else did come in through a window? I don't like this, Camilla. I don't like it at all."

"No more do I."

He strode down the church aisle and then back, to fling himself down beside me. "Look. You may find the suggestion presumptuous and offensive. But your best protection, it would seem to me, would be to have the treasure found and claimed. Two minds are better than one, and I know that house like the inside of my hand. Why do we not work together instead of in competition, and divide the booty?"

I sat for a long time struggling with myself before I was able to nod slowly. "You are right, it would be more fair. Wychwood House belonged to you, didn't it, before I'd ever seen it. But you see, I have already found the treasure."

He stared. I flushed, unfastened the top buttons of my basque and drew it out. The heavy gold gleamed in the shadows against my dull black serge and the pearl was luminous. I unhooked the clasp and placed the locket in his hand. "Take it. You will have better knowledge than I of who would be the most reputable London dealers."

He shook his head, still looking at it dazedly. "No. You found this before any agreement to share was spoken of. You've won; it is yours by right."

"No. Please. I think Lady Kersey would have wanted it this way."

"Lady Kersey," Jeremy said grimly, "wanted fun. She could not resist meddling, in life or death. She won't win this time. The locket's yours, and that is flat. Besides, Camilla, I don't think this *is* the treasure. I think this is a temptation, to see if we're dull enough to settle for less than all."

"You mean it isn't real?"

"Oh, it's real, and worth a pretty penny. But Grandmother used to speak tantalizingly of 'prize beyond price' and 'shaking up the sacred cows of Empire.' There's nothing scandalous here. Everyone knows about poor Katherine Parr and her opportunistic Thomas." He closed my fingers around the locket gently. "Keep it. You were concerned for security for your sister, weren't you? Put this aside or sell it, and you'll feel better. Though you may never need it for that use. Wychwood House is yours, you know; you've won it fair. No," he said swiftly, at my protest, "it's given itself to you these past months, more than it ever did to me. I love it, yes, but what really bothered me the most was losing not Wychwood but my trust in Grandmother. So you stay here; I'm sure on the strength of that locket we can persuade Sir Percival to hand you over the deed. And let us seek together, cousin, for real fortune. I hope one day I'll see that thing hanging round your neck on something more appropriate than mourning serge."

I stroked the gold with a regretful finger. "I

must sell it and make Nell go south, though she doesn't want to. And have Wychwood House repaired. It's terrible of me—but I almost can't bear to part with this."

Jeremy was frowning. "What continually puzzles me is why you are so destitute of funds. In her letter to me, Grandmother made quite plain that she was providing you with income to maintain a position suitable to your station. Which to her mind, believe me, meant something lavish."

"There is barely money for food," I said with blunt honesty. "Thank God, I've been able to augment that with my tutoring."

"Not with Rafe and Dan and Georgina, you have not." Jeremy looked at me closely. "There is something wrong there, too, is there, lady? I shall see to that. A little gossip's rather fun, but not when it turns vicious. Rafe well deserves every horsewhipping he's ever earned!"

"You've known from the first, haven't you, that it was Rafe who . . . did things?"

"What one knows one cannot always prove. I don't like making unsupported accusations. But—yes, I was sure. Rafe was the sort of child who tore the wings off butterflies for sport."

"It's so incredible. Like a nightmare come to life."

Jeremy's face darkened. "I hoped I'd dropped enough hints to stop the nightmare. They're not sure how much I know, you see, and that troubles them. And I have his knife; I thought holding that over his head would generate sufficient threat to keep things in control. But if Rafe was in your house the other night—" I shuddered, and he stopped. "Come, I'll see you home. Try to put all this from your mind, and after Christmas we'll face it together."

It was so plausible, so logical, that I could not but believe his story. My bitterness and antagonism had slipped away. We talked quite pleasantly as he walked me home, and I even invited him for Christmas dinner.

When I entered the house again, dusk had long since fallen and Georgina reported that Philip had called while I was out. "But I told him Miss Nell was sleeping, and sent him off," she added virtuously.

Nell, learning of this when we brought her down to supper, was disturbed, and she was in a state of anxiety, too, about the weather. Snow was still falling, and she had begged to be taken in her invalid-chair to the late-evening service at the church. But by the time we had finished our meal the air, though cold, was clear and still. Charles, coming later to escort us, made nonsense of my reservations. He said, as Jeremy had often done, "You make her into an invalid by your hovering." So I bundled Nell up tightly and we took her out into the magic night.

The church had the winter scent of smoking footstoves and burning tallow, of bayberry and pine. Candles glowed everywhere, and the apocalyptic window had shrunken into the shadows. *Some say that ever 'gainst that season comes wherein our Saviour's birth is celebrated . . . no fairy takes, nor witch hath power to charm, so hallowed and so gracious is the time . . .* I could not help myself—despite Jeremy's good advice and my stern resolve, my thoughts strayed, even on this night of nights, to the Old Religion.

The Manor House pew was filled with Lady Margaret's visiting relations. Philip was there, too, his face dead-white. He looked so burnt out and defeated that when I glanced at him involuntarily, I as quickly looked away.

I did not intend to look toward that pew again. But later, as the choir voices soared in the oratorio, I felt on me so strong a pull that my eyes could not resist. Philip was looking straight toward us with a face of such inexpressible anguish that I reeled as from a blow. Beside me, Nell gave a cry of mingled pity, fear and pain. I hid my face in my hands, and when I looked again, Philip was gone and Nell was lying back, her eyes closed, marble-pale.

After the services we moved home slowly as the bells in the tower flung the Devil's Knell to the night sky. One thousand, eight hundred, sixty-three. I lay awake for hours, feeling the vibrations of those bells and remembering the look on Philip's face.

Christmas was quiet too, and grey, a day of slow tempo and memories and small, unexpected joys. To please Nell, I wore the locket on its golden chain against my plain black serge. Laura and her father noticed it at once, and the story Jeremy and I had agreed on—"a gift left for me by Lady Kersey"—was repeated again when Charles arrived. So the news of the token became public, naturally and simply, and I hoped that that would put an end to others' searching.

There was an awkward moment when Jeremy appeared, for I had forgotten to tell Nell, and Charles looked none too pleased.

Laura looked from one to the other of us and grew very quiet, and Dr. Quinn, nattering on obliviously, rescued us from our embarrassment. So it was a pleasant Christmas; happy, I hoped, for Nell, and as painless as it was possible to be for me.

Charles brought me a book, and when they all had gone I discovered on the table a small box directed to me and signed with Jeremy's name. *If I presume upon too short acquaintanceship, I claim the right on grounds of cousinship. This was Grandmother's, and I think she'd like you to have it*. Inside lay a gold watch, exquisitely engraved. I did not intend to wear it.

I told Nell the whole story, of course, omitting only the account of the intruder. "It explains," Nell said slowly, "a great deal." Her eyes were grave, and I could feel her watching me all the while I was preparing her for bed.

"Don't worry," I said deliberately. "It will be helpful having a masculine connection to call on for assistance when we need it. But otherwise . . . I have no intention of allowing any more entanglements." And wondered whether it was Katherine's or Kersey's ghost of laughter that I seemed to hear.

On Saturday, though there was no sun, there was thaw. Snow turned to a slushy river in the street, melted on rooftops and ran down the eaves. Georgina arrived with the latest village rumor. "Our Nate's been put on board wages come next weekend. Her Ladyship's closing Manor House and going upalong to relatives in Scotland till the spring."

Nell and I stared at each other. "But she can't," Nell said softly. "Philip hates the cold. And there's no piano at his uncle's castle."

Clever, clever lady, I thought with grinding futility. And how cruel. To give Nell comfort, I relented in my determination not to dine at the Manor before the Mummers' Morris, Sunday night.

"I'm tired," Nell said abruptly. "I think I'll spend the afternoon in bed and be rested for tomorrow. No, Camilla, you can stay with your own work. Georgina will see to me."

I heard them whispering upstairs for a good part of the afternoon, but for once I did not reprove Georgina, I could not begrudge Nell that small companionship. I sat down and composed a letter to Sir Percival, telling him of my discovery of the token and enclosing a copy of Lady Kersey's letter; I set forth, carefully, my claim to Wychwood House, and asked advice on whether it was possible to sell properties in the trust. Then I crossed the river to put the letter in the mail sack at the Copper Maid's.

I felt a bit better when this was done. Men and boys trudged past me, followed by village children. All preparation for the Morris were being made today, in deference to tomorrow's proper Sunday-keeping. It seemed odd that a ritual which undoubtedly had pagan roots was tolerated on a Sunday, but Laura had told me that with the Church of England's comfortable way of adapting to local custom, the rector would bless the Morris Bells and say a prayer for the reformers at tomorrow's service.

Sunday was cold and grey, with a raw wind, and Nell was in a fever that I would make her stay at home. Georgina was in and out, full of portentous rumors. One of the main performers, the Betty, had slipped on ice, with a resultant broken leg. The Morris might be canceled; the Betty's speciality would be omitted; a substitute had been procured. By midafternoon a sullen sun had turned the sky yellow and the wind had died. And in the end we went, Nell and I, as I had known we would.

Nell was wearing her best dress underneath layers of wraps; two pink spots burned in the pallor of her face and she was so radiant it hurt me to look at her. I put on the black silk Mrs. Lee had dyed, and at the last moment, in a bravura recklessness, Queen Katherine's locket. The coachman called in the closed carriage and we were swept to the Manor House along a drive that was lit with flaring torches.

The house was overbright with candlelight and crystal, heavy with the scent of greens and hothouse flowers. I was introduced, so kindly, to a score of people in faultless evening attire and glowing diamonds. Lady Margaret had invited county neighbors as well as relatives to observe the annual rite. Dinner was copious and excellent, but before it was time to go outdoors my head was throbbing.

Our attendance at the Morris was as formally ordered as a call upon the Queen. The Scottish uncle who escorted me was austerely cold. Two footmen carried Nell up in her chair, well muffled, as were the rest of us, in Manor furs. Chill met us on the threshold, accompanied us as we proceeded up the marble stairs to the Italian garden.

The villagers bowed or bobbed curtseys as we passed.

My eyes were dazzled by ice and pitch and fire. If the garden by summer twilight was a Roman grotto, by winter night it was a Druid grove. Great poles had been thrust into the ground and wound with pitch-daubed rags. These were now burning brightly, and on the upper level a pyre had been erected. The Manor party being settled, the populace approached with a mixture of surly servility and awe. I saw Georgina and Rosie, giggling; Doth and Nate. Somewhat apart, in a sheltered space, were Dr. Quinn and Laura, the rector and Charles Roach. A stalwart man, clad in cream shepherd's smock and trousers ringed with bells, strode forward. Lady Margaret nodded, and from off by the stairs came a wavering thread of violin tune.

The man, having bowed, jogged solemnly three times around the pyre, withdrew, returned with a flaming bough. He was followed by another figure with a scythe. The Whiffler, the purifier of the sacred ground—the roots of this celebration went back even further than I had thought. The ground was ritualistically cleared; the burning branch thrown on. The pyre burst into crackling light.

Involuntarily I gasped, and I was not alone. The flames leaping high, illumined the marble figure in the grotto so that the grinning face seemed to change expression eerily, evilly, like a satyr. Something white, like a heap of snow, lay on the fountain stone, something that fluttered and riffled in the breeze. A dark streak, like congealed wine, ran from it.

In the old days it was a sacrificial stone . . . Philip's words, that summer evening, pounded in my brain. I turned my face away, but without having to look again, I knew. Another of my white cocks had met a ritual knife.

"It's blood . . ." "Blood for the stone . . ." The ripple of sound was running, running round, at first scarcely more than a whisper and then swelling. "The Old Ones . . ." "The Old Religion . . ." *Why had I come?* My head was pounding madly, and I felt Nell's trembling hand slip into mine.

"Remove that." It was Lady Margaret's voice, firm, precise, not raised with any emotion at all but clearly carrying. "Take that object away and please proceed."

I could not but admire her. There was a moment of silence, and then her orders were obeyed.

The Whiffler repeated his purifying in an uneasy silence. Would I have seen as much in the Morris, I wondered, had my senses not been sharpened by the Book of Shadows? Did the ritual affect the others just as strangely, or did familiarity dull the edge? I must ask Laura, my mind thought hazily.

Fiddlers Variations, the General Entry, the Morris, Entry of the Hobby-Horse and the Betty—the events proceeded in their proper fashion. The Morris Men, their faces blackened beyond recognition, danced solemnly, their great feet leaping, their bells on red ribands jingling to the night sky. Up in the air and down, round and down again. Their swords with their red cords flashed as they wove intricate patterns. Was this so different from what had taken place at Hallowe'en in the graveyard circle? It sprang, surely, from the same atavistic roots—only this, the public ritual, had been domesticated, church-blessed, its meaning lost.

But not to me. The sense of recognition grew with the steady pounding. These were the figures from the Old Religion, from all old religions; the Fool-King-Father figure who must die with the dying year and be born again as the Knight and Son; the hermaphroditic Betty, symbolizing the polarized opposites within us which must be integrated into one organic whole; the Hobby-Horse distortion of the horned god, its power perverted from regeneration to lust alone. This was corruption, this was what was meant by one's eyes being opened—this frozen inability of mine to look upon the pageantry and be anything but fascinated by its darker implications. How inordinately glad I was that I, not Nell, had found the Book of Shadows.

The Betty with its man's coat, woman's bonnet and enormous hoops was jogging clockwise round the circle in counterpoint to the Hobby with his grinning iron head. "I see they found a substitute for the Betty, after all," Lady Margaret murmured. "Who is it?"

Philip was watching intently. "Yes," he responded, and "I don't know." He's lying, I thought.

The pace was accelerating now, the figures made darts into the crowd, and there were shrieks of delight from village maidens. Members of our party moved forward for a better view. Nell's fingers gripped mine urgently. "You go, too, so you can tell me what I cannot see!"

To voice my reluctance would be to explain the very things I did not want to have her think of. I moved forward, slowly, and was swallowed in the standing crowd.

The crowd was a living entity, seething and shifting. The fire leaped high; in the grotto the pagan boy's face grinned. I was cold, and the fire drew me almost against my will. The figures behind me shifted again, and I stood alone. The iron horse's jaws snapped, close behind me, with an enormous crack.

A shudder shot through me, and I whirled. The Hobby-Horse loomed beside me, its jaws grinning as the satyr grinned. Its leathern skirt, daubed nauseously with pitch, swung at mine. In the old days, anointing by the Hobby's skirts had meant the blessing of fecundity; I had read somewhere that pitch had become a traditional substitute for the Elixir of Life of the Old Religion. I had read, with a sick fascination, of the compounding of the true Elixir in the Book of Shadows . . .

Crack! The jaws snapped at my hair. The Hobby grinned. Through the little viewing window of its leather neck, Rafe Smith's face jeered at me, his eyes sly and knowing.

I could not help myself; I screamed. I ran toward the crowd, and laughing, mocking figures caught me and spun me out again as they had the village girls. Only Rosie and Georgina, with their bold slantwise glances, had deliberately courted the Hobby's chasing, the popping over them of the leathern skirt in the tradition that had caused much ribaldry in the old days.

It afforded much laughter and bawdy comment now. I ran and the Hobby pounded down toward me, and my eyes superimposed a vivid image of the horned god with Rafe Smith's face upon that grinning mask. And the crowd roared and shouted, loving the sight of the strange woman, the outsider, running from their pagan figurehead as for her very life. My lungs were close to bursting, and my breath turned in them like fire. The garden, the crowd receded, except as vibrating waves of sound. To my disordered brain, it was every flight, actual or spiritual, that I had ever known. I was fleeing for my sanity, from the grinning mask that was the mirror image of one's shadow self.

There was an opening like a tunnel through the faceless crowd, and at its end a fantastic figure loomed. I ran toward it, with the Hobby at my heels. And then hands reached out to me with sanctuary, and from the Betty's painted visage a familiar voice spoke, saying, "Camilla, come!" With instinct beyond the bounds of thought, I flung myself into Jeremy's arms.

IV

THE SPELL'S WOUND UP

17

Rossford-under-Wychwood
January, 1864

I WAS shuddering and sobbing, and he held me. Held me tight, and as the satyric face loomed near, stretched out the stick he held and drew a circle round us. Afterward I was to wonder how many others recognized that sign. But I knew, and Rafe knew; he fell back a step, involuntarily thrown off guard. It was the sign, both in the Church and in the Old Religion, of sanctuary. And then Jeremy's arms, still locking me tight, formed the shape of the cross, the barrier and protector, his two fingers extended in the sign of the Horned God. It was the anathema, the instinctual ritual gesture as old as time, the banishment of the evil one. And all the while Jeremy's eyes held Rafe's in a battle of power.

All this happened in an instant, before all the people, amid the jeers and laughter. It seemed, I suppose, a new exciting flourish on the traditional fooling. But not to all.

Invisibly, under the surface, cords were tightening, and I could feel the currents pass.

Jeremy, using himself as a shield, backed with me toward the Manor party's seats. Then Charles was there, saying, "I'll look after her. You have your act to do." And Jeremy: "I must; I've no choice. I'll be back as soon as I can. Keep her out of it." Both speaking as if I were an object inanimate to be passed between them.

"I don't want looking after," I exclaimed violently. "I want to get away." I was shaking uncontrollably, and to my horror I could not walk unaided. "Please, please, just get me back to Nell."

Jeremy had plunged back into the ring, and using his stick as a sword, was chasing Rafe. The crowd's attention was diverted. Charles steered me to my seat, and Nell's hands reached out to pull me down. Her eyes were searching and enormous. "Stay by me. Are you all right? Lady Margaret, please, would you take Camilla to the house and give her tea?"

I exclaimed hastily, "No! I am all right. If we could just go home."

"I think you must have some tea," Nell insisted quietly. "Please, Lady Margaret, will you come?" She was deeply frightened, but her voice had the authority of the ages in it.

"I'll go," Philip said swiftly. Lady Margaret shook her head. "I think not. Your place is here." She did not even look at him, but Philip sagged as though drained. I saw Nell stiffen, and a startled look, almost of recognition, flitted across her face. Then her lashes dropped, and she held tightly to me.

Lady Margaret was signaling two attendants to carry Nell's chair down the icy steps. Another assisted me, for my limbs were behaving strangely. After the icy air the Manor House seemed hot and close, too close. We were served tea in a small sitting room and Nell made me drink two cups, insisting Lady Margaret join us. From outside, distantly, came the sound of revels and an occasional reflected flare. A slow warmth was stealing through my veins, and I felt dazed and lethargic.

"If you would be so kind . . . could the coachman be instructed to drive us home?" Lady Margaret was eager to be rid of us, I was sure, and I had no wish to look upon the revelry again. A bell was rung and orders given, and then at last Nell and I were alone together in the closed carriage and the sights and sounds of the garden were swallowed up in darkness.

Nell's earlier feverish energy had been exhausted and she was very pale. But she was the mother now, touchingly concerned, insisting with gentle firmness that I sleep with her in the secret room. And it was a comfort to me to feel her near, although long after she was slumbering I lay awake, haunted by insights I could now no more ignore.

Jeremy was involved in the village manifestations of the Old Religion. The look on Rafe's face tonight when Jeremy drew the circle around me had been proof. As clearly as if it had been put in words. Jeremy had been warning, *This woman is safe. She is untouchable*, and Rafe had yielded, unwillingly, as to authority.

And it had been to Jeremy that I had run. I had not stood secure in intellectual conviction that the ritual mummery was empty fooling. Nor had I used the force of my own will, nor turned to Charles Roach, who was standing near. I had run out of sheer instinct to the Betty, that atavistic symbol of the union between the two paradoxical forces in man's nature. I had run to Jeremy.

Toward morning a soft thud like cat's feet

against the windows told me the night was ending in wet snow. It turned, with the coming of grey light, to a steady rain. The day was slow, drugged, still, like a great moth dragging itself from a cocoon. Nell was drained and aching, and I reproached myself for having drained her, but she shook her head. "We promised to look after one another, did we not? I *want* you to let me be your strength, Camilla."

I needed that. I felt uprooted and cut off—not from others, precisely, but from myself. I found myself, without deliberate thought wearing the token outside my basque, where I could hold it in my hand as a source of comfort. *Katherine, Katherine, is that what you felt when the firm-set earth on which you'd built your life turned out to be shifting sand?*

I felt, acutely, the need for a confidante and wise advisor, the chance to sit with someone whose judgment I respected, to think aloud and have my disordered mind set straight. Not to be told what to do, although at moments I might have the longing to run back to childhood Eden. I knew too much, my eyes had been opened; I was irrevocably aware of the serpent in the garden. What I needed was a sounding board and mirror, and I had none here. Nell, however willing, was too young; I had no right to put that burden on her. And with the others—where there was affinity, there was too little detachment and too little trust. Oh, Lady Margaret had been right when she said one could not learn from those with whom one was too personally involved. Infernally right; that was her danger.

I was back again to Lady Margaret, like a great black velvet spider brooding over the web of the spellbound village. Not in my most irrational nightmares did I imagine her the force behind the outbreaks of the Old Religion being blamed on me. Her calm rationality made the thought absurd. Yet in a way, might that very uncombatable rightness of hers not be the catalyst? I was learning, too well, that the darker drives in our natures, if rigidly repressed, could break wildly free.

Laura, for many reasons, could not advise me, but she would understand. I wanted to go to her, but could not; wanted her to come knock down the icy dam of my control. But as the afternoon passed, there was no sign of her. The streets were empty; the village had withdrawn behind its walls. I untrimmed the

Christmas tree and sent Georgina to the cellar with the ornaments, and even she, today, was silent.

Toward twilight a knock came at the door. It was Georgina's brother, Nate, who stood there. He gave me, to my surprise, a note in Laura's hand. "Please, can you come? Lady Margaret is gravely ill and I need help in nursing." The scrawled writing had an urgency that set off a tremor of alarm within me, for Laura was usually so exquisitely neat.

"I shall come at once," I said, and went to tell Georgina she must stay with Nell. Georgina nodded; she had known of the Manor calamity all along, my village-tuned senses told me, and for some reason had not wished to speak about it. But there was no time to puzzle on that now. I bid her not alarm my sister, and hurried off.

A preternatural, after-festivities orderliness hung over the Manor House. Philip met me in the hallway, where he had been loitering. "Mrs. Giles wants you to come right upstairs."

"Philip, how is your mother?"

"It's too soon to know. She ate something, apparently, that she oughtn't. At any rate," Philip added strangely, "we shan't be going up to Scotland after all, now, shall we?"

Two maids were hovering in the upstairs hall and showed me, with those odd half-glances that were now familiar, to Lady Margaret's room. It was a stately apartment, but I noticed little save for the writhing figure on the bed and Laura bending over it. She looked up, her face haggard, as I entered.

"Camilla. Thank God. I didn't know whom else to send for. The only female house-guest is elderly and prostrated, and the servants are suffering from a bout of superstition."

"Where is your father?"

"I made him go lie down. He's been working over her for hours. Here, come help hold her. She'll hurt or exhaust herself if we let her thrash like that. And I must force more of this mixture down her. We can't risk her not having rid herself of all the poison."

Lady Margaret, lying so, had lost her powers of intimidation. What I felt toward her now was only pity. We worked over her for a difficult, unpleasant hour. Then there were voices upraised outside.

"Get out of the way. I'm going in, and there's no time to argue."

"It's Jeremy." Laura flew to the door, and he strode in swiftly.

"Philip fetched me. Have you found out yet what caused it? What are her symptoms?"

Laura, after one startled look, recited tersely, "Rapid pulse and perspiration, lack of moisture, dilation of the pupils, stiffness, twitching of the muscles. It must be food poisoning of some kind. Nothing helps; she just grows weaker, and now the servants are mumbling that she's bewitched."

"They would," Jeremy snapped grimly. "How did it escape your notice that her symptoms were identical with those blasted sheep? Tell your father to treat her for atropine poisoning."

Laura stared at him, and ran. I could hear her footsteps clattering on the stairs. Jeremy stood gazing at the elaborately draped bed and its pitiable occupant. "Poor stupid woman. Yes, she is stupid to think she can make things not exist by choosing not to see them. If she dies, the villagers will say it's because unsanctified blood was spilled on the grotto stone. But you and I will know it took a human being to feed datura to those sheep, or to Lady M. Nemesis—Christian or pagan—

does not usually just drop down from the sky."

I looked at him in shock. "Are you saying she was deliberately poisoned?"

"I'm saying this," Jeremy said gravely. "Sin, evil, negative vibrations—call it what you will, it does exist. But it can only operate through human agencies. And the line between victim and victimizer is very, very fine." He stopped, and his tone softened. "You're tired, and the doctor will be back here in a minute. Philip's downstairs wrestling with his private demons. Why don't you go to him?"

"I doubt he wants me."

Jeremy said bluntly, "When has want had anything to do with need?"

I went. I walked slowly, and Philip was so lost in his dark thoughts he did not hear me come. He was sitting in the little room at his piano, his hands resting soundlessly on the keys. I stood in the doorway, unsure how to proceed, and then the floor creaked and he did look up. His eyes were unsurprised and his voice sounded rusty and disused.

"How odd. I could play now and it wouldn't bother *her*. She wouldn't hear. But I . . . can't. I wonder if I ever will."

I went up behind him, careful not to touch him though I longed to hug him like a child. "You must not punish yourself. Guilt and regret are corrosives; they cannot change what's past, only eat away from within until they destroy the living. And there is no point in blaming oneself for what one feels. Feelings are neither good nor evil, they simply *are*. All one is responsible for is one's own actions, not one's thoughts or emotions, or another's."

Philip's eyes flickered. "It's strange to hear you say that." He did not turn, and silence hung down between us like a curtain. Then he brought his hands down, hard, upon the keys, in a discord that reverberated in the stillness of the room. He started to cry, awkwardly, his head hunched upon his arms, but when I reached toward him he jerked himself away. "You don't understand—there are all sorts of sins. Even if one is not responsible for another's actions, one can be guilty of not stopping them."

Someone else was in the room. Jeremy had entered; whether he had been listening, I could not tell, but he strode to Philip's side and shook him roughly. "It's all right. Your mother's starting to come round and she'll be all right. Do you hear me? Do you hear me, boy?"

Philip, with lurching sobs, just shook his head. "You're just saying that. You don't know, nobody knows. What's done cannot be undone. Oh, my God—"

"You'd better say 'Oh, God,' " Jeremy said grimly. "You've got too far away from that lately, hadn't you? Yes, I thought so. Try listening for an answer, instead of dictating what it ought to be. And you might try praying for some understanding that synthesis, not polarization, is the key to life. Or paradox, if you prefer a less scientific word. That's what you can't accept yet, isn't it, that opposites are but two sides of the same human coin?"

Philip tried to speak, and couldn't, and all at once with a muffled oath, flung himself like a child in Jeremy's arms. Over his dark head, Jeremy's eyes told me to go.

I found Laura in the upper hall, her head resting wearily against the wall. She opened her eyes as I approached. "She'll be all right now. Thank God, Jeremy recognized. *I* ought to have, but I didn't let myself—How's Philip?"

"Blaming himself for not wanting to be a

dutiful son. Jeremy's with him; he'll be better now, I think."

Laura nodded slowly. "Jeremy has a way with people once they've dropped their guard." She ran her hands across her face and down her throat.

I leaned forward. "Laura, what is it? You're frightened, aren't you?"

Alarm leaped to her eyes. "Hush. It mustn't show. We can't talk here. Walk home with me. Mrs. Greene's come; she's an excellent nurse. Father's sent me home to rest, and there's something I must check."

We walked together through the mist, but we did not talk. Laura had retreated again into silence, but I knew that she was deeply troubled. When she unlocked her door and went straight to the dispensary, I followed. She opened the locked cupboard where she kept the pharmacopoeia, and a tremor went through her. I thought for a moment she was about to faint. I steered her to a chair, and after a moment she swallowed hard and sat up straight.

"I shall be all right. It is, after all, only confirmation of what I thought. But oh, Camilla, what will Father do?" I waited, and after a moment she went on more strongly. "Lady

Margaret was in on Saturday, complaining that she found it hard to sleep. She could not relax, she had too much on her mind." Laura looked at me briefly. "I gathered there had been a difficult scene with Philip. She wanted to be sure, after the excitement of the Morris, that she would rest. Father gave her his standard potion. Father's tired to death. His eyesight and concentration aren't what they used to be. I've told you, Camilla. I knew one day . . ." She could not finish. She pointed to the shelf where two identical bottles stood side by side, labeled in spidery writing: *Eye drops. Sleeping mixture*. "The eye drops," Laura said, "are atropine."

I made a small, involuntary sound.

"If he would just retire," Laura said tiredly, "but he won't hear of it. If there's a public inquiry now, it will kill him. He's tried so hard; he's given his life to help this village, Camilla, and it's eaten his heart out. *You* know."

Yes, I knew. I made Laura tea and an omelette, and saw she ate it, and when I knew she was resting I went on to my own house, deep in thought. An elderly doctor, a mistake in dispensing medicine; how neat and tidy.

But it did not explain the atropine fed to the sheep.

For an instant, as in my nightmare, I had a vision of us all in an Old One's circle, with the cords pulled tight. There were too many connecting threads of love and hate and fear; too many separate, unrelated occurrences: the ritual at the grave circle, the sacrifice on the stone, the incidents at Wychwood House. It was possible to believe Rafe Smith was behind them, prompted by the threat I represented to the villagers or by sheer malignity. Georgina involved in them with him I could accept, though she was, I thought, torn in two directions in her feelings toward me. But many of the currents of antipathy toward me seemed, before, to have come from Lady Margaret. And now Lady Margaret herself was victim. It made no sense.

The line between victim and victimizer, Jeremy had said, was so very fine. He knew too much. *I* knew too much; too little. I felt as if I were on the brink of some profound discovery that slipped and vanished away from me into the mist.

Lady Margaret recovered slowly. All talk of her journeying to Scotland with her children was competely dropped. During the rest of Christmas week I alternated with Laura and Mrs. Greene in nursing her, with Georgina staying by my sister while I did so. Lady Margaret's illness had affected Nell. She grew more pale and still, with a strange fatalistic calmness, as though she herself were waiting for some doom. When I tried to rouse her, she said only, gently, "You must not worry," and, with the ruthlessness of innocence, "Philip will be free now. That is what matters."

Acceptance might be enough for her, but it was not for me. I had within me some force, angel or demon, that drove me on to know. I sat alone in the weary evenings by the fire in Kersey's Room and felt the warmth of Katherine's beneficient spirit, and Katherine's own intellectual curiosity was in my mind.

There were too many loose ends and unanswered questions. It helped to set them into orderly propositions:

An effort was being made to revive the Old Religion. In quest of excitement, in rebellion against Lady Margaret's ordered universe, as genuine religion or a quest for power?

More than one person was trying to drive

me from the village, either to remove my influence or to gain access to Wychwood House. The attempts took the form of direct threats or frights, actions charged against me or undisprovable rumors.

There had been attempts, both before and since my coming, to break into the house. But Jeremy said it had not been he, the night of cat-and-mouse terror, and I believed him.

There still might be, on the premises, another priceless treasure.

Jeremy was sure there ought to be more money in the trust.

Lady Margaret, whom I had seen, still saw, as victimizer, was now a victim.

Jeremy was in some way connected with the Old Religion.

Who had put the Book of Shadows behind those newly arranged books for me to find?

I felt as one often does when doing research—satiated with too many facts in no consistent order, nagged by the conviction that the connecting link lay just within one's grasp if one could but see.

New Year's Eve passed quietly. Georgina stayed with Nell, for I was taking the night watch at Lady Margaret's side. I came home at dawn to fall into my bed. And late New

Year's Day, when Laura stopped by on her way home from the Manor, I learned that hydra-headed rumor, strangely silent since the Mummers' Morris, again was stirring. At midnight, as the old year ended, the Copper Maid had walked.

"Within a week, of course, everyone will swear she was the cause of Lady Margaret's illness. I ought to be grateful, I suppose," Laura said tiredly. "Lady Margaret herself seems disinclined to seek its cause, and better the Copper Maid takes the blame than Father. Still, I shall have to find a way to make him give up practice."

An old year was ended, a new year begun, and what would it bring us but more of the same? Nell was no better. She was able to sit up, to move with a bit more ease, but that was all. If her frightening attacks of pain and panic were diminishing, they had been followed by resignation that tore my heart. My own life, which I had thought so splendidly disciplined and organized, seemed a succession of futile darts into darkness, leading nowhere. I could understand how in the old days the belief arose of evil spirits sucking their victim's blood. Our own vitality, Nell's and mine, was being drained drop by slow drop, as the blood of pigs had been at slaughtering time.

We dwelt in a state of suspended animation. Holiday was over, the work of the new year would begin with the Blessing of the Ploughs in church next Sunday. This interval between was a time of waiting, and the village lay in the chill and slush while the dark forest brooded on the hills of Wychwood Rise.

Nell was troubled; she would not let me speak of going south, or admit to the ache in her bones from the raw damp. She asked regularly after Philip, but he had closeted himself in the fastness of his tower apartment and would speak to no one. I could feel her aching to comfort him, but he did not come.

When I reached home after my morning nursing stint on Saturday, I found a letter from Sir Percival Parrish. It was quite likely that I could claim Wychwood House on grounds of having fulfilled Lady Kersey's terms, "Especially since the other potential heir has written to waive all claims upon the dwelling." *Jeremy* had written so, and not even told me. "As to your right to anticipate the principal in the trust, I cannot say. If you can procure the document for me, and a list of all properties and transactions pertaining to it, I will look into the matter." That necessitated a visit to Charles Roach's office, but Nell was so drawn and ill that I was loath to leave her.

But Nell, on hearing Sir Percival's letter, said quickly, "Go at once. I must bear this, I know that now. And one does what one has to do, you taught me that."

One does what one has to do. Including giving up the house of one's heart if necessary for a sister's welfare, or marrying, for her security, where there was at least respect and companionship, if there was no love.

Charles Roach was not at his office. He had been called to the Manor House, the clerk said, by Lady Margaret. When I told him what I wanted, he got the deed box and opened it for me.

"I will take this with me and examine it at home." The clerk looked alarmed, but I scooped the box up, nodded decisively, and left. If I worked quickly, I could get the papers Sir Percival requested ready for the afternoon mail.

I took the deed box to my bedroom, where I could shut and lock the door, beginning to realize why having one's servants know how to read could be annoying. I cleared a table, lit the lamp, and spread out the papers—a bewildering array. Rough drafts of documents, foolscap on which Charles had been making notes, lists of securities, receipts for purchases and sales. At length I found the trust document itself, signed with Kersey's flourish, and a witnessed list of properties attached.

How did one represent the present value of such things? Charles did not seem to know, but Sir Percival would. I made a careful copy of the list to send him. It occurred to me he might require precise data on the securities—their original purchase price and dates, registration, proof of ownership. My stepfather had always had a need for such when engaged in sales of antiques and incunabula. I began a search for the proper certificates and receipts.

It was a baffling search, and I grew more and more perplexed. It almost seemed as if halves of two separate, similar estates had become mixed in this single box. Sales of securities had been made in the past two years; checks had been issued to Charles Roach as trustee. To Charles Roach, not to the trust. Other checks had been paid from the trust to him; that must be quite proper, since he was the administrator. But nearly all of the original properties of the trust seemed to be gone. They had been sold, for the most part, about a year ago.

I frowned. There ought to be records, then, to account for reinvestment of proceeds, but there were none. The next flurry of purchases, small ones, had commenced a bare few months ago. The receipts were made out to Charles Roach, Esq., not to the trust. And—this was what caused a worm of uneasiness to squirm—the purchases were all for duplicates of properties the trust had earlier contained.

I sat back, feeling faint.

I was being unfair; my mind was leaping to unwarranted conclusions. Certainly Charles, as trustee, had the right to buy and sell as he saw fit. But why the beginning of exact replacement? More important, where were the proceeds unaccounted for after the original sales? There were no records, no bank-books, no pound notes.

The room felt cold, and there was a ringing in my ears. I reassembled the contents of the deed box carefully, conscious that my limbs were trembling. I closed the box and tucked it beneath the undergarments in my bedroom chest; I hung the keys on Katherine's locket-chain inside my basque. Then, almost mechanically, I donned my outer wraps and ran downstairs, calling to Nell that I was going for a walk. I needed openness and air. The foundations of trust and belief on which I had been constructing my life had been severely shaken.

The villagers who had hunted and grazed flocks across Wychwood fields were not alone in having cause not to want me here. Jeremy was not the only person with reason to want Wychwood kept shut, or sold, or rented—or to want private access to it. My throat caught. I had only Charles's word for it, hadn't I, that he had entered that night in pursuit of an intruder? I had only Charles's word for many things.

Charles had said that little of value had been placed in the trust fund, but that was not true. He had said those items had decreased in value, and that was not true either. They had been sold, their proceeds unaccounted for, a year ago. Just after Lady Kersey died. Just when Charles had acquired his little house, commenced furnishing his office in that copy of Sir Percival's style.

I walked up the common, through the lych gate and the cemetery, scarcely noticing where I was going. I passed the yew tree and its circle, and mounted Wychwood Rise, and the fog and mist enfolded me. But I was preoccupied with groping through the clearing mists of my own mind.

A few months ago those missing stocks began to be mysteriously replaced—after I had unexpectedly arrived, claimed right of occupancy and the maintenance money, asked too many questions. Just before that frightening nighttime visitation, I had demanded a list of all securities for Sir Percival, announcing a determination to convert some to cash before the ending of the year. If Charles *had* been . . . borrowing, he must have been desperate. And if he had known about a hidden treasure, legally to belong to whoever found it . . .

Windows were opening too fast for my mind to follow, but certain things stood clear. Charles had had reason, other than the one he'd given me, for being in the house that night. At very least, a prowler would have frightened any properly timid lady out of a desire to live there. And reason too, I thought sickly, to come courting. A husband would have management of his wife's property, with little chance for a fuss to be made over missing items.

Money—the lust for which, according to the saying, was the root of all evil. That was what really lay behind the pressures to drive me from Wychwood House. Not superstition, nor the Old Ones, nor malignant forces. Those elements all were present, but as window dressing, like the velvets and laces which had concealed the token in the portrait. Money, and what it symbolized—security, position, power. In one way or another, my coming had been a threat to all here who possessed those things, or were possessed by the drive to have them. *I* was possessed by those very drives myself.

I had climbed now to a kind of clearing. The fog enshrouded me like wet velvet, so thick I could not see the trees. Memory transported me back to the deck of a war-darkened ocean liner on just such a night, when the blood in my temples had throbbed *calamity* and the long-buried instinctual powers within me had stirred to life. I had had a sense, ever since, of moving in a fog—but had it been, completely, the mist of a spellbound village or the mist in my own eyes?

I had mistrusted Jeremy from the first, the more so as my irrational nature responded to him. I had trusted Charles by very reason that he was so logical, so rational, so sane. In both instances, I had been wrong.

One must be guided by both head and *heart*, Lady Kersey had written, and in my blind intellectual pride I had trusted only in the first. *Blind following of instincts is not always wise*, she had added, and I had missed the qualifying words. Kersey had chided Jeremy for following impulse at expense of reason; could that worldly too-far-seeing woman have been warning me against the opposite? *The birthright that is in your blood, the pulls in paradoxical directions* . . . so often, so intensely, since coming here, I had felt those pulls, had discerned them as opposites, not paradoxes. "Synthesis, not polarization, is the key to life," Jeremy had told Philip. "That's what you can't accept . . . that opposites are but two sides of the same human coin."

I stood alone in the damp, caressing mist, and there passed before me, like a vast panorama, all the polarities of my life. I was not thinking any more of the shock and disillusion of Charles's embezzlement, I was confronting my own soul. What infinite peace one could find—not a peace free from tension, but free within it—if those polarities did not require "correct labeling," after all. "Positive/negative," "good/evil," "right/wrong" . . . if they were two sides of single coins, and their pulls were not in opposite directions, but to the core of one's own self, "the heart of rest."

In instinctive trust, I had fled to Jeremy, not Charles, the night of the Mummers' Morris. *Blind* following of instinct is not always wise, I long had known, but intuition could be, perhaps; "felt thought" could lead one swiftly to a path which wisdom and logic in time would reinforce. It was instinct which had led me to Wychwood House, and to the token; instinct which had impelled me to Jeremy, despite—yes, there was consistency here—despite the intuition which from the first had warned me he could be a threat. He *was* dangerous, not to my self, but to my defenses, my carefully constructed barriers against loneliness and leaps of faith, and love.

They were barriers raised in self-protection, yet until they fell I would be forever trapped in a circle of fear. I could not yet wholly trust the intuitive, non-rational side of my own nature, but until I took that leap of faith, I would be an alien and a stranger—to others and to myself. Amid all the miasma of perceptions swirling like mists around me, that much was firm and sure as the rocks beneath my feet. It was time I came out of the ivory tower and joined the human race.

The leap of faith—St. Thomas Aquinas had written of that in his carefully structured argument for a unity between rational and irrational perceptions. Katherine Parr must have studied it and been influenced by it; I, in my determined blindness, had warred against it. But I stood at a precipice now and knew not where to turn.

And then through the mist a form materialized, moving toward me. The form became a figure, and it was Jeremy. And I moved toward him, straight into his arms, as I had done before. There was no moment of definite decision, I simply knew; there were no words spoken, for there was no need. We came together as friends who had known each other from the dawn of time; as strangers who, as from long journeyings, had found in one another the heart of rest.

"How did you know to come here?" I said at last.

"Georgina told me you had gone out walking. You fool, don't you know it isn't safe for you up here alone?"

"I'm in no danger. I—I've found out what's been behind it all, the attacks and threats. I was wrong. I'd be more dangerous dead than I am alive."

Jeremy looked at me. "What in the name of God are you talking about?"

"It was Charles," I said dully. "He's been embezzling from the trust; you were right, there should have been more money there. It must have all seemed so perfectly safe. Kersey was dead, and I across the ocean, with a war on. There was little likelihood I would appear to make my claim. He didn't know about you, of course. Then I came to Wychwood, and there was no money . . . What could he do but try to scare me off?"

"Can you prove this?" Jeremy asked tautly.

"I took the papers from his office while he was away this afternoon. That's how I learned. But you see, I'm in no physical danger. Especially since Sir Percival knows I've found the token and claimed the house.

If anything suspicious happened to me now, it would all come out."

"Have you written to Sir Percival about this yet?"

I shook my head.

"Then I am going to, at once, and I think I shall ride to Oxford and post it there." Jeremy took me by the shoulders and turned me round to face him, his expression grim. "Will you do something for me? Take Nell and go stay at Quinn Cottage, and don't let Laura leave your side."

"But there's no reason, and I certainly won't leave Wychwood House unguarded, especially now—"

"I don't care if Charles Roach or Rafe Smith or every other thief in the neighborhood breaks in to hunt the treasure," Jeremy said violently. "My dear idiot, will you use your brains? You're not safe, not yet. Yes, if you met with obvious foul play, the trust would be examined and the truth exposed. But . . . an accident? If you slipped on the rocks while walking in the mist? Or made a fatal mistake with those herbs you've been playing with? Or took an overdose of sleeping draught? You're reputed of late to be under great nervous strain. This village recently has been all too prone to accidents."

I stared at him and my protests dwindled into a cold, hard knot of fear. "You're not thinking about the sheep and Lady Margaret—"

"I'm not sure what I'm thinking," Jeremy said bluntly. "But Charles Roach would not have known how to witch those sheep." He frowned, more to himself than me. "Something's wrong somewhere. Oh, it all adds up, too neatly. Something's out of focus; there's a piece missing somewhere." He looked at my troubled face and his own brow cleared. "No use worrying at it now. I'll take you home and then go straight to Oxford. I think I shall spend the night there; telegraph Sir Percival and wait for a reply. We shall reason this out together, on my return. We have a great deal that we must talk of, don't we? Oh, my dear, you must not start to cry. Where's that calm, disciplined detachment you're so proud of?" But he was smiling, and he held me close for a long time without speaking.

We came down from the hillside, still in silence, and when we reached my own door he kissed my hands. "I shall go at once, and come to you as soon as I've heard from Sir Percival. You go to Laura, and try to put it from your mind."

He was gone into the mist, and I lifted the latch of Wychwood House, thinking his instructions were easier said than followed. I went into the hall, started to lay aside my cloak, and stopped. Despite my earlier brave words, a serpent of fear began to uncoil deep within me. Nell was in Kersey's room, drinking tea, and she was not alone.

"My dear, I was growing worried. I have been waiting for you for some time." Charles Roach was rising, smiling, gesturing toward my chair. "I've come for the deed box. You ought not to have carried it off, you know. But come and drink your tea. It's all here and ready."

18

Rossford-under-Wychwood
January, 1864

I THANKED God for those long years of discipline, of hiding emotion under the cool mask of reserve. I came in, smiled, held my hands out to the fire. "I'm so sorry, I was out walking on the hills. No, no tea, thank you." I remembered Jeremy's words about accidents, and repressed a shudder.

"Then I must be going. The deed box, please, my dear? I shall get the papers all in order for you tonight, and call tomorrow morning. We can go over them together. It was really not right of you to have carried them off. Not only are they so complex as to be easily misunderstood, but as trustee I am legally responsible for them."

He was coming toward me, smiling kindly, holding out his hand.

Say nothing, Jeremy had told me, but I could not do it. I took a deep breath, and looked him in the face, and lied. "It is too late. I have already mailed the papers to Sir Percival. I'm truly sorry for the trouble this will cause you. But I had to do it. You can understand, can't you, that there's no point in calling now?"

He understood; a mixture of emotions passed through his eyes. Then he bowed swiftly, murmured a conventional farewell, and took his leave. I barred the door behind him, feeling weak and very tired.

Nell was looking at me strangely. "You were very abrupt, considering that he'd come courting." I swung round sharply, and she added, "He was here for some time, you know. We talked a good deal. *He* talked, rather. He has great hopes, and he seems to think his feelings are reciprocated."

"I'm afraid his hopes just ran up against reality," I answered shortly. Then I looked at Nell and forced a smile. "I'm sorry to disappoint your matchmaking instincts, darling, but there's not a chance in the world I'd ever marry him."

An odd expression crossed Nell's face. "I'm sorry for him," she said at last, surprisingly. "He couldn't know."

"Know what?"

"That it's dangerous to love you." I flashed

her a startled glance, and she returned a steady, troubled gaze. "Camilla, haven't you noticed? You're set apart, somehow. Maybe that's why you seem like one of the Old Ones. There's a kind of power holding you off from others. Every time someone cares too much about you, or cares *against* you . . . something happens."

I stared at her, and that tide of wholly irrational panic that had possessed me at the grave circle stirred within me. "But that's ridiculous." I struggled to make my voice quite firm and calm. "Why, after all, you're the closest to me, and no harm has come to *you.*"

"Hasn't it?" Nell said, so quietly, and dropped her eyes.

I took her two hands tightly. "Nell, look at me! Are you trying to say Martin's death, your accident . . .? That's ridiculous, you've been listening to too many of Georgina's superstitious tales."

"I lied to you," Nell said slowly, "in that letter. I wasn't glad for you . . . I was afraid you'd be so happy with Martin, you'd leave me in England and forget me. I was jealous, and then I fell." She pulled her hands away to hide her face. "So it served me right, you see, what happened to me."

"Oh, darling, darling." I put my arms around her and held her tight. "Things don't happen that way. People aren't punished for wanting the wrong things. And you don't have to be afraid you'll lose me, ever."

"But it does happen," Nell corrected dully. She straightened and looked at me, and a hopeless expression filled her face. "You can't understand, can you? But you will someday."

"Nell, listen to me. You must not feel guilty, or blame yourself for your accident. And you mustn't listen any more to superstition. Promise me that." She nodded slowly, but I could tell she did so just to please me. I rose and stood regarding her, deeply troubled.

Something was wrong, as Jeremy had said; there was more at the root of the spellbound village than Charles's embezzling. I was back again where intuition had led me earlier, to a sense of seething unidentifiable evil, and the children as its innocent and helpless pawns. First Philip, and now Nell, possessed by a despairing and irrational sense of guilt. *And may God have mercy on us all.*

"Come," I said to Nell with false brightness. "We're going across to Quinn Cottage to spend the night."

Laura was surprised to see us, but she gave us a warm welcome. "Of course you can stay! It will be good for Father, he's grown so in upon himself of late." Her eyes met mine. So Dr. Quinn had realized the error made in Lady Margaret's prescription. *Or was it error? There have been a great many accidents in the village lately.*

Why was I becoming steadily more alarmed, and more afraid?

To Laura, when we were alone, I said, "Jeremy told me to come here. He thinks it's dangerous for us in Wychwood House alone."

Laura looked at me. "So he has talked to you. He's been very worried." She said, "You do realize, don't you, he's in love with you?"

I could not speak, and she went on steadily, "It's not surprising. It was inevitable, I think. In many ways, you're two sides of the same coin."

How very strange that she should pick up the same phrase in which I had been thinking earlier.

"I am very happy for you both," Laura said. "I am, truly."

"Nell says it's bad luck to care about me, for good or ill. She's taken a notion there's something about me that brings misfortune."

Laura shook her head. "The air of Wychwood Rise, I think, is poisoning us all."

It was a pleasant evening, but I could not shake off the feeling that it was an escape from reality back to the ivory tower. On Sunday morning I went to church with Laura for the Blessing of the Ploughs. Charles Roach was not there; the Manor pew was empty. The day dragged. I was restless, and Nell tense and troubled, picking up my mood. It was late afternoon when Jeremy appeared.

"I've heard from Sir Percival. He's very much shocked, and taking steps at once. By morning Roach will be arrested, and you'll have no further danger from that quarter. I hope," Jeremy added grimly, "he's not got wind of the fact we've tumbled to him."

"He was at the house yesterday when I returned. He'd discovered the papers gone, and come for them." At the expression on Jeremy's face, I added hastily, "I said I knew, that I'd sent them on already to Sir Percival. It seemed safest, to let him think it was already too late for prevention. And besides, I had to tell him."

Jeremy looked at me. "Yes, you would, wouldn't you? The bottomless well of your compassion continually amazes me in one who so professes the value of detachment. Don't look at me that way, love, I understand. But I think I had better pay a call on Roach at once, to make sure he does comprehend there's no point in trickery or flight to avoid the making of restitution."

I rose, and he said swiftly, "No. You are staying right here. You understand? I'll be back as soon as I can."

Laura shut the door behind him and turned back, frowning. "What *is* all this? If something's really wrong . . ."

"You might as well know," I said dully. "By tomorrow the whole village will. Charles Roach was embezzling from my trust fund and I found it out. That's why the rumors, the attempts to drive me off—so he'd not have to pay me out money that wasn't there."

Laura sat down slowly. "I can't believe it."

"Oh, it's true, all right." I felt suddenly very weary. "Let's not speak of it. I don't want Nell to find out unless she has to. She's worrying over too many things, and she's taken a notion to do some matchmaking between Charles Roach and me."

We did not expect Jeremy to come quickly back, but in a breathlessly short space of time he was there, dwarfing Quinn Cottage's low-ceilinged parlor. The expression on his face brought Laura and me instantly to our feet.

"Where's your father?"

"Taking his Sunday nap. Jeremy, what's hap—"

"Get him. Quickly."

Laura flashed one look at Jeremy's eyes and hurried out. We could hear the snap of her hoops as she rushed past the newel-post on the stairs. I swung round to Jeremy. "What is it? *Charles*?"

Jeremy took my arm and forced a smile. "Come and sit down."

"No." I clasped my hands together tightly. "I want to know."

Jeremy looked at me and nodded. "The whole truth, come what may? All right, then." But he crossed the room and stood a few seconds staring into the flames before he turned round bluntly. "Charles is dead."

I had known it. Had half expected it.

My mouth was dry. "What—how did it happen?"

"I don't know yet. The house was shut up tight, and that bothered me. So I went round to the law office and peered through the back window. He was in his inner sanctum, slumped at his desk. I let myself in." Jeremy smiled without humor. "I'm becoming quite good at breaking and entering. The lamp had burnt itself out, and he was cold. He must have gone straight back there from Wychwood. Apparently he couldn't face the thought of disgrace, and took steps to avoid it."

What a wealth of meanings were implied in that word "apparently."

"I've sent word to the chief constable—under my own name." Jeremy's mouth twisted. "Lord Jeremy Lavenham's a more useful identity for discovering dead bodies than the cryptic Bushel." He came over and rubbed my shoulders. "Ah, my love, don't look like that. I know what you're thinking, and it's bootless self-flagellation to blame yourself. My love. That's the first time I've called you that seriously, isn't it? But not the last."

"I can't help feeling responsible. If I hadn't told him—"

"But that put the burden of self-determination onto him." Jeremy turned me round squarely. "Where's your scholar's integrity? Truth at all costs. You did what you had to do. And if he chose this means of meeting exposure—then so did he."

"You said 'if.' "

"Did I?" Jeremy looked at me and shrugged. "My skeptic's mind again. Why should it only be in books that things work out so very tidily?"

Tidy. That was what had been disturbing me. Everything so neat and pat.

"But you don't believe it," I said slowly.

"Let's just leave it that I'm going to offer Dr. Quinn the use of the laboratory—and suggest an analysis of the remains might be in order." He came to me swiftly. "In any event, you must not blame yourself. However it happened, you're not responsible."

How I wanted to accept that, but I could not. My coming to Wychwood had been the catalyst for all that followed.

Dr. Quinn came downstairs, carrying his bag, and left with Jeremy. I went upstairs to tell Nell we were going home. I ought to have remembered she could read me like a book. She took one look and sat bolt upright, and commenced to tremble. "Something's happened. No—no, don't try to hide it from me. I must know!"

"Mr. Roach is dead." I caught at her hands and held them against me, and said sharply, "*No*. I know what you're imagining, and it isn't true. This had nothing to do with any feelings he had for me. He was not in love with me, nor I with him, and we both knew it."

I was not prepared for the intensity of her reaction. Cold beads of moisture stood out on her forehead, and she shook as though she had the ague. "No, you're wrong. He had to have cared, otherwise the Old Ones wouldn't let—"

"Nell, *listen* to me!" I grabbed her by the shoulders and fairly shook her. "I hadn't wanted you to have to know. He was stealing from us, and I found out, and told him so. He was only pretending tender feelings to keep me from finding out."

Strangely, as though a magic potion had canceled out all tension, Nell's face cleared. "So it's all right, then," she said, astonishingly. "He was meant to— Camilla, don't you see? The Old Ones are looking out for you. Like the villagers who owned those sheep, and Lady Margaret—he tried to do you harm and he was punished."

"Stop that! The Old Ones had not a thing to do with it. Apparently"—how automatically I found myself using Jeremy's words—"apparently he couldn't face the disgrace of exposure, and killed himself."

"That's all right, dear." Nell patted my hand, looking at me in that way that so alarmed me, with the look of an old, old woman talking to a child. "You don't have to understand. You're protected, that is all that matters."

She smiled tenderly, fell back against the pillows and closed her eyes.

I sat back, aghast and silent, contemplating her frail figure. I had been so concerned about her health and physical welfare—why had I not realized there were other dangers? Philip's stories, Georgina's superstitions and Nell's vivid imagination, her propensity for fancy—I ought to have known, I who had been haunted all these years, deep beneath conscious thought, by remembrance of a voodoo ceremony and a Book of Shadows. Oh, Laura had been right in thinking the air from Wychwood Rise was poisoned. Some force, someone, was reaching out tentacles of the Old Religion to ensnare the children.

Thank God it was physically impossible for Nell to have been at the rites in the grave circle, in the Italian garden. I had never thought I could be grateful for my sister's handicap, but I was now. But the others—Rafe, Georgina . . . I would not, could not, let my mind think further.

Jeremy came back, at last, saying all the formalities had been attended to. He helped me take Nell home. After her outburst she was drained and pale, silent. She had a very bad night, clinging to me and moaning. It meant neither of us was able to think, which was a blessing.

I rose up in the morning feeling drugged, and I was still at the breakfast table when the door knocker sounded and Amy Ross was there.

"Why, Amy, dear." I covered my astonishment. "Are you ready to resume your lessons?"

"I hope you don't mind. I needed to get out. I can't stop thinking." She had, I think, lost weight; her bones were too close to the surface of her small face and she looked ghost-haunted.

"How is your mother?"

"Better. I'm not allowed to see her. She says I make her nervous." Amy's hands were tense and restless. "Please, Miss Jardine, can we read?"

I set her some Latin to translate, feeling that it might help to occupy her troubled mind. She worked at it with a kind of dogged desperation, but after a time she faltered and grew still.

"What is it, dear?" I gazed over her shoulder at her stopped finger. "*Inexorabilis*? Inexorable." That word that had so characterized for me the relentless tide of events of the past few months. "You know what that means, don't you?"

"Unyielding, unalterable, that even prayers can't change, doesn't it?" Amy stopped completely, and a hot tear spilled down on her hand.

"Amy, dear." I bent toward her quickly. "Put that book away. Do you want to talk?"

"No. I—I can't. I've been so bad. You don't know." Her tears were coming freely now, with a kind of hopeless fatalism. "Mama's been so ill . . . I didn't know. I've been such a disappointment to her, and I've hurt her. And it can't be stopped, can it? Like those one-way lych gates—you don't know, till you've gone too far, that there's no turning back. But I didn't mean—" She pressed her hand up, hard, against her mouth, while I gazed at her in considerable alarm.

"I really think that you had better tell me. Please do. One always feels better, you know, when something's shared."

"I can't. I swore an oath—and it's no use, anyway. Once the powers have been called down, they can't be stopped, and if one's bound to serve—" Amy stopped abruptly, looking terrified. Then, in a violent rush, she flung herself into my arms and hugged me hard. "Goodbye. You've been good to me. I'm truly sorry for the trouble I've caused."

She stumbled out as I stared after her, a wild surmise flashing across my brain. The expression in Amy's eyes . . . Something nagged at my memory; then, with a cold stab of recognition, I understood. Just so had my own face stared back at me from the mirror, a stranger's face, when at her age I'd fled back to my own room from a ritual fire.

Amy behind the dangerous currents of the Old Religion? I could not believe it. But Amy caught in its toils, a sick and fascinated victim—yes. She was so suggestible. And there were others who could play upon that vulnerability, who knew the old ways and had the necessary craft. Raphael. Georgina. Jeremy . . . *No*, both instinct and reason rebelled against that panic-prompted thought. Jeremy would never knowingly corrupt the children. But Philip . . . Philip had been so intrigued by Jeremy's strangeness, until he perceived him as a rival. Philip was fascinated by the Old Ones. Philip, as Charles had said, loved to throw rocks into still-seeming ponds and watch the ripples.

My mind fled from the dark images it was projecting. I threw myself into my research the rest of that endless day. I kept away from Nell, who was burrowed in a cocoon of featherbeds and pain. Nell was so sensitive to my thoughts and moods, she was already too much affected by the Old Religion's spell. I had let Philip and Georgina talk to her too unwisely. *Nell* . . . I could not bear to have her innocence blighted by too-early knowledge of dark forces. A sudden vision of that dream I'd had, of all of us in spell-working circle and Nell in center, a mute victim, flashed over me, and I pressed my hands across my eyes.

I turned in desperation to translating Latin:

discipline good for the student is good for the teacher too. But here, also, I found escape to the ivory tower blocked. I came, without warning, up against familiar lines.

> I hate and I love. Why . . . I do not
> know, but
> I feel it, and I am in torment.

Toward midafternoon Laura walked in unannounced. I had forgotten to lock the door today; it seemed now a futile and needless gesture. "I hope you don't mind. I had to come to you." Laura flung back her hood, and her face looked unutterably weary.

"I'm glad you did." I scanned her closely, concern turning to alarm. "What has happened? Not your father and Lady Margaret's medicine—"

"It's worse than that," Laura said starkly. "I've come from the Manor. Amy Ross has had an overdose of laudanum."

Cold spread through my veins like an icy tide. "Another . . . accident?"

"I'm afraid not. She'd written a note, and the first thing she said was why did we bring her back, she was so bad, and she had to go before she got so much worse she was afraid to." We looked at each other, sickness in our eyes.

"I can't believe it." I sat down slowly.

"Nor can I. I'm getting so I don't know what one can believe. Well, Father pulled her through; she'll be all right physically, anyway." Laura walked to the window and stood looking out at the still grey village. "I swear to God, I wonder sometimes if there is something to the old wives' tales about how Wychwood Forest is malignant, cursed. There are so many separate, unrelated evils happening."

"Not unrelated," I heard my own voice saying. "Like the separate cords used to cast spells in the old rituals—all intersecting at one common core."

"And God alone knows what that is. God . . . or the Other."

"The 'other' is something in ourselves, of that much I'm sure," I said slowly. "The pull away from God, toward selfishness, self-gratification, power, evil—whatever name one names it." I quoted the old Prayer Book formula, " '. . . envy, hatred, malice and all uncharitableness.' "

Laura's head came up. "The same words I've been thinking. There is nothing new under the sun, is there? It's all as old as time. But no less frightening when it comes home to one's own circle." She stopped and closed her eyes. "That poor child. I may have done something unwise. She was so distraught, blaming herself somehow for her mother's illness. I had to tell her the truth, that there could have been an accident with the medicine, not her fault at all. Well, it's in the lap of the gods now. I'd best go home; I don't like leaving Father alone these days. The strain's telling on him." Laura took a deep breath. "Perhaps it would be better for us if the whole truth *could* come out, whatever happens."

"Truth at any cost? That's what Jeremy says."

"Jeremy." Laura's voice was a whisper, not meant for my ears, but it's tone caught me at the quick. I moved toward her, and she put her hand out. "No. You must not feel guilty. Promise me that. We have had enough of quiet and secrets in this village." She came and kissed me, and murmuring, "I must go," left swiftly.

She had been gone but a few minutes when Jeremy appeared and flung himself heavily in the chair before the fire. "Lord, Lord, what a world this is we live in."

"You look tired to death."

"I am, now that you mention it." Jeremy rubbed his hand across his brow. "To death—the words that come to mind."

"What have you been doing?"

Jeremy started to say something, stopped, seemed to change his mind. "Will you come out with me?" he said at last. "I've brought the trap. Let us run away from all mysteries for an hour or so. We both need escape for a time to where the air is clear."

I went with him gladly, out into a world awash with January thaw. The Cotswold stone glowed with a deceptive, futile radiance through the haze. We rode in silence, lost in our own thoughts, and after several miles the air did seem purer and wan shafts of sunlight arrowed through the gloom. We had come out upon an open ridge that looked across two counties, and opposite us on a neighboring rise was a large white building, its architecture alien and forbidding.

Jeremy let his breath out in a kind of sob. "There is no escape, then, is there? Our ghosts are not tied conveniently to Wychwood Rise. They travel with us, in ourselves."

"What is that place?"

"The County Madhouse. An object lesson to us both. *That* is the fate of those who become so deeply involved in one facet of their lives that they lose their balance of reality. We keep them as we do our rarer monsters, and on fine days the populace comes to be entertained by their antics."

"Jeremy, how horrible."

He shifted restlessly. "We're both safe, aren't we? No matter how we try, our touchstone of reality intrudes. Who shall speak first, you or I?"

"What's happening with Charles Roach?"

"He's being buried tomorrow afternoon. Death labeled 'accident' for the rector's ears, and 'suicide' in the chief constable's private eyes. He leaped on the death-to-avoid-exposure theory with cries of joy, and Dr. Quinn's convinced it's all as clear as water. Everyone's satisfied but me and thee."

"You found out something, then."

Jeremy contemplated his boots ironically. "How little we know ourselves, really, do we? And the more we think we do, the greater is our folly. A day ago I'd have sworn an oath I was long past ever wanting to run back to blessed ignorance." He was silent for a moment. "Yes, I found out. The estimable Charles died of taxine poisoning."

"*Taxine.*"

Jeremy shot me a look. "You were expecting atropine? To be honest, so was I. And I think a suggestion to Lady Margaret that she investigate all the business Roach transacted for her, very carefully, would be in order. He was handling affairs for her, you know, as well as you. No, it was taxine, all right. Not deadly nightshade; deadly yew."

"*Yew!*"

"As from the tree in the grave circle, or the hedge beyond your walls. The berries are highly toxic; every country child knows that. Charles Roach might not. Perhaps."

"Are you saying it might not have been suicide?"

"I? I have already said far too much." Jeremy made a bitter, grandiose gesture. "The sin of Adam, the need to *know*. Well, I'm cured now, at least, of rushing in on impetuous curiosity alone. Knowledge without wisdom can be a dangerous thing. Too late one finds one has drawn down the powers, set forces in motion that cannot be stopped. Witness poor foolish Charles. What starts with a bit of borrowing ends with a handful of yew. Why yew berries, anyway? Why not the proper manly bullet through the head? And why no note?"

"It's not so simple, is it?" I said slowly. "Charles. Lady Margaret. The sheep. The Old Religion. Philip's traumas. Amy Ross taking an overdose of laudanum. They're all tied together, and we both know it."

Jeremy looked at me oddly. "How can you be so sure?"

"Because I've been doing research in a Book of Shadows."

Jeremy's eyebrows rose. "Where *did* you find one?"

"You know what it is, then?"

"You knew I would. And no, I'm not a member of the Craft, if that's your next question."

"You didn't hide the book for me to find?"

"I'd no more leave one of those things around," Jeremy said bluntly, "than I would a bowl of candy-coated poison. Where did you find it?"

"Behind the books in the case beside the fireplace. After I'd fine-tooth-combed every shelf in the house in search of one." A wave of sickness washed over me. "Who, do you suppose? And who could have, or would have, given Charles Roach taxine? We've all been inhaling poison vapors. Nobody's safe, nobody's innocent. We're all drowning in a sea of guilt, and that *is* possession. And oh, dear God, I'm so very tired."

"So much for running away," Jeremy said heavily, and picked up the reins and turned us back toward home.

The day was well into twilight when we arrived, but the lamps in the front windows had not yet been lit. Jeremy pulled up at the door and got down, then turned back toward me. "Lord, Lord, it lacketh only this."

"What is it?"

"Another small epistle of esteem. Hung on the knocker this time, with no *athone*." He pulled it down, and we squinted at it in the dimness.

A row of figures ran across the top, recognizable as symbols. Sheep. Walled fields. A woman marked with a ducal coronet. A man in lawyer's robes. A child. Separated from them by a cross, the familiar figure of a woman dressed in black. Beneath them, lines of verse.

For the past one hundred year,
Nothing have we had to fear.
Now the curse has all come back—
Copper Doom has turned to black.

Jeremy crumpled it bitterly in his hand. "All my intellectual curiosity and all my pride, and I can't protect you from the likes of this."

I put my hand on his shoulder. "Let it go now. Come inside and I'll make you tea."

We stepped in silence into the still, dark hall. There was no sign of Georgina's presence, and Kersey's Room was cloaked in shadows. Jeremy started toward the fireplace, but I said quickly, "No. I have a need, somehow, to keep from light."

"So have we all." Jeremy flung himself down in the nearest chair. "Drowning in a sea of guilt, you said. Who do you think it was came dashing into the village, ferreting out traces of the Old Ones, poking and prying for juicy bits to study? Who talked much too freely to young Ross, delighted to show off and flattered by his interest? If the village wants to throw stones, it should start with me, not you."

"Oh, my dear." I looked at him. "It *is*

possession, isn't it? Guilt. And suspicion. The effort to shift the burden from one's own conscience to another's. You were right when you said that things once put in motion cannot be stopped. We started asking questions, and we must go on to the bitter end—till the whole truth's out, no matter what the cost. Otherwise none of us will be able to look each other in the eye."

"Easily said, when one does not know the cost," Jeremy said heavily. "Dear God, I wish I could protect you from it. But I can't. No one can. We're in too far, all tied in it together. God, God, God." His face dropped on his hands.

I did the only thing I could do—went to him, put my arms around him and held him tightly, his head against my breast. "Oh, my love. Don't. We *are* together, we'll see it through together. And we'll find the truth."

"Truth. There still are a few great absolutes remaining, aren't there? Thank God for that. Truth, love, pursuit of self-knowledge, work. They'll be our sanity, and we'll hold to them." He rose and stood looking at me for a long moment, kissed my hands, and left.

I turned and moved toward the center table, lost in thought. There were boxed matches there, and I struck one and lit the lamp. It was across that circle of warm light that I looked, startled, into my sister's face.

Nell, sitting by the fireplace, hid in shadows. Nell, an unseen, involuntary witness to our private scene. Nell, looked at me mutely, lost, sad, despairing. I ran to her quickly. "Oh, darling, it's not what you think. Well, yes, it is, but it won't shut you out. Nothing could. It's just making the circle bigger, letting in more affection. Oh, Nell, please be happy for me, for I do love him."

"Of course I want you to be happy." Nell said slowly. "It's all I've ever wanted, to make you safe and happy. So everything turns out like a storybook, after all. Not a dark fairy tale." She shivered, groping for her blanket. "I shall be very glad when this is all over."

"It will be soon, I promise you. We'll see to it."

"You really mean that, don't you?" Nell asked gravely. Her eyes searched my face. Suddenly her expression was transfigured by a tender smile. "I do love you. I've always loved you. You know that, don't you?"

I hugged her hard, and could not speak.

Nell retired early that night, and so did I;

we were both exhausted. But long after she was shut safe away in the secret room with its protecting door, I lay awake. I stared up at the carved tester and the dark images I had conjured earlier rose up to haunt me. More and more strongly came the feeling that the missing knowledge, the touchstone piece that would make all the rest of the puzzle fall into focus, lay within me. Unperceived, unrecognized as yet, but *there*. It was I, I only, who could find it.

But not here. Here my vision was too clouded. And all at once, quietly and clearly, I understood where I must go. I made no conscious decision, yet I was rising, I was dressing methodically, I was slipping downstairs, careful to make no sound. Out the door, into the moonlit night. Up the street past the common, through the lych gate, the cemetery beyond. Up and up, deliberately, calmly, to the grave circle on the hill. It was here, in the vulnerability of old fears, I had first struggled with the aura of evil that possessed the village. It was here, armored now with the paradox of head and heart, that I must face it down.

The white stones gleamed like marble in their mysterious circle, but there were no waves of conflict, no negative energies present now. Perhaps the ritual of Samhain, the laying to rest of Gypsy Aaron's spirit, had banished them. The grave circle was purged and at peace; the air beneath the dark, mysterious yew was sweet.

It was from behind me that the restless forces came.

I do not know when I first became conscious of their presence. They grew and swelled, became one body, one pulsing source of malignant power, such as had seized me on that first encounter here. It was not here now, but behind me, back in the direction from which I'd come. And I was no more its helpless victim. I knew it for what it was, knew the potential for it within myself, and therefore, knowing, I was free.

But still, still it reached me, pulling as for a final confrontation. And I could not close my eyes. I turned, and looked.

The village was so still, sleeping in the moonlight. So still and peaceful. The thatch of Tarr Farm, Quinn Cottage, Wychwood was like silver, and silver were the slow ripples of water in the river. No lights burned, and on the street and common, nothing stirred. But in the walled garden of Wychwood, a figure moved.

A figure that was the fountainhead of the pulsing power, the form of a young girl moving through a ritual dance, her hair like molten copper down her back.

It was some vision, some figment of the legend of the Copper Maid, thrown in my mind's eye by my moon-dazzled senses. It was not real, could not be real. But still it pulled me, like the irresistible magnetism of some terrible truth. Down from the hill I came, as though sleepwalking, as though I were imprisoned by a spell. Straight to the wall of yew, unerringly, and through the aperture hitherto unperceived but now so clear. Into the secret garden, like a shadow, like a wraith without a sound. To be brought up in the path, shocked, confronted by a knowledge I could no longer refuse to know.

The spell was wound up, the picture which had lurked just beyond the boundaries of awareness now was clear. For still another time in my life, I stared into the alien visage of the Stranger in a hitherto-familiar face. Stared at the dear figure loved better than life, known, I thought, better than I knew myself. The world whirled, then settled, crazily askew. The blood drummed in my temples, and all the apocalyptic demons screamed a name that echoed and reechoed in my horror-struck brain. Nell. *Nell.* NELL.

19

Rossford-under-Wychwood
January, 1864

FOR an instant we stood there, or an hour. Time had no meaning. Silence hung between us with the weight of centuries. Then I reached out, involuntarily, and Nell's mouth opened. From Nell's lips a stranger's voice, hate-filled, accusing, screamed: "Don't look at me like that! I did it for you! For you! *For you*! *To take care of you*!"

I shrank back, and Nell moved toward me. Walking. Nell, whom I had not seen standing these long months. She took two steps, three, then a shadow passed over her face, a shudder shook her. My own Nell's voice cried out in whimpering panic, her arms reached desperately. She swayed and fell.

She was doll-like, lying there on the damp ground. Her white nightdress glowed like phosphorus in the moonlight, and her hair tumbled round her shoulders, red-gold like the legendary Copper Maid's. *The Copper Maid, who'd not been seen for generations, but who had begun to walk again, once we had come.*

A tumult of comprehensions churned around me, but I pushed it resolutely to one side. Nell could not lie here thus. Unconscious, she looked smaller than ever, and more frail, ghost-possessed. I slid my arms beneath her, carefully, and as I did so her hand dropped away, the fingers uncurling like petals of a flower. Something fell from them. A clump of knotted silken cords. So small a thing, to touch my heart with ice and turn my blood to water in my veins.

I scooped the things up swiftly, as if they were alive, and thrust them in my pocket. Then, like an automaton, rigidly, mechanically, I lifted Nell and carried her inside. past the fire-place, where the ingle-nook door swung open on the gaping stairs. Up, through the deserted corridor, the empty room, through the cupboard to the secret chamber, to lay Nell down at last on her own bed. She looked so tiny and so vulnerable, so helpless. I covered her, and she stirred, and her own voice murmured, "Camilla?" like a weary child.

"Yes. I'm here."

Her fingers groped, caught my hand tight against her. "Stay here. Don't leave me! You mustn't ever leave me!"

"I won't. I promise." Thank God for my years of emotional control, I was able to hold together till she was asleep and I was in my room alone. The the waves of truth crashed upon me, sucking me into their force like helpless flotsam, and I could fight no more. My eyes were opened. I yielded to the reality which had lain dormant behind the shut door of my protective love, but which I could no more deny.

Oh, I had been right in thinking some malignant force was abroad in Rossford, right that none would believe me if I spoke the truth. But wrong, wrong in my identification of that evil's source. The power of Lady Margaret's love, like tentacles, had reached out to bind Philip close, to control the villagers and to hold us off. But her influence, harmful and misguided though it was, had been furthered by another presence more forceful, more possessive and more malignant.

Nell.

Nell—throwing herself from her window

because she thought she was going to lose me through my marriage. Nell—the night I came to London, crying, "We must be very good to one another, for we are all each other has now . . . I'll never, never leave you!"

Nell—playing one against another the people whom she loved and who loved her; people who feared for her, people who feared *her*. Myself. Philip, Amy—my throat caught and my eyes widened as the small canvas of my mind widened to become a panorama. Jeremy, who had warned her with his "Blessed be." Poor old Dr. Quinn, wrongly suspected. Lady Margaret, who had been determined to keep Philip from us. Charles, who had been wooing me, who had been engaging in an attempt to steal our treasure. The sheep of the villagers who had talked against us.

Nell, able to walk and never telling. Nell, creeping at night down the secret stairs to dance in the moonlight among the graves on Wychwood Rise. Nell, her hair coincidentally red, bringing to life the legend of the Copper Maid and spreading terror, superstition and fear. Nell, using the force of her personality—and helplessness—to compel Philip and Amy to do her bidding. Nell, finding, as I had done, a Book of Shadows, working the same spell I once had worked to "bewitch" farm animals. Nell, putting datura and yew into cups of tea.

Nell, who loved me too deeply, too completely.

Darkness swept down upon me, and in that darkness, like echoes in a dungeon, came the memory of Jeremy's voice as we rode home from the asylum.

"Persons who were ill were often thought witches in the old days. Now and then these old shire families would breed a monster, or a poor, sick unfortunate. Rather than expose it to the village's hands, they would build a secret room and hold it fast, making a world for it within their own four walls." My "How terrible!" and Jeremy's "Yes, but an act of love. And kinder, all in all. It was, after all, their monster."

Nell. She was a monster, but she was my own. All she had done had sprung from that terrible, misguided love for me. And what was more—

The darkness lapped at the shores of sense again, but I fought it fiercely. Nell's obsessive need was only half the story. And the other half—I drew a long and painful breath. Lady

Margaret had been right, then, hadn't she? The other half was that, knowingly or not, I had encouraged Nell's and Philip's dependency, having some need for it deep within myself. Only when I had begun to change, to reach out as a whole person, had the troubles come.

Possession, witchcraft, the villagers had called it. There were all kinds of witches and all kinds of possessions. *May God have mercy on us all.*

Truth, one of the last great absolutes, was out at last. "No matter what the cost," I'd said, and Jeremy: "I wish I could protect you from it. But I can't." He knew. His wits, unclouded by family ties, had guessed before me. And we could not go back to ignorance, nor stop the forces we had set in motion.

I was too tired to grapple with it now. Exhaustion, like blessed oblivion, washed over me, and I slept. I awoke very early with the silver dawn, but it was some hours before I could bring myself to go into the secret room. Nell lay sleeping, looking small and fragile, and there were circles like dark stains underneath her eyes. The dark carved frame and posters of the bed were like cage bars.

She looked so vulnerable, like a mute victim, and the nightmare that had haunted my dreams flooded back.

All of us in a circle, caught by cords. Nell in center. Victim? No. Catalyst and cause. If she was still and drained, it was because her malignant forces flowed out along the cords to poison us. It was our lives, our spirits, our wholeness she sucked to replenish hers.

Nell stirred and her eyelids fluttered. Her voice, like a child's voice, murmured drowsily, "Camilla?"

"Yes."

Nell's lips curled in a contented smile. She pushed herself up sleepily on the pillows. "It's morning, isn't it?" Her gaze grew puzzled. "Why do you look at me so strangely? What is it, dear?"

I reached into my pocket and flung its contents on the bed. A handful of silken cords.

The look of relief and ecstatic joy that filled Nell's face made a chill run through me. "You know! I'm so glad. I've wanted to tell you, but I've not known how."

"You were working spells in the garden." I took a leap in the dark. "Against Jeremy. You've been able to walk all this time. You've lied to me."

"Not lied," Nell said swiftly. "Never lied. And not all this time. Only since All Hallow's . . . like a miracle. But you wouldn't believe in the Old Ones, so you'd have been shocked. But it's all right now, I won't have to keep the secret any more." She reached out to me, and her face was radiant. "Oh, Camilla, I promised I'd look after you. I knew I had to, as a sacred trust, once I found out that I had the power."

"Once you found out you could pull the wool over my eyes," I heard my voice say coldly. "You didn't fall out of the window, did you? You threw yourself to get attention, and Amy knew it."

Nell's eyes clouded with hurt. "No! I meant to die. I'd been so bad, and you no longer needed me. Then—when I lived—I knew God had a purpose for me. I wished your Martin dead, and he did die, and it was up to me to protect you in his place—keep you safe from ever being hurt again. You weren't meant to belong to anyone else but me, you see. I knew it then."

I could only stand there dumbly, watching her.

"I had the power," Nell's voice went on in that musing tone. "I'd always thought I had, but I wasn't sure. Then we came here and people were cruel to you. I had to protect you and I knew I had to use it."

"It was your Book of Shadows, then," my lips said stiffly.

"It was Papa's. I found it long ago. It was very naughty of you to take it from me."

Nell was regarding me with a tender, tolerant smile that made me tremble. "All the superstition, all the outbreaks of the Old Religion, *you* brought that here."

"No! It was here already." Nell's eyes took on a mystical light. "Philip . . . I knew as soon as I saw him that he was one of the Children of the Sun. Philip drew the power down on me and made me walk again." She flashed me a pitying look. "*You* have power. You could have been one of us. But you'd have been afraid."

"The atropine poisoning. The sheep. Lady Margaret. The taxine in Charles Roach's tea."

"But I had to do it," Nell said gently. "They were hurting you. If they died, they brought it on themselves, you see? But you must not fear. They will not hurt you now, no one will ever hurt you. We will be everything to one another, as we used to be, and I will protect you."

She sounded like a mother speaking to a very young child. She was looking at me with the face of Michelangelo's Madonna, her eyes filled with pure love, and that was the greatest horror of it all.

I could not stay there, looking at the pure innocence of her face. I stumbled out, locking the cupboard shut, and groped my way out to the upper hall. I clung to the newelpost at the stairhead, and nausea swept me.

Nell. *Nell.* What would become of her? Child of Lucifer, a fallen angel, dangerous to others and to herself. Nell who, newborn and bereft like Katherine's orphaned infant, had been put in my hungry arms with the admonition that I must be a mother to her. Nell, who had dazzled me since I was nine . . . I must not give way to memory and emotion, for therein lay madness. Hold to the touchstone of reality, Jeremy had said.

Nell was a murderess; Nell was not sane. The noose, or the asylum. Everything that was in me, head and heart together, screamed out *No*. It must not be. We would protect her, Jeremy and I. But Nell had killed, and could kill again. No one was safe with her, save only I. *Jeremy* was not safe. The burden of whatever was to happen lay with me alone.

There can be other accidents, a voice of temptation whispered; *there are herbs in the garden that lead to sweet and dreamless sleep*.

No. No matter what she'd done, I could not face my God with the knowledge that I had caused my sister's death. Nor could I allow Nell to go free, harming others and being harmed by them. I must do as those bygone ancestors had done, keep Nell shut up here, and make a world for her, a world apart. And dedicate myself to be her keeper. Nothing else would hold others off from discovering the truth. Nothing else would keep Nell from seeking to escape. I dropped my head against the newel-post and my breath was like a sob.

In love, guilt, compassion, Nell must be allowed to win. We must be all in all to one another. Let one person enter, and he was not safe. Nell was not safe. So no one must come between us. Not even—God and my love, forgive me—not even Jeremy.

One does what one has to do. I moved through the day as if mesmerized, telling Georgina in a stiff parody of my normal voice that Nell was not well, was not to be disturbed, was not to have any visitors at all. I sent word to Aaron Smith that he was to come install locked bars on the cupboard, on the inglenook door; Nell could not be allowed to wander free at will.

Aaron Smith was not available until tomorrow, for today he was gravedigger at Charles Roach's funeral. Charles—victim, victimizer. So were we all. And Nell the most. I could pity her, pity her terribly, but I could not yet forgive.

In midafternoon Jeremy came to the door. "I'm on my way to church for the funeral. I stopped to see if you would want to come."

"No. I can't go out. And I can't ask you in."

He gave one look at me and came in firmly, shutting the door behind him. "What has happened? You look as if you'd seen beyond the gates of Hell."

"I think I have." He took a step toward me, and I flung up a hand to hold him off. "No! We can't. We must hold on to reality, as you said. And I've not been doing that, not since the Morris. I've been living in a world of dreams."

"Camilla, look at me! What in God's name are you trying to say?"

"That I have other responsibilities I've been forgetting. I'm not free." My hands went to Katherine's golden locket, and I lifted it off from round my neck, put it in his hands, closed his fingers over it. "Take it. Please. It's all that I can give you—perhaps ever."

Jeremy grabbed me by the shoulders and shook me roughly. "I won't let you do this."

"I must. One does what one has to do. Help me! Don't make it harder for me." I stumbled blindly from his touch, and he stood regarding me across the eternity of space that yawned between us.

"One does what one must," he said quietly. "I, too, you know. Don't think for one moment, lady, that this is the end."

But it had to be. I did not look at him as he turned and went. I must armor my private heart, for I dared not be vulnerable to his love.

I shut myself into the stillroom and drowned myself in *The Education of a Christian Woman*, seeking Katherine's wisdom, seeking understanding. And when at twilight I saw Philip's twisted figure toiling up Wychwood Rise, I flew upstairs to confront Nell in the secret room.

"*Was Philip here?*"

Nell was curled on the tester bed like a

kitten, her face bewildered innocence. "What made you ask?"

"Don't play games. The time for that is past. You let him in, didn't you, up the fireplace stairs? He's not to come here any more, do you understand? Not ever."

Nell's face altered. "I saw Mr. Bushel."

"You won't again. You wanted us to be all in all to one another. Very well, that is the way it will have to be." I moved out of the reach of her outstretched arms.

I went downstairs, and Georgina brought me my solitary tea. *Georgina.* What should I do about her? I could not manage this house alone. Would the bars on the cupboard be sufficient protection to keep her and Nell apart? She knew too much already; did I have enough power over her to keep her silent? I would think about that tomorrow. The decisions already made had drained me dry.

What had Hamlet said? That each day's duty done, each day's absence from felicity, made the next easier? This day was endless, and when at last night fell, Georgina was gone and the house was still, I could hold back no more. My weary body refused the dictates of my mind, and I gave way to tears.

There was a creaking. The inglenook door

had opened, and then Nell stood there. The Nell I had so loved, frail and tender. Her red-gold hair hung down her back like a copper veil and her arms were outstretched in forgiving pity.

"Ah, Camilla. My own dear Camilla. It will be all right, we'll make it all right, you'll see." Her arms went round me, and all the memories of my first days in England came back to me. She was the mother now, and I the child. She held me tight, rocking me and crooning. She made herb tea.

"Drink it, it will help you sleep. Sleep with me tonight in the secret room, Camilla, please!" Her eyes looked at me with anxious pleading above the rim of her steaming cup.

I must try, I would have to try. "Love given grudgingly is no love at all, and it is a terrible thing," Nell had said long ago, "to be someone's duty." If I could not dedicate myself to Nell with heart as well as mind, I was in truth condemning her to a prison. So I acceded to her wish, and I disposed of the unwanted tea in a potted plant when she could not see.

Nell fell asleep quickly, but I could not. When her breathing grew slow and quiet, I crept out of bed, out of the room, closing both panel and cupboard door behind me. All the anguish and tumult of my heart pulled me to the sanctuary of Kersey's Room. I lit one lamp and sat there in the stillness, and slowly, slowly, the warmth and benevolence of Katherine's presence formed around me.

Katherine, lady wiser than I, how do I bear it? How do I forgive?

Involuntarily my hand went up to where the token had hung, and hung no more. My fingers felt in memory every curve of the burnished gold; my mind's eye saw the poignant contents. Three locks of hair. Katherine's gold, Seymour's brown-auburn, their daughter's red-gold curl.

A curl of red-gold hair. Like Nell's. Like the mythical Copper Maid.

Red-gold hair from a beloved young girl. But not their daughter. Never their daughter. The truth sprang before me with a blaze of light.

Have you ever wondered how superstitions start? Like a tumult of bells Jeremy's words rang in my brain. *Sometime in the 1540's a young girl walked here, where she ought not be. A girl with red-gold hair. Why is it, do you suppose, that no one has ever inquired into the identity of the original Copper Maid?*

I knew, I knew why now. In the sixteenth century, as in the nineteenth, villages were fiercely protective of their own. Lips had been sealed, the secret not passed on, and in another generation the reason behind whatever catastrophe had been visited on the village had been lost. *I hate and I love . . . I am in torment.* A young girl had walked where she ought not to be, and heads had rolled. Ultimately, Thomas Seymour's own.

There had been a young girl of Nell's own age, with Nell's own copper hair, in Thomas's life. In Katherine's. A girl with Nell's gift for magic, who according to legend had been so badly, mysteriously hurt, she had never risked any trust in love again. A girl in whose youth there had been a period about which history was blankly, almost deliberately silent. A girl to whom Thomas had incautiously proposed marriage soon after Katherine's death. Who had been in unexplained seclusion in the Cotswolds during Katherine's lying-in. Who had, despite deep bonds between them, not been allowed at Katherine's funeral. Who'd been sent away from Katherine's household, in some strange, never-spelled-out disgrace. From Katherine's household, where dwelt Thomas Seymour, lecher, opportunist, with an eye to any pretty maid.

Nell was not the first witch-child to be possessed by that fatal mixture, the sensuality and instincts of a woman in the innocent vulnerability of a child.

A bewitching, dangerously catalytic red-haired girl who had been old enough for secret assignations, young enough not to comprehend their terrible folly. Who was a humanist scholar, and even at thirteen could write "*I hate and I love*" on a secret window, and known its meaning in both mind and heart. Who had been loved by Katherine, and had betrayed that love. It was Katherine's spirit who possessed this house, but it was not Katherine's secret that the house possessed.

Katherine's stepdaughter, the original Copper Maid, the ultimate red-haired enchantress. Elizabeth. Elizabeth Tudor loves Thomas Seymour. "*I hate and I love.*"

Three locks of hair. Three lives intertwined by star-crossed loves. The locket itself, love token—Henry VIII to Katherine, to Seymour, to Elizabeth. Elizabeth learning so young that Thomas, her first love, was no more faithful to her than Henry, her father and sovereign lord, had been to her mother

Anne Boleyn. It had been *Elizabeth* speaking, in that memento mori Lady Kersey had penned. As a clue—to the other part of the treasure, to a pledge.

A love-letter pledge from Elizabeth to Thomas Seymour, revealing the secret of the centuries? A priceless treasure that would be, indeed. And Katherine, knowing—for she would have known. Katherine, tortured by love for both of them, by anguish at how they had betrayed that trust. Katherine, torn by head and heart, like a mirror image of myself.

Mirror. Like a sleepwalker I rose and crossed the room, stared at my reflection in the tarnished glass. *Yes*, cried the voice of that other self within me. *Yes*, echoed Katherine's spirit. And the very air of the room commenced to vibrate.

I lifted it down, the mirror; laid it face down on the table; picked up the letter-opener dagger and very carefully began prying off the back. And within minutes they were in my hands. Thin, brittle paper, so old, so very old. I spread the first out carefully with trembling fingers.

The words leaped up at me, the angular letters familiar from a dozen facsimiles in scholar's books. Familiar on the window but for the fact they had been scratched not with a pen but with a diamond on a young girl's despairing hand.

My lord, my liege, my love—Never again in her whole life would she commit herself so freely. She had learned much of treachery and danger, a girl not yet fifteen, waiting in a secret room to tryst with the lover who never came. Waiting, while at Sudeley, Katherine lay in painful labor. Waiting until, imprudently, she had wandered on Wychwood Rise, giving rise to the legend of the Copper Maid. She would have been seen, would have been hustled off by followers who were older, wiser and more cautious. Calamity would have followed; heads would have rolled from those not loyal, who could not be trusted with the scandalous secret.

A love letter, the outpourings of an impassioned, trusting girl. And at bottom, the endorsement, the mark that made it valued beyond price. The signature in her own hand. *Elizabeth.*

Feverishly I opened the other letters. The first tore at my heart. In the same angular writing, an anguished plea for Katherine's forgiveness. *I hope all goes well with you, and with the babe. I send you for the child a coverlet made for me at my birth by the Queen my mother . . . Dear Madam, never, never have I ceased to love you, to hold you in respect. I have sinned against you, and am in torment. I pray your Highness, in the boundless goodness of her heart, to send forgiveness . . .*

And Katherine's answer, formal, brief, austere, giving thanks for the gift, advising decorous behavior. Nothing more, no miracle, no grace, and the taste in my mouth was dust and ashes. Then I saw it, the Latin motto, twisted in tiny letters like an ornament around the signature of Katherine the Queen. Prudent Katherine, who would not risk private matters falling into dangerous hands.

Omnia vincit amor. Classical motto proper and correct, but Elizabeth would have grasped at it with a surge of joy. *Love conquers all.* Katherine knew everything and, knowing, was still able to transcend both hurt and hate with love.

Tout comprendre, c'est tout pardonner. To understand all is to forgive all. The terrible burden, like a weight upon my lungs, was gone. The weight which had assailed me, stopping up my breath when I stood in the grave circle and confronted the Doom Window which was an allegory of my inner self.

Weight of conflict, weight of sin—not, as I had thought, from some outside source of malevolent power but from within ourselves. *Vainglory . . . envy, hatred, malice, and all uncharitableness.*

Katherine had known them, must have known them, for she was very human—as her infatuation with Thomas Seymour proved. But Katherine, rather than being possessed by them, had overcome. Knowing all—of herself, Thomas, Elizabeth—she had at last been able to forgive all, and still love.

I could not wholly do that yet, but I was on the way. The warmth of Katherine's spirit was all around me, the aura of her presence and an odor like incense in sweet-pungent smoke.

An odor of smoke . . . My head jerked up, and like air at a crash of thunder, my senses cleared. This was no metaphysical aura, no manifestation from the afterworld. Grey streamers of thick haze curled down the stairwell, reaching out to me beckoning, insidious fingers. Fire.

20

Rossford-under-Wychwood
January, 1864

JEREMY had said not to use the chimney of the secret chamber, and I had not heeded. Jeremy had said beware of sparks on new unseasoned thatch, and I had forgotten. I bolted for the stairs, and the smoke flung a smothering blanket over me, driving me backward, gagging. I buried my nose and mouth in the sleeve of my nightdress and struggled on.

The smoke was pouring from about the secret room, and in the outer chamber, flames licked through the ceiling insufficiently repaired. The noxious fumes were thick in the cupboard that concealed the panel door. I clawed at it desperately, but it would not budge. It had jammed, as it had done before, the night of Jeremy's midnight visit. I screamed Nell's name, frantically, but no sound came from beyond the barricaded wall where she lay sleeping.

Back again, stumbling through the hall, choking and coughing. Somewhere, the precious Tudor letters fell from my grasp and I did not even know. Down the stairs, half falling, through rooms thick now with that inexorable pungent mist. To the inglenook in the fireplace, fumbling with the metal panel. It opened. God, it opened. Up, on hands and knees, through the thick close blackness of the passage, palms bruised by stones, entangling gown impeding. Wall, hard and unyielding, at passage end. Grope for the door. Push hard, throw weight with rising panic.

The door would not open; it was as tightly shut as if it had been jammed and barred.

Down, bumping and jolting on narrow, twisting stairs. Air in Kersey's Room now like an iron vise that gripped one's lungs. To the bell-pull, throwing myself like a dead weight upon it, not even wondering whether the village would come in answer.

The tapestry panel, weakened by my pull, tore from its moorings, precipitating me to the floor. The air was clearer here. I crawled, guided by some desperate instinct, to the stairs and up . . . up . . . back through the serpentine coils of grey clouds to the cupboard door. The bell had rung four times, five. Someone would come, someone had to come. The door would open. I pulled, pried, hammered. Nails breaking, fingers bleeding.

Behind me, flames reached hungrily for the bed hangings, caught, raced down them in a blaze of light. Flames licked avidly toward my nightdress billowing in the draft, and I did not heed. Choking, sobbing, muttering every prayer I'd ever known, I labored till breath was all but gone, and strength, and hope.

Then arms went round me, jerking me away. I fought and struggled, and Jeremy's voice shouted hoarsely, "No use—know that door—"

I clawed at him. "I have to—*Nell!*"

"I know. Have to get in from outside." He dragged me off forcibly; sheltered me under his arm as we stumbled downstairs, out into the blessed air.

There were people there, familiar faces taut over rhythmic labors. Georgina, Laban Greene and Daniel, Aaron Smith—a bucket brigade extended from the river. Laura's arms went round me. "Come away."

"I can't—Nell's in there—"

"*Nell!*" Philip catapulted through the

crowd to me, his voice anguished. "Where is she? Is she all right? I've got to—"

"She's in there. We can't get at her—"

"*Oh, my God*!" Philip's face was a mask of torment. "We've got to— Something's gone wrong! It wasn't meant to be this way!"

I grabbed at him. "*What way?* What's happening here? You *know*, don't you?"

"It was only supposed to be a little fire! I swear to God. Just an excuse, a shock, to explain why she could walk again! Otherwise I'd never—"

"You set it, didn't you? You've been a part of it, that's what you meant by guilt. All this time you've known what she was, and yet you've *helped* her." I was shaking him like some limp creature caught by a terrier, and he let me, until Jeremy jerked him free.

"I had to. I . . . loved her, and she needed me." His voice was low and sick, and I understood, oh, how I understood. He was in my arms, sobbing like a child, and I held him tightly.

Jeremy was staring upward, rubbing a soot-stained arm across his sweating brow. "Can't go up the roof, too much smoke and danger. Laban, your tall haying ladder . . ."

"Daniel!" Laban Greene ordered, and Dan

dashed off. Across the river, back; the ladder dragged, thrown against the wall of the secret garden. Jeremy vaulting upward, over; the ladder following, flung against the house. Jeremy mounting; the ladder looking so frail. Jeremy hammering against the quatrefoil window. My own voice shouting, "That's *Elizabeth's* writing." He not hearing. Glass shattering with a crash. Jeremy thrusting his head through, drawing back. "She's there, unconscious. But it's too narrow. I can't get through."

I wrenched myself from Laura's grasp, ran forward. Jeremy shouted, "*No*! Don't let her!" and Laban Greene's arms went round me with a grip of steel. It was Philip who plunged toward the secret garden.

"I can do it. I'm small. Help me, please!" His voice a sob. Aaron Smith lifting him, tossing him over the wall light as a playing ball. Jeremy, descending; then Philip's slight figure crawling up the ladder like a grotesque spider, the moonlight cruel upon his twisted back. Philip, vanishing through the quatrefoil where Elizabeth had scratched her anguish on just such a night. *I hate and I love . . .*

Then . . . nothing. Waiting. Stillness. Buckets splashing water in a futile rhythm. Laura's voice, whispering the words of the old prayer, joined by Mrs. Greene: "God, merciful and compassionate, . . . grant us Thy help in this our need." I struggled against the bonds that held me, and Laban Greene's voice said reassuringly, "Be no need to fear. Us'll get to th' maid, if so be God wills."

A murmur like a sigh, swelling, rising. Philip stumbling out the front door, doggedly carrying Nell's limp figure, Jeremy's arms supportively around him. Laban Greene released me and I ran to them, just as they sank with her to the street. Philip lifted a haggard face. "There was no fire there, and little smoke. But she's so cold."

I flung myself on Nell, pressing my ear frantically against her breast. Looking up at Jeremy, my eyes pleading for a denial he could not give.

"It's too late," Jeremy said quietly. "She's gone. I knew it at once."

Philip was shaking his head in a dazed stupor. "It can't be. There's no reason. That's not the way it was supposed to be."

"Yes, it was," I heard my own voice saying. "She told you only what she wanted you to know. There were meant to be two deaths, blamed on smoke. But the real reason was the herbal tea." Nell, insisting I drink with her, sleep with her in the secret room. Nell, when I wasn't looking, jamming the door catches to prevent a rescue that she did not wish. Nell, knowing she was no longer the focus of my whole heart, determining to possess me through shared death. And failing—powerless now to compel me because, my eyes being opened, I, too, possessed power. And the power of love, of wholeness always outweighed the powers of darkness.

Jeremy's hand was on my shoulder. He said gently, "The spell's wound up. Now you're free to love her. And forgive."

But I already had done that, before . . . I would never cease to be grateful to the grace of God which had enabled that to happen. And to Katherine, who had shown the way.

Katherine. I stared up at Jeremy, aghast. Then I was on my feet and running toward the house, Jeremy tearing after. He caught me on the doorstep. "In the name of God, woman, what are you doing?"

"The treasure—I found the treasure. Letters from Queen Elizabeth, in her own hand.

I dropped them upstairs, somewhere near the flames."

"Let them go." I struggled forward, and he interposed himself between and held me tightly. "*Let them go*. The hall's an inferno. We've already found what's really beyond price. Do you think I'll risk that by letting you go in there for a piece of *paper*?"

He led me, weary, beyond tears, to where Laura was kneeling by Nell's side.

"We'll take her to Father's office," Laura said. "You shall come too. I'll sit up with her if you like, but you must sleep."

I did not think I could, but Laura was wiser far than I. Healing sleep, blessed oblivion, folded around me like a soft caress.

When I awoke, the room was filled with winter sun and Laura was beside me. I struggled upward. "Why did you let me sleep? There's so much to be seen to."

"It's better you rested. There's no need; everything's being done." Laura hesitated, then went on with a matter-of-fact kindness for which I blessed her. "The village has rallied round. Georgina and I have dressed Nell in her favorite gown, and Lady Margaret sent down flowers. The rector's with her now; he'll arrrange the funeral for tomorrow if that suits you. Jeremy's having Aaron Smith make a coffin. Amy sends her love. She's better; that's one ray of light in darkness. And Philip's downstairs. He's been waiting for hours to see you. I'll send him away if you're not up to it."

"No. I'll come." I rose, and dressed, after Laura had left me, in the black gown she somehow had procured for me from Wychwood House. Mourning for Martin; mourning for Nell. The old life now was totally, completely gone. But soon, soon there would be an end to mourning.

Katherine's golden locket lay on the dresser. Jeremy must have brought it, amidst all he had had to cope with, as a talisman. I picked it up, tears rushing to my eyes. But I did not open it to look at the lock of red-gold hair.

Philip was pacing restlessly in the parlor when I entered. Behind me I heard Laura softly shut the door, leaving us alone together. We stared at one another across a boundless space of laden silence.

Philip looked suffering and exhausted, and there were burns and bruises on him. But despite the weariness the strain was gone out of his eyes, and there was a new serenity in his face. A man's face . . . he was no more the tortured Pan of the walled garden.

I held out my hands to him, and he came and kissed them. There were dark circles under his eyes that made me exclaim involuntarily, "My dear, are you all right?"

"Yes. Are *you*?"

"I shall be, now." There was a pause. "I'm glad you came," I said at last. "I want to thank you—it was very brave of you, what you did last night."

"I had to," he said simply.

"Yes, I know."

"You do know, all of it, don't you?" Philip regarded me with a kind of wonder.

"Not all. Enough to guess that Nell was behind all the bewitchments. And that she could not have done them on her own."

"No. If I'd said no to her—but I could not."

"Tell me," I said gently. "It will help."

"Confession good for the soul?" Philip's voice flickered with a flash of his old dark humor. At first I thought that he would not obey, but then the words came slowly, matter-of-factly, constructing knot by knot a web of horror. A village isolated, imprisoned in primordial patterns and superstitions,

Jeremy, investigating old lore, sharing his discoveries unwisely with an impressionable boy. A boy in whom irrational forces raged for freedom—as they did in Rafe Smith, in Georgina. And the others—Charles, driven for status; Lady Margaret, driven to control; Amy, too easily influenced, with her load of guilt. Oh, the village had been like a garden of rank fruit, ripe for picking. But the plucker, the catalytic agent, had been Nell.

Nell, initiated into the Great Rite, seeking a kind of healing and absolution and discovering what she called "the power." Oh, it was Rafe who had been responsible for the bloody tokens at my door; it was Jeremy and Charles seeking the hidden treasure. It had been the villagers' instinctive suspicion of the alien, and Lady Margaret's automatic response to my rival influence, which had created the climate of malignant tension. But Nell had sensed and used it, just as she had used Amy to spread the jimson weed on the hillside where it did not grow. Nell had been the spellbinder, weaving together all the disparate threads. The others, for all the troubles they had wrought, had been just pawns.

It was just happenstance, not an atavistic

pattern, that had recreated events from my own buried past. Or perhaps not; perhaps if I had never succumbed to the temptation of the Book of Shadows, had not left it, long ago in Charleston, where Nell first had found it . . . I must not think of that; I must let the dead past bury its dead, and allow Philip to find the gift of rebirth too.

"I always knew you were bound to find out someday," Philip said. "I . . . almost prayed you would. At first it all seemed so innocent, and right. Then, when I knew better, I could not stop. *You* could have."

"I'm not sure." I shuddered, remembering long memories. "Perhaps it would have been just cowardice."

"Or wisdom." He stood still, with an expression I could not read. "And can you—will you be able to—forgive?"

"Oh, my dear, we *all* need forgiveness. How can we then withold it?"

He lifted his eyes then, and for an instant, as had happened once or twice before, I was able to look straight into his soul. A sharply indrawn breath, like pain, and he moved away. When he spoke again, it was with his back to me. "I came to tell you we're going away. To Italy. My sister's weak, but better, and my mother too. The shock of these calamities has wakened her, I think. Anyway, she now agrees the southern sun will be beneficial to us all."

I did not speak, and he swung round, his words coming in a rush. "Thank you. For everything. You were the first truly good thing that ever happened to me. I'll never forget you, ever."

He was gone. I was alone. Laura came, made me eat, made me drink hot tea slowly. She took me to see the rector, and I nodded agreement like an automaton to his arrangements. She went with me to the dispensary, where Nell was lying, candles burning at her head and feet. Mrs. Greene was keeping vigil in a corner, knitting; she looked up at me with a compassionate smile.

I stood in a long silence looking down at the frail figure with its cloud of red-gold hair, its look of peace, all marks of suffering gone. Sister, stranger, my shadow self. *And may God have mercy on us all.*

In the midafternoon Jeremy arrived, and without speech, without thinking, I went straight into his arms. He held me, wordlessly, for a comforting time. At last he stepped back, and his voice was gentle.

"Come outside. The day's like spring, and you can do nothing here. We'll go across the way and view the damage."

How like Jeremy to know that looking at the reality of the destruction was what I had to do.

The air was warm and fresh. I filled my lungs with a great uplifting breath of it, and only then realized what had changed. There was no grey haze upon the village now. The sky over Wychwood Rise was bright, bright blue, as it had been at Sudeley.

"The spell is gone," Jeremy said, watching me.

Across the common, Wychwood House still glowed, radiantly, on its corner. The thatch was scorched, and in some places gone. Much damage had been done—to ceilings, plaster, precious paneling. But the house itself miraculously endured.

We stood in the still, healing peace of Kersey's Room, and the sun streamed in, carrying me in memory to the gracious ruins of Katherine's banqueting hall, where her magic first had cast the cords that now bound Jeremy and me. Jeremy—my friend, my complement, my love.

"I'm happy," I said aloud. "It may be terrible to say, but I am happy."

"It's not terrible. Never terrible."

I moved toward the fireplace slowly. "Philip came to visit me this morning. To say goodbye. They're off to Italy, the three of them."

"So he, too, is free," Jeremy said. "I'm glad for him. But you'll miss him, won't you?"

"Yes. But in any event, we would never meet again."

Jeremy's eyebrows rose. "He told you that?"

"He did not have to."

Jeremy nodded. He understood; he would always understand. "He did love you, you know, in his fashion."

"He loved Nell, too. It was more than fascination. He knew about her, and wanted terribly to help her. And it near destroyed him."

"But not entirely. In people, as in your herbs, that which can kill can also sometimes cure." He looked at me. "They were lovers, you know, most likely."

"Nell's a child!" But I had known it, ever since Nell said that Philip had drawn down the powers on her.

"Philip's seventeen. And Nell was . . . a child of Lucifer."

Lucifer's child, a fallen angel. Child of darkness, child of light. I had a sudden vision of Nell and Philip as I once had seen them in the luminous gloaming of the walled garden. He so dark, she spun-gold fair, both with those strange dark eyes with the golden lights, like the Children of the Sun. Those ancient Greeks had understood such things. Children in years they were, but half as old as time. Nell was a Lilith-woman, her frail child's body racked not just with pain but with adult loves and passions she half comprehended and could not control. *I could understand that, couldn't I?*

"Children of darkness, children of light," Jeremy said gently. I nodded, my eyes blind with tears. He said, "She gained her heart's desires, which is more than most of us can say. And she chose her end. Who can say her life was not, for her, complete, and happier than most?"

Child of darkness, child of light. Her life blazed briefly, but so very bright. Nell, my sister.

"You had two protégés," Jeremy said quietly. "One at least grew whole. That means something, does it not, even if the price is that the cords must break?"

How did I feel about Philip? Lonely. Sad. With a deep nostalgia for what was gone, what could never be. And a deep joy over what he would become. "I'm grateful," I said at last, "for all he taught me. For whatever I was able to give to him. And very, very happy he's his own man at last. At whatever cost."

Jeremy smiled. "There speaks the true teacher. Oh, yes, you are, my love. Your gift lies with people, not in the ivory tower."

"So is yours."

"So shall we join them, then, and work together. And laugh, and fight, and make up, and grow, and learn. And Wychwood House will again cast its beneficient circle, with you its presiding genius. That's what genius originally meant, you know—the collective spirit of the house."

"That's Katherine, then." I swung round. "Jeremy, you were here earlier, weren't you? Did you find the letters?"

He shook his head. "They are all gone, save for a crumbled ash where you must have dropped them. What was in them, anyway?"

"A love letter from Elizabeth to Seymour, and one from her to Katherine, begging forgiveness. And Katherine's, granting it."

Jeremy whistled softly. "So now the Tudor triangle will remain a private secret, and Kersey's scandal not shake historians, nor fill our pockets. Well, we'll live well and truly, love, without it."

"Did you really mean what you said last night, about our finding each other being the treasure beyond price?"

"Can you doubt it, after the burns and bruises I acquired to rescue you?" Jeremy stopped, and all at once began to laugh. "That damnable, maddening grandmother of mine. I always thought there was a method to her madness. She flung us together, Beatrice and Benedict, a union of head and heart. She succeeded in transforming both of us according to her wisdom, and in leaving her legacy simultaneously to the two persons whom she cared for most. So she wins, after all."

"No. *We* win."

There was a silence. Then Jeremy said, "I did find something when I searched." He brought it out, smoke-smudged and wrinkled. The Book of Shadows.

I stood for a long time looking down at it without opening it. Then I moved with it to the fireplace. "Do you mind?" I flung it on the hearth, and struck a match, and lit it. Jeremy came up behind me, pulling from his pocket something he added to the flames. A black-handled knife. We stood together and watched them burn until nothing remained of them but their forms in ashes. Jeremy reached out with the poker and broke them up, and a faint powdering of soot scattered in the golden air like benediction.

The words that had been haunting my brain all day with new meaning rose to my lips. " 'Neither principalities, nor powers, nor things present, nor things to come, nor life nor death nor any other creature, will be able to separate us from the love of God.' "

Jeremy's gaze went from me to the empty hearth. " 'This rough magic I here abjure, I'll break my staff, and deeper than did ever plummet sound, I'll drown my book,' Fire, water; destruction, purification and new birth. The Old Ones sleep at peace again, I think, and we are free." He turned to me, and smiled, and held out his hand. "Now life begins."

I walked with my love out into the sunlight of Wychwood Rise.

Omnia vincit amor. Love conquers all.

This book is published under the
auspices of the
ULVERSCROFT FOUNDATION,
a registered charity, whose primary object
is to assist those who experience difficulty
in reading print of normal size.

In response to approaches from the medical world, the Foundation is also helping to purchase the latest, most sophisticated medical equipment desperately needed by major eye hospitals for the diagnosis and treatment of eye diseases.

If you would like to know more about the
ULVERSCROFT FOUNDATION,
and how you can help to further its work,
please write for details to:

THE ULVERSCROFT FOUNDATION
The Green, Bradgate Road
Anstey
Leicestershire
England